UPHOLD AND DEFEND

UPHOLD AND DEFEND

WE THE PEOPLE SHALL NOT BE INFRINGED

Stephen S. Hoag

IngramSpark

ISBN: 979-8-988466-369

First Printing, 2024

Cover Art offered by SelfPubBookCovers.com, Art and design credit goes to Mary 60

www.upholdanddefend.life

Published by Ingramspark

Disclaimer Statement

It is important for the reader to note that this is a work of fiction and that any reference of characters to real people is purely coincidental and unintended. This is pure entertainment, any reference to real agencies, places or businesses are simply for situational orientation only. No affiliation or endorsements exist, and defamation is certainly not the purpose of mention.

The author and the publisher are not responsible or liable for any injury, damage or loss incurred by an individual attempting to misuse any information or act on any fictitious plot depicted in this book. This novel is not intended to be an instruction manual, and readers are not advised to use it as such.

Contents

List of Characters

- Merrill Konager- Head of the Oneida UAD resistance group.
- Ramsey Himmel - Civilian member of Oneida resistance group.
- Kaiden Alvin Sawyer- New member of the Pioneer Patriot Cluster.
- Ciera Lowman- Ex Academy Administrator. Kaiden's true love.
- John Shay- Director of Clear Water Farm.
- Angie Foster- Assistant Director of CWF.
- Neil Lee- Zeta Cluster President at Tenny Hill Academy.
- Melvin Brooks- Security Chief at Clear Water Farms.
- Crenshaw, Greg- Seargent/Captain of the Pioneer rescue squad.
- Jerry Reeder- Member of the Pioneer Outpost.
- Betsy Stoiber- One of the female members of the Pioneer Outpost.
- Shiloh Mead- One of the few female Cadet survivors.
- Steve West- Cadet survivor.
- Paul- Cadet survivor.
- Allen McKinney- Leader of the Cadet movement.
- Donnie Canter- Member of the Pioneer Outpost.
- Reese Johnson- Member of the Pioneer Outpost.
- Jones Herring- Cadet survivor.
- Rudy Lancaster- Post Office Clerk in the Town of Piseco.
- Hank Quaid- Machinist in the Town of Piseco.
- Abba Jenson- Mountain Market owner.
- Brian Hardy- Met Ciera at Town Hall meeting.
- Toadie- One of Brian Hardy's younger gang members.
- Jen, Bill and Fife- Hardy's men who joined Patriots at Lake Pleasant.

- Gutierrez, Hermon- "Official" Federal Government Representative.
- Mayor Cole Arden- Lake Pleasant Town Administrator.
- Hal Avery- Lake Pleasant Chief of Police.
- Victor Coaler- Cadet that came to CW farm with Neil Lee.
- Sandy Kemp- Pioneer Outpost member.
- Marko Briggs- Leader of the resistance in Poland N.Y.
- Trip Salantro, Nevel Burns, and Mack Heedy. Three recruits the Patriots picked up in Poland N.Y.
- Hanson, Commander- Commander of the Federal base at Herkimer.
- Kendrell, Agent- Commander Hanson's aid.
- Profit, Teejay- Pioneer Outpost member.
- Donnie Tilfer- Pioneer Outpost member.
- Nick Malner- Pioneer Outpost member.
- Marshal Kelly- Prisoner released to Crenshaw in Herkimer.
- Klem Ambrose- Herkimer's acting Fire Chief.
- Arron Michaels- Herkimer Policeman who joined the Patriots.
- Marvin Halper- Herkimer Police Chief.
- Kurt Mendel- Cadet survivor.
- Robert Metcalf- Pioneer Outpost member.
- William Dunlop- Drone technician who spied for the Oneida Militia.
- Lyle Ramshaw- Herkimer policeman who joined the Patriots.
- Nance Lackland- Herkimer policeman who joined the Patriots.
- Sky Winiker- Herkimer policeman who joined the Patriots.
- Ramsey Himmel- Leader of the 'Boy's from Oneida".
- Merrill Konager- Black man from the 'Boy's from Oneida'.
- John Pearlman- Feds Oneida base Drone operator.
- Jester Mann- Farmer who allowed the convoy to park at his farm.
- Jenson Greein- Designated laborer for the Oneonta City Brigade.
- Kent- Brigade patrol leader.
- Danial Ferenczi- Oneonta Police Chief.
- Riley Mason- Cadet survivor.

- Ben Haines- Oneonta Sargent ex-policeman.
- Jake Ferenczi- Oneonta policeman.
- Glen Greenwise- Pioneer Outpost member.
- Andy Finn- New Pioneer Outpost member.
- Irene Stalouti- Cadet Company Lieutenant
- Casey Brown- Jester Mann's neighbor.
- Jeremiah Greein- Laborer working for Citizens Brigade.

1

SHATTERED

Merrill Konager sat at the dinner table staring at his wife Renay in disbelief. Oddly they were both home on the same day, a weekday no less. Both companies they worked for had temporarily closed so they found themselves with some extra time on their hands. Riots in downtown Syracuse made it too dangerous to travel into the city anyway. Their house was built in one of the newer gated Glendale communities located near Syracuse in the neighboring town of Oneida. Glendale, a neighborhood that sprung from a growing demand for accommodation's situated outside the city but where living was in range of a bearable commute. The home was beautiful, the furnishings that surrounded the couple and their two children told of an affluent lifestyle. They reeked of what progressives would call "white privilege". The only problem with that label was that this family was of Black African descent, the reference to 'Black' made to differentiate them from citizens of 'White' African descent.

Oneida used to be a small college town. Due to the popularity of its University, it grew over the years and transformed into something resembling a city, but not quite. Certainly not like Syracuse with the infamous 'Syracuse University'. Merrill worked as a lawyer at Strews and Laman in Syracuse and was very good at what he did. The fact that he was not a partner would be pointed out as proof of discrimination by the left all in a continuing effort to drive a wedge between people and stoke the flames of racism in America. Merrill was happy with his position, he thanked God for everything he had and the affluent lifestyle that he and his family were able to afford. His wife didn't have to work but she maintained a job at the Teachers Credit Union as a financial advisor also making the forty-minute commute to Syracuse five days a week.

Riots in downtown Syracuse had gotten progressively worse over the last three months and after hearing the latest news reports, Merrill and Renay became very concerned. The reports told of three deaths associated with the riots and showed that violent crime was spreading to outlying areas at record levels. The Konager's had good reason to be concerned. Extreme liberal members of the progressive party led by professors and staff at the University persistently stirred up students with anti-capitalist rhetoric spurning a tornado of hateful dissent.

A look of concern formed on Merrill's face as he watched a news cast on TV that described the events that led to the death of a homeowner in a neighborhood just ten miles away from them. Video clips of the violent encounter accompanied the news segment as well as pictures of damage done to Oneida city hall during yesterday's riot. Merrill was staring at one of those small portable TV's sitting on the kitchen counter. Lately it was "on" every waking hour which had always been against house rules... until now. In the background the reporter went on an oratory of fresh reports detailing the present economic situation the US found itself in. Prior to this Merrill had been able to placate his wife's fears but now after constantly hearing a barrage of recent bad news, it was impossible to put a cap on the anxiety they both felt. Undoubtedly it was the same for people all over the State, probably throughout the country.

"Merrill this crap has been going on for years now".

"I know Renay, you don't have to say it. I was the one who thought it wasn't possible for it to go this far. I was wrong. The government shut down the internet and the US economy's going down the tubes" Merrill said.

"You told me the riots in town were just a passing thing the students were cooking up and it would eventually go away" Renay reminded him.

Merrill ignored the comment and continued "Well tearing down the statues... I didn't think it was a big deal. I certainly didn't think it would affect us. Then the students occupied the town hall and a hundred of them have been camping out in the square ever since. Now they've burned down city hall and they've gone and killed someone. All the while stomping on people who speak up and condemn their actions". Merrill shook his head.

"It's gone too far Merrill. I never thought this could happen in America" Renay told him.

"But it is happening" Merrill glanced at the TV. "I knew we were in for trouble when our own mayor wouldn't authorize the police investigation and arrest those arsonists. Damn, I knew something was wrong. What I thought were 'students' ended up being members of that New World Order group, or else it was students that were recruited; I don't know which. And 'Black Lives Mater' is there too. I was 'for' BLM at first because black lives do matter. But not at the expense of other people's lives. The murder, I can't believe it. Since then, I've learned what BLM really stands for and it appalls me that a group dedicated to black people can alternately be so hateful towards Jews and dedicated to the Marxist cause and ideology. How on earth could that become popular in America? What's the matter with people these days? They don't even know what they're advocating for. And the socialists don't even hide it anymore. They say they want to take down the American system. Look there it is on TV now". Renay turned to look.

On the screen a reporter had a microphone held up to the face of a man with a black mask and helmet on. It was obvious he was one of the protesters. He was asked "...and what is the reason you are out here protesting tonight".

"Why would they dress like that if it's a peaceful protest?" Renay questioned.

"Shhh, let me hear this" Merrill demanded.

The white man dressed in black made a face into the camera and pointed his finger yelling "We are going to come to your neighborhood and f***in take down your white privilege you 'beep, beep, beep". The reporter quickly pulled the microphone away and moved so the man was not in the picture. "Sorry about that folks, this is live TV and we're getting some strong words from a protester with strong opinions...". The protester kept sticking his head into the shot behind the reporter and flipping viewers the bird.

Renay looked at her husband with genuine concern. "Merrill... do you think they'll come to our neighborhood?".

"I don't know honey..." Merrill said, but then he saw how concerned she was and changed direction. "Oh, don't worry, they won't come here". He reached out and took her hand trying to give it more meaning as he did his best to console her. "We have security and Ramsey told us...".

Renay cut him off. "Ramsey Himmel is the neighborhood extremist. He's always been on the hyper side of things. He's been talking about this for months now".

"Yeah, well maybe he was right" Merrill commented. "This is getting worse". He pressed the issue. "It's national news honey, the rioters were down on Portland street last night. They set fire to one of the houses and caused a lot of damage smashing up a few of the other ones. One of the owners was killed Renay, killed! They called the cops, but they never showed up until two hours later. I think Mayor Staten doesn't want clips of his policemen beating up on protesters. It wouldn't look good for his re-election campaign if that was getting around. And that's just one neighborhood over from ours Renay".

"So, what are we going to do if they come here?".

Merrill had to think about that. He also thought about their two kids, age eight and eleven. How was he going to protect them. There were no guns in the house, the ban made it impossible to get one legally. Besides, Renay would never have allowed a gun in the house anyway. All he had were his golf clubs and the kid's baseball bats. He had some exposure to guns from the impromptu lectures and the 'show and tell' put on by Ramsey in his "Uphold and Defend" meetup group. Sometimes meetings centered around the use of firearms. That was the first time he ever held an AR-15. The only time he fired one was at the barbeque Ramsey held last spring at his cousin's farm. They had a 200-yard range set up out back. Before that, as far as self-defense is concerned, Merrill only had a few classes in karate to his credit, the ones he took years ago in college. Suddenly he felt very inadequate against an angry mob.

"I don't know honey; we'll have to cross that bridge when we come to it". With that, he turned off the TV and ended the conversation.

That night the bridge crossed them. Two and a half hours after Merrill and Renay went to bed, around a quarter to twelve, there was a very loud banging at the front door. It woke Merrill up from a sound sleep.

"Honey that's got to be a neighbor or the cops" Renay exclaimed. "No one else would be allowed through the gate at this time of night.

Merrill groaned and mustered up a "I'll go see".

Whoever it was, they were persistent. The banging continued until Merrill came to the door. Merrill looked out the glass wing on the side of the door and recognized Ramsey Himmel and one of his other neighbors before he opened the door. By that time Renay was standing at the top of the stairs behind him wrapping a robe around herself. Merrill opened the door and Ramsey, his neighbor, burst through.

"Thank god you answered! I was just about to break it down" Ramsey said.

Ramsey was an army veteran that Merrill was good friends with on a level that neighbors would be (or should be). A select number of people around town were well acquainted with Ramsey and knew of his exploits and experience in the army as well as his political standing. Ramsey made sure his friends knew exactly where he was coming from in his UAD meetups. Merrill and Renay got invitations to attend, but only made it on a few occasions.

"Uphold and Defend is a movement" Ramsey would say. Opponents of his "movement" and his "conspiracy theories" called UAD a right-wing militia organization. Ramsey founded the organization three years earlier. Since then, attendance had increased, and the organization flourished because more and more of his "conspiracy theories" were coming true and people took notice. Yet Merrill was cautious and asked the pertinent question up front. "Why should I join your organization Ramsey? It's not like anyone is going to take over the United States. We don't need guns".

Ramsey's answer is what made Merrill join up. He said "Merrill, what was the first thing the Government of Ukraine did when Russia invaded their country?" Jokingly Merrill answered "Panic". That got everyone to laugh but Ramsey got serious and answered the question for him. "No, the first thing they did was to hand out rifles to the citizens". Ramsey paused to let that sink in. Everyone became quiet. "They handed out guns to citizens who didn't know a thing about how to use them except which way to point it". That got a chuckle from attendees. "A little late at that point don't you think? The 'Uphold And Defend' organization is dedicated to teaching citizens about the U.S constitution and how to defend yourself. How to defend yourself and your family in the event of a catastrophe, a catastrophe in which a gun might be needed to save lives. I implore you not to wait until the tragedy comes to your doorstep but to get involved now so that you'll be familiar with the weapon if an event should ever present itself".

It took a few days for Merrill to think about it, eventually he sort of joined by offering his legal services to the organization. More out of feeling an obligation to help a neighbor than to fully participate. He only attended a handful of meetings, but by the time this night was over, Merrill wished he had attended a lot more.

"What? What's going on Ramsey. Why at this time of night... what's up with the guns? You're not supposed to have those, aren't they illegal now?".

Both Ramsey and another neighbor were standing there holding a rifle in their hands. Merrill recognized the man standing next to him. It was Sid, another neighbor who lived a few houses down.

"Never mind that now, there's trouble at the front gate" Ramsey said with an urgency that told him this was serious. "Look!".

Ramsey swung his arm and pointed out the open door and down the road towards the far end of the street. The Konager's house was in the middle of a cul-de-sac and had a straight line of sight down the middle of the street to the gatehouse about 500 yards away. You could see it in the distance from their front door but at that distance details were sketchy.

Merrill looked as best he could through sleepy eyes but only saw that something was going on. Although he knew Ramsey well enough to trust him, he couldn't believe that guns would be necessary to solve this problem. Still, he thought "*But if Ramsey was worried about it, then maybe I should be too*".

Abnormal light flickered around the gate house exposing the fact that there was a large group of people down there whose shadows danced around as they moved about. "I can't see, what are they doing" Merrill said.

Ramsey walked in and moved quickly to the large living room window that overlooked the street. "Sid" he demanded. "Set your rifle up so Merrill can see. Sid unfolded the tripod on his rifle, sat it on the window sill and pointed the rifle at the gate house. Looking through the scope he adjusted the lens before turning and offering the view to Merrill. "Here, take a look Merrill".

Merrill knelt and placed his eye up against the lens of the rifle scope. He was familiar with this rifle and its scope; it was the same one he had fired it at Ramsey's cousins farm during one of Ramsey's UAD meetings. Merrill adjusted the scope and after a bit of searching he was able to line up the cross hairs on the gate house. When he did, the whole scene became clear.

"Oh my God!" Merrill exclaimed. "There must be a hundred people down there.

Renay appeared at Merrill's side. "What do you see Merrill? What's going on?".

"Shit! There's smoke coming from the gate house and there's a whole bunch of people shaking the front gate trying to tear it down. Damn, there must be a couple hundred of them. The gate looks awfully loose; I think it's going to give way".

Ramsey walked over to the open front door. He put his eye to the scope of his own rifle and focused on the same event. "They're going to ram it with a car!" he yelled.

A man dressed in black with a black mask on was one of the rioters who seemed to be in charge (at least in charge of some of them). He was urging the people who gathered at the fence to move aside. Then he instructed his guys to start pushing a car to get it moving towards the gate. It was the communities security vehicle. How they got it was anyone's guess. From what Merrill could tell, it looked like no one was in it. At the last moment, the guy lit a flare and threw it into one of the car's open windows. The car burst into flames just before it hit the main gate. When it hit, the car hesitated for just a moment before its momentum carried it through. The gate broke and gave way. The metal bars came off its track and fell to the ground.

The rioters cheered. The car was on a slight downhill section of the road, so it picked up speed and rolled on into the neighborhood. The rioters followed. Now completely engulfed in flames that poured out of the windows, the car continued rolling down the street for forty yards or so before it started to veer off to one side. In its wake was a line of fire marking its path on the pavement. The gasoline they had poured into it must have been leaking out. The flaming battering ram bounced over a curb and steered itself into the yard of the first house on the right, coming to rest only after striking the owners car parked in the driveway.

"Oh my gosh they got in!" Merrill yelled as he watched through Sid's rifle scope. He gave a play-by-play account of it to his wife. "The gates are down, the rioters are running in. They're running up and standing in front of the first two houses on the block. Our neighbor,

I don't know his name I just wave to him when I drive by... a burning car just hit his car and... it's catching fire! He and his two sons just came out... they got hockey sticks in their hands and... they're trying to fend off the rioters. All these people, they're swarming onto his property throwing things". Merrill paused as the action unfolded. "They got bricks, stones or bottles or something and they're throwing them... smashing windows. They got torches too. Holy shit! The guy just creamed one of the rioters with a hockey stick... they're fighting in his front yard... he got jumped... he's down. Oh no! They're kicking the be Jesus out of him. Oooo! Ohhhh! He's on the ground and someone just kicked him square in the face. He's out! His wife, I think, is at the front door totally frantic. She's screaming at them and they're yelling at her. Wow! They're running up to her... shit! They just punched her in the face. She's down too. Oh my God, they're throwing a lit torch into the house. Shit! There might be children in there!".

The rioters were prepared. You could tell that this was premeditated. They were carrying polls with rolls of toilet paper soaked in gasoline strapped to the end with chicken wire to hold it together. One was lit on fire and all the others were lit off that one.

"POW!" an extremely loud unexpected sound of a gunshot came as a complete surprise to the Konager's. The sound reverberated deeply throughout the house. It scared Merrill so, that he jumped and hit his eyebrow hard on the rifle scope. Startled, Renay fell backwards with a gasp and raised both hands to her ears. When Merrill looked around for the source, he saw Ramsey laying prone in the hallway with his rifle supported on its bipod. The stock was nestled in his arms and the barrel was pointing out the front door in the rioters direction. It fired again "Pow!". Everyone covered their ears.

It wasn't by accident that Ramsey Himmel and Sid Evel showed up at Merrill's front door. Ramsey, together with a small group of like-minded neighbors, had discussed the topic of defending their neighborhood in their "Uphold and Defend" meetings. While assessing various hypothetical situations, Ramsey pointed out the tactical advantage of the Konager's house. It was ideally situated and had a commanding view of the street with the front stone wall giving good cover.

Ramsey Himmel had been a sniper want-ta-bee ever since he saw the movie Lone Survivor when he was a kid. Ever since, he had become enthralled with anything military and gobbled up anything attributed to the sniper's trade. He coveted the ability to reach out and touch someone. For years he indulged himself in the intricacies of the art, and endeavored to purchase the equipment and train himself to the degree that he could. He read everything on the subject and due to a May article in Guns & Weapons magazine, he chose the tried-and-true Remington 700 to be his sniper/hunting rifle. But that was mainly due to budget constraints. It was only $813.00 + tax at the time.

Ramsey told everyone that accuracy was the most important issue. The 700's accuracy was impressive. It shot below 1" MOA right out of the box. 2013 was also the first year Remington offered the rifle chambered in 300 blackout, a new round said to have an edge over the popular .308. Designed to flatten the curve and achieve an even greater degree of accuracy, the 300 blackout was a perfect choice for a sniper. All of that was before he became eligible. As soon as they let him, Ramsey joined the army.

Sid opened the living room window that Merrill was looking out. He yelled at Merrill "get out of the way!". Merrill just looked up at him like he was speaking a different language. Sid pulled Merrill up, knelt in his place and looked through his rifle scope to focus on what was happening. Sid picked out one of the guys still kicking his neighbor who was now motionless on the ground. A split second later- "Pow!" his rifle echoed the same loud report. The guy he was aiming at jerked, stopped what he was doing and went stiff. Then he spun a half turn before falling over like a tree hitting the ground.

Renay turned with her hands over her ears and ran into the interior of the house seeking refuge from the noise and from the shock of what was happening. She ran upstairs to tend to the kids. It was a good thing too because if she was able to see what transpired she would have been sickened by the sight. About 300 yards down the street in front of the house that was being attacked, there was a protester who was just about to throw another lit torch into the open door of the house. Ramsey's rifle sounded and the guy spun around after being hit by a bullet that tore into his body. Smoke came from the barrel of Ramsey's rifle. He manipulated the bolt, chambered another round and put the scope to his eye again. Tonight, he didn't have to think about windage. He placed the 300 yd hash mark on the target, aimed and fired at one of two guys who came out of the house carrying a big, large screen TV. The closer one of the two let go of the TV, fell to his knees and then fell onto the steps clutching his mid-section. His body wiggled around for a moment on the ground and then went still. When his partner in crime realized what had happened, he dropped his side of the TV and ran into the crowd as fast as he could.

Ramsey settled the cross hairs of his scope on the guy who punched the lady in the face. That asshole was standing on the front steps of the house yelling victoriously and jumping up and down over her body with his hands in the air performing 'Rocky's' victory dance. He was so euphorically involved (or drug induced) that he hadn't noticed his comrade go down on the steps next to him. Ramsey aimed for the guy's body but since he was jumping all around... the bullet struck him in the head. His body tumbled down the front steps of the home. After each gun shot that came from Ramsey and Sid's rifle, a body fell. At first the rioters didn't know what was happening. But after hearing multiple gun shots above the racket made by their fellow rioters they understood. People standing around suddenly became frightened for their own lives. They turned and started to run back the way they came. It was a trickle at first but then word spread causing a panic among the throng of attackers. "Shooter!" some of them were yelling as they ran. Soon there was a stampede of people running back toward the gate.

Ramsey picked his targets based on the degree of violence the guy was perpetrating. If they were throwing a torch into the house, he shot them. If they were beating up on his neighbors or throwing a brick through a window, they got shot. A rioter who was smashing out the windows of a car on the other side of the street got shot. All the people standing around in the background peacefully, he left alone, including a local news woman he saw roaming around with a camera man in tow.

Watching the crowd as they ran, the crosshairs of Ramsey's scope focused and settled on the same guy who seemed to be charge of the burning car idea. He was standing near the gate looking around, eyeing everything that was going on. Ramsey had him in his sights. The guy paused and looked down the street seemingly right at Ramsey or at least in the direction where he believed the shots were coming from. He raised his left hand high in the air and gave Ramsey the middle finger, then his right hand pulled a pistol out from his belt. He fired three times in Ramsey's direction. They found out later that one of the bullets struck the house. Luckily it didn't hit anyone, including the kids or Merrill's wife upstairs. Ramsey almost pulled the trigger on the guy, but the guy turned and joined the mad rush for safety. There were too many people in the way for a clean shot. "I'll remember that face dude" Ramsey said out loud.

Fifteen minutes later the rioters were gone. In their wake they left a path of destruction. The gate house, two cars and a home were on fire. The front gate was inoperable and busted up. Five cars had their windows smashed; mailboxes were uprooted. One neighbor was dead, three needed hospitalization and four others suffered multiple bruises from the fights they got in. That along with rioter's dead bodies strewn all over the place made it look like a war zone. Ramsey and Sid ditched the rifles, and along with Merrill, ran down the street to the burning house to see what they could do to help.

* * *

The next day, on the small TV sitting on the Konager's kitchen counter, a local news reporter described the incident:

"...resident forces in the Glendale neighborhood took the law into their own hands last night and shot at members of a peaceful protest. Four killed and six critically wounded, it's been a costly night for free speech. Our own Marion Hemmingway was on the scene. Here's her report:"

The network switched over and showed video from the night before taken by their "on the spot reporter". The same one Ramsey had seen in his scope.

"Yes John, this is Marion Hemmingway standing here outside the Glendale neighborhood where a peaceful protest has formed. Let's get a one-on-one account of what they're doing here". Marion walked over to where a protester was standing and asked the women "Mam, why are you and these people here protesting at this community?".

The interviewee was a white woman dressed in black. She had a black backpack on, a bandana that covered her face and she had a black helmet on her head. Marion placed the microphone near her mouth.

"We are here to address the un-equal treatment of black people in America. This neighborhood is a prime disgraceful example of 'White Privilege', something that has been perpetrated by the rich for far too long. We are bringing our message to them that it will no longer be tolerated. We demand reparations for slavery and for the degradation of the working class. Without us

> they would have nothing!". She yelled the last part and turned to her friends standing around her for support. They all yelled "YEAH!" and shook their signs and threw their fists in the air while chanting "No Justice No Peace! No Justice No Peace!". One sign said "BLM" another said "TEAR IT DOWN!".
>
> "There you have it" Marion said as she took back the microphone and started to walk away. The camera followed her. "...a stirring plea for peaceful change coming from a woman who has surly felt the disparity...".

In the background the camera happened to show a partial view of one side of the community's gate house which sat just outside the front gate. Smoke emanated from a broken window. The video with Marion in the foreground switched to clips that were obviously taken at various moments throughout the night. Each showed various groups of people standing around with signs and chanting. Then they went back to Marion who was clearly shaken and speaking in a shocked tone.

> "These protesters here were seeking to peacefully exercise their first amendment rights and to get their message across. Just now we witnessed a violent reaction as they were viciously attacked by security forces protecting the rich who dwell inside these walls". The background video changed to an interview with another protester.
>
> "This land is not theirs! It was stolen. We can't afford to hire protection for ourselves, for the members participating in this march..." she said.

> The Protester standing next to her bent into the mike and shouted "These white people never had to work hard in their lives!".

The woman turned and yelled at the houses in the background. The picture switched back to their correspondent:

> "They are defenseless against firearms! They are unarmed. The rich got their security, their guns... what do the protesters have? Nothing".

Marion motioned an arm towards the gate behind her. Once again, the camera (inadvertently?) caught a glimpse of the gate house which was now completely engulfed in flames. Then the scene was cut to show various clips of protesters huddled together chanting and holding up signs. No scenes of any protester creating havoc or destroying anything were ever shown. The only clip of a protester in a fight with one of the homeowners showed the homeowner striking the protester with a hockey stick. That was cut short so that the protesters response was not seen.

> "...and they were attacked with a hockey stick for voicing their opinion" Marion confirmed. "Now this is graphic so get the children to leave the room. The protesters..." she paused...

The network capped it all off with a disturbing clip of a guy happily cheering and jumping up and down on the steps of a home when he was shot. They were discrete enough to block out the head blowing apart but made sure viewers saw the body crumble to the ground.

> "...they came to make a point, and for that, some valiantly lost their lives. A disturbing end to a just cause...". Marion paused for effect. "Four dead in Glendale. When are we going to get the guns out of the hands of people who so nonchalantly use them to murder the innocent? Something's got to change. This is Marion Hemmingway, back to you John".

"That's not how it happened!" Merrill stood up and shouted at the TV. He was now standing there in the kitchen with his hands on his head incensed about what he had just heard. Simultaneously he was expressing his anger to Renay who stood at the sink. "I can't believe they're reporting it like that. That's nowhere near what happened. These people flagrantly distort the news to fit their own agenda. This is absurd. I'll never trust the news ever again".

"This is going to turn against us Merrill. I knew it" Renay said. They're acting like we are the ones who attacked them".

"We had to ditch the rifles when the cops and fire department finally showed up, or else they probably would have arrested us. Ramsey told them that a security guard hired by the association did the shooting".

"Oh my God, you mean for protecting ourselves and our home we could go to jail? Why aren't the Police arresting those people who attacked us?" Renay asked.

"They said they weren't allowed to interfere with a first amendment rally".

"What! You've got to be kidding me. They have more rights than we do?".

"From the sentiment I felt out there... it looks that way. I don't know Renay, the police seemed to be buying the story. We should be alright" Merrill tried to console her. "Don't worry I happen to know some good lawyers..." Merrill told his wife.

Merrill shook his head, walked over, and hugged his wife.

2

FALL OUT

Kaiden climbed out of the tunnel and scurried through the hatch into the Bunker building's auditorium, pulling his legs out just in time before the cover automatically closed on his foot. "*How quickly things change*" he thought. Within seconds he was squatting low in the dark silence at the base of the podium in the middle of the auditorium. "*No backup here*" he said to himself, "*I'm on my own*".

Illuminated by dim secondary lighting Kaiden could only see the outline of the auditorium's perimeter walls which enabled him to just barely make out the movement of a dark figure running fast up the aisle to the main exit at the rear of the hall. It was the traitor Remy Horton. "*The bastard's running to the Feds with information that'll make my world come to an end. I got to stop this guy*". That thought kept repeating itself in Kaiden's mind. The Glock 45 he clutched in his hand came up quickly. He pointed it at the moving body intending to fire, but Remy reached the double doors and burst through them before he could pull the trigger.

"*Shit! I'm not sure I could have hit him anyway*". Doubt made him hesitate. "*I've got to think! What's the best way to do this?*". There wasn't any time to think. He got up off his knees and ran after him.

"A gunshot will surely bring the Feds down on me, but I've got no choice. I should use my silenced Beretta not the Glock". That was an afterthought. The beretta was sitting in a holster strapped to his thigh. The Glock in his hand was extra firepower that he was glad he brought along. *"I just might be needing this. Damn, that would have been the fastest way to end this. If only I could have gotten off a shot".* The seriousness of the moment wasn't lost. *"I can't believe I've got to do this... kill this guy. Doesn't matter. I'll end this now. For Ciera, and for the sake of the others".* Kaiden ran up the aisle and burst through the double doors on the heels of the traitor.

On the other side of those doors was the building's large main lobby. After Kaiden burst through he saw Remy on his knees in the center of the lobby with his hands up over his head and his gun on the floor in front of him. He was giving himself up and looking away towards the building's main entrance. Stationed there at a desk on the far side of the lobby were three men, two of them had pistols pointed directly at Remy's chest. They were shouting at him "Get down! Get down on the ground!".

No one was supposed to be in that auditorium. The guards had searched it three times already and came up empty. Remy's sudden appearance surprised the hell out of them. The sound of a second infiltrator bursting through the doors left everyone dumbfounded for just an instant. An instant that Kaiden took full advantage of. In a flash the barrel of his Glock pointed at the traitor kneeling on the floor. Remy turned and when he saw Kaiden, instantly a shocked expression formed on his face. In the next instant it was replaced by one of terrified alarm.

"Bang!" Kaiden's gun went off. Then all hell broke loose as the feds turned their weapons in Kaiden's direction and fired. Kaiden ducked and rolled coming up on one knee while firing at the first agent his sights landed on. Bullets flew just inches over his head. Quickly he fell to the side without taking his eyes off the agents or from the sights on the barrel of his gun. When his body hit the ground, a sharp pain welled up from a half healed broken rib. He put it out of his mind and didn't allow it to register. After the split second that it took, Kaiden re-adjusted his aim onto the target in front of him and fired twice.

A second agent clutched his gut, and the man went down. Always moving with bullets following him, Kaiden rolled back onto one knee, never remaining in a single position for more than a second. His gun blazed as he went. Bullets fired by the remaining agent passed through the space Kaiden had just occupied. From a sitting position on the floor Kaiden fired until the Glock pistol emptied. The last remaining agent crumbled to the floor.

All the noise meant the game was up. Surely other agents were on their way. Quickly Kaiden returned to the middle of the lobby where Remy had been kneeling. There was a large streak of blood and a trail of it on the floor leading off into the hallway that led out of the lobby going toward the rest rooms on the left-hand side. Remy couldn't have crawled very far down the hall. Kaiden's first shot had struck Remy somewhere in the upper torso and he was in the process of bleeding out. When Kaiden came upon him the worm was slithering his way down the hall trying to get away from his source of agony. Kaiden looked down at the sorry sight the guy was in, only without the sympathy that would normally accompany anyone else in that condition.

"You sorry ass son of a bitch" Kaiden told him. "Taken down by the same gun you tried taking us down with" Kaiden hovered above the slow-moving bloody slug beneath him. Violently Kaiden threw the Glock at him. "Why would you make me do this?" he yelled.

As if he never heard him, or didn't feel the gun strike his back, Remy continued crawling. Kaiden pulled the silenced Beretta 92 from its holster and aimed it at Remy's head. "Doof!" the dull sound of a silenced gunshot brought the body to a standstill. Without ceremony Kaiden nodded his head. "It had to be done" he said out loud.

A noise coming from inside the building made him aware that agents must have come in from another door and were now leap frogging down the hallway and coming fast in his direction. He turned and started to run. At the same moment, Black Jack agents dressed in swat type gear burst through the building's front doors. His only choice was to run back through the double doors leading back into the auditorium. Bullets zinged through the air and peppered the door as he ran through it. The small glass window in the center of one of them shattered. Once inside he ran in an all-out sprint down the aisle and sped past the podium. *"Can't go there"* he thought. *"Hell, I can't believe I'm still alive"*. Bypassing the stairs, he leaped and rolled onto the stage. At the top of his roll, he turned and fired a shot at the doors just as agents came running through. The shot missed flesh but made them pause for a second giving him time to exit the stage and duck behind curtains that led backstage. Kaiden was familiar with the layout from attending a handful of board meetings here. From a choice of hallways, he took the one on the right which he knew led to a bathroom in the back. The rear service entrance to the stage was just beyond that. Continuing down the hall brought him to the back door where he came out onto the rear loading dock. Again, skipping the stairs, he jumped onto the driveway below and ran all out into the parking lot beyond.

Five or six agents following Kaiden were cautious and hesitant as the barrels of their rifles peered around curtains and corners. When they entered the backstage area, it was immediately evident that there were quite a few ways that their fugitive could have gone. They split up to cover all possibilities.

Kaiden found his way into the shadows of the trees and bushes that lined the parking lot and the area between him and the road. Looking back, he felt confident that he had put a few seconds between him and his pursuers. He slowed down to a fast walk to keep from eliciting any unneeded attention. The front entrance of the Bunker building came alive with activity. More vehicles arrived at the scene of the disturbance. Kaiden got out of there just before agents surrounded the building.

3

CLOSE CALL

Kaiden sat on a large rock out in front of a wooden hut located somewhere in the Adirondack Mountains. Many a hiker must have had their picture taken or perhaps a selfie snapped on this unique piece of granite. Now it was his turn to honor the rock. He was sitting on top of it in a meditative posture with his legs folded and his eyes closed. During meditation he tried not to think or concentrate on anything, or at least as little internal chatter as possible.

"Meditation is an attempt to stop the monkey inside your brain from chattering and to allow yourself a different experience" Kaiden pictured his Tai Chi teacher and remembered his words. Still, it was impossible to get himself to stop thinking about his present situation and keep fresh memories from rolling around in his mind's eye. The more he tried to erase it, the more it appeared. Practicing Tai Chi helped, so he got up off the rock and walked over to the only small flat section of ground in the whole camp. There he started the slow-motion exercise. Concentrating on the movements allowed him to block everything else out.

Ciera pulled out her phone and took a picture of Kaiden meditating on the rock and now one of him practicing Tai Chi. The phone didn't connect to the grid anymore, but it still took pictures. She was sitting up on the wooden deck of the three-sided hut still wrapped in her sleeping bag. There were more people sleeping in similar sleeping bags next to her. They were all inside the hut lined up in a row. Her hair was disheveled, and she looked like she had just woken up.

It was cold up in the mountains on this late spring morning. Cool morning air was nice, but it made leaving a warm sleeping bag something that Ciera thought was not in her best interest. She lingered there for a while watching Kaiden move slowly through the Tai Chi form. The whole scene with Kaiden in the foreground and a beautiful view of the mountains with green foliage in the background made for a great picture. And it made her wish they could stay here forever. Especially after all the turmoil they had just been through. Ciera had her own account of previous events rolling around in her mind and she too couldn't help but think of them now. Was it a few weeks or a month ago, she didn't know anymore, her whole life had changed and went in a different direction for the second time.

The trek out from the Academy was one thing, but the exodus out of Clear Water Farms was quite another. Ciera revisited the event in her mind starting with their hike back from their trip up Skanelis Mountain:

"I'll always remember this trek and our camp out on Skanelis Mountain" she said to Kaiden. "It was absolutely the best". Ciera felt the need to keep focusing on something that was good. Anything that was... good.

"Yeah, because we weren't on the move and always having to keep an eye out for someone trying to kill us huh? After reaching the safety of Clear Water Farms it's a great feeling to be able to relax for once and enjoy being out on the mountain" Kaiden stated.

"Oh, and I don't suppose it had anything to do with the sex now did it?" Ciera asked with a sarcastic pucker on her face.

Kaiden smiled and grabbed her pulling her close. He kissed her with a gleam in his eye. "Now that was absolutely the finest moment of my life".

She smiled at that. "This is our last day off so let's make the best of it. After the meeting this morning, we can meet and greet, but then let's go have some fun and play ping pong in the barn. I heard they got a table" Ciera told him.

"Okay but I haven't got a chance to roam around the farm and get accustomed to what's going to be our new life for who knows how long. I'd like to walk around".

They had three days off to get acclimated, yet they chose to go on a little excursion on the mountain to get some alone time. "Today we'll be put 'on schedule' as they call it at Clearwater farms. I wonder what position they'll give us and what task we'll be assigned" Ciera said.

"Don't forget about our meeting at 9 o'clock this morning with the farm director John Shay" Kaiden reminded her.

"Then we better hike it out of here now".

When they arrived at the classic white colonial framed Clearwater farm house, John Shay and his assistant Aggie Foster were there ready to receive them. His chief of security Melvin Brooks was there too.

"Greetings" John offered.

"It's great to meet you John" Kaiden and Ciera both said. They shook hands. "And you Angie" they shook hers too.

"Yes, we've heard about some of your exploits from Sargent Crenshaw. Your group calls him 'Captain' which I guess means that he has been field promoted. Well done, I must say to you all. You brought in the funds that will get us through this crisis and keep us afloat for years to come. The Clear Water Militia thanks you for that and we all thank you for your service".

"Have there been any other Cadets coming in from the Academy?" Kaiden asked.

"Yes, five other's arrived just this morning. Ah, look. Here they come now".

Walking up to the farm house porch and through the front door were six Patriots. One of them was their very own Captain Greg Crenshaw, yet one of the others caught Ciera's attention.

"Neil Lee!" Ciera screamed.

"Hello Ciera" Neil said with a smile. She went up to him with open arms and hugged him. "My God. You made it out of Tenny Hill alive. It's so good to know that there are others who made it. We were wondering what happened to everyone".

"We had quite a time of it" Neil told her. "Originally there were six Cadets that made it out with me but… some of them weren't so lucky.

"Oh". Ciera said. Her glee faded as well as the smile on her face. "What happened?".

"Well, that's why we're here. We just rolled in this morning, and I'm here to give Director Shay an account of our exodus".

"Yes, come Neil, we can do this now" John said. "Then you can get cleaned up and situated. Besides, everyone here should hear this".

"Yes, I'd like to hear this too" Crenshaw said. Everyone found a place sitting at the table or they stood nearby within earshot.

Neil began "The fucking Feds" he shook his head. "I stayed at the Academy thinking it would never come to this. But as soon as the Feds attacked, I knew we were done for. I heard of events like this happening elsewhere in Texas and Florida, but I never thought it would happen to us at the Academy. At least not to the extent that it did.

I was surprised that we won that first skirmish on the first night. But it just prolonged the inevitable. When they broke through the next day, I was in Chilton Hall with what remained of my Cluster's crew. There were just four of us, the rest had taken off days earlier at the first hint of trouble. We at Zeta don't have a house you know; we meet and work or I should say 'worked' out of Chilton Hall. That was our station. Anyway, as soon as we heard the order to vacate, we took off on foot to the farm house in Rio Linda. Most of them at the farm were preparing to fight it out but we took a vote and decided to hike it out of there. And I'm not ashamed of our decision". Neil looked at his partner who nodded his head in solidarity.

"From the hut on top of Tenny Mountain, we could hear the fight going on down below us. We kept a low profile. Didn't dare venture out onto Bald Ledge in case anyone saw us. From the people we ran into on the trail... we heard stories, bad stories about what was going on down there. Grim to say the least. We heard some were killed. Everyone else scattered". Neil's voice cracked as emotion crept into his words. "We thought we would stay up there and hide but then we heard the Feds were coming so we moved and hiked it out of there going east. We ran into one of the Feds patrols on the way out; we were forced to shoot it out. That's where we lost Erin and Jimmy". Neil paused and rubbed his face and took a deep breath.

"From that point on the Feds were on our trail. We were being hunted like animals. More than once we barely escaped their drag net. I'm not proud of it, but we stole a truck. Drove it up Kortright Road and ran right into a roadblock...".

"Holy shit! That was you guys?" Kaiden stated rather than asked. "We saw that fight!".

"What! You were there?" Neil asked in disbelief.

"Yeah, at Bloomville, right? We were crossing the river at that very moment. I saw the whole thing. I'm so sorry man. We were in a really vulnerable position, and it was impossible to help". Kaiden glanced at Crenshaw. "The Feds would have come down on us and we would have lost our load".

"We sure could have used your help" Neil said with a notable degree of disgust in his voice. "Lost three at that intersection. Vic Coaler and I barely got away with our lives. Got this wound for all my trouble" Neil put his hand on his bandaged arm. "Had to disappear into the woods or else they would have got us. Continued east and stumbled into these guys from Pi Cluster" Neil pointed his thumb at the three Cadets that had come in with him. "We hiked and dodged our way east paralleling Route 10. Caught various rides north and eventually made it here with a few minor but no major events. At least no one else got killed. The country's economy is collapsing and everyone's starting to go nuts. It's crazy out there. Some people are doing some bad ass shit man".

Ciera chimed in "Yeah, tell me about it. And on top of that you can't tell someone's political preference in all of this. With anyone you meet you got a fifty/fifty chance that they're either with you or against you.

Neil, we found out that Remy Horton was a traitor. He sold us out and set us up".

"Remy Horton?" Neil said with an incredulous look that turned into a frown.

"Yeah, that bastard" Kaiden stated emphatically. "He was working with the Feds. He placed a tracking device in the handle of a .45 that he gave to Ciera…".

"What!" Neil stood up and looked at Ciera with drastic concern spreading deeply across his face. He said "Remy came to me just before all the shit went down. He gave me a .45 too! I thought he was an angel from heaven because I didn't have a weapon at the time. It saved my life; I shot an agent with it". His voice trailed off as he thought about it.

"Holy shit Neil, where's that Glock now?" Kaiden yelled at him.

Neil looked at John "I gave it to security at the gate when I came in".

For a split second they all glanced at each other, then reality sank in. Kaiden spoke first "That bastard gave a Glock pistol with a tracking device in the handle to all the cluster leaders… he was counting on them to scatter and lead them to the outpost locations after the attack! The Feds know where we are, we've got to get the motherload out of here now!".

A type of controlled panic ensued. Crenshaw barked orders at Kaiden, Kaiden spoke sternly to Ciera and the Director started shouting orders at Melvin Brooks "Take us to Code 2! (Code 2 was the order to prepare for an attack) And lock this place down now!". Then Shay spoke directly to Brooks. "Prepare for an attack! Send someone to get that Glock and have them drive it out of here as fast as you can. It may not do us any good, but it just might lead them away from us without looking too deeply into this section of the woods".

Crenshaw walked up to John Shay and grabbed him by the arm. "Where's the rat pack?".

John hesitated as if trying to decide whether to give up his new found source of wealth. He had confiscated the rat pack and its contents and put it all under the watchful eye of his security team. For a second it looked like he wasn't going to let it go. If not for a strong sense of loyalty to the cause and the fact that John was a Christian and an honorable man, he probably would have fought hard to keep it. But patriotic duty overtook his own desire George Washington style.

John spoke to the group but addressed his security chief "Melvin, take them to the barn, give them the RP then escort them out on the back trail". John turned to Crenshaw and Kaiden "We hid it in a storage room in the barn. Melvin will release it to you along with all your things and your weapons. You are the best people to get it out of here… assemble your team, your mission is to get that rat pack to Allen McKinney, at all costs! Go do it! ASAP!".

Melvin Brooks shouted into his radio "Code 2! Code 2! Prepare people, this is not a drill". That's all he had to say and suddenly the whole Outpost came alive and shifted into high gear. Brooks told Crenshaw "Meet me in the barn after you get your things" and then he ran out. Crenshaw, Kaiden and Ciera ran from the farmhouse and joined several Clear Water members already scurrying from place to place. Crenshaw shouted "Kaiden, we're headed to the village to gather the team and their equipment. Prepare everyone to leave now! We'll all meet at the barn in ten minutes. Let's move it, quickly!".

Fifteen minutes later, Melvin stood outside the barn and greeted Crenshaw and the twelve Patriots that he brought with him. Neil Lee and Vic Coaler were standing there too. They all had their SKP's on (standard kit packs), but it was clear that they didn't have enough time to pack properly or set themselves up like they would have if they had more warning. All of them were in a bit of a disheveled state.

"Twelve? Where are the others?" Melvin asked.

"This is all we could find" Ciera told Melvin.

"Where's Shiloh?" Kaiden asked. Have you seen her?

"Shiloh's down by the river" Paul yelled.

Kaiden reacted immediately. "What? Near the bridge?".

"Yeah, by the bridge where they go swimming".

"I'll get her" Kaiden said. Without hesitation he turned and ran toward the river.

The distinct sound of gunfire rose from the entrance side of the compound. Instantly Melvin's radio came alive with a frantic voice from one of his security guards. "Intruders at border point Victor! I repeat intruders at Victor!". "Point Victor" was code for the front gate where the Patriots bus was parked.

The pop of an AR-15 was heard over everything else. Its frequency grew and quickly turned into what sounded like a battle. Right on its heels came the ominous sound of grenade explosions, first at the perimeter of Clear Water Farms. Then one exploded in the middle of the compound. That one was loud, and the message it sent was clear. Everyone ducked, Melvin looked at Crenshaw with a worried look on his face and yelled "Contact! We got to get you and that rat pack out of here. Follow me." He turned and ran fast toward the barn yelling into his radio as he went. "Prepare! CODE ONE! CODE ONE! I repeat PREPARE CODE ONE! We're under attack!" Brooks waved the guards aside at the barn door and entered. Crenshaw entered with the Patriots right on his heels. With a quick walk, Melvin led them to an open door at the center of the barn. One of his men was walking out with the bugged Glock in his hand. "Get rid of that. Throw it in the river for all I care" Melvin told him. Then Melvin led all of them into the room. His hands were trembling.

On the outside it looked like a double large, enclosed horse stall. It had a solid door with a small window with bars on it. This one had been converted into a jail cell. When Crenshaw entered, it was immediately apparent that it was now being used as a storage room. Inside were all the Patriot's confiscated rifles leaning up against one wall. Some of the supplies they had stored on the bus were stacked there too. "Quickly!" Crenshaw yelled. "Get your weapons and make sure all your magazines are fully loaded". One thing was obviously missing- the rat pack.

Kaiden appeared on the river bank right behind Shilo where she was sitting on a rock next to the water's edge, her bare feet soaking in the cold-water runoff that flowed down from the mountain.

"Shiloh!" Kaiden yelled loudly with angst in his voice. "Shiloh!" he repeated when she didn't immediately respond. Noise from the freely flowing river masked his voice.

Shiloh heard something and turned slowly to see Kaiden running down the river bank toward her. As he ran, he yelled louder "Shilo! You've got to come with me. Now!".

The tone of his voice got her attention. Shiloh stood up with a puzzled look not understanding the severity of the situation. Kaiden got closer yet yelled with the same intensity. "Shiloh, we're at code two, you've got to come with me now!".

"Code 2, what the hell's code 2?". That's when the sound of small arms fire came from the woods on the other side of the river. The crack of rifle fire started slowly, then quickly intensified into something alarming.

"That's not target practice" Kaiden said when he reached her. "Grab your boots and come with me".

Shiloh sat down to put on her boots, but Kaiden scolded her. "We don't have time for that. Take em with you, we've got to go now". Kaiden turned his request into a demand when he grabbed her by the arm and pulled her to her feet. She got the point, nailed home by even more gunfire echoing out of the woods behind them. She complied and followed him without complaint to the top of the river bank, but after stumbling over roots and rocks she stood her ground and would have no more of it. She insisted on sitting down to put her boots on.

The sound of a helicopter's engine preceded its appearance by only a few moments. It came out of nowhere and zoomed over the river bridge. It's low-level flight was shocking enough, but when it started shooting at people it became deadly serious. A CWF member crossing the bridge got hit and went down. Some of the bullets came Kaiden and Shiloh's way but only traced line in the dirt behind them. That turned both into a frantic run up the road towards the barn.

The chopper continued toward its main target and flew past them right up to the south side of the farm house. Most inside never heard it until it was right on top of them. John and Angie ran and looked out a farmhouse window just before bullets spewed from the craft strafing two electric golf carts parked in the driveway in front of the farmhouse. Tires popped, and pieces of it flew making them inoperable and now useless as an option for escape.

John moved fast to shield Angie and pushed her to the center of the living room floor just as the chopper turned its attention and its fire power on the front side of the farmhouse. Perforating lead popped through the walls and ceiling, zipping past the two of them as they huddled together. The building tore up with bullets plinking here and there while making pounding noises on the roof like they were getting hit with softball size hail.

Two farmhouse security guards on the front porch responded and returned fire. The chopper turned its gun on the threat and fired its machine gun running a stitch of bullets across the porch and across one of the guards chests. The man spun around and went down. More militia members from various positions around the Outpost recognized the threat and joined in with return fire of their own.

Inside the helicopter, on an inferred screen, pilots could see the red outline depicting the position of human targets inside the building. The helicopter swung around the other side of the farm house to both dodge bullets and to fire into the walls at the red blotches on the monitor. The gunner shot the building up on each side of the building that the chopper swung to. Wood siding splintered and window glass shattered at every point the gun focused on.

Clearwater militia members who watched from a distance looked on in horror while feeling sorry for anyone inside that farmhouse. Crouched underneath one of the windows, one of Neil Lee's guys got hit when multiple holes appeared in the wall in front of him. He turned around with a look of horror on his face and then fell to the floor. In the middle of the living room floor John clung to Angie with a protective embrace. He raised his head among the carnage of bullets that churned things up and knocked things down all around them. There was a sharp tug on his sleeve and then Angie's body went limp. He looked down at her, the love of his life, the one he was trying to protect. She was bleeding profusely from a bullet wound to the chest. Life went out of her eyes as he held her in his arms.

Inside the barn, Melvin, Crenshaw, Kaiden and Ciera gathered outside the door to the storage room, each looking for guidance from the other. The Patriots, after arming themselves, assembled to each side of them checking and preparing their weapons in anticipation of a fight.

"What now?" Crenshaw asked Melvin. "Where's the rat pack?".

Melvin didn't answer but spoke into his walkie talkie "Report, report".

Out of the black box in his hand came a frantic voice "We got heavy intrusion at the front gate! Shots fired. We're being driven back. Casualties". Melvin's radio had multiple lines. A second security member reported in. "Boarder point 3, Renaissance reporting, I see multiple contacts approaching our position, some in ATV's..." Gunfire was heard in the background and the man said no more.

Into his hand-held radio Melvin yelled "Code 1, Emergency defensive posture code 1. Everyone, report to your stations!". He looked at Crenshaw and then Kaiden. "That's from our position on the south side, it means they're flanking us. If they've got the numbers to do that, we're in trouble".

Smoke began to emanate from one of the farmhouse windows on the south side. The flash of small arms fire coming from a few of the other windows showed that there were still defenders in there fighting back. In the distance out in the field beyond the driveway a line of what looked like soldiers with rifles in their hands were crossing and moving in their direction. Men riding ATV's with a tripod mounted machine gun supported the action. Already they had overwhelmed the security team on that side and were now moving in fast. A CWF sniper in position somewhere in the compound shot and hit an agent crossing the field.

John Shay, in total shock from seeing his wife die right in front of him, got up and walked calmly through a hail of bullets up the stairs to the farm house second floor. He was a zombie that seemed not to notice the bullets that zinged past him. It was amazing that he didn't get hit. Once in the hallway at the top of the stairs he pulled the attic stairs down from the ceiling and climbed up into the attic.

On top of the roof of the farm house, shutters that surrounded what looked like a bell tower fell to the side exposing the silhouette of a person inside. Agents in the helicopter, smiling while enjoying the results of the bullets they dispensed, suddenly found themselves looking down the barrel of an M2 machine gun that protruded out of the bell tower. They only had enough time for the smile to fade from their face when the menace chattered and spit out flame and lead. The chopper had no chance, it was hovering just above the bell tower and took a direct hit from a long spray of bullets. The pilot tried to veer away but a bullet found him, and he was never able to straighten out the craft. It followed an arch trajectory and slammed full force into the ground. The blades hit first then the chopper disintegrated before exploding into a fireball positively killing all on board.

John stood in the middle of that bell tower firing away amongst the noise and constant barrage of empty shell casings that flew and bounced off the floor. After the helicopter went down, he turned his attention to the enemy approaching through the adjacent corn field. Satisfaction came to him only when he hit one of the ATV's speeding across the field. Its driver turned too sharp, and the ATV flipped over. Behind the ATV, two figures went down from a left to right spray of bullets from his Ma Duce. He became invigorated by his success and yelled out "Yeah that's right! Come closer so I can shoot you, you bastards! Come and get it baby, yeah, that's it!". Another agent crossing the field went down.

Smoke coming from the fire in the farmhouse started to pour up from the floorboards underneath John. It soon engulfed the entire bell tower. At this point John might have gone insane because he just kept loading, firing and choking. Soon you couldn't see him at all in the smoke, it was so thick. The wind would blow it clear and then you could see him, still there firing but then once again the black smoke would engulf him. He had that angry 'I don't give a shit' look on his face as he continued to pull the trigger and fight without concern for his own life.

Two of Melvin's security guards came running in to the barn with bad news "There's an Armored BearCat coming up the front drive'.

"Shit! They punched through already? Melvin blurted out. "Let's hope the boys are in position" They all ran to the wide exterior barn door and looked out.

Running, Kaiden pulled on Shiloh's hand forcing her to run in the right direction toward the barn. Looking over his shoulder he saw the enemy. A BearCat was moving fast up the driveway with the gunner firing at targets as it went. Bullets were striking objects around the two of them and another CWF member just ten yards away went down.

The BearCat was tearing up the gravel driveway about to descend upon the compound with conviction. But just before the vehicle got to the wooden bridge over the stream, the bridge blew up in a huge fireball and was torn to pieces. Instead of crossing, the Cat fell into the stream bed and plowed into the bridge's concrete support wall. Neither the occupants nor the vehicle was able to move.

"YEAH!" welled up from the group as well as exuberant high fives at various defensive positions around the compound. It was quite an accomplishment. In the first few minutes of the battle, they had already taken out the chopper, a BearCat and a few ATV's. But the celebration was short lived. The farmhouse, including the bell tower, was now engulfed in flames. John's M2 had fallen silent, and Melvin knew what that meant. He couldn't believe it. John was dead.

A second BearCat drove up behind the first and stopped just before the blown-out bridge. About twelve Black Jacks holding rifles exited the back of the vehicle. Those men quickly dispersed down into the stream bed which gave them cover. In addition, the ones who were able, climbed out of the disabled cat to join them. More Agents ran up the road behind them. Soon a steady volley of fire was peppering the defenders' positions from that side as well as from the south where the flanking team of agents and ATV's had gotten into attack position on the near side of the field.

Kaiden and Shiloh made it to the barn completely out of breath. "They're right behind us!" he yelled at Melvin.

Melvin was shocked. But the seriousness of the situation and concern for their lives snapped him back to reality. The farm was in serious jeopardy. "We're about to be overrun" He yelled at Crenshaw. "Quickly, come with me. I got a plan".

4

JOB WELL DONE

Way too quickly it had become obvious to Melvin Brooks that the Feds were going to succeed at closing in and would soon over-run the compound. Brooks changed tactics quickly and went from defense into survival mode. He turned and led Crenshaw's team back into the barn and back into the same jail cell/storage room that they had gotten their weapons from. In the corner of that room was a well-hidden wooden hatch in the floor which when opened exposed a service ramp with a set of stairs that led down into the storage area below, that's where he directed the Patriots to go.

Before he closed the hatch behind them all, Brooks gave some last-minute instruction: "Down there you will find that this is where we have hidden the rat pack. You and that pack must survive at all costs. Do not enter this fight no matter what you hear. I'll close the hatch behind you and hide it as best I can. Stay down for a few days until things quiet down. Don't make any noise! Wait till dark and find your way out to the Skanellis Mountain trailhead. Kaiden and Ciera know where it is". He spoke to Kaiden- "The trail you and Ciera started up on Mt. Skanellis splits off at the base about a mile up…".

"Yes sir, we saw it" Kaiden replied.

"It goes west. I know it's going to be tough, but this is the only chance we have to get the load out of here and into the hands of people who deserve it. You're all we got".

"We won't fail you sir".

With that, Melvin closed the hatch on a bunch of worried faces. Their lives were in his hands. He tried his best to make the outline of the hatch in the floor disappear by stamping horse manure into the cracks and throwing a little sandy dirt on top of it. Next Melvin did a curious thing. He had one of his guys bolt the door from the outside making it look like he was locked in, then he put hand cuffs on his wrists and sat down in the middle of the room.

It was the hardest thing that Kaiden and his fifteen companions had ever done. To pack in that room and stay quiet without moving. It was extremely nerve racking. They had been down there for hours now, waiting, waiting for what felt like a whole lot longer than it actually was.

There was only enough room for each of them to turn around and just barely enough room to sit and stretch their legs. CWF had stored dehydrated food and other supplies down there as well, making it positively crowded and uncomfortable for a large group of people to be down there. The storage room had a dirt floor, so they were able to dig a hole in one corner for use as a toilet. It was such a hassle to get to it and very embarrassing to use it. Crenshaw was afraid it would wreak and give them away, so everyone tried not to use it. It was enough to drive someone crazy.

* * *

The Feds Special Agent in Charge (SAIC) was respectfully called "Captain" on these missions. On this one, his name was Hermon Gutierrez. He stood in front of the collapsed Clear Water farm house surveying the damage. Smoke emanated from its charred remains with fire still burning in a few places. The Captain had his hands on his hips looking around with indifference. Lying on the ground scattered around the compound were the lifeless bodies of the men and women of the Clear Water Militia. Smoke and the smell of burnt remains floated in the air. His men moved back and forth across the compound with their rifles slung low while they finished securing the premises. Subordinates were busy taking inventory. His Sargent compiled those reports and was reading them out loud to the captain from a digital note book.

"Looks like we achieved the advantage of surprise Sir. Got thirty-nine of em', thirty dead and nine prisoners. Eight of those are wounded, six seriously. Probably won't last the night".

"Did any escape?".

"No sir, I don't think so. We got em' surrounded pretty good and our drone had the rear covered. There were no reports of anyone getting out" the Sargent said.

"What's the stats on ours?".

"Eight dead, thirteen wounded".

Gutierrez was shocked but all he allowed himself to say was "Damn it!" Then he asked "Any further resistance?".

"All resistance has been quelled sir; we're completing mop up operations now".

"Have you found anything of value among all this garbage Sargent?".

"We're trying to bust into that safe we found in the remains of the farm house now. Otherwise, no large stash of money at any other location Sir. Nothing else reported in the main compound besides that large cache of weapons, ammunition, and tons of dehydrated food we found in the barn. Looks like they could have held out against a siege for years with all that stuff".

"Anything in the outer area buildings?".

"Nothing yet Sir, Hodges unit is out there now".

"Tell him to send out a patrol to look for any strays or evidence of survivors just to be sure, otherwise Sargent we're done here. Let's wrap up the bodies and get the hell out of here".

Clear Water Farms had a significant number of trained personnel to defend against an attack and they were very well supplied but their director John Shay hadn't prepared them for a war. Allen McKinney had advised all cluster outposts to strengthen their defenses. Some took his advice more seriously than others. Definitely a bit of "It could never happen here" was evident at CWF. The Feds arrival as well as the intensity of their attack was a shock to all. Everyone at the Farm had been caught off guard and yet they put up a valiant fight against a far superior force. Some militia members refused to give up but ultimately one position at a time was overwhelmed and then Federal agents flowed freely into the compound. Black Jackets, sometimes called 'Black Jacks" surrounded the barn. They took out its defenders and then stormed the building. Eventually they burst through the lock on the jail cell door with rifles and flash lights pointing in all directions. Every Militia member hiding under the floor could hear Melvin Brooks scream "Don't shoot! Don't shoot! I'm a prisoner here! Don't shoot!". The Feds questioned him and escorted him out. Brooks gave them a fake name and told them he was a conscientious objector and that he had turned against the Militia's cause. "For committing such a sin, the Militia locked me up in this cell" he told them.

For now, the Feds accepted his story, took him prisoner, and left without any further scrutiny. Brooks accomplished his goal. Mainly saving his own ass. They didn't suspect the room was used for anything else except a jail cell and never searched hard enough to find the hatch in the floor. Occasionally, an agent would come back, enter the room and look around. But there wasn't much to see so he always left in short order. At one point they threw a bunch of CWF prisoners in there and used it as a temporary holding cell. Crenshaw ordered his crew to stay put and forbid any movement, sound or contact even with their own people.

The next day the Feds removed the prisoners and things calmed down to almost no movement around the farm at all. Still, Crenshaw allowed more time to pass in the hope that they would leave before trying to make a move. The team spent two days hiding underneath those floorboards. Down there, packed in boxes next to them, were the same items that the Feds had found stored in various other places around the farm. Looking around, the Patriots found themselves jammed up against boxes of dehydrated meal packs, ammunition, various items of survival gear including winter clothing and other supplies. It ended up being convenient to have these items at their disposal and they took full advantage of it. In the meantime, they lived on granola bars and dry cereal from the meal packs and were able to prepare and stock up on ammunition and other items that they knew they would need.

All CWF property and its contents was confiscated by the Federal government. An act that was constitutionally illegal but one that had recently become routine. They had weaponized "confiscation" and used it against perceived enemies to weaken their ability to function. It was also the IRS's preferred technique used to tap into new revenue sources. Their job: to enforce the "New Laws", new laws that congress never voted on or approved. Laws which turned "We The People" into "they the enemy".

During daylight hours the Feds ushered in work crews that stripped the farm of everything of value; Cars, farm equipment, guns, ammunition, and the stockpile of survival food and gear they had found. On the third day the horses were removed from the barn and taken away on a transport. Without a working farm house, the place wasn't worth much, especially in such a remote location.

At night on the third day the level of activity as well as the Feds onsite presence diminished to the point where Crenshaw decided that it was time to make their move. First, very cautiously, reconnaissance was sent out to determine what they were up against. For the first time a member of the team crept out of the hatch and into the shadows to determine the strength of the enemy's presence. They reported back that only a skeleton crew of either federal agents or hired security had been left behind to guard the property. The location of vehicles and the guards were observed and noted.

At 2:00AM the entire Patriot team slid out of the underground storage room. Six of them painstakingly pushed the 300-pound rat pack up the ramp and into the jail cell while the others took up positions in and around the barn. Outside, the Feds still had a Bearcat and two Humvee's stationed at the opposite (entrance) side of a temporary military type replacement bridge that they had set up next to the blown out one. Also, they had set up three manned positions within the compound where two guards were stationed at each location.

"Damn, how many of them BearCats do they have?" Kaiden said to Crenshaw as they peered out the barn door.

"Enough to keep us on the run" he replied. "But at this stage of the game I'm betting that security is here to keep people out rather than to keep anyone in. I'm betting their attention will be focused outward toward the front entrance rather than toward the back of the property".

At daylight, 12:00PM and then in the evening, 6:00PM, the Feds sent out patrols that roamed the compound and checked in with the guard posts. Such a patrol was out that night. Headlights from their vehicle gave away their position.

Crenshaw and the entire crew, one at a time, maneuvered around both the vehicle and the guards and made it to the rear of the property without being seen. Kaiden and Ciera led the team to the beginning of the Skanelis Mountain Trail where the lot of them hiked it out of there as fast as they could go. Once again, it was back to dealing with the motherload. No one relished the idea of pushing it over a rough hiking trail. They knew what they were in for.

About a mile up Skanelis Mountain Trail they took a left turn at the junction of an unnamed trail and headed west just as Brooks had advised. From there they made a clean getaway and disappeared into the foot hills with every one of them wondering where they were going next.

5

SURVIVAL AT ALL COST

It proved to be a tough hike as any of the Patriots pushing and pulling that damn three-hundred-pound rat pack would attest to. Everyone thought that they were finally done with what they un-affectionally called "The Motherload" but here they found themselves hauling it... again. As soon as the team reached what Crenshaw considered a safe distance away, he ordered a ten-minute rest and held an impromptu meeting with the now fourteen other members of his team.

Out of breath Crenshaw told them all "A plan is only as good as our desire to carry it out. And we frickin did it! Even though none of this was planned. I'm proud of you guy's. I want to congratulate all of you on a job well done. Most of them smiled at that but a worried/concerned look quickly replaced it.

"I don't know" Kaiden stated. "Everything depends on whether the Feds are on to us".

"How confident are we that they're not following us?" Jerry asked. Jerry Reeder was Crenshaw's right-hand man, a Seargent in training, a great shot, and one of the Patriots Crenshaw assigned the job of erasing their tracks along the trail as they went.

"They don't have a tracker on us now and they don't even know we're alive" Crenshaw said. "I'd say we're free and clear".

"Yeah, but how confident are we that Melvin Brooks won't talk or anyone else for that matter?" Ciera stated more than asked.

"And all the gold in the world can't help us survive out here in the Adirondack Mountains. Where're we going?" Betsy Stoiber asked. Betsy was one of the three remaining female members of the group.

"I don't know. We're just going to follow this trail and see where it leads" Crenshaw said.

Crenshaw had them stock up on food and clothing from the storage room, so they were well supplied. Some took jackets from an old trunk to prepare for colder weather in the mountains. Due to the way things went down at the farm all anyone had time to do was to grab their back pack. The jackets they took and the clothes on their backs were all they had to their name. Luckily, they got their weapons back just before the curtain came down.

The standard equipment kit in each of their back packs gave them most everything they would need to survive in an emergency like the one they were in. It was part of their SOP (Standard Operating Procedure) for a reason. Hence the basis for requiring every Cadet to keep their "go bag" packed, ready to go, and within arm's reach. Now the why of it was crystal clear.

A Patriot named Donnie Canter spoke up "I don't care if they're on our tail, I welcome it. I'd rather fight than run. They killed my friends..." he said as he stared off into space. "I never signed on for this hide and run bullshit. I can't stand it".

"Yeah, they could attack at any moment" Jerry said. "But I'm with Donnie. I'd rather be on the offensive. I say we go back and kick some ass".

Crenshaw jumped on that "I'm afraid that wouldn't be the most prudent thing to do. 'Defense' is the way we are going to play this for a while until we can turn it around. If it ever gets turned around. But delivering this rat pack to Allen McKinney will enable us to do just that. I know. Things are so screwed up. Yes, you joined and swore allegiance to our cause with the belief that this was something you could do to fight back. But I need every one of you to remember the higher goal: 'We the People' are going to fight to force our government to reinstate the Constitution and then this time… to abide by it".

It had always been obvious that Crenshaw was an enthusiastic constitutionalist. He took this opportunity to plug the cause. He told them "Most of us thought that our government could never turn against us and label people who think like us as 'extremists'. A few among us, like Allen McKinney, believed that government alienation was not only possible but inevitable. I can hear the anti-gunners now, they constantly said "Why do you think you need guns to fight against a tyrannical government? That's just silly". This nails the point home; governments tend to gravitate towards a top down ever tightening rule of its people, people who they increasingly see as subjects, not as equals. Government, combined with the corrupt side of human nature, eventually forms a cancer that consumes the people it's designed to protect. When it gets out of control and loses its ability to function effectively; the oppressed, meaning us, the very people calling for a cure, become the enemy of the disease.

All we're demanding is to get back to the way we were. Get back to the guiding principles of the Constitution which history has proven to be the way for personal freedom to thrive. But no, we see that the disease dislikes the cure. We are very inconvenient to its survival. Yes, they are right. We would limit their ability to manipulate and physically squeeze more money out of a system that no longer has any more to give. They can't stand the thought of limitation. The cure is to re-instate the Constitution and empower congress. That will eliminate the ability of the disease to metastasize".

Jerry stuck in a comment "Well the Constitution didn't do such a good job of it before now, did it". Some people murmured in agreement.

"No, it's not the constitution, 'We The People' didn't do such a good job of it. We let this happen".

Ciera chimed in. Her conviction to the cause had been cemented in stone due to recent events and she added fire to the argument. "We're going to have to get used to the fact that we're at war with these progressive socialists. They want to take away our liberty along with every ounce of profit stemming from any work we do. It's not a conspiracy theory now, they've made their move, we know it's true and we know they'll do anything to maintain their power.

This is a total disregard for our right to pursue happiness and that cold hard fact changes everything, everything! It changes all you have become comfortable with and puts us smack dab at odds with a rogue government that has crossed the line. It's become an ever-expanding force whose tentacles are reaching out to invade our lives. Each one with a syphoning effect that eats away at our substance.

Now you know that we, you and I, will have to physically fight at one point or another. We will face them! Here or at our next stop or in some future battle. It doesn't matter. I think we all need to consider our sworn oath to each other and understand exactly what that means. I want revenge as much as any of you. Believe me, oh boy do I want revenge. But we can't afford the luxury of confrontation right now. Our cargo is the most important mission that any one of us could be on. We got a second chance here to get this through, and it's imperative that we do. Let me assure you that getting this rat pack back to the Patriot Outpost is the most important thing that any one of us could ever do for the cause. Now that will be sweet revenge, wouldn't it?".

"That's if we can make it without being captured or killed" Jerry said.

Ciera and Crenshaw gave each other a glance because they both knew that it was a very plausible outcome to this adventure. Even though Ciera out ranked Crenshaw, Ciera allowed him to take command of the Pioneer team without pulling rank. After all, it was his team, and he had successfully kept them all alive up to this point. That drew a lot of respect from the entire group.

Crenshaw turned to them and acknowledged Ciera's rank by saying "The Lieutenant's right. I propose that we all dig down deep and pledge to deliver the motherload. Getting it back into the fold will be the best form of revenge that we could possibly shovel on the Feds. We'll have to lay low for a while in the mountains to make sure they're not following us. We're going to follow this trail until we find a good place to hold up. I got a plan as to how we're going to proceed". He looked at Ciera. "I'll discuss that with you later". Then he said to everyone "We weren't prepared for any of this so we're going to have to work together to make it through. Are you with me?".

"Aye!". "Here, here". "We're with you man!" shouted the members of the Patriots who were now composed of members from more than one cluster.

Crenshaw hiked them hard for seven days to get the team and that damn rat pack as far away as possible. Their load slowed them down to an average of about six miles per day. It was difficult to know what to do when they encountered other hikers. A large group such as theirs was not unheard of but a group of this size with some of them carrying firearms and looking as "military" as they did surely would raise a few eyebrows. When they came across two particular hikers, Crenshaw avoided answering strategic questions and concentrated on gathering information. He asked them if they had a spare map of the area. They did not, but they allowed Crenshaw to study the single map they had. They were able to produce a pen and paper so Crenshaw could write notes.

From signs and their hand drawn map they found out that the unnamed trail Brooks set them on eventually led them to one called Botheration Pond Trail which then connected into Puffer Pond Brook Trail. That trail took them west, into the heart of the Siamese Wilderness. Continuing on, which felt like forever, they rolled across a slew of other trails with names like Kings Flow East, Round Pond, and Kunjamuk Trail. Whenever they came across a fork, Crenshaw opted to stay on the path that promised to keep them as isolated from other people as possible. He stuck to the same mode of operation that allowed them to stay undetected on the march out of the Academy. Luckily, the area they were in offered plenty of isolation.

Although the trail had been well maintained by various volunteer groups (one of the signs boasted that fact) it was rough going. Especially when the rat pack crew encountered downed trees or a steep climb.

To minimize the military appearance of the team, Crenshaw made all but two of them pack their rifles out of sight in their backpacks. That was the beauty of the SU16, and why the Academy chose that weapon as the weapon of choice. It folded up small and fit into their pack, yet it can be deployed quickly. Jerry and Kaiden carried what were the group's two sniper rifles slung across their backs. A .308 Winchester SX-AR and a Les Baer .308 SA Match rifle with a stainless-steel barrel and a Night-force 5.5-22X 56 mm NXS scope. Both had a long barrel (24 inches) which made them impossible to hide. So, they slung them over their shoulders and proclaimed they were hunters. The Winchester was the Academy's choice for a semi auto 'hunting' rifle but mostly because it wasn't that popular of a rifle, so they were able to buy a bunch of them for half the price of a good quality AR-10. Cadets who passed sniper training and had received the coveted sniper patch were allowed to buy a sniper rifle of their choosing if it fit standard Cadet requirements which just meant that it had to be light in weight, chambered in .308, semi-automatic was preferred, and of course it had to be accurate as hell. The Winchester SX-AR was all of that.

One luxury they encountered on the trail was when they came upon a shelter. A shelter is a small hut or lean two type wooden structure with a floor and a roof that can hold varying numbers of people depending on its size. Invested local groups build these shelters in strategic places along the trail for the benefit of overnight hikers. Similar structures are called "AMC huts" in the white mountains of New Hampshire and are close in style to the one the Academy built on top of Tenny Mountain. Sometimes they have four walls and a door but mostly they are just three sided with one open side facing a fire pit. It's a much more convenient place to stay than having to find a flat area of ground to set up a tent. Sometimes there's a shelter located as close as eight or ten miles apart, others are fewer and farther in between, either way they all have one thing in common, there's a clean source of drinking water nearby.

After seven days of hiking along with a little down time thrown in for much needed rest, Crenshaw and crew made it over to the Northville Placid Trail which ran north and south in the middle of the Siamese Wilderness. Crenshaw guided the crew south on that until they came across another AMC hut. Everyone liked this campsite. It was located next to a lake in a consumer-friendly valley setting; meaning it wouldn't be as cold as it would have been if they stumbled across a hut at a higher elevation. Plus, it had a clean drinkable source of flowing water nearby. The hut was nicely built and was one of the few with four enclosed sides and a door. Although it could only accommodate eight of them and their equipment comfortably the others could tent in an area right next to the hut. Remarkably it had a small hibachi style stove sitting inside a stone fire place which meant that it was possible to cook and warm the place up with a fire if needed. Lookouts sent back along the trail in the direction they had come reported no evidence that they were being followed, knowing that they all voted to extend their stay at this location and hold up for a while. The troop settled in and made plans for the next stage of their journey.

Crenshaw wanted to avoid as much exposure as possible, yet he knew that if they decided to stay for any length of time, they would need supplies. Having touched the evil that man is capable of, everyone was wary about coming off the trail and injecting themselves back into a society where evil perpetuates. They felt relatively safe in the valley, and no one wanted to spoil that feeling.

But it was inevitable, their food started to run out and they were forced to plan a trip. The trip into town would be the first of a two-part plan to get the team back on the road and moving in the direction of the Pioneer Outpost. They couldn't stay in the mountains; cold nights reminded them that the weather was fickle in the mountains, even in the summer. A squad was chosen to make the trek into town to get supplies but also to have badly needed repairs done on the rat pack. The frame on the rat pack had cracked and a piece of aluminum needed to be welded on to strengthen the joint. They also needed to replace the bearings on one of the wheels as well as to address some other minor issues. The rat pack was unloaded, and the precious metal was hidden in an inconspicuous location not far from the camp site. Lieutenant Lowman would lead the five-person squad and take the mostly empty rat pack into town. Of course, Kaiden volunteered to go with her.

* * *

Just off the trail leading into town, sitting in a hut, and still immersed in her own thoughts, Ciera came back to reality just as Kaiden walked up. She was still sitting there on the wooden floor of the hut engrossed in strong memories with her sleeping bag pulled up around her.

"What did you dose off again" Kaiden asked her. He swooped in, sat down next to her, and grabbed her with a big playful bear hug. It made her smile. She giggled when he tried to kiss her neck. There was a weak attempt to push him away but then she gasped out loud when he tried to slide his cold hands inside the sleeping bag and touch warm bare skin.

"Oh no you don't" she said. "You'll have to warm those up first before I let you in here". She successfully pushed his hands out but took them and pulled them into her belly and curled herself around them to attempt to warm them up. Kaiden laughed.

"Hey guys, get a hut will you" one of the sleeping bags lying on the floor next to them spoke.

Kaiden leaned in close to Ciera and whispered "Not a bad idea" just before he kissed her. But then he turned and said to the four lifeless sleeping bags "Alright guys, it's time to get up. We've got some miles to put behind us. Let's shake two legs. We leave in twenty".

The hut they had stayed in was the last hut on the Northville Placid trail before the final stretch going south into the town of Piseco. The hikers knew they were close when they hit paved road at the outskirts of town. Following it they were surprised when the first thing they came upon was the Piseco Post Office. They were also surprised to see that it was open. The airport situated next to the post office was no surprise. Crenshaw had it marked on his hand made map. After minimizing their gun footprint by packing them away, they were able to obtain a real map of the area from inside the post office. Now the lay of the land was a whole lot easier to understand.

"My name's Rudy Lancaster, nice to meet you" the Post Office Clerk told them. "It's not often I see a group of people all dressed in camo. You guy's almost look military". Kaiden shook the guys hand and explained.

"Nah, not military. We're an explorers group on a hike and we were told to wear our uniforms. But hey, I'm not going to knock it, these pants are great for hiking, I love em'. We've been out there for a week. Just came in to town to see if we can get a welding job done on that cart". Kaiden poked his thumb in the direction of the parking lot.

"Oh gosh, there's basically nothing here in Piseco except town folk, an airstrip and this here Post Office" said the clerk. "But you can find a machine shop on route 8 going north into Speculator or you can go south on 8. There's a motorcycle repair shop that a way. Either of them could do a welding job fer ya".

"Thank you, Post Master Rudy Lancaster" Kaiden saluted him. "We'll try the machine shop first".

"Rudy, we haven't heard any news for over a week now. How's things going out there" Ciera asked.

"Yes, is there anything we need to know?" Kaiden added.

"Oh, you haven't heard. Martial law's been declared, the country's gone to shit. Normally not much national stuff affects us here, Piseco and Speculator is a small town. But this is different, I can tell you that. This is trouble. I hear there's trouble in some of the larger towns and cities mostly. Riots. These folk here don't have anything to complain about even though they still do. We're a peaceful bunch. But I guess I got to warn you, watch out for the sheriff. He and his deputy are taking this seriously. They're roaming around and not taking shit from nobody".

"Well thanks for the warning. He's got nothing to worry about with us. We're a peaceful bunch" Kaiden said with a smile. "Oh, are planes still taking off from here?".

"Some. The rest of them planes out there haven't moved for a while. I guess everyone's trying to figure out a way to get or to pay for gas. The government's in turmoil. My paycheck has stopped coming along with a lot of other things. You're lucky you found me here. I'm only here because I got nothing else to do so I came in for a few hours" Rudy said.

"Any news about what the governments doing about this?" Kaiden asked.

"Well supposedly they're going to roll out a new currency, something like a worldwide digital coin or so they say, but they haven't got it worked out yet. I wish they'd hurry up. Internet's still down. I'm sure they would have to repair that first. In the meantime, nobody knows what's going to happen. But what's more important is 'when' will something happen. People are starting to panic. I don't even know if there's anyone at the machine shop up there. Some businesses are open, and some are not. Even the stock markets closed, can you beat that?".

"Wow, I figured as much" Kaiden commented.

"We got some movement though. Yesterday I got an official Federal memorandum delivered by our new Federal representative. One of the few things that has been delivered recently. He posted it over there and gave me a bunch of copies to hand out. It's on the bulletin board, you can take one with you". Kaiden and Ciera walked over and read it.

> Official United States Document of Notification.
>
> From:
>
> The Department of Justice in conjunction with the President of the United States of America.

A STATE OF EMERGENCY HAS BEEN DECLARED

In pursuant of the Federal Government's inherent Constitutional responsibility to protect and serve the public at large, Martial Law is hereby officially declared for the 50 states bound by union. Hence forth, Supreme authority is now granted and bestowed upon the Federal Government of The United States of America to address the crisis more adequately and effectively. The Supreme Court, chaired by the President will now have the power to exercise exclusive legislation and administer like authority in all States to target the crisis more precisely without un due delay. Hither to, all State and Local Governments are now relinquished and subsequently determined subservient to the will and laws of Federal authority. Furthermore, the States are required to relinquish all State-owned property to the newly empowered Federal Government to allow the accomplishment of responsibilities. We the people through the Federal government now assume responsibility for economic restoration and demand compliance from all administrations to abide by such laws of design to maintain unification of the United States of America and effectuallize a return to previous state. This action is deemed essential and is granted by the people, for the National Security of the people. Central law clarification will follow.

Signed,
President Richfield and Counsel

"Wow!" Kaiden said with a gasp. All the ramifications of what he just read were swirling in his mind. "I can't believe this. Do you know what this means!".

"Effectuallize?" Ciera said. "Now they're even making up new words. Yeah, I know what it means, it's the end of our republic that's what it means".

Kaiden didn't wait for anything more. He turned and shouted over to Rudy at the counter. "What the hell is this!".

"Well, we think it means the Federal Government is going to kick it in gear and get something done. No one in Congress can agree on the best way to go. Couldn't get anything passed. I welcome it. Maybe now we can get things moving".

"You don't mind that the Federal Government has just taken over and you have just lost all your Constitutional rights?".

"No, I don't think we've lost our rights. I think we have just shed some inefficient bureaucracy. I hope they can fix this, maybe my paycheck will start showing up again".

It was immediately apparent that Rudy was on the government dole and wasn't going to be sympathetic to the Patriots cause. "I see. Ok thanks again for the information Rudy. Can I have a copy of that?".

"Sure can. I gave most of em' to the Sheriff to hand out. There's gunna be a town meeting tomorrow night at 7PM At Lake Pleasant Town Hall to discuss it".

"Ok, thanks Rudy. Have a good day" Kaiden said.

"Hey, come to think about it, take down this address. Its Hanks. Hank Quaid. The guy lives just down the street in the corner house. He works at the machine shop I referred you too. If it ain't open, then he'll be home. I think he'll be able to help you out".

"Alright, thanks Rudy" Kaiden turned to go.

"But he don't take no dollar bills" the clerk yelled after him.

The address they got was just down the road, so they stopped at Hank Quaid's house to see if anyone was home. Four of them waited on the corner with the RP and two went up to the door without their guns. Their attempt to not alarm the occupants didn't work. Someone inside was peering out the window, he saw the guys on the corner and became suspicious. Their camo uniforms didn't help either. The guy yelled through the window without pleasantries and without unlocking the door. "What do you want?".

"Are you Hank? We heard you're a welder and that you could help us out" Kaiden said.

He looked them over. After seeing Ciera standing there with her best smile on, he said "Yeah, I'm Hank. Hold on a minute". There was some rustling inside, some rattling at the door and then it opened.

"Yeah, what can I do for you?".

Hank had a shotgun in his arms which he held in a manner that made it conspicuous. He looked to be about thirty years old and from the looks of things he had been doing just fine up until the Collapse. It was a nice house, and a fairly new pickup truck was parked in the driveway. In the conversation that followed Hank told them that he was not working now, he had been instructed to take a vacation until this crisis was straightened out. "I'm home... at limbo" he said when it came to work. Even still they were able to strike a deal for a welding job. Ciera used her natural ability to charm the guy and quickly diffused his apprehension, but she had to give him her speech about the value of money before he would accept a single silver eagle coin for the work that needed to be done.

"Hank the dollar has lost all its value, so you've got to stop thinking in terms of 'the dollar'; although I'm going to contradict myself and tell you the value of this coin in dollars just to enable me to give you some kind of indication about where we're at. I know that doesn't make any sense. None of this does. This one silver eagle coin is one ounce of silver". She took one out of her pocket and showed it to him. "It will be worth something like over two hundred dollars in last year's dollar value if it isn't already" (that was totally arbitrary, but she went with it anyway). "But there I go again... I'm talking about dollars which really doesn't mean anything anymore. No one's accepting the dollar now because they don't trust it. So, what really matters is what you and I think this coin is worth. In other words, how valuable is it to us? Right now, I can imagine that everyone will be trying to barter right? You've got to give a bunch of stuff for a bunch of stuff, right? (Ciera got him nodding his head yes). So how valuable would it be to be able to use this coin to get a bunch of stuff in trade (she held up the silver metal) and all for a little coin like this one?".

"I'd say that would be a whole lot better than carrying around a bunch of 'stuff' to trade" Hank said.

"Precisely! Very valuable. Because something that could do that would be in high demand right now, or if not, very soon it's going to be. And you know, when something is in high demand, people will trade a whole lot for it. Well, it's the same thing here. People will give a lot for this". She held up the pretty shiny silver coin between her two fingers.

"You, in turn, can take this coin and buy a lot of stuff because right now there is no other way to do it without lugging around truckloads of stuff to trade. People out there are desperately seeking a means to transact business. This is it. This coin accomplishes that. Anyone will take this as a legal tender. You, see?

Ciera prattled back and forth with Hank for a while until he believed her and gave in. "Ok, I'll take it" Hank said. Then he offered to drive the six of them and the rat pack up to the machine shop in his pickup truck. After a bit more coaxing Ciera got him to lend them the truck so they could drive into town while he was doing the repairs. Hank was obviously enamored with Ciera but, not to give her all the credit, he might have been enamored with the silver coin as well. Being a machinist, Hank went on and on about what was needed. "You're gunna need a welded brace right here to shore up that frame and might as well put one on the other side too so it don't do the same thing there. I can see you've been carrying a lot of weight in this thing. The wheels are good but the rubber's getting chewed up here. This one needs a new bearing. I'd put another brace on the wheel support… I can get parts from Jay's bike store…" he went on.

In the truck while driving into town Kaiden high fived Ciera. "Nice going" he said.

Ciera commented "…pure psychology".

Kaiden fired back "Oh, flirting with him and sashaying that ass of yours had nothing to do with it huh?".

Ciera smiled "...well maybe that had a little to do with it". She laughed and punched him hard on the shoulder.

Having Hank's truck to drive around allowed them to accomplish things in a lot shorter period of time. While driving over to the small town of Speculator N.Y. they found they were able to move around without the constant fear of violence or road blocks. Rudy was right, the people here were peaceful and pleasant to deal with. Although it wasn't the town's folk they were watching out for. Here there seemed to be no need to shoulder their rifles, so they left them in their packs. But their packs always stayed within arm's reach.

Ciera gave her magic "Value of money" speech everywhere they went. Some people needed a little more 'help' than others to get comfortable with... not the precious metal itself but equating it to an upgraded level of perceived value. Others didn't need the speech at all, they were already there.

First, and above all else, one of those speeches got them all an extremely, much desired pizza dinner at the Old Country Pizza restaurant in down town Speculator. They ate exceedingly well in exchange for a silver eagle. Another coin got them some new clothes and hiking boots at a small mom and pop retail outlet. Then after driving back to Piseco and stopping in at the Irondequoit Inn, a gold coin got them all a two-week rental on a really nice cabin. The owners were impressed and more than willing to take payment in gold coin. How much of it (in weight) was the only thing they haggled over. Conveniently the Inn was located just down the road from the Post Office and the Northville Placid trail head. The cabin they rented slept six and that night the Patriots slept in a bed or on a soft mattress for the first time in a long while. With such a meal and a bed, they were feeling a bit guilty.

Kaiden and Jerry got up early the next day to take advantage of what Kaiden called "lake energy". They went down and practiced Tai

Chi at a cleared beach like section of land next to water that reflected the surrounding scenery like a glass mirror. The Irondequoit Inn is more like a resort in its setting. Quaint cabins, lake front and beautiful scenery is right outside your door. The others slept in, but not for long. They were all on a mission.

At first it was hard to get around because they had given Hank's truck back the night before. The clerk at the Inn told them "Sorry guy's, we normally run a shuttle into town for our guests but due to the crash we're not offering that service. You're on your own".

Before Kaiden's squad left Crenshaw on the trail, he made it clear that he loved the bus idea. "Try and find us a bus" he told them. "It worked well last time, and I'd love to duplicate it. Then get back here to the camp site with those supplies. We're going to need them".

Acquiring transportation had to be next on their list of things to do to facilitate obtaining supplies. Ciera decided it would be easier for the two of them to hitch hike into Speculator. They left Jerry in charge and at nine o'clock, Ciera and Kaiden set out walking.

It just happened that within walking distance of the Inn on Route 8 was Piseco Elementary school. Ciera was elated, it was an easy walk and there were two yellow school buses parked side by side in the parking lot. No one was at the school. It was closed and deserted. It was frustrating, there was no one to talk too about renting one of those buses. To gather information from neighbors they wandered around for an hour looking for people to talk to. The people they encountered either didn't know who to contact or if they did know a phone number or an address, it didn't do them any good. The cell towers were down, and they couldn't drive to a distant address. Everyone asked Ciera and Kaiden if they knew why the cell phones were still down. No one had an answer.

One consolation was that one of the people they spoke with gave them the name of a person they could reach who worked at the Mountain Market in Speculator. "He'll have the supplies your looking for or know where to get them" the guy told them.

Walking, as well as walking with a pack, had become more normal than riding so it wasn't the fact that they had to walk, it was just that they were now walking on a road which was boring as hell. It took a long time to hitch a ride. There weren't many cars that came by. Finally, one stopped and took them all the way into the town of Speculator. The old man and his wife who picked them up were kind enough to drop them off at the market.

Bargaining with the market's owner was easy. Heck, he had a sign on the door that said "Sorry... No Dollars Accepted. Silver, Gold or Barter Only". There was no need for Ciera's 'value of money' speech, they just had to haggle over the number of silver coins in trade. Abba Jenson was the owners name. He told them "I can get you some of the things on this list like beef jerky and granola, but I'll have to scrounge up the dehydrated food packs" he told them.

"But can you get them?" Kaiden asked.

"I can get it. I know a guy that has been stockpiling this stuff for quite a while now. He'll be more than willing to part with some of it, especially for silver coin".

A deal was struck. Their supplies would be ready for pick up first thing the following morning. With their shopping list pretty much filled the two of them hitched back to the Irondequoit Inn. It was getting late. Once again it took a long time to hitch a ride. They walked what felt like most of the way before being picked up.

"Damn I'm beat" Kaiden said when the two of them finally arrived back at the Inn's parking lot.

"Yeah, it's already 6 o'clock in the afternoon and we don't have a lead on a bus. Might have to get to a larger town" Ciera said.

Kaiden stopped in his tracks. "Wait a minute. What's that". Off in the corner of the Inn's parking lot sat a small bus. They both looked at each other and raised their eyebrows as the possibility dawned on them. Why didn't we think of that before?" Kaiden said.

"Wow, the clerk told us this morning that their shuttle wasn't being used. I don't know why I didn't think of it either" Ciera said.

It was a StarCraft Allstar bus. More of a 'shuttle' than a bus really. The Inn used it as a perk for patrons. During season it ran on a regular schedule into town and was available to transport groups to special events. Ciera went to talk to the owner about renting it.

Kaiden was still staring at the bus when Ciera came back. "They were more than willing to rent it to us" She was smiling while dangling the keys in front of him. "It's even got a toilet in the back" she said. Kaiden smiled back and grabbed the keys and then he grabbed her around the waist and pulled her close. They kissed in celebration of their good luck.

It was smaller than the yellow cheese bus they had previously, but it was perfect. The bus had fifteen seats and sat 30+ with a fair amount of storage space in the back compartment. There was more luggage space in compartments located on each side. Since their team was smaller now than it had been on their trek to CWF, it would do nicely. That evening they used it to drive the squad over to Lake Pleasant Town Hall. They arrived at 6:30 for the town meeting that started at 7PM.

6

DOCTOR IN THE HOUSE

Lake Pleasant Town Hall is not a very large building, but it served its purpose. It offered a large capacity meeting room for the surrounding area in which meetings like this one could take place. The fire code said it could legally seat one hundred and twenty with standing room for forty-five. Now the room was filled to capacity with overflow that was forced to stand in the back or outside. People arrived in every type of transportation thinkable. There was an unusual appearance of a handful of people on horseback which provided an interesting 'sign' of the times. Many bicycles lined an outside wall and there were some who arrived on foot even though it had probably been a long walk. There was also a large showing of people who felt the meeting was important enough to spend the gas and drive their car or motorcycle. Some even drove an electric golf cart. The parking lot was packed.

In total five members of the squad came to the meeting. Reese Johnson stayed behind to guard the cabin and their belongings. He was a Patriot that claimed he wasn't interested in the politics of their situation, so he volunteered to stay behind. Ciera made the rest of them go early so they would get there in time to get a seat.

Two local cops in uniform stood at the entrance of the building and two more stood against the wall inside the hall. Electricity had not come back on, which explained the loud muffled noise of a generator located somewhere on the other side of the building. It powered the lights and the microphone on the sound system that spewed music from speakers on the table situated at the head of the room.

Four Black Jacks with pistols holstered at their sides came in and ushered tonight's speaker to a seat at the table at the head of the room. Three town administrators stood up and received them with hand shakes. Jerry whispered "Black Jacks!" when he saw them. Just the sight of their uniform gave Ciera the creeps. Memories of the attack at the Academy and at Clearwater Farms came rushing back and made her body shake. Their roll here was unclear. After the guests were seated and settled in, one of the town administrators turned off the music and spoke into a microphone.

"People of the town of Lake Pleasant, Speculator and Piseco and beyond… welcome. This meeting has commenced". The place was buzzing. "Please quiet down so we can proceed. We have news that we would like to pass on to you and things we have to discuss". That did the trick. Everyone wanted to hear the news so independent conversations died down to nil.

"Thank you. Tonight's meeting developed from a special request by our new Federal Representative who is present here tonight. I will introduce him, and we can get the latest news about the state of our Union. His name is General Hermon Gutierrez. Will you please stand-up sir". The man stood and waved to week applause from the crowd.

"His official title is 'Official' the staff member said (The crowd chuckled). We also have the honor of hearing from our own mayor, Mayor Cole Arden. He's here tonight and wants to say a few words. So, without further a due, I give you your Town Administrator- Cole Arden".

Officially Mr. Cole Arden's position was designated as 'head administrator' but everyone called him Mayor. There was little applause because people wanted to hear what he had to say.

"Ok, thank you all for coming. I understand that in times like these local meetings like this one are much more difficult to get to. We have also found that emergencies stemming from our current situation are also much more difficult to address. Government services are not functioning very well as you might imagine. At the moment, we do not have the resources to operate at full capacity, but we are working on it. If anyone has a service you can offer, time you can contribute as a volunteer, or something of material value you can contribute, please see me or someone on my staff after the meeting. Right now, I want to share the latest news from Washington".

An attendee yelled "Why is the power still out?".

Someone else yelled "What are they doing about the dollar?".

"Order!" a staff member yelled.

"They are working on the power..." the Mayor started to say.

"Niagara Power doesn't need fuel it's powered by river flow. It can't go down!" the same attendee yelled.

"Even Niagara Power's facility runs on computers. The computers are down" the Mayor told them. "Look, the government is reacting to this crisis and implementing a system to bring everything back on line. If you'll let me speak, I'll tell you this...

We got an official notice from our Federal Representative yesterday, the one posted on the back wall. I hope all of you have gotten a chance to read it. If you haven't, I'll paraphrase and add some additional news. But wait..." the Mayor paused and looked over at Official Gutierrez. "Now that I'm thinking about it, why not hear it from the man himself. Official Gutierrez, would you?".

"Sure, Mayor I'd be happy too". The microphone was passed over and the Official spoke with a thick Spanish accent. "Last Thursday the Federal Government enacted an executive order called "The Supreme Authority Act". This is a declaration of the implementation of a state of government authority which now supersedes all State and Local governments and Administrations..." The noise level in the room rose. Mayor Arden held his hands up to quiet the crowd.

Gutierrez continued "This order is in response to the crisis at hand. This is a severe situation that has forced your Federal Government to act and take the reins because our system, the way it stood, was unable to launch a quick, precise response that would facilitate an adequate solution. Congress was too slow and argued themselves into dead lock from which no action came forth. The president was forced to act through executive action. It had to be done. In bypassing Congress..." A murmur among the crowd came alive again. Gutierrez spoke louder over the noise. "...he has joined up with the nine members of the Supreme Court, added members, and formed an authoritative body that has produced and launched a plan of action. A plan for recovery that is being implemented...".

"By who? And by who's authority?" yelled someone in the crowd.

"By the President of The United States, President Richfield" the Official said into the microphone. "And by the power invested in him. For now, he has declared martial law..." Statements of displeasure and independent conversation welled up from the crowd making the level of noise rise to the point where the Official couldn't speak over it.

"He doesn't have the authority to do that!" someone yelled.

Gutierrez put the microphone down on the table and looked to the people seated next to him for support. After a moment he turned back, picked up the microphone again and asked for quiet. The crowd eventually toned it down and the Official continued.

"People, this is not detrimental to our cause. Quite the opposite. Don't you want the country to recover from this? And recover quickly I might add? We are going to get your government working again. We are going to get the farms working again. I see this as the quickest way to mend the evil that has crept into our system of gove...".

"How about the Constitution?" another yelled.

"Look, the Constitution is what got us here in the first place" Gutierrez said. His body language showed signs of frustration from which his true feelings began to emerge. The thought that *'These people just don't get it'* was starting to show through his mannerism.

"It's flawed!" Gutierrez yelled. "We need to move beyond it and amend it to reflect the needs that modern society and the twenty first century have placed upon us. The Constitution hell! The Constitution has allowed rampant corruption to thrive in America. Right now, we need a more decisive style of government to guide the throngs of people we now have within our boarders. It's the only way to get us out of this...".

"You mean illegal immigrants!" someone yelled.

Gutierrez ignored the comment and continued. "Otherwise, this chaos will continue!" His voice had gotten louder but then he softened it and backed down. "Look, the President said that martial law and ruling by executive order is only temporary. Once this nightmare has passed, we can get back to our Democratic roots and start again. At this time of crisis our government needs to be guided by a strong leader.

Also, I must inform you that there's a lot of violence going on in Texas and California right now, have you heard? We've got Cartels at our border who are taking advantage of this crisis and are now fighting to take back land that they say we stole from them. There's already a majority of Hispanic people living in Texas and California, and they are helping the Cartels".

"They won't win!" someone yelled. "We'll fight!".

Official Gutierrez couldn't help himself. He said "Hell, I say give it back to them. Save the money and the lives that will be lost in fighting it...". The response to his statements created a level of noise that rose to where the Official laid the microphone down in front of him again and turned to his cohorts to wait for the crowd to calm down.

That was it for one lady. The woman rose from her seat and marched up to the table and stood in front of Gutierrez. She leaned over as if to say something but instead grabbed the microphone from the table and turned to the audience. Gutierrez looked over and saw his security team start to move but he waved them off to avoid a conflict. He sat down and let her speak. The woman was Ciera Lowman.

Recent events still fresh in her mind formed the catalyst that put fire into her voice. "I can't believe what I'm hearing! When I hear lies like this I have to speak!" Ciera yelled.

Everyone in the room quieted down and listened. "If we lose this now, we will never get it back. We are Americans… who's success has been created by the very Constitution that this guy trashes. They have been subverting the Constitution for decades, that's why we are in such trouble now. Our politicians haven't been abiding by it at all. You can't blatantly disregard the Constitution and then turn around and say that the Constitution is the problem. They are the problem! Without our constitution you and I would not be here. Or if you want to argue that we would, I know for a fact that we would not be as well off. Yes, I said 'well off' in spite of recent events.

In the past our capitalist system has created wealth for its citizens like no other country in the history of the world. But not anymore. Due to an ever-tightening noose around our necks called taxes and government restrictions, we are all being milked into poverty. The middle class is no longer. People are either hurting or rich. Do you enjoy paying over half of your income to the government?".

"No" was the answer that welled up from what seemed like the whole audience.

"Our elected officials, these people (Ciera waved her arm at the table) have set us up. We are now slaves for their sole benefit! They all talk like this guy" Ciera jabbed her thumb at the Official. The Official stood up with an angry look on his face. Ciera moved away to avoid him and continued "…this proclamation from our president has suspended our rights, our unalienable rights granted to us by God and written into the Constitution. Something that by definition CANNOT BE TAKEN AWAY! But they are doing just that. 'Government' does not have the authority to suspend our rights, period. Our rights are not granted to us by the government. They are granted to us by God! By declaring martial law, they have stripped us of our rights. The government can now do whatever the hell they want with impunity. They are putting you into an ever-tightening box. Can you feel it? Can you feel yourself sliding deeper into servitude. This guy (she thumbed the Official again) mentioned 'leader'. He meant 'Authoritarian'. He meant 'Tyrant". Yup, that's the only truthful thing he's said tonight. Understand the ramifications of this word. From now on the government runs things not you, certainly not 'We The People'". The 'council' that is helping the president run things, it's made up of people who have not been elected to that position. This is what happens when the government takes over..." Ciera raised her arm and pointed at the crowd "YOU LOOSE!". She shouted that last statement and then turned and threw the microphone back down on the table behind her and gave their Federal representative an angry stare. An act of defiance that fully expressed her disgust with officials who were always trying to pull the wool over the eyes of the citizens.

The audience built upon Ciera's lead. Shouts emerged from the crowd joined by demanding voices that agreed with her assessment. Ciera had struck a nerve. As she walked back to her seat people gave her high fives. One shouted at her "You should be President!". But when she got to her row, she didn't sit down. Ciera motioned for the four of her crew to follow her out. She was done with this. Gutierrez saw her leaving. He turned to one of his men standing against the wall and nodded.

Darkness had descended while they were in the meeting. Ciera and crew exited the double doors of the building and threaded their way through the group of people who were waiting outside for tidbits of information to emerge from the meeting. Ciera didn't notice, she was furious. But Kaiden did. Two people had followed them out.

"Hey, wait!" a guy in the crowd yelled. "Wait!".

He was insistent. "Hey, hold up, I heard what you said in there". Ciera turned to confront the guy. Kaiden stepped forward but Ciera put out her arm. "Hold on" she said to Kaiden.

The guy came up with his hand out expecting to shake her hand. Ciera waited for the nature of this to reveal itself before she took it.

"That was a great little speech you gave there" the guy said.

"Little?" Ciera said.

"Oh, I didn't mean it like that. I loved it. From what I heard I can tell that you and I agree on a lot of things. My name is Brian Hardy, I own a place down on Lake Pleasant. It's normally just a summer place for us but my family and I bugged out of New Jersey when the crisis hit. A lot of people up here now did the same. That's why there's so many of us at the meeting tonight. We're looking for answers". Brian was an older guy, about 55 with a long beard. Positively on the heavy side. Probably rode a motorcycle to the meeting from the way he dressed.

"Oh ok, well Brian, my name's Ciera..." She was about to reach out and shake his hand when a rather large, rude security guard entered the conversation and stepped between her and Brian.

"Yeah, it seems there's a lot of people who want to know who you are lady. I need you to come with me right now". The guy was the same security guard that Official Gutierrez had nodded to. He grabbed the arm Ciera had extended, clamped on and pulled. Ciera resisted his action by sinking into her feet and relaxing Tai Chi style. The guy couldn't easily move her.

Way too quickly the guy got mad. "Sweetie I wouldn't do that if I were you. I'm a Federal Agent. You can either come with me or I can arrest you right now. What's it gunna be?".

Ciera made it look easy. She circled her elbow counter clockwise and folded it back over the guy's forearm. With a shove downward and forward his hand lost its grip on her arm. Kaiden's punch to the guy's face came a split second after. The guard reared back from the blow and fell into the hands of his two partners who were standing behind him. They grabbed him to keep him from falling. It took a moment for the guy to shake it off but then he came right back at Kaiden.

Before the two got within striking range, Brian stepped between them with his arms out trying to keep the two from coming together. He was at least as big as the agent so his hand against the agents chest had an effect.

Brian yelled at the guard "HEY, HEY what the hell's going on here?"

"I'm placing her under arrest. Get out of my way, this is official business!" the irate agent said.

"What the fuck man! Are we arresting people for having a different opinion now?".

"Shut up and get out of my way before I arrest you too!" the agent snapped.

That did it. Brian pushed the guy back and stood his ground. The agent stepped back, pulled out his side arm and looked back at his adversary. Only, he quickly realized that this probably wasn't going to be the smartest thing he'd ever done. Many of the people in the crowd standing around them had stepped back at the first sign of trouble but they had been replaced by a large number of Brian's friends who filtered out of the crowd and stepped forward. There must have been at least ten guys standing there along with Brian's wife (they found that out later) who now surrounded the agents. And of course, there was Kaiden and crew now standing in front of Ciera. At the same time the security guard pulled his gun, all of Brian's friends pulled theirs too.

Kaiden smiled. He had never seen a Mexican standoff like this except on TV. This was a whole lot different though, real bullets could go flying at any moment.

Looking around, the guards got nervous from seeing so many guns pointed at them. Brian told him "This is not your lucky day". At that moment two local cops came running up to address the confrontation.

"Brian what the hell's going on here?" The first cop yelled.

Brian yelled back at the cop without taking his eyes off the guard. "Hal, stand down, we got this". Hal Avery was the Chief of police, and it was immediately apparent that they knew each other. His words made the cop stop and stand there without any further action.

Brian told the agent "If you shoot me, you all will die tonight, and I think that's going to really spoil your evening Sir. Now let's keep this civil. You can put that away and walk back into the building or we can start shooting. Which one's it gunna be?".

The agent didn't have to think about it for long. He put his gun away and the other two followed suit. "This is not the end of this" he said to everyone. "You're messing with a Federal matter here and pretty soon it's not going to be YOUR lucky day. It's illegal for you all to have those guns" he said as he glanced around.

"Yeah, but what are you going to do about it" someone yelled.

With that he turned and walked back into the building. As he passed the cops that were standing there, he said "And what are you going to do about this?".

"I ain't going to do nothing" Hal told him. The agent gave the cop a fierce stare as they passed each other.

Brian turned to Ciera and Kaiden "Ok, we've been warned".

"I need to warn you too" Kaiden said. "We've dealt with these people before. They will go to any extreme to bring you in line. I wish I had time to tell you what's been going on, but we've got to get out of here" Kaiden said it as much to Ciera as he did to Brian".

Brian got serious and said "Thanks for the warning. Lines have been drawn and we're finding out who's standing on which side. We have a group that is more than ready to defend our freedom… and yours. If you would like to join us, you are more than welcome".

"We just might take you up on that. But we have some loose ends to take care of first. How can we contact you?

"Lake Pleasant Fire lane 23. You'll find me there".

7

YOU'RE NOT IN KANSAS

First thing the next day, Kaiden drove to the market in the shuttle with Ciera and Jerry Reeder. If it were up to Kaiden he wouldn't have gone into town, and he wouldn't have picked up the two hitch hikers on their way there, but Ciera made him go and she made him stop and pick up the hitch hikers too.

Kaiden complained the whole way. "This is not a good idea. We don't want to run into those feds we saw last night. I think we should kick caution up a few notches, things are getting dangerous out here. Remember Crenshaw told us to keep a low profile".

"Hey, if we were hitching, we would have wanted them to pick us up right?" she said. Kaiden couldn't argue.

"Speculator's a small town" Kaiden said. "It's more like I'm worried that those Feds from last night are still roaming around here.

"No one saw us walk to the bus last night. We all walked back to the bus with some going different ways so that we could avoid that possibility. No one knows this shuttle was our ride and luckily, they're not into road blocks around here. Not yet anyway" Ciera said.

"That's true we haven't seen any road blocks but with our luck, being Federal Agent magnets and all, I wouldn't put it past running into them" Kaiden said.

Ciera didn't argue the point. She just said "We have no choice; we have to get these supplies".

When they got to the market There were a lot of people there looking to trade things. It looked like a mini flea market had sprung up in the market's parking lot. When Abba Jenson saw them, he welcomed Kaiden and Ciera.

"Hello my friends. It's good to see you. I have the items you ordered. Thank you so much for your purchase. If there is anything else I can get you, please don't hesitate to ask". Then Abba said to Ciera "Great speech you made last night. You got everyone fired up".

"Oh, you were there?" Ciera asked.

"Way to keep a low-profile Ciera" Kaiden said under his breath.

Ciera told Abba "I had to speak. We can't let these people get away with their lies. Besides, we made some friends".

"And some enemy's" Kaiden added under his breath.

"I left right after I had my say. Did I miss anything Mr. Jensen?

"Oh, so you don't' know. You started quite a backlash with that speech. After that, every time that Official said something the audience hammered him. Though for good reason I say".

"What did he say?" Ciera asked.

"Let's see. The guy stated that the Feds are stepping up gun confiscation. He wanted everyone to give up their weapons to deter a visit by the ATF. He also reminded us that trading with gold and silver is illegal... then something about confiscating that too. That got me. I mean the only other thing we have right now is gold and silver. I was one of the people who hammered him on that one. Don't worry I'll take gold or silver in trade from you guys anytime".

"Thanks. But what do they expect us to do, barter from now on?" Kaiden said.

"Well, the guy was trying to tell us that it would all be fixed real soon. But then he contradicted himself and said that the government will take gold or silver in payment of taxes. Can you believe it? We aren't allowed to use it, but they can.

The thing that got everyone really mad was his last statement or at least the last statement that he was allowed to make. He said that the government is still operational and that taxes will still have to be paid to keep the government running and since the internet and phones are still down, someone from the IRS would be coming around to Collect payment from local businesses. Oh yeah and get this- gold and silver is the preferred method of payment. Can you believe it?

"Yes, I believe it. Nothing they do makes sense unless you look at the big picture" Ciera said. "It's what I've been telling everyone. Gold and silver have become a very sought after commodity and they want to suck it out of the population".

"That was the last thing he said because so many got in his face and started yelling and screaming that the guy's security detail picked him up and took him out of there. Luckily so, I think he would have gotten lynched if he stuck around".

"Well, well. It's good to see that people are finally reacting" Kaiden said.

Ciera looked like she was thinking hard and said "Yeah there's hope".

Hank was at the meeting too. They spoke with him at length while picking up the rat pack on the way back to the Inn. Repairs had been finished and "The rat" was good to go. Hank expressed similar comments about the meeting but also made his position clear "I'm a Democrat. Voted like that my whole life but I don't like what's going on now. This is too much. My party has moved to the extreme left and I don't like what that stands for, not anymore. I stand for the flag and kneel only to the cross. Now a days that statement will get me kicked out of the Democrat party. I actually like some of the ideas that socialism brings to the party, but I agree with you Ciera, I don't think that socialism should come with a loss of our rights. That's not what America is about". He looked at Ciera, smiled and said "And everyone knows your views on the subject that's for sure Ciera. Great speech".

"Yeah, everyone knows what Ciera thinks. Even the hitch hikers knew you" Kaiden said sarcastically.

Ciera elbowed Kaiden "Hey come on, don't be so negative. Go put the rat pack in the bus, let's get moving". She thanked Hank for his work, and they talked while the boys loaded the rat pack. Ciera was pleasantly surprised and flattered when Hank asked her if she wanted to come over for dinner.

"Oh Hank, that is so nice of you. I like a man who makes his intentions clear. Especially one who is willing to cook dinner for me" she gave him her signature smile and touched him on the arm. "I hope we continue to be friends after I make my situation clear. I'm tied up in that department now if you know what I mean. So, I can't. But thanks. It was sweet of you to offer".

Hank was head over heels in love with the rear view as she walked out of his building. He stood there and shook his head from side to side.

"We need gas" Kaiden informed her when she got back on board the bus.

Back at the cabin, Kaiden and the guys loaded supplies and strapped them onto the rat pack. Ciera held a meeting with everyone to settle on a plan to hike the 'bitch' back out to Crenshaw and crew. Every other day someone conjured up another name for the rat pack.

"Ok. Guys. Listen up. Crenshaw and the rest of the crew need these supplies like yesterday. Only four of us are needed to hike it back to them. It doesn't weigh but half with just the supplies on it so it shouldn't be the bitch that she normally is. I propose Jerry, Alex, Vic, and Reese take it back. Yes, I am asking permission for Kaiden and I to stay here. Yes, for the obvious reason that I want Kaiden with me. Yes, you guys are doing the bitch work while we stay here in the comfort of this cabin. No, it's not just to be alone with each other but that 'is' one reason. The other is that there is still work for me to do here. I've got to find enough gas to fill the tank on that bus. Yes, it's not fair. But I'm asking you to do it anyway". She looked at them for an answer.

Jerry spoke up first "Fine by me". Two others said the same, but Reese came back with "One: I don't want to go. Two: It's still going to be a bitch even without the weight. Three: Yeah, it's not fair. Four: Ciera you don't need our permission so thanks for asking, but Five: I'll go because I don't want to make this a problem".

"Ohhhh you guys are the best". Ciera went over and hugged Reese and then hugged the others in turn. Then she told them "Ok prepare. You leave as soon as you're ready.

Everyone was thinking about the job ahead so there wasn't much conversation when Kaiden and Ciera drove them all to the trail head. Everyone was concentrating on what lay ahead. Even after dropping them and the RP off the two of them didn't have much to say to each other on the way back to the cabin. But as soon as they got back and closed the door, clothes started flying everywhere.

A generator at the Inn only ran for an hour and fifteen minutes in the morning and for two hours in the evening starting at five o'clock. This, they found, allowed the refrigerators and freezers to function while using the bare minimum amount of fuel. But it would only work if the cooler doors weren't opened too much in between.

Ciera and Kaiden marveled at the luxury of a hot shower and the presence of electricity while they got dressed to go at 6:00. "I need to get a grip on the mood of the people around here. We need to know which way they're leaning" Ciera said as she brushed her hair.

"Maybe we should have stuck around at the meeting last night. Sounds like we would have found out" Kaiden said.

"No, I want to know how they are going to react to what they heard after they've had time to think about it. Not the rantings of a mob reaction" Ciera said.

"Ok, let's go see Brian first. I'm dying to find out what he thought but more importantly, what he and his friends are going to do about it".

Fire lane 23 wasn't that difficult to find (it was the one right after fire lane 22) but Brian's house proved to be elusive. There was more than one cottage on the lane and the lane snaked around a bit before running up alongside the lake. One person they asked said "Keep going, it's the one with all the bikes parked in front". Sure enough, the cottage with about fifteen motorcycles and a handful of cars parked out front was Brian's.

"Hey! You found me" Brian said as he walked up to them and shook their hands. "This is Alisha, my wife (they shook hands). I didn't know if you would take me up on the invite or not".

"Nice house! Ciera chimed. "I love it".

"Well, it's an old cottage, not totally good looking but beautiful in the sense of how it looks sitting there nestled in the woods with the lake in the background" Brian said.

No matter the age or condition, anyone would have fallen in love with it. The only detraction from the picture-perfect view of a 'cabin in the woods next to a lake', was the addition of a tent site on the left-hand side. There, about eight different color tents were randomly pitched among the trees.

"It's been in my family for years" Brian said as they stared at it. But I don't own all of it right now. I inherited the place from my parents. The inheritance tax I owed on the place made it impossible for us to keep it (Brian hugged his wife). So, we sold shares of it to drum up the money. I offered a deal to the motorcycle club I belong to in New Jersey and luckily, enough people took me up on it. Everyone chipped in and made it our clubs 'go to' place in the summer. But come on in, let me show you around. I want you to meet the gang".

"The gang" had certain connotations that ended up not being quite what Kaiden envisioned. That night as they all stood and sat around a campfire by the lake, Kaiden confided in Brian "I got to tell you, I thought when you said "gang" that you were going to introduce me to a bunch of rough redneck outlaws. You guys are not quite what I expected".

"Hey, wait a minute..." someone who overheard said. "We drink a lot of beer!" he said it while holding up the beer he was working on. There was a whoop and a holler from some of the others in agreement.

Brian told him "Well I'm sure you saw the Gold Wings, the Road Glide and a Vulcan Voyager out there. Not exactly an outlaw's bike. Most of us are professional business men and women but we do have a few rowdies and some young'uns here.

Katie over there owns 'Miss Priss' flower shop in Hackensack and her husband's a service manager at Seacore plumbing. Tomas, we call him Tommaso, owns the Ludwig Bike Shop from which we all are born". Brian gave a deep bow to Tommaso who held up his beer in return. "Me, I'm an electrician. Or was. I owned my business, but I'm retired now. That young'un over there is Jackie, we call him Toadie. He's one of Misty's kids. Misty's not here right now. Her husband Leo over there made it up but she didn't come up with him. Supposed to meet us here but she hasn't shown up yet. We don't know what happened to her.

When we saw the shit hit'in the fan down in Jersey, we sent word to our members to bee line it up here to ride this out. Those who left early got here without much of a problem, those who left later have war stories to tell. It got crazy in the city and even on the roads near here. We had stocked this place with enough provisions to last for quite a while; just for an emergency such as this. My wife had the foresight to help make it a great bug out place. Now we're wondering how long we can last with the number of people we got. It'll be getting harder to get supplies now. People are starting to clam up.

All twenty-five of us come from different fields but we are generally of the same mind. Or else they wouldn't be here. A few of our members had opposite political viewpoints, but as I mentioned last night, everyone here has chosen our side. I made sure that anyone who wants to live on this property cannot be in favor of the asinine things that have gotten us into this mess. And of course, no one here would allow anyone to take away our guns. We made sure those people knew they were not welcome. In fact, everyone here owns a gun. It's like a pre requisite. We're well supplied in that area too by the way, but we could use more rifles. Got plenty of hand guns. You can't travel very well on bikes with rifles slung across your back. Toadie over there doesn't quite agree with my politics but he owns a gun and will not give it up. He thinks he has a case for socialism but we're working on him. Ask him about it when you get a chance".

"I will" Kaiden said. "Brian I kind of guessed at your politics when we met last night. And from what I gather I see that we're on the same side. But what I would really like to know is the demeanor of the people who live around here. What's their inclination? I told you that my crew and I have been basically hiking through the wilderness ever since the crisis went down. We would like to know how Americans are reacting to this. Got any news?".

"Yeah, last night was a real indicator alright. People are hurting or if they are not yet feeling the hurt, they know that if things continue the way they're going then we'll all be in serious trouble soon. I've spoken to my neighbors and some of the merchants in town but sometimes people are cautious and will say anything and agree with anything just to avoid a confrontation. Last night I felt the true pulse of the town and it was angry. You know that we ended up kicking the Fed's rep out of there, right?".

"We heard" Kaiden said.

"We didn't like what we were hearing. The Official, and I take it, a few of the people who were on his side, left with him. After that an impromptu meeting was formed with the Mayor and the people who remained. A surprising number of them are fired up and genuinely pissed off at what's going down. I felt the intensity of their objections, and I'm here to tell you that they are as devoted to rejecting the Fed's takeover as I am".

"Did you talk about what it would mean to go against these people?" Kaiden asked.

"Yes, we did".

"I don't mean are they going to go and vote them out. I mean, did you talk about what it's really going to take to get these people out of power?" Kaiden asked.

"Yes, we did".

"Wait, I'm talking about the full ramifications of what that involves. Because I'm here to tell you. These socialists took over slowly and methodically. They were successful because we were complacent and unwilling to stand up and fight the good fight. Now it's too late to change the course through politics. We must acknowledge the trampling of our rights and that to maintain them, and the structure of our republic, now you're going to have to take up arms to stop them. We're wondering if you and people like you are willing to go there".

Brian looked at Ciera and then Kaiden "I know what this means. I've seen this coming for some time now. I'm an ISIS War vet. I'm not sure if 'they' really know what it means, the rest of the people in this town, they probably don't know the true reality of it. But we here talked about it. And I can tell you that they are 100 percent behind the effort to rebuff these assholes. Hell, the local cops were there and even the Mayor agreed. But like I said, I don't know if that's just the Mayor's politics and he's playing both sides or what. He knows he's just lost his job or if not that, he sure as hell realizes that he's about to become a puppet for the new regime".

Ciera told Brian "From our experience with these people, the Officials job is to stick his nose into the works of the town government and seek out the most profitable businesses around here. He'll tap into any profit he finds and take it in the name of taxes. He'll enforce restrictive laws and install socialist party policy and socialist puppets into the new order around here.

I think they've been planning this for quite a while. These Black Jacks showed up way too quickly. They're inserting their people even before the power comes back on. I'm guessing that it's easier to set up before people can effectively react. If this crisis was a spontaneous event, I don't believe they would have been this prepared, they wouldn't have enough time to get such a network together. That Gutierrez official is going to report this to his superiors. Sooner rather than later, he'll be back with support".

"What do you mean by support?" Brian asked.

"I mean more than the four-man security team he had with him at the meeting. He'll be back with enough firepower to assert himself. Brian, we're not in Kansas anymore" Ciera said. She added "I've got a story to tell you. And then I need to ask you, what are we going to do about it?".

8

OPERATION RESTART

You could now call the White House an armed compound. The existing walls and fence surrounding the famous house were now reinforced with multiple rows of razor wire strung across the top going 360 around the entire property. Also, someone trying to get in would have to stumble over a secondary wall of razor wire running parallel to the perimeter fence on the lawn about fifteen feet away. Large, sandbagged guard posts with a second story observation tower had been built every hundred yards or so. Sticking out between sandbags in the tower watching the no man zone was the barrel of an M240B machine gun. A gun that no civilian was allowed to own or use for their own protection.

Inside, in one of the fancy conference rooms, all the lights were on, and the heater was running. Coffee had been served by servants. A meeting was in progress with ex-president Richfield sitting at the head of the table. Ten men and two women sat around him. One person was in uniform; all the others were in business attire. If you were looking at video of the meeting, it would look like they had not been touched at all by the crisis that surrounded them. Everyone was there to report their findings pertaining to the department they were assigned to. One of Richfield's affiliates was in the middle of their report:

> "...Throughout most of the country, power is still down, infrastructure has collapsed. I would say that at this point we are very vulnerable to outside interference. I intend to shore this up and get results with operation 'Restart'. Details are in the packet in front of you".

"Thank you Mr. Koneham I hope the ATF can produce the results you have outlined" Richfield said and then turned to the one in uniform. "General, I was assured that we would have the reins on this within weeks not months".

General Whitney replied "Sir we will. Don't worry. We knew there would be resistance, but our main problem is that the collapse of the net occurred way before schedule. If you remember I'm the one who pushed for allowing the gun confiscation program to play out for a minimum of a year before instigating 'the event'".

President Richfield looked at his people, then at one of them in particular. That gentleman answered even before the question was asked "Yes, I was told that we had a better grip on the 'catalyst event' than we did". The guy quickly expanded on the defense of his position.

"Sir the timing of certain components proved to be more difficult to control than we thought...".

"Yeah, yeah, I heard all about it. But people... we knew it would happen; we should have been better prepared. Please continue General".

"At the start, resistance to our forces showed up in the expected form of protests, marches, and defections. There was a surprisingly high number of defections as well as attendees at many of these demonstrations. But today, now that the shortages have kicked in, it has taken a toll on their ability to mount a significant response. People are finding it much harder to push back without adequate support... as planned. Due to shortages of basic necessities, and the Media's campaign to pit one group against the other, people have not been able to establish the same size crowds with any numbers that are able to overwhelm our Security forces. Right now, they are fighting amongst themselves as much as they are fighting us".

"Good, exactly what we hoped for. Thank you General. Alright now let's hear from our chief economic advisor Mr. Allen Harris".

"Yes sir". Harris looked down at the papers sitting in front of him. Then said "Thank you, it gives me great pleasure to announce that we have canceled all debt that the government, I mean, the previous government, had accumulated. We are starting fresh. It was just a matter of twisting a few arms".

"Here, here!" many of them shouted.

"Due to the implementation of the pre-positioning drive, we have our own people embedded in the banking industry. Operations are greatly influenced. Inserted IRS-ART members have achieved clear control of certain named banks and will soon lead us to a position of dominant control, then we can proceed as planned. Interest charged on government loans is now against the law..." Applause erupted from everyone around the table. When it subsided Harris continued "Profit on government loans has been eliminated…".

Richfield broke in "Don't worry ladies and gentlemen, profits are not against the law to make, they're just against the law to keep". Richfield said it with a big grin. Everyone laughed even though they heard that joke many times before.

Harris continued "We have been successful in distributing 'New Government Script' currency, or whatever you will eventually decide to call it. Profits stemming from all 'script' activity will now flow… into government coughers. This is only one of our sources of income, but it will give us a big boost enabling us to naturally move into phase two-wage control. With its implementation, the government will be able to get projects completed without the (excessive) expense that labor has tacked on to the final product. Without the inflated prices charged by corporations who have raped us in the past, we are on track for significant achievement in the future.

Income Taxes will be eliminated but still indirectly paid by the worker in the form of lower wages. The savings will be rolled into 'company profit' and will be skimmed off by the IRS. We are simply going to take it before they see it in their pay, offset of course by the services the government will provide the worker in the form of products, healthcare, education and security. That should appease them. Of course, we will be the supplier of the very job they are working at so their livelihood will depend on us. If they don't like it, we will give the job to someone else who does. We are in control of who gets what and of course the ones who comply will be rewarded".

"That's great Mr. Harris, what are you doing when you run into resistance to reform by white supremacists?".

"Sir, IRS-ART representatives have the authority to send anyone deemed to be hindering the implementation of the Restart Program to the Manassas labor camp. This camp will serve a dual purpose. One, it will be a significant deterrent to dissent once the word gets around. Two, it will become our best source of free labor.

As stated in the operational laws described in 'phase two'. Our representatives are authorized to eliminate anyone resisting the new order. Most industries have been nationalized and are now under operational control of the state, the "United One State" as some people are calling us now. We don't have time to waste at this stage of the game. It is imperative that our power becomes system wide, we must achieve absolute sovereignty. This is the only way we are going to stamp out the greed of the lingering capitalist system".

"Good. Next, Mr. Anthony Knowles. Let's hear your report on the IRS-ART.

"Yes sir. Our 'Asset Reclamation Team' has done a fine job securing assets. The resources we have placed at our disposal have been producing an ever-increasing stock of physical holdings. The program has proven to be vital to our ability to sustain ourselves through the 'worthless dollar" transition period. Our efforts have given us solid collateral that will insure our ability to secure outside financing from Saudi Arabia and other sources. Financing that is essential to our ability to pull us out of the initial downturn.

We now control pretty much all media outlets and are working to tie up some loose ends. We are demanding complete compliance and cooperation to pull our constituents up and out of the ashes that the capitalist system has buried us in.

Anyone resisting our efforts will have their land, building and or assets expropriated and awarded to the State. The State reserves the right to redistribute these lands and assets to people that are fit to inherit them. All the great warehouses are now under our jurisdiction and can be distributed at our discretion". Mr. Doarsky paused, indicating he was done.

"Mrs. Crestivo, status on education?".

"Yes sir. The structure of the educational system has been gearing up over the last decade, it will be initiated and finalized during 'Phase Three' of the general plan. We are ready.

First, we need infrastructure to build and to allow for the formation of strong central control. Then we can implement the new system. Yes, education will be free, for almost everyone, but certainly the students accepted into the program who will be participating in the State sanctioned programs. This will be offered to all immigrants and students that we deem eligible".

"And what's the plan for the ones who are not?" Richfield asked.

"They will be steered into vocational training camps. We are gearing up for that now and will expand these facilities and bring them on line as needed".

"Ok. Maria Escobar, would you please comment on the state of the economy" Richfield asked. "As if I didn't know" he added. A chuckle fluttered around the table.

"Yes sir. Presently we are getting control of runaway prices and inflation. Once we attain full control, drop the dollar completely and stop transactions by any other means, such as gold or silver and barter, we will have the ability to force the population to completely rely on government script for payment of all services and products. Then we can more easily move government script into the realm of digital currency. Prices for the sale of assets Mr. Harris talked about and the cost of goods produced in the new system will be set so they cannot run away from anyone's ability to pay for them. Price control is our main weapon we can use to regain control of the economy. Then we will insert the digital dollar or whatever you are going to call it".

Richfield broke in "Mrs. Escobar, I always heard that price controls are the cause of future supply problems. How are you going to solve that?"

"Sir, I will oversee the valuation of products personally and make sure that the prices we set are fair and allow for people to thrive. Believe me, we are smarter and better at this than our socialist predecessors".

"Alright. Benson. You're our tech advisor. Inform us on the progress of the surveillance system".

"Yes sir. First, we had to confiscate and secure the surveillance equipment from local law enforcement. Convincing the right workers to run the technology was more difficult than we thought but we have that taken care of now. We've been able to set up electricity in most of our government buildings with equipment we put in place prior to the melt down. That is a tremendous advantage in getting our surveillance equipment up and running".

"Yes, but when will it be operational?" Richfield asked.

"We're already operational in most major cities as we speak sir. Sections of rural areas that we cannot monitor at present are insignificant in the scheme of things, but more sections of those areas are being covered daily. Fully operational... I'd say within two or three months".

"Good. Our goal gentlemon, and I didn't miss-speak. I see here in my notes that the new word for 'ladies and gentlemen' is 'Gentlemon'. It combines 'men' and 'women' into 'mon'. It's gender neutral, inclusive and we will all use it instead of gentle 'men' from this point on. Anyway- gentlemon" Richfield looked around the table at the men and women. "We must find out who and where our enemies are. Drones can be effectively employed to identify protests and the dissenters who attend them. I trust our teams are standing by ready to go in and root them out".

Richfield looked down toward the opposite end of the table and nodded his head toward the man sitting there. The man nodded back showing his approval. Then to the people seated to his left and right he said "Accelerate the timetable so we meet our deadlines for operation restart. Continue inserting our assets, get them in place before the people know what's happening. We don't want to give them any more time to think".

"How about the military sir? Someone to his left asked.

Richfield told them all "As planned, the limited military assets we still have in country are on standby. We have one rogue General in Florida and one in Texas that we are still negotiating with now. They are insinuating that if we use military assets on civilians they will 'enter the fray on the other side'. Those were their exact words. We are only going to use the military if the A.R.T. can't achieve the results we're looking for. We will deal with the Generals, we will have them all under control soon. Is this acceptable Mr. Wu?" All eyes went to the person sitting at the opposite end of the table.

Mr. Wu nodded his head and spoke with a thick Chinese accent "Yes, bring operation re-start up to speed as quickly as possible".

* * *

Syracuse N.Y.: The relatively new Command Center for Hacia's north eastern territories contained a large situation room which was now buzzing with IRS-ART members. Personnel, some in uniform, some not, were moving briskly around the room between a menagerie of lit computer screens and equipment. Previously, this was Google's old reginal headquarters, but it was re-named after the controlling interest in Google's empire had been bought out for an absurd amount of money by the Hacia enterprise. No one knows for sure, but the rumor is 'Twenty-two hundred billion dollars' worth of absurdity. The new owners changed the name to "Hacia" which means to go towards in Spanish. At the time, no one knew what they were really shooting for, but many suspected.

Some people sat at desks monitoring relatively small setups while others stood in front of three huge screens with headsets covering their ears. Those people paced back and forth speaking into wrap around microphones alternately looking at a hand-held computer and the large screen in front of them. Everyone went about their business seemingly unhindered by any outside influence. They had good clothes, electricity, and a water cooler in the hall. Food was available in the cafeteria. Even their paychecks still arrived on Friday, only they were now being paid in the form of "government script" which was redeemable at the new company store located in the confiscated Costco building.

One of the agents who managed the Command Center roamed the floor in a shirt and tie giving orders and directing attention to certain hot spots located on a map depicted on one of the large monitors. Earlier in the day this division sent out a surprisingly large number of hired 'Officials' to their assigned areas in this second attempt to insert them into the political matrix of upstate New York and surrounding areas.

Recruits had been chosen from the mass of desperate people looking for work. The ART division of the IRS was hiring. Only people of a certain political lean and of a preferred race had been hired to fill the lucrative positions of "Federal Officials". Official benefits offered were few, but a steady salary was a major attraction. The unofficial benefits (bribes) were the main attraction. This governing structure was being set up and duplicated all across the country with varying degrees of success.

In areas where trouble had been reported during Phase One, they now sent their "representatives" back, only this time, with an escort. Hot spots had been identified and noted on the big screen map. Bright normal colored areas were designated as "controlled". Those sections of the state were right next to shaded areas that depicted places where resistance had been encountered. The word came down from above that there was an unacceptable amount of shaded area on the New York State map. Therefore, they commenced Phase II of the operation and sent out what they called "restart patrols".

As the spearhead of that effort in upstate New York, a large convoy of about fifty surplus High Mobility Multipurpose Wheeled Vehicles (HMMWV) more commonly known as "Humvee's" but also called "Hummer's", drove off the parking lot of the Hacia building which housed the Syracuse Federal Command Center. Each one was an up-armored version of the M-1151 Humvee dressed in a heavy armor package along with a 50 caliber M2 machine gun mounted in a turret on top. These military style vehicles mixed in evenly with about seventy-five cargo vans and suburban SUV's as they all left the lot together. Their gas tanks were topped off with fuel drawn from six onsite aboveground 60,000-gallon fuel tanks, one set held gasoline, another diesel and two held aviation fuel. Trailing behind the convoy were two heavily guarded 3,000-gallon tanker trucks designated specifically for refueling any Federal vehicle that required it in the field, all in an effort to assure the mobility of the vehicles and the success of the restart mission.

Some vehicles peeled off right after they exited the gate and went in the opposite direction from the main convoy. The majority of the vehicles snaked their way through the streets of Syracuse going east breezing their way through two check points and a road block on the New York State Thruway 90. While the whole lot of them drove down the highway, every so often two M-1151's and two or three other vehicles formed up in their designated patrol and peeled off from the main convoy initiating an exit. This scenario repeated itself all the way to Albany.

* * *

Federal Official Hernando Gutierrez arrived unannounced at Mayor Arden's house in Lake Pleasant N.Y. at 1:30PM. Four members of his eighteen-man squad were standing behind him at the front door. They were armed and dressed in black SWAT style uniforms. *"I should just break this door down"* he said to himself. Refraining, he just banged harder on the door.

"Federal Agents" he yelled.

Parked out front were three of those impressive M-1151 Humvees, a black van and a black SUV. The turrets on top of the Humvees had the barrel of a 50-caliber machine gun pointed at the house. When the Mayor opened the door, Gutierrez wiped the surprised look off the Mayor's face by saying "Come with me, we need to talk".

Looking beyond Gutierrez the Mayor couldn't help but notice the threat. By design for sure. His surprise expression was replaced by a serious look of concern. There was no other choice but to comply.

Fifteen minutes later the lot of them arrived at Lake Pleasant Town Hall. The rest of the squad remained outside to guard the vehicles and secure the premises while the Lieutenant and four of his men escorted Official Gutierrez and the Mayor into the Mayor's office. The office was a room off the main town hall that was sectioned off with dividers for the four members of the town's administration including one secretary. Any words spoken at the Mayors desk could be heard by others if anyone else was at their desk, but at the moment, the room was void of personnel.

Cole..., can I call you Cole?" Gutierrez said when they sat down at the Mayors desk. The Mayor nodded.

Gutierrez continued "I've got other townships to visit today so I will be brief. You and this immediate area are my responsibility but you're not the only area I oversee. I'm a busy man so I'll get right to it. What is your political conviction, Cole?".

"I'm a Democrat" Cole said.

"Sir." Gutierrez said. "From now on you will address me as 'Sir'".

"Yes... sir. My whole family votes democrat" Cole told him.

Gutierrez replied "Well that doesn't mean shit but at least it's better than Republican. Ok, listen up. From now on there will be no more town meetings. No more discussions. I am here to tell you how this is going to work. Keep in mind my goal is to get the people in this area to begin working for their own good and for the good of the community. Hell, for the good of their neighbors. My goal is now your goal, got it? You will follow my instructions to the tee. And your people will follow your instructions. If not, you will report the names and addresses of anyone who is non-compliant, and we will take it from there.

What I'm doing here is offering you the honor of being my go-to man in this area. It comes with certain benefits and yes, some compensation. At this point that might be in the form of gasoline, food... things like that until we can get company script or digital coin. In return all I need is your cooperation and your connections. Especially with the local police. But what I need most is your loyalty. If you screw me, I will roll over you and move on to someone else who better deserves my kindness. Are we clear?".

"Yes... sir, certainly. I would greatly appreciate the opportunity to work with the government...".

"Work 'for' the government" Gutierrez corrected him.

"Yes".

"Yes sir! Gutierrez said in a stern tone. "Understand the pecking order here Mayor. And understand the meaning of 'I will roll over you'.

Mayor Cole looked up at the four men in uniform with rifles standing in the four corners of his office. "I understand you precisely sir" he said.

"Good I'm glad we have an understanding, and your cooperation. Someday soon we will celebrate that fact". Gutierrez stood and they shook hands. Gutierrez turned to leave but then turned back. "Oh, the first order of business is that I need you to compile a list of people who own guns in this area. Include the names of people who are most likely to impede a smooth transition to our New Order. Let's start with the woman who made that speech the other night at the town meeting. I want her here" Gutierrez jabbed his finger into the desktop. "Also, my men tell me there was a guy involved in a ruckus outside the place. Do you know who they are?

"No sir I've never seen that lady before. Definitely not a local resident. There are a lot of 'out of towners' up here at the moment and I didn't hear about any ruckus outside the meeting...".

"There was a guy who threatened my men, almost turned into a shootout. I want their names and place of residence ASAP. Make it a top priority. I'll be back tomorrow to discuss some of the new laws and the new way we're going to be doing things. I'll need those names and addresses at that time so get cranking".

"Yes sir".

Mayor Arden went home and discussed what went down at the meeting with his wife. The two of them had a serious decision to make. One with dire consequences no matter which way they decided to go. The path of least resistance would be to join the government and participate in their endeavor to correct the country's ills. That path offered perks that would only flow into cooperative hands, yet it would involve going against people they considered to be good friends.

9

SAY IT AIN'T SO

When agent Gutierrez showed up again at the Mayor's house two days later Cole noticed that the Feds convoy was one Humvee short. Gutierrez himself looked rattled and was quite terse in manner. Mayor Arden cut the small talk and handed him a list of names. "These are the people who I know to have weapons in this area" the Mayor said. He showed Gutierrez a page long list with two priority targets at the top- Ciera Lowman and Brian Hardy. The Mayor explained "These are the two you want. She's the one that caused the scene at the Town meeting the other night, and this guy Brian and his crew are the ones with the guns. Got the information from my police chief" the Mayor said while pointing at Brian Hardy's name.

Gutierrez and his men hit Brian's house first because it was just across the street and a few fire lanes down the road from the administration building. They rolled up to the cottage fast to insure the element of surprise and about twelve soldiers jumped out of two Humvee's and a black SUV. They spread out around the place with guns drawn, positively prepared for battle. There was no sign of anyone outside the cabin and there were no motorcycles. Not even a pitched tent. While the place was being surrounded, Gutierrez followed behind six of his men who stormed the front door. Without knocking they busted in.

Two very frightened occupants were inside, it was an old couple. “We’re here to see Brian Hardy. Where is he!” Gutierrez yelled at them. While his men spread out and searched the inside of the house, Gutierrez got answers.

“He’s not here. He’ll be back tomorrow” the old man claimed.

“See if that’s true” Gutierrez told the soldier next to him who turned and went with the others to search the house. “I promise you that you won’t be harmed if you give me the information I need. I want to know where the guns are?”.

“There are no guns here” the old man told him. Gutierrez smacked him hard across the face. Threateningly, as if he was going to do the same to the old lady, he turned to her and asked in a cold stern voice “Where are the guns?”.

She stood up to him and said “I wouldn’t tell you even if I knew, you piece of shit!”.

Gutierrez stepped forward and looked like he was about to hit her when his man came up to his side and said “We searched the place sir, they’re not here. We’re still searching for guns but haven’t found any yet”. Gutierrez turned back to the old woman and got in her face “You like the word ‘shit’ lady? Well, if we find any guns now, I’m going to have my men beat the living ‘shit’ out of you”. He turned and went outside to let her sit with that.

They searched alright. Gutierrez men tore the place apart. But found nothing.

* * *

Everything was going pretty good at a time when things were disintegrating all around them. Ciera was able to get the RP fixed, obtain supplies including three tents, and secure a vehicle. She was also able to purchase some gas although not enough for a full tank. People were starting to get stingy with their gasoline supply, it was getting to the point where no one wanted to let any of it go, at least not that easily and certainly not for ‘dollars’. The price of gas rose to between fifty and one hundred dollars a gallon. Ciera completed Crenshaw's list of things to do and to get by getting an indication of the publics demeanor. *"All of that while making some friends"* she thought.

Staying in the cabin was plush. It made her mood. She strolled around the porch throughout the afternoon and sat on the swing drinking tea. She kept busy by cleaning up the place as diligently as if she owned it and then packed supplies into her back pack... oblivious to the van that pulled up down the road.

At first the van hung back with the bulk of it out of sight, but the men inside kept an open line of sight to the cabin's front door for three hours prior. They communicated by radio with their boss, reporting that only the girl occupied cabin #14. "No other personnel sighted going in or out sir" the man said into the radio.

"That's good" Gutierrez replied from the SUV he was sitting in. "Vehicle two, three and four, pay her a visit. Go".

Two supporting Humvees took off from their set back positions down the road from the Inn and descended upon the cabin. The third van joined Gutierrez SUV and all four raced up the road and came to a sudden halt at the front walkway. Full of confidence, Gutierrez stepped out and joined his men. He strolled up to the front door behind six soldiers who hustled up to the porch. Two of them peeled off and stood at the bottom of the steps. Gutierrez didn't order his men to surround the place, he wasn't here for guns, that wasn't the threat. The threat was this woman's ideas. He was here to make sure she didn't spread them around anymore.

Instead of knocking four soldiers busted in as they had done at Brian Hardy's house. It had become their mode of operation, exactly like they were taught in training. The four entered while screaming "Federal agents! Put your hands on your head". Ciera was standing in the middle of the living room when suddenly there were four rifles pointed at her. She didn't look surprised, she just stared at Gutierrez as he walked in behind his men. Halfheartedly she raised her hands. He looked around and motioned for the two soldiers on his right to go search the rest of the cabin.

"What are you going to shoot me? You could have just knocked you know" Ciera said.

"You could have gone with my men the other night and avoided this whole thing" Gutierrez snapped.

"Hell, this way we can sit on the couch and have some tea, would you like some?" Ciera said in a calm voice.

That made Gutierrez angry. He was about to launch into a tirade, but Ciera was standing there in a skimpy tank top and cutoff jeans looking hot as hell, suddenly there were other things playing on his mind. She had a cup of tea in her hand with no weapons in sight. He had the drop on this lovely lady, and she looked harmless enough. Originally, he planned to just shoot her and get it over with. But when he saw her standing there, he changed his mind. *"Such a waste to shoot that"* he thought.

"No tea, but let's sit and talk young lady, I need to tell you about your big mistake and how you can make up for it".

Gutierrez sat on the couch and patted the seat next to him, motioning for Ciera to sit. As soon as she sat down next to him you could hear a commotion in the back room. Someone shouted "Hands on your head or you die!". Then there was the sound of five consecutive gunshots. Gutierrez smiled knowing his men had just shot this woman's accomplices.

Hearing the gunshots, Jerry and three other Patriots in the loft above the living room sprang up from their hiding place and slung their rifles over the railing pointing them down at the soldiers below. Gutierrez men reacted by backing up and raising their rifles. Big mistake. The four Patriots fired at the same time. It was loud. Two soldiers went down, one fired his weapon, but the bullet only pierced the wall.

Ciera pulled a knife out of the back of her boot and in one smooth motion sprang up from the couch. In a flash she clutched the Officials hair, pulled his head back and instantly had the blade touching Gutierrez throat. He made the mistake of reacting. His hands came up and he tried to pull the knife off his throat. It just made her tighten her grip and press harder. The blade cut into his neck. His men walked out from the hall leading to the rear bed rooms. Gutierrez was shocked at what he saw. It wasn't his men. Kaiden and Vic Coaler were standing there with their rifles pointing at him. The smoking guns they were holding told the story- his men were dead.

Seeing that no one was going to come to his aid Gutierrez yelled "Ok! Ok!". He put his hands back down. Blood started to trickle down his neck.

From outside the cabin came the sound of gunfire. On queue Crenshaw and his nine Patriots attacked the soldiers standing aimlessly around their vehicles. From the bushes, behind trees, and in between the cabin and the lake came an intense number of popping sounds that preceded the bullets that tore into Gutierrez men. Four of them were hit with the first volley knocking them down. A sniper round took out one of the gunners on a Humvee. None of them expected an attack, let alone of this magnitude. That same sniper took out another Fed soldier at the bottom of the steps near the cabin. Five of them ducked down behind their vehicles before the Feds figured out where the gunfire was coming from. The one still in the turret on the second 50 cal had to turn around 180 degrees away from the cabin to fire into the forest. That's when the front door of the cabin opened, and the Patriots came rushing out with Gutierrez. Through open windows and from the porch, the Patriots opened fire on the Feds. A second soldier at the bottom of the porch steps went down. The rest of the enemy found themselves caught in a heavy crossfire.

Gutierrez patrol was devastated. A Federal agent standing next to the van was hit. Seconds after that another went down clutching his shoulder. Confused on which way to address which threat, the remaining gunner turned his 50 cal back to the cabin and was about to open up when he saw his boss standing there on the porch. There was a women behind him with a knife to his throat. The few agents still alive saw how the situation had become untenable real fast and just as fast they lost their desire to continue risking their lives. These were not professional soldiers. Most of them were illegal immigrants that only spoke Spanish. The Feds recruited them to serve on patrols as the force behind the elimination of American resistance, A job in which they were more than willing to participate. They were issued a uniform and a rifle but were dealt only enough training to get by. It wasn't a priority. All of their weapons dropped to the ground and their hands went up. None of them expected to run into an ambush with that much fire power arrayed against them.

Ciera yelled at Gutierrez "Tell them to stand down or I'm going to open you up!" Still clutching his hair, she shook his head hard.

Gutierrez waved his hands with his palms down signaling the Humvee's gunner to cease. The gunner obeyed by pointing the barrel of the 50 cal to the sky, but the driver had a different plan. He started up the Humvee. And to keep himself and the vehicle from getting captured, he floored it and took off.

Kaiden spoke into a hand-held radio "We got the drop on em' but a Humvee's coming your way. She's all yours".

From the wood line across the street from the cabin, Crenshaw, with his Patriots by his side, ran up from their positions and confronted the few remaining soldiers around the vehicles.

"On your knees! On your knees!" the Patriots yelled with their rifles pointed at their heads. They didn't resist and were consequently taken prisoner.

That second Humvee though, tore off in the dirt and then hit the pavement with screaming tires. In a matter of seconds, it was out of sight. Thinking they had removed themselves (and the Humvee) from a very precarious situation, the driver and the gunner smiled to themselves. Seconds later the Humvee rounded a bend in the road and was forced to come to a screeching halt. In front of them were two Police cars and the Inn's shuttle bus parked across the road. The vehicles successfully blocked it off so they could not pass. To get around, they would have had to traverse a rather deep drainage ditch on one side or go through a forest of trees on the other. Four men responsible for the obstruction were in position behind the vehicles holding rifles pointed at the Humvee. One of them stood up and flagged down the Humvee. It was the Chief of police, Chief Avery, with a bull horn in his hand.

In response, the Humvee's gunner on the 50-cal opened fire. It was a clear attempt at punishing the people who got in their way, for the act would not have gotten them through the roadblock. The Chief dove for dirt real fast as bullets plunged into his vehicle. Smoke and noise poured out of that gun, so much so that for just a minute the Feds were distracted and never heard the motorcycle coming up from behind.

That dirt bike had one brave dude from Brian Hardy's group riding it with an open throttle. The guy sure knew how to handle a bike. With fire coming out of the tailpipe and fire coming out of the riders eyes the bike screamed out of the woods and bore down on the Humvee with vengeance. He had just heard how these people had beaten his grandfather and grandmother and was hell bent. He hit all gears and went sailing up to the Humvee in an all-out attempt to get to it before that gun could turn around and spray him with life-ending metal. To achieve that goal, he had to go way too fast for any kind of a sane dismount. The bike approached looking like it was going to crash into the back of that Humvee, instead the guy hit the rear brake and locked it up. The rear tire skidded and then the bike fishtailed sideways. Expertly he laid the bike down and rode on top of it like he was surfing in Maui for just a moment while it slid across pavement. His speed diminished to the point where he stepped off the bike and started running toward the Humvee amazingly without getting tripped up. The guy ran up, jumped on the back and crawled up to the Humvee's turret.

Now the gunner heard the commotion behind him and was in the process of turning the 50 cal around to meet the threat. A frightened look appeared on the guys face when he came face to face with someone standing there on the Humvee looking down on him with a pistol in his hand.

In the coming days after the battle while standing around a campfire 'Toadie', the stunt rider in the incident, told his story "It was all in slow motion. I don't know if I could do that dismount again if I tried. When I finally got up on top of the Humvee and looked down into the turret the guy looked terrified man. He was frantically trying to pull out a pistol from a holster on his side. I had to, it was either him or me. I aimed at his head and fired".

The 50 cal went silent.

Two cars and six bikes came screaming up the road behind Toadie and his motorcycle. They all screeched to a halt in a position that blocked off any chance of retreat. The dead gunner slumped to the floor of the Humvee and Toadie started firing into the cab through the turrets hatch in the roof. The Humvee's driver saw that if he continued resisting, he would end up as dead as his gunner. He yelled out "Ok, ok, I give up. I give up! I GIVE UP!" at the top of his lungs. "I'm coming out!". The driver opened the door and exited the vehicle with his hands up over his head and then fell to his knees.

Brian's gang got out of their cars high five'in it with anyone in reach while screaming "Yeah that's how you do it!", "You show 'em Toadie!" Then they all raced toward the Humvee brandishing pistols in their hands. Covering them, Brian held a Savage hunting rifle aimed at the Humvee. He smiled at his elated friends as they ran past him. "That's how you capture a fifty-cal machine gun" Brian said to no one in particular.

* * *

At the Inn, Crenshaw and his Patriots had to deal with the aftermath. Prisoners, vehicles, weapons, wounded and... the dead. They made the prisoners strip and took all their uniforms.

The Inn keeper was shocked and mad at the same time realizing that there had just been a battle fought in their back yard. She stood there yelling at Crenshaw, Ciera and Kaiden.

"You all have to get out of here, leave now! We don't want violence here" she told them.

Luckily Mayor Arden showed up and took the irate lady to the side and explained things. He knew her and called her by her first name

"Susan". Eventually he calmed her down and talked her out of any immediate action on her part. Probably what did the trick was the fact that he promised that the damage would be paid for. Still, she was one pissed off lady.

After that conversation the Mayor walked up to Ciera, Kaiden and Crenshaw with a smile on his face. "She'll let you stay, at least until your prepaid rental period is up" he said. Then they all shook hands and were properly introduced.

"Great job guys" the Mayor said. "And without a single casualty on our side. Nicely done. I was hoping for the best. Looks like we got it".

"Well, if it wasn't for your heads up it would have definitely gone the other way. Thank you, Mayor Arden. Thank you for your patriotism" Crenshaw told him.

In a serious voice the Mayor replied "I made the most difficult decision I have ever made in my life. It was a decision in which I had to declare which side of this mess I was going to stand on. One that will probably define how I die but one that will most definitely define how I'm going to live. My conclusion was that these people are not going to get control and change my way of life. Our way of life. Not without a fight. When I found out it was Brian Hardy they were after I made my decision and went to warn him. Brian told me about your situation, the fact that you guys are from the Cadet organization and about the fight you had with these people, not pretty. I can hardly believe it. But at that point I knew that things were a hell of a lot more serious than I thought. Your tale made it 'deadly' serious.

"Sir, it's important to understand that we are at war with these people because of what they did to us, and what they're doing to the country" Ciera interjected.

"Yes, that fact is opening my eyes to a lot of things Ciera. I'm beginning to get the picture. Anyway, Brian knew where you guys were staying so that's when he bee lined it over here to warn you. I didn't know what you would do about it but when Brian came back to me with your plan, I was shocked. I got to tell you; I didn't think we needed to use force. Kept thinking that our government would never do this to us, not in America. But they wanted that list of names, I had to come to grips with that. I knew what they were going to do with it. They were going to go out and visit each one on it and take their guns away by force. I swear, this is not the America we grew up in, it's not the America I want my grandkids to grow up in.

The ambush? I thought the plan was suicide. I heard you were a Cadet Ciera, but I didn't know you had a seriously equipped crew like this behind you" the Mayor motioned to Crenshaw. "I'm aware of the Cadet organization and some of the shocking news that came out about you guys down there. The rendition I heard from Brian is the opposite of what I heard on the news. I'd like to hear more about that. I'm glad to meet you Captain, yet sad it's under these circumstances" the Mayor shook Crenshaw's hand again.

"As instructed, I put Brian and Ciera's name and address at the top of the list I gave to Gutierrez. Wasn't too difficult, they were after you two anyway. Brian and crew had scrambled to get the hell out of his cottage the day before to avoid confrontation, which was smart. His group couldn't handle the firepower the Feds had. Only, I just heard that they beat up on old grandpa Perkins…".

"Oh no" Ciera cried out.

"Yeah, the old man wouldn't tell them where Brian was, so he took a beating. They got mad when they didn't find any guns. Slapped them around a bit. They're tending to them now. Didn't think they'd go that far. Didn't know why they were so riled up about you Ciera, but they went after you next. The rest is history be it good or bad".

"Sir, what are we going to do with the prisoners?" Crenshaw asked.

"I'll take charge of the prisoners if you will bury the dead. We got a temporary holding cell at the station, it's small but we can put them in there for now. I'll warn you; we're going to have to let them go eventually. I mean, we can't execute them, and we don't have the resources to hold them. Normally we'd send them over to Schenectady's Jail but…".

"Mayor please, if you let them go Gutierrez is gunna come back with more guns".

The Mayor looked worried. "Got any ideas?".

"Well at least drop them off in the middle of the wilderness and let them fend for themselves" Kaiden offered.

"Interesting idea" the Mayor said with a smile. "I'll have to think about that one".

"Before we let them go, give us a chance to interrogate them. We might be able to get something useful". Crenshaw said.

"Okay, send someone over tomorrow, I'll tell Chief Avery you're coming. I'm curious about what they've got to say too. But I've got to cut this short, I've got to go. There's some pressing business and plenty of things to shore up after this mess. We're in a different ball game now and there's going to be a lot of explaining and convincing to do. There are some preppers and groups I know who are stocked up and prepared for this. And others who have been caught completely off guard. I've got to reach out to them. Great to meet you all" the Mayor said.

"I understand. I'm glad to meet you too sir. And I sure am glad you're with us" Crenshaw said. The Mayor saluted, turned, and walked away.

After the Mayor left, Kaiden stood in front of Crenshaw and told him "I'm really glad you showed up too. Couldn't have pulled this off without you".

"Yeah, thank you" Ciera chimed in. "We were literally in the middle of a conversation with Brian trying to figure out what we could do when you appeared. What timing".

A voice came in over the radio that Kaiden was holding. He excused himself from the group to take the transmission. Kaiden had been conversing with Brian Hardy throughout the event getting updates and relaying the information to Crenshaw. Brian had four Motorola hand held radio's that he distributed between the main players of the operation, good communication ended up being instrumental in the execution of their plan.

Crenshaw told Ciera "Well we sure didn't plan it this way. We ran out of supplies and were forced to come off the trail. Met the squad hauling the rat pack on our way out. They were a bit too late with supplies, but they gave us the run down on your situation and where you were. I didn't know that the Feds were on to you. That was a surprise. I told you to keep a low profile, Ciera. What happened?".

"Sorry" Ciera said. "I had no idea".

"Where is it now sir? The rat pack" Kaiden asked.

"We took as much of the supplies as we could carry and stashed the rest along with the rat in the woods where we met your guys. It's a half day hike out to get it. I knew we'd be back for it. There was no sense in lugging it all the way back here, we would just have to lug it back again when we go back for the motherload. And it would have slowed us down. Besides, the thought of showers and some decent food sounded really good to us at the time. Nice repair job on the rat pack by the way".

"How about the load?" Ciera pressed.

"Did you leave anyone there to guard it?" Kaiden asked.

"Oh, the motherload's fine hidden where it is. Still in the same spot we put it before you left. It's all wrapped in plastic, it'll be ok. Haven't seen any hikers out there for the last four days. There's not a lot of traffic going through there right now. I'm confident no one will find it". Crenshaw leaned in closer to them and in a low voice said "I also didn't want to leave anyone there alone. Temptation's a funny thing you know. It can get to the best of us..." Then he raised his voice back to normal. "... It's lucky that I did, that's the only reason I had everyone with me. I agree, if we didn't have the numbers, we couldn't have pulled this off".

Brian Hardy's car was following the captured Humvee as it drove into the Inn's parking lot. Standing and sitting on top of the vehicle were a bunch of his guys that were hoot'in and holler'in in celebration of their newly acquired trophy. They parked and it took a minute for Brian to walk up to the Patriot leaders.

"Did anyone order a Humvee? Brian said jokingly.

They all laughed and shook hands while patting each other on the back. There were smiles all around. When he got to Ciera, he hugged her and picked her up and swung her around. It was a Joyous occasion, especially for the Patriots. They had won their first battle against the Feds.

To the Patriots, it was payback. Finally, they had a chance to go on the offensive and it felt good. Tonight, they would celebrate. Before his crew left, Brian confronted Crenshaw. Shiloh was standing next to him. "I was hoping I wouldn't have to fight you for the Humvee. I'd like to keep it if you don't mind".

"No fight from me. Brian, you can have it, you and your guys deserve it. You took a big risk. Besides, it's looking like it might be difficult for us to find gas for the vehicles we got, so yeah you can have it".

"Great, thanks. I was counting on adding that 50 caliber machine gun to my arsenal. I heard you confiscated a number of M16A1's too. Would it be too much to ask if you could throw a few our way?".

Crenshaw chuckled. "Yeah, I know you could use some rifles instead of those pea shooters you got. I can spare a few".

"Hmmm" Brian acted like he was thinking. "Some ammo too?".

Crenshaw laughed and patted Brian on the back saying "I'll throw in some ammo too. It looks like the Feds used the van as their supply truck. Besides the ten M16's we took off the men, we also found four HK 416's. It looks like the Feds are distributing a small number of HK's to their men, probably for the officers. The rest are getting surplus M16's. There was also a nice supply of .223 ammo in the van oh and... an October surprise. We found an M79 grenade launcher with a couple cases of 40mm HE shells to go with it. I can't believe the Feds are issuing a Viet Nam era M16, they must have brought those out from mothballed inventory, why they're not distributing the new(er) M203's I'll never know. Probably getting rid of the old stuff first. The M79 is a sweet fire and forget weapon for sure but I didn't think they still had those".

Brian raised his eyebrows at the news.

"No, you can't have that. I've got to hang on to the heavy stuff" Crenshaw said with a laugh. Then more seriously "Unfortunately we might be needing that heavy stuff. But I do want to help you guys out since you were such a factor in today's success" Crenshaw reached into his pocket, pulled out four gold coins and handed them to Brian. I'll throw these in as a token of our appreciation".

"Wow, now that's a deal!" Brian said. He had a big grin on his face when he shook Crenshaw's hand.

10

BACK TO BUSINESS

After a mish mash dinner of dehydrated food packs mixed half and half with fresh food that Ciera was able to scrounge up at the market, Crenshaw called for a meeting and had everyone huddle around the front porch of the cabin. Shiloh was by his side with an SU-16 rifle slung across her back. She looked... different. So much more serious after participating in the attack today. Her smile was gone. The act of killing another human being creates a whole new base of experience from which to draw from.

Crenshaw began "I wanted to congratulate you all. You won your first skirmish with these sons a bitches".

"Yeah!" the guys cheered.

"I thought about this long and hard. I want to congratulate you but also, I want to warn you. We had the element of surprise on our side today. It was the main factor that led us to victory. Do not get cocky. Without it, it might have been a different story. We are up against a well-supplied and well-equipped enemy. Maybe not well trained but that fact can change depending upon who we run into. I didn't intend to fight, but since we did, it has put us in kind of a hard spot. We're going to have to leave this place".

"Aww no! Nooo" many of the Patriots moaned.

Jerry Reeder spoke up "We just got here man". Jerry was Crenshaw's Sargent in training, he was one who always seemed to be within arm's reach. "I haven't gotten a chance to sleep in a real bed for a while and I was looking forward to it".

"We're going to have to leave. I fear that our action here will attract some unwanted attention. Sooner or later the Feds will be back, and they'll be looking to find out what happened here. Especially if the town lets the prisoners go. And I got to tell you that the Mayor has hinted that they're going to do just that".

"What? No way. No! Why?" was repeated by many in the group.

Another standing close by was Betsy Stoiber. After hearing that, she spoke up. "If they let them go then I agree, the Feds will be back within a few days with more fire power".

Crenshaw nodded and said "Unfortunately the Mayor doesn't see the gravity of our situation or the full ramifications of the mess we're all in. But this town simply doesn't have the manpower or the resources to tend to and harbor prisoners. No one's prepared for this shit. They would have to send them over to Schenectady's jailhouse and they'd have a whole lot of explaining to do to get them locked up. It looks like everything from this point on depends on what areas the feds have under their control. We just don't know who's who".

"Execute the bastards" someone yelled.

"We can't do that. That would make us as bad as they are, and we are not them" Crenshaw said in a sharp tone.

Donnie stepped forward. "Cap, I would kill those bastards in a heartbeat. Maybe it wasn't these guys, but their kind shot and killed Nigel, Mike and Mindy McLachlan back at CW Farms. I'm sorry, but if they're on the same side as those mother fuckers then they don't deserve to live". Others in the group spoke up in agreement.

"Ok guys, I hear you. I hear you. This is the dirty, dirty business that comes up in a time of war. I'll tell you right now, if you do something like that, it will be the stink that gets on you and it will never come off. You'll smell it for the rest of your lives, and I know that you will regret it each time you get a whiff. I know! This is crazy shit. Here it is I'm congratulating you for killing today, then I tell you that it's not a noble thing to do. Welcome to the hypocrisy of it all. And believe me, it's only just begun.

We need to be gone before the Feds show up. We're not running away. As I've said before, my job is to keep you focused on this mission. We must try to avoid letting things get in our way. Guys, here's the plan. We're going to use the Feds vehicles and the shuttle bus to get back to the Outpost. It's a great turn of events because we got a ride, but it can also be a negative. For one thing, it might be difficult for us to find enough gas to get all the vehicles back to the Pioneer Outpost. And on the other hand, just driving around in them could attract trouble. But we sure as hell can't hike all the way there. I'm counting on the two Humvees and the 50 to help bust us through. I'm thinking that the uniforms we took off the prisoners will come in handy. I'm warming up to the idea that we can put them on and drive through as Feds".

"Oh, that'll guarantee that we get shot at" Jones said. That got a laugh from the group.

"Well, it looks like either way we're going to run into trouble from one side or the other. It'll be better than before, we've got radios and the CB working for us now, that's a definite upgrade.

Tomorrow morning I'll take four of us and hit the trail to go back and pick up the motherload. Ciera will take the vehicles and move to another campsite of her choosing. Changing locations will make us harder to find. Wait for us to come off the trail, pick us up and we're on our way" Crenshaw said. "Okay. That's all for tonight. Let's enjoy this place while we can. Oh, and my half of the crew gets the beds tonight".

"Yeah!" half of the Patriots cheered the idea, the other half booed.

* * *

The next morning before leaving, Crenshaw told Ciera "Remember, low profile". He took Jerry Reeder, Shiloh, and three other Patriots with him. Ciera dropped them all off on the Northville Placid Trail going north. They planned to pick up the rat pack on the way to the camp site. "We should be back in two- or three-days max" Crenshaw told her. "Find a place to bury the bodies. And find enough gas to get us out of here! And Ciera…".

"Yeah, yeah, I know…" Ciera said. "Stay out of trouble" they both said it at the same time. He had repeated that last request quite a few times that morning.

Ciera and her squad could have stayed at the cabin for another three nights before they planned to meet Crenshaw back at the trail head on the third day, they were paid up for another week. But she told the Patriots to prepare to leave that same morning, then went in to settle on payment for damages with the Inn's owner.

Kaiden advised Ciera "Make sure they know that we're leaving today. If someone comes looking for us, they'll find out that we've moved out of the area, and it'll throw them off. Besides maybe you can apply some of that money to the damage bill".

"Can't do that. Then they won't let us take the bus and they'll tell anyone asking that we left. I think it would be better if people believed we were still here or that we were coming back. I got the cabin and the bus rented for another week. It's bad enough that we're going to be taking the bus without their permission. We're just going to have to square up with them when we finally return it".

The Inn's owner wanted her to pay a hefty amount for damages. As far as Ciera was concerned the bill was inflated to an absurd amount. Either the owners thinking was still clouded by old term dollar concepts, or the lady was trying to take advantage of this girl who kept coming up with gold coins to pay for everything. Ciera stood her ground and offered them three gold coins, about a quarter of what they were asking, in a take it or leave it bid to settle the bill.

"It takes two to make a fight" Ciera told the lady. "Send the balance of the bill to the Federal government". The lady took the coins.

With all the holes in it, it was amazing that there was still some gas left in the police car's gas tank. The car wouldn't run and had to be pushed off to the side of the road where it still sat. Kaiden had the guys siphon out as much as they could, and they poured it into the Humvee. That was enough to fill it's tank to about two thirds. They needed more. That fact produced an early morning gas run.

After they performed the gruesome task of burying the bodies, all three vehicles roamed the area looking for gas. No one seemed willing to sell them any. The gas station's owner was nowhere to be found and even Mr. Jenson, the markets owner, couldn't or wouldn't part with any more. The effects of the crash were quickly becoming serious.

"I don't know how long this shit storm's going to last" the store owner said. "I'm going to need all the gas I got now". Not even an offer of more money made him budge. The same attitude must have prevailed with the town folk too. No other cars were on the road today except the Patriots.

So, it had to be done. Kaiden led them to the school yard where they had previously discovered the two yellow school buses sitting side by side in the parking lot. Quickly and with as little of a footprint as possible they hooked up a tube and syphoned out enough gas to finish filling the tanks in the three vehicles. Ciera felt bad, she didn't know who or where to leave a coin to erase the fact that they had just stolen it.

Successful at finding gas and lucky that no one harassed them (maybe because they were driving around in Federal vehicles?), the guys drove the vehicles and followed Ciera and Kaiden who rode the Humvee. Kaiden drove on the back roads of Lake Pleasant in search of a place to set up a temporary camp for a few days. It was nice to have radios to communicate with the other vehicles. They practiced radio procedures and switched channels as well as used privacy codes to keep from being monitored. With great interest Ciera monitored CB radio chatter for any news. She dropped in on a few conversations where she heard some local chatter about the state of the union and a few theories about the what and the why of it. They all smiled when they heard someone talking about a gun battle at the Irondequoit Inn. None of the details were accurate except for the statement that "...bullets were flying".

After driving around Lake Pleasant and the surrounding area, they found a site not too far away off a secondary dirt road near the lake. It was a spot that couldn't be seen from the main road which suited their needs. They spent the afternoon at the site setting up camp. Not being seen was paramount.

* * *

Kaiden and Vic got the job of interrogating the prisoners. They drove over to the police department first thing the next morning. Kaiden had a plan but wasn't quite sure if he would be allowed to implement it. Chief Avery allowed them the freedom to proceed because he was more than angry that his patrol car got shot up.

Vic and two police deputies (one of them had just been deputized in an attempt to beef up their numbers) stood outside the jail cell with rifles pointed at the five Black Jack prisoners. One of the prisoners was not there, he had a bad gunshot wound and had to be taken to a doctor last night for treatment. The rest of them were standing behind bars in their underwear. The look on their faces varied. Two of them looked frightened at the thought of their immediate future. The others looked mad.

Kaiden yelled at the prisoners "Ok, listen up. I'm going to interview you one at a time. To make this easier for me and positively easier on you, I need to know if there's anyone in there who wants to have a pleasant conversation with me without us having to kick the shit out of you first?

One of the prisoners spoke to the others in Spanish and relayed what Kaiden had just said.

"I will" one of the prisoners spoke up while stepping forward. Gutierrez told the guy to shut up and get back in line. A prisoner behind him kicked the guy in the back.

"The next person who touches that man gets shot!" Kaiden yelled. And I would just love to lighten the number of prisoners in here. Go ahead, test me. Tell that to them" Kaiden told the interpreter. The interpreter mumbled something to his guys in Spanish.

Vic removed the guy who wanted to speak from the cell and had him cuffed to a chair in Chief Avery's office. Kaiden walked in and looked him up and down and then asked "What's your name?".

"Phillip" the prisoner said in perfect English.

"You sure it's not Phillipe?".

"No, I'm American. I just joined these guys because I thought we were going to help keep the peace, not harass folks for their guns. I just needed a job man".

"But you were willing to accept whatever the 'job' entailed right? Including killing your own fellow citizens!" Kaiden shouted in a stern voice.

"I didn't know we were going to kill anyone, once that shit started, I wanted out".

"So, you did kill someone?".

Phillip looked up at Kaiden with a depressed look on his face wondering what was going to happen if he answered truthfully. "Not me. But they did. It happened when someone resisted giving up their weapons. We've been on the winning side of a couple of shootouts, but we did lose one just the other day, plus they captured one of our Humvee's".

Kaiden glanced at Chief Avery making eye contact. Both of them raised their eyebrows. Kaiden continued and asked him questions: "Where did you come from? Where is your base of operation? How many are there? What type of weapons do they have? Any drones? How many vehicles? What's their procedure, when do they move out and when do they return? What are the names of the leaders? What areas do they control? Where do they store their weapons and ammunition?".

Phillip was cooperative and willing to answer to the best of his knowledge so Kaiden went on trying to gleam as much information out of him as he could.

"What news have you heard about how things are going out there? Kaiden asked.

"The government is re-organizing..." Phillip said.

"I know that, tell me something I don't know".

"There're rumors about a coup that started all this. They say that President Richfield is now just a puppet of the World Party counsel. That's what they call themselves. Those are the people who are calling the shots now. I heard about some nasty infighting between the parties when the shit hit the fan. Security details turned into hit squads. They murdered each other for control of the government".

"What about the military? Why didn't they intervene?" Kaiden asked.

"I heard most of their resources are tied up in the Iranian war and technically they aren't, or 'weren't' allowed by law to deploy on American soil. Plus, the armed branch of the IRS, the ART was already there 'handling things'. Only they came in on the side of the progressives which tipped the scale in their favor. Together they delivered a knockout punch to most of the Republican opposition. Afterwards the ART put out a statement blaming the Republicans for the downfall of the economy and the attempted coup. They said the Republicans tried to take over and the Democrats are reacting by taking back control".

"A coup in America? Jeese, no one thought it could ever happen. Anything else? How's the country reacting?" Kaiden asked.

"There's push back against the Federal Government in several areas still controlled by Republicans. But I guess I've got to say that there's a lot of old school Democrats on their side too, so I really don't know what to call them" Phillip said.

"Well, I'm not a Republican or a Democrat, I'm a conservative. There's a big difference. But tell me Phillip, who are we up against out there?".

Phillip replied "All over, but especially down south, it's us against a horde of illegal immigrants with major Cartel support and they suspect even the Mexican Government. Months before when the Progressives tore the rest of the Trump wall down the refugees were free to set up camp where ever they pleased. They say some of them were terrorist training camps. Even the border patrol had to retreat because the Feds weren't interested in confronting them with force. The Dems got that 'Open Door' policy; it's been going on for decades now. The Cartel sent in Capitan's who trained and funded what they were calling "Especial Fuerzar de El Gente" meaning Special Force of the People. Some fire fights had occurred previously, but the fighting started in earnest when the economy collapsed. That undermined everything and made us vulnerable. Most of the local resistance is tied up in dealing with that.

In this area, I see it mostly as a city against the rural population. Bands of city folk are starting to roam around the rural areas. Individual farmers are ineffective in defending against them. Food is becoming harder to get and people are beginning to run out of stuff. Nothing is working like it used too. We, I mean 'the Feds', are training squads to go out and help local governments get the farms working again. I thought that's what 'we' we're doing".

"Help?" Kaiden said in a sharp voice. "You mean they're recruiting people to go out and forcefully insert themselves into State and local governments and businesses, demanding that they produce for the 'state'? That's help? No, that's called Socialism".

Phillip looked down like he was disappointed in himself for being a part of what he was about to confess. "Yes" he said. Then he looked up at Kaiden. "But what's so bad about that? What are we supposed to do? If we run out of food? I mean we have to eat... right?".

"Phillip, our government is creating the problem so that they can step in as the solution. They're pulling the constitution right out from under your feet and ushering in a new political agenda in the name of a national emergency. Now they've demagogued you into participating. Forcing farmers to produce at set prices effectively eliminates choice and free will. It commits everyone to slavery. Let alone the fact that they're stealing guns from law abiding citizens". Now Kaiden was yelling "How about working for a society that promotes the freedom to create and allows people to produce an abundance of the very thing you are going out to steal?".

"That system failed us..." Phillip started to say.

"No, you're wrong, it hasn't. I can't believe I keep hearing that. That's a perfect example of socialist propaganda designed to keep you from understanding the truth and allow the people behind it to slip into a position of power. The truth is that 'people' have failed the American system. They have failed it by refusing to adhere to the very principles that made it work".

"The people have to support the government, so the government can support the people" Phillip said.

"Ahhh, there it is" Kaiden said. "The socialist agenda. But yes, I agree with it only on a base level. The government should provide a safety net for people who are hurting. That's it. Only, you know what governments turn into Phillip? My high school history teacher said it best; Throughout history, governments evolve and outgrow their original mandate and turn into a steam roller that swells up in size behind the ever-increasing number of people it supports. It gets bigger and bigger and goes faster and faster until at one point that steam roller runs over the very citizens it was designed to serve. After seeing that steamroller come to life in America, I decided that I can no longer support the beast that's going to kill us. And we can now rightfully say that this beast is here and 'is' literally rolling over us, can't we Phillip".

"It's Gutierrez, he's the one!" Phillip cried out. "He's a mean son of a bitch. Calls himself "General". He ain't no General. He's the one who ordered us to do it. He doesn't care about nobody".

From the responses Kaiden got he determined that this guy was just another pawn in the game, just like Chief Reynold's new deputy who has no idea what he's in for. It also occurred to Kaiden that he himself went out and stole gasoline just the day before, he'd committed a crime in the name of survival. And now he was about to bust this guy just for trying to survive. But that didn't eliminate any responsibility (for either of them), it did give Kaiden an idea though. After he got all the information he wanted, he told Phillip "Okay, you've been very helpful to us. Now I'm going to release you…".

Phillip was shocked. "You're going to release me?".

Vic gave Kaiden a frown and the deputies glanced at the Chief.

"Yes" Kaiden said. I'm going to see which one of your buddies in there will be as cooperative with me as you have. The ones that cooperate will get clothes, a jacket, and a free ride out of town. One of us will take you and any of your cohorts that cooperate out to the town limits and let you go". Kaiden got down to his level and looked Phillip in the eyes. "I advise that you and the others start walking as fast as you can away from here and don't ever come back. If you do, you will be shot on sight. Next, I'm going to tell Gutierrez that you told us everything we wanted to hear and that you even wanted to join our side. I'll drop Gutierrez off last, in the same spot we drop you off. If he's as much of a threat as you say he is, then he's not going to be too thrilled to see you. I'd walk fast, very fast. Fast enough to make sure that a meeting between you two never occurs". Kaiden used the rest of the afternoon to interrogate the others, at the end he gave each the same deal and had the deputy drive them to a drop off point outside town limits..

Afterwards, Chief Avery told Kaiden "Thanks. I didn't know how we were going to get rid of those prisoners. That was a very equitable idea. Wish I thought of it".

Later that day, Ciera, Vic, Jones, Kurt Mendel and Robin Metcalf and the others busied themselves with the task of building a fire pit at their campsite. When Kaiden walked up and joined the group they pressed him for news.

"Current news is hard to come by" Kaiden told the circle of Patriots. "From the 'interviews' this morning I got bits and pieces of information, not much in the way of solid news on the state of the union. There's a lot of theories out there but I think they're a little light on facts. Until now we relied on the internet for everything and suddenly… bam! We're thrown back onto pen and paper. It's exactly what many people feared would happen. All those conspiracy theorists, looks like a lot of them have come true. I don't really know what to believe. Brian says everyone thinks that at any minute the net is going to pop back up. The anticipation stifles any motivation to do anything. It's like they're all waiting around for someone else, for the tech companies or for the government to fix things".

Ciera walked over to Kaiden and put her arms around him and hugged him. Then she stood behind him and massaged his shoulders. "I can see that" she said. "Any investment in alternatives at this point would be a total waste the second the net pops back up".

"So, we got nothing" Vic declared. Nothing official but those notices posted at the post office. And they just read like Federal propaganda".

"Yeah. There's one thing I heard that was very interesting" Kaiden said. "One of the prisoners told me that their Syracuse headquarters is in the Hacia Reginal Headquarters building. The old Google building. There's a defensive wall around the entire property now and all the Feds operations are based out of there. I wonder what the Hacia corporation has to do with all of this".

"Hacia bought out Google a few years back" Betsy enlightened him. "They own the internet. I've heard rumors that they've bought off so many politicians that they own the government too".

"Last I heard the Republicans were trying to pass a bill that would have declared them a monopoly and would have broken up the conglomerate" Vic contributed.

Ciera chimed in "They were trying to pass a very unpopular law that restricted Hacia's ability to control the internet. Everything on the net must pass through their algorithm and get their stamp of approval. They've become the government of the net. Even the Democrats were demanding access to a shut off switch for the net. Looks like they found it".

Kaiden couldn't help but conclude and he threw it out there for everyone to try on. "Could it be that the Hacia corporation, in cahoots with the progressive party, just overthrew the American Government?". They all stared at Kurt who was trying to light a fire in the pit they had just finished building. That theory was something that would have been so absurd just a year ago yet now sounded like a real possibility.

Kaiden continued and told them more about what he had extracted from the prisoners. When they heard about how he released them they all laughed.

"What about Gutierrez?" Betsy wanted to know.

"They're still holding the head honcho and his sidekick. I just lightened the load on the town by releasing some of his men.

"You met with Brian after that? What did he say about what he intends to do?" Ciera asked.

"Those guys are gearing up" Kaiden told them. "They think the Feds will be back and they say there'll be a definite confrontation if they come in here with the intent of becoming supreme ruler. He's working with the Mayor and the local cops on forming a militia, one that will respond to an outside threat. Now that they know there 'is' an outside threat. Brian asked a lot of questions about our organization. He wanted to make sure that I would relay to you all, that there is a standing invitation for us to join them".

"Nice to know. Finally, someone on our side. I was beginning to think it was us against the world" Ciera said.

* * *

On the morning of the third day after Crenshaw left, a voice came in over the radio. "Beach Baby Bingo to Bloody Sally come in". Kaiden started cracking up when he heard it. "Who put Crenshaw in charge of the call signs?" he asked Ciera. They hadn't made up new call signs yet, which must have been the point Crenshaw was making. "Uh, Beach Baby Bingo this is Bloody Sally we got ya, come in".

"Ready for pick up there Sally, over".

Kaiden drove the shuttlebus over to the trail head and found the six Patriots lying around on the embankment using their packs as either a back rest or a pillow depending on how tired one was. All of them got up and cheered when the bus arrived. It was like they were congratulating themselves for being successful at bringing out the motherload. But Kaiden knew it was because the job of pushing and pulling that thing over some very difficult terrain was over. Hanks welding job had been put to the test and it held up nicely under the stress. It was obvious that the guys were happy to be done with it and voiced that opinion while loading it into the rear cargo bay of the bus. It took all of them to run it up a ramp and get it in there but that was better than unloading and then restacking the metal. This way if they had to take it out in a hurry, they would know how to do it and the rat could instantly be mobile.

"Thank God Ciera found us a bus that can handle this thing cause I'm done pushin it" Jerry said. He brushed his hands together signaling that he had just relinquished the task.

Back at their campsite, Kaiden let Crenshaw and crew settle in before submitting a verbal report. Crenshaw absorbed every detail and when it was time, he held a meeting out in front of the bus. All the major players and a few minor ones were there for the discussion that ensued. He summarized their situation and went over the information that Kaiden had gotten from the prisoners to make sure everyone was up to date. In his summary he let Kaiden know that he didn't agree with his theory behind letting three of the prisoners go and why 'from this point on' no one else had the authority to make those kind of decisions except him or Ciera. Crenshaw said he understood the reasoning but wasn't happy about it. Information gotten from prisoner interrogations was discussed next and it immediately sparked a debate.

Kaiden argued for taking advantage of the situation given to them. "I figure we can use their uniforms and their vehicles to get us through the roadblocks. It's perfect. It'll be just like one of their teams returning to their base in Syracuse and just like one of their teams going out on a mission on the south side of Syracuse. The paperwork we found in the Humvee will get us through the roadblocks".

"Yeah, but that won't be the case on the south side" Crenshaw interjected. "I read the paperwork; it describes the area assigned. It'll look really odd that we're roaming around on the south side of Syracuse. I don't like it" Crenshaw frowned. "If we get caught, it'd be like taking the load and handing it over to the Feds. Poof, they got it. All our work for nothing. That would be devastating to me, and to our cause. It'll send us right back to square one".

Kaiden pressed the issue "If we go now, we got a good chance that we can just waltz right on by em', then we can get the load back to the patriots sooner rather than later. But the paperwork we got will only be good for a short period of time, a couple of days more at the most. The window is closing. We can't use it if we wait. Hell, if we go any other way there's a chance we'll get attacked by some militia and lose the load to them. This way we might even be able to drive all the way through to Pennsylvania unhindered. The risk of getting caught is going to be just as great no matter which way we go".

"That's true" Jones spoke up. "But I'm not relishing the idea of getting attacked by a band of militia mistaking us for the Feds".

"That is if there are any other militia's fighting back. I don't think people are reacting to this yet" Victor Coaler said. "We really haven't seen any organized resistance. This thing caught us all by surprise. No one was thinking that the government would flip like this".

Ciera added her two cents "We 'are' the organized resistance people! Get that through your heads. I think we're going to find plenty of Brian Hardy's out there. Hell, we've been hiding, and we haven't seen shit yet. But this way we don't have to go the back roads. Jones is right, we'd probably get shot at. But I think Kaiden's right too. This might be the only chance we have to get back to the Outpost fast before anyone can organize more resistance than is already being arrayed against us. I think this is our chance".

Vic spoke up "There's one other option that no one is coming to grips with. There might not be a Pioneer Outpost anymore". He paused to let that sink in. "Then we could be walking right into a trap, they could be waiting for us". Everyone was quiet as they digested that possibility. Vic continued. "If so, we'd do better by staying put. We could go back to Lake Pleasant, hide the load, join Hardy and operate out of there. When we're strong enough we can strike out for the Outpost next year or better yet, have them come to us! Hell, I don't want to risk my life and make this any more complicated than it need be. We got Brian Hardy's gang on our side. I say we hunker down with them till things straighten out. We get out when we get more information. Maybe the net will be back up and things will be getting back to normal, who knows".

"Ok, ok. I've heard enough" Crenshaw said. "I'm going to put this topic to rest. I've heard both sides and I've thought this through. I made up my mind. Jerry, if we didn't have this unique situation thrown into our laps, I wouldn't even consider it. We would stay put like you said. But with what we've been given… this can work. We need to move fast while we can. Who knows how strong they are now, but one thing is for sure, things are going to get worse before they get better. I've decided, we're going straight through. Half of us will dress as Feds, the rest will be on the bus playing the part of prisoners. The cover story will be that we are bringing them in for interrogation. We'll bring Gutierrez with us. He can speak Spanish when needed and help get us through…".

"But Cap! If he gets a chance and turns us in, we're all dead" Jerry objected.

"He won't if he values his life" Crenshaw replied. He looked each one of them in the eye, Kaiden had never seen him look so resolute. In a serious tone Crenshaw said "Guys, this is no game. Things have gone way past serious, and I've got to tell you, this could get rough. But if it does, I'm going to need people who are on board and who are going to step up and do what it takes to deliver the motherload. I need people who are steadfast in their convictions and in full agreement with me and this mission. If you come with me, I'll need you to do exactly what I ask, especially in situations that might call for putting a bullet into Gutierrez if he turns us in. Ruthless. That's the kind of grit that it's going to take for us to make it. Now let's take a vote. Who wants to go with me? Raise your hand". Everyone in the group raised their hand.

"We leave at 9:00AM tomorrow morning". Crenshaw told them. He turned and walked away leaving them to talk among themselves.

11

PULSE OF THE NATION

Early the next morning, just after dawn, the fifteen members of the Patriot organization scurried around preparing the shuttle and the Humvee for the trip. Today would be the first day of what was hoped to be a two-day trip back to the Patriot Outpost. A trip that could normally be accomplished in just one day if they were still living in the good old days.

The plan was to take the four vehicles to maintain the look of a Fed patrol. One Humvee with its highly visible 50 cal machine gun would lead as a deterrent, followed by the shuttle bus in the middle of the pack. The SUV and the van would bring up the rear. It was more vehicle than they needed for the fifteen militia members that were going, but it was a better strategic way of escorting the mother load. They just had to worry about getting enough fuel along the way.

Eight of them in total wore the Federal uniforms that had been taken off the prisoners and the dead. Those were also tasked as the designated drivers. Crenshaw, Kaiden and two others standing behind him, looked positively out of place wearing black jack uniforms with HK-416 rifles cradled in their arms. All the others were still in their Cadet/Patriot uniforms playing the part of prisoners on the bus. Ciera was put in charge of the bus. She and her 'prisoners' had access to weapons stashed under the seats and would be tasked with protecting the motherload should it become necessary.

Jerry Reeder and another Patriot named Sandy Kemp, were tasked with getting the prisoner Gutierrez dressed in uniform and released from jail. That had been accomplished early that morning and they were now escorting the prisoner up to meet Crenshaw in the staging area that formed in the Irondequoit Inn's parking lot.

"Ahh, Gutierrez" Crenshaw said when Jerry presented him.

"You're going to keep me in these cuffs?" Gutierrez complained while holding up his two bound hands.

"Of course. What would you do?" Crenshaw asked without leaving room for an answer. "This is how it's going to go Gutierrez" Crenshaw stepped towards him and got inches away from his face. "You will be riding up front in the Humvee. If we encounter any of your people, it will be in your best interest to help convince them that all is well and that we are reporting back to headquarters with prisoners. If need be, you will talk us through any roadblock…".

"And why would I do that?" Gutierrez asked.

"Because if you don't, you instantly become useless to our cause. Once that happens, the primary job of the soldier sitting behind you will be, above all else, to put a bullet in you. If you don't cooperate, your life here on earth will end. If you help us, we will drop you off somewhere where your people will find you. You have my word on that, you'll see the light of another day". Crenshaw stared at Gutierrez. "Answer this question... are you willing to die for these people? Do you understand the gravity of your situation?".

Gutierrez had a lot of things that he wanted to say but he simply replied "Got it".

Crenshaw nodded to Jerry and Jerry escorted Gutierrez over to the Humvee. He loaded the prisoner into the passenger seat and cuffed him to a metal bar underneath the seat. Crenshaw was about to give the load em' up signal when he recognized Brian Hardy's car as it drove into the Inn's parking lot. It stopped in front of them, and five guys got out.

"We heard you were leaving today" Brian Hardy said. "I'm glad we caught you before you left".

Crenshaw greeted them "Good morning. This is unexpected. What can I do for you guys?".

"Our group had a major pow wow last night. We got down to it and discussed, debated, and argued over our future. These guys have decided to ask you if they can join your Patriot organization". Brian motioned to the four-standing next to him.

"Oh" Crenshaw said a little puzzled. He turned to the four guys and recognized seventeen-year-old motorcycle hero 'Toadie' standing there among them. Toadie was honored for his role in the 'Battle at Irondequoit Inn' (as it has since been called).

Crenshaw asked him directly "Toadie, speak for the group. Why do you want to join us?".

Toadie glanced around at his friends and then replied "We all decided that there is something big happening here and we want to be a part of it. We don't want to wait it out in this town. My grandfather fought in the Viet Nam war. Now he's badly injured from the beating he took at the hands of these guys. If anyone can do that to someone who has served his country so honorably like my grandfather, then they do not deserve to be in control of our destiny".

Kaiden admired the guy's passion. "Well said, but someone told me that you were the one making an argument for socialism, is that true?".

"Your right" Toadie said. "I have. But... number one. I have learned a lot since then. Recent events have changed everything. Number two, if you know your history, even the citizens of Britain and Romania gave the reigns to the socialist party after WWII. Many of those 'socialists' fought hard against Fascism and won". He looked at his friends and then turned back to Crenshaw. "We want to help you fight these guys".

"That's good to hear" Crenshaw said. "What's your names?".

"I'm Toadie, this is Jen, that's Bill, and Fife is what we call that guy".

Crenshaw looked them over. "OK, yes, we can use you. You are welcome to join us. We are going to need Patriots like you". The new members smiled from ear to ear and nodded with approval.

"Do you have any weapons?" Crenshaw asked them.

"Two of us have pistols and I have one of the Feds rifles" Toadie replied.

"Yeah, you earned it kid. Ok, we'll work with that. Since we don't have any more Fed uniforms, you all will play the part of prisoners on the bus. See Lieutenant Lowman, she's in charge of the shuttle. She'll fill you in on the plan and your responsibilities. Go and stow your gear, keep your weapons handy and get ready to move out". Then Crenshaw yelled to everyone "Saddle up! Prepare to move out!".

Militia members loaded into their assigned vehicles and took their places. Now there were two in each vehicle dressed in Federal uniforms. In the Humvee there were three. Profit stood in the turret manning the fifty-caliber gun, Kaiden drove, and Crenshaw sat in the back seat with his rifle pointed at Gutierrez. Gutierrez was given the privilege of sitting in the front passengers seat. On the surface, the convoy looked legit.

Kaiden looked around from the driver's seat in the Humvee. "If our passes and paperwork are still good this could actually work" he said to Crenshaw.

Crenshaw mumbled "Yeah it better for all our sake". Then he waved his hand out the window and gave the signal for the vehicles to move out.

They left the parking lot and took off down the road leaving Brian standing there wondering what his nephew and his guys had gotten themselves into. He couldn't talk them out of it. The boys thought it was going to be the adventure of a lifetime. Brian knew it was going to be a life-changing event. He was simply hoping that they would make it through whatever was happening to this country.

* * *

It was a chilly spring day. A gray haze covered the sky as the three vehicles headed out across route 8 going west.

"Team Leader to Back door man. This is Team Leader, radio check, radio check".

"Team Leader, this is 'Back door man' we read you loud and clear" Profit said.

"Rodger Back door man. Team Leader to Lifesaver, radio check, radio check".

"Team Leader this is Lifesaver, 10/10 on this end we read you loud and clear" Ciera said into the radio's hand set.

For the first hour and a half of driving, the countryside was all forest with an occasional home thrown in making some wonder what in the hell they did for a living out here. Then the more frequent scene of an old farmhouse sitting next to the only cleared piece of land for miles around became more common. When seen from a distance the fields started to look like green/brown blankets tucked into the rolling hillsides. Kaiden didn't see much of it, he sat in the driver's seat of the Humvee searching the road ahead for danger. Crenshaw sat in the back going over the paperwork they had gotten off the Feds.

Hardly a car passed them on the road at that time of the morning. They were lucky, the convoy didn't run into any road blocks. This time Crenshaw had a map from the Feds which he was counting on to get them around the major populated areas. The small town of Poland N.Y. was up ahead but it wasn't one of the areas he was worried about. It probably had about the same number of inhabitants as Speculator. In many ways it looked just like it. Some say a lot of these small towns look alike. But all Crenshaw was concentrating on was what their reaction would be if they ran into trouble around the next curve or over the next hill. He was literally praying to God that his crew would perform the way they were trained.

It was quiet when they rolled into the town of Poland. Crenshaw ordered the convoy to stop at the post office in the center of town.

"Why stop here Cap?" Kaiden asked Crenshaw. "Aren't we trying to keep a low profile?".

Crenshaw was the one who insisted they maintain a low profile. "Yeah, but we also need information" he replied.

The sign out front on main street said "General Store". After taking note of the two men standing at the front door with rifles in their hands the convoy pulled into the back parking lot. It was a little confusing. The sign on the back door of the same building said "Post Office". There were three men standing outside that door, all of them armed. One was sitting in a rocker underneath an awning with a shotgun in his lap. Crenshaw and Kaiden walked up cautiously with rifles at the ready but relaxed when one of the men waved them forward with a welcoming gesture. The men allowed Crenshaw and Kaiden to enter, a lot having to do with the 50 cal on the Humvee that was pointed in their direction, but also because of the uniforms. After passing through the back door, they found themselves in a section that was clearly dedicated to all things Postal. Taking ten more steps across worn plank flooring and they were standing in the middle of a General Store that seemed to sell everything including penny candy behind a glass counter. Of course, now a days it costs quite a bit more than just a penny.

"Hello" they said to the old man behind the counter.

"Hello, you boys are back" the clerk said with a little tension in the air due to the uniforms they wore (he didn't shake their hands or introduce himself). "Come on in. Are you delivering mail, looking for supplies or picking up the prisoners?".

That last statement made Kaiden's eyebrows go up, he glanced at Crenshaw to see if he had the same reaction. "Ah… (Crenshaw returned Kaiden's glance) we're here to do the Kings bidding" Crenshaw said with a joking smile which somewhat relieved the tension in the air.

"Ah, good. It's about time you guy's got here. Where's General Gutierrez?" the clerk asked Crenshaw.

Winging it Crenshaw replied "General? Ah he's… in the Humvee".

"We reported this four days ago. What took ya so long?" the clerk asked".

Crenshaw looked at Kaiden then back at the clerk. "Well… you know, we had to wait for paperwork and all that shit to come down from above. Things are not flowing like they used to. It's not my fault, don't blame me".

"Oh no, I wasn't. It's just that I don't want the responsibility of hanging on to it. If it got stolen it would be my ass. And we ain't set up to hold prisoners ya know". The clerk walked over to a rack on the wall and pulled off some keys. "The whole town wants this shit gone. Follow me".

Kaiden gave Crenshaw a 'What the hell' look. Crenshaw raised his eyebrows and shrugged his shoulders as he fell in line behind the clerk who walked out the back door.

Outside, the clerk scouted out his visitors. When he saw Gutierrez sitting in the passenger seat of the Humvee, he waved to him. Disgust showed on Gutierrez face, but he nodded his head and gave a weak salute in response. Profit's rifle now pointed at the back of his head giving him the motivation to cooperate. That was all the clerk needed to confirm that this was legit and that he'd get the proper credit for doing what Gutierrez had asked him to do. He handed the keys to one of his men. "Craig, open the garage". Craig did what the old man asked.

On the other side of the parking lot was an old, not in fantastic shape, rather large for the area, steel building. A rusty sign that looked like it was about to fall off hung above the double garage doors. It read "AUTO REPAIR". Craig told them "Wait here". He walked over to a side door, used the keys on the lock and disappeared inside.

When the garage door swung open, Crenshaw and Kaiden stood there with a surprised look on their faces. Inside was one of the Fed's Humvees. It was an exact duplicate of the two they took from Gutierrez in Piseco, complete with the barrel of that 50-cal machine gun jutting out from the turret. Instantly they noticed the cracked driver side glass and dings/holes in the shell. Definitely caused by multiple bullet strikes.

Craig opened the door and pulled a folder out that was on the seat of the Humvee and then said "She's all yours gentleman" then added "And follow me, there's more". Craig led them farther inside and guided them around the Humvee to the other side of the garage. On the floor were two 4' x 4' wooden crates both about half full, one with hand guns and the other had boxes of ammunition in it. Seemingly every make and model of hand gun ever made was represented in that box. Leaning against the wall behind it was a row of rifles. There must have been fifty or so of all types both hunting, and AR-15 style rifles. Right away Kaiden noticed an AK-47 and then an old M1 carbine with a wooden stock. Next to it was a new M1A SOCOM 16 that really caught his eye. That was the coveted model CQB that was held in high regard by the Cadets at the Academy. More than a few Cadets owned one. Chambered in .308 made it a powerful long-range weapon; a lot more accurate than the Kel Tec SU16 they started this trip with. With its short 16.25" barrel the SOCOM handled well, pointed well and hit well. It's handicap was weight. At about ten pounds it wasn't a rifle that was considered appropriate for carrying on long hikes (some would say even on short hikes). So, it was 'out' as far as hikers were concerned but 'in' for a troop of Patriots driving around in cars and trucks.

Craig handed the folder he had in his hands to Crenshaw. "Here are the names and addresses of the people around here that owned these guns. We convinced most of them to turn in their weapons" he said with a smile. "It's amazing how much cooperation you get when the consequence for having one of these is death. Still there are some hold-outs, those got a star next to em".

Crenshaw looked at the guy "All but you and your buddies I suspect?".

The guy stepped up to Crenshaw and said "Hey! We had a deal man. We help you confiscate these guns, and we get to keep ours. We're going to need them to keep the peace around here. You saw what happened to your patrol! We got the guns and the guys who did that. Got the Humvee back for ya too. You got the names and addresses right there, just like you wanted. We held up our side of the bargain, now you hold up yours".

On the fly Crenshaw did his best to play the part. "Don't tell me what the bargain is! The bargain is whatever the General says it is. You're lucky your dealing with me here instead of Gutierrez. He'd slit your throat you talk to him like that". Crenshaw got up into his face "You keep doing what you're doing, and I'll put in a good word for you.

You can keep your guns. But don't screw it up. Don't make us regret it or we'll come back here and take lives as well as your guns. Got it!".

Craig backed down "Ok, Ok. Got it... there's one more thing". He turned around and walked to a door in the back and opened it. He stood there and motioned for Crenshaw to look inside.

"What's this?" Crenshaw asked. Looking in he saw a mostly empty room with three men sitting on the floor. Two were on the younger side, maybe late twenties. The other was an older man about fifty-five or so. Right away he noticed the smell. It was bad, like the men in there didn't have access to a toilet. Their hands and feet were bound, they looked dirty, and they sat there staring back at him with a defeated look on their faces.

"These are the ones" Craig said. "At least these are the ones still alive. The others are dead, we captured these guys when we found out they's the ones who done it".

Crenshaw was starting to get it. "Oh, and where are our guys?".

"Well dead of course. We told you, it's all in the report we gave you when you were here last week. We buried them at the site. Didn't figure you wanted em back" Craig said with a sarcastic grin.

A lightbulb went off in Crenshaw's head and he switched into high gear. He turned to Kaiden "Get Jerry, Jenkins and Tarloff. Load up these weapons and store them in the luggage compartment on the shuttle. Then take these men, hose em' down and try and get them some clean clothes". For Craig's ears Crenshaw said "Then lock them up on the prisoner transport. And do it fast you hear?".

"Yes sir" Kaiden said. He turned to go.

"Oh, and Kaiden" Crenshaw stopped him. "You can leave the ball and powder musket here". Kaiden glanced at the row of rifles leaning against the wall and saw the civil war era musket. He laughed at the thought.

The convoy remained in that parking lot a lot longer than Crenshaw wanted. But it ended up being worth it. It was like Christmas. Another armed Humvee fell into their lap. Unfortunately, the 50-cals ammunition box was missing along with anything else that might have been inside the vehicle. They inherited some decent weapons from the cache and the three prisoners, who what? Shot up a Federal vehicle?" Crenshaw was determined to get the answer to that, but he didn't want to risk asking the town folk too many questions about something he was supposed to already know. That would draw suspicion. He was hoping to slide on out of here without any need for unnecessary ruckus.

Manny Laear the store clerk (pronounced "La-air") ended up being the towns head administrator, or so he claimed. Crenshaw didn't know the story and didn't ask. He just wanted to get his guys going without getting involved any more than they already were. There was only one close call when Manny Laear insisted, he speak with Gutierrez. They threw a towel over the cuffs on Gutierrez hands and Crenshaw brought Manny to the Humvee's passenger side window allowing them to talk. Crenshaw stood close by to monitor the conversation. They had to speak English, so he understood everything Gutierrez said. The scene was intense for the entire time though. Crenshaw didn't know if at any moment he was going to have to pull out his pistol and blow the two of them away. He would have shot Gutierrez first, that's for sure. The conversation ended up innocent enough and was kept short. But Gutierrez cooperated with the Patriots and passed the first test.

Everyone played their part and continued the ruse right up to Crenshaw's meeting with the three new prisoners. Before that meeting could take place however, they had to be cleaned up out of necessity. Even in the cool morning air they were forced to strip and were washed down out behind the garage with buckets of water from a well pump. It was the best that could be done under the circumstances. Members of the Patriots had scrounged up a towel and some clean shirts for them, but no one had any spare pants or were willing to give up any of their underwear. Therefore, after rinsing out their old ones the prisoners just put them back on.

The owner of the General store refused to sell any of the used blue jeans they had. Crenshaw didn't push the issue. In fact, the guy refused to sell anything to anyone. The owner said the store was closed due to the crisis and the guards were there to keep people from ransacking the place. That's why there were no customers the entire time the Patriots were there. It was possible to force the issue and take what they needed "for the Federal government" but a decision was made to avoid the conflict.

Finally, Crenshaw walked onto the shuttle to have a conversation with their new prisoners/guests. He addressed the three of them where they sat on the bus. "Gentlemen, I'm glad to meet you. I am Captain Crenshaw of the Cadet Militia organization. I need you to answer so that I know your demeaner and your involvement. From what I gathered; someone attacked the Feds patrol. Ball-z move I must say. Was it you?".

They looked at each other and were not immediately forthcoming with an answer. "Gentlemen I don't have time for this..." Crenshaw started to say.

The older man spoke up. "Cadet Militia? What's that?".

"You first, answer the question".

"Ok, it's simple. They came for our guns, and we gave them our ammunition".

"Cute, I bet that's on a T-shirt somewhere". Crenshaw said.

He continued. "Evidently you weren't prepared enough, how many of your group were killed?".

The man looked down at the floor "Three" he said.

"And you got captured? How?" Crenshaw asked.

"We didn't know that Laear and his cronies had made a deal with you guys. Damn, they're people I've known my whole life. They pretended to be with us but then turned. Caught us by surprise and locked us up. Thought by turning us in they'd get some kind of reward or score some points".

"It became evident that this was the group that had attacked Gutierrez and his men. Somehow, they took out one of Gutierrez Humvee's. Inadvertently the act might have been the reason the Patriots succeeded in the battle at the Irondequoit Inn. If the Feds had another 50 cal in that fight and the men to man it, the results could have been disastrous for the Patriots. The advantage could easily have swung the other way.

"Are there more of you?" Crenshaw asked. The man fell silent and just stared at Crenshaw with contempt.

"Ok, I understand. I should explain first. What's your name?".

"I'm Marko Briggs, that's Trip Salantro and Nevel Burns" Marko said proudly.

"You're the leader of your group?" No response.

"Well Marko I've got news for you". Crenshaw looked over at Ciera, smiled, and then turned back to Marko. "Today's your lucky day. We are not Federal agents. We are members of a group called 'The Cadet Militia'. We ran into Gutierrez and his men up in Piseco. Only up there the town was behind us. We won. We took their shit, put on their uniforms and are now driving their vehicles to an undisclosed location". Crenshaw paused and looked for a response. Marko glanced at his cohorts and then back at Crenshaw with disbelief.

"It's true. I'll prove it" Crenshaw said. "You see the other prisoners sitting in the seats here?".

Marko looked around. "Yeah".

"Guys, oh and gals (he saw Betsy Stoiber sitting in one of the seats opposite them) show them".

Betsy and four other Patriot 'prisoners' sitting in the seat across the aisle reached under their seat, pulled out their coveted Heckler Kotch 416's, stood up and simply held them cradled in their arms with the barrel pointed menacingly in their direction.

Marko said "That doesn't prove anything. Those are Federal issued HC 416's they're holding. You could all be Feds. This whole thing could be a set up".

"I guess that's true Marko. But let me ask you. We are going to drive you to the location of your choice, hand you your weapons back and drop you and your friends off. Now, if we were really Feds, would we do that? Especially knowing that you probably will come back here to this General store and shoot up our supposed partners in crime".

"No, I guess not, not unless for some reason you want us to shoot them up" Marko said.

"You know, I never thought of that angle. From your standpoint I guess that could be true as well". Crenshaw turned to Ciera "Ciera how can we prove that we are not Feds?".

"...you can help us take out those collaborators at the General store" Marko said firmly.

"Wow. What do you mean? Kill them?" Ciera asked with raised eyebrows.

"Whatever need be done. I won't take any prisoners that's for sure" Marko replied in a cold tone.

Ciera looked at Crenshaw and said "No we're not going to go and murder those civilians...".

Crenshaw held up his hand. "Mr. Briggs, sorry we can't help you do that; we can't get involved in this fight. We have to slip out of here without event, so we don't draw any more attention than we have to. I used this little meet and greet at the General store as a test to see how effective we were at passing ourselves off as Feds. Didn't know we'd run into you".

"Well Captain, if your little test went wrong would you have shot them? And how 'did' you get those uniforms?" Marko asked.

Crenshaw glanced at Ciera.

"Did you take them off dead Federal agents?" Marko asked.

With a sigh Crenshaw answered" a few, yes. We did".

"How's that any different than what I'm asking for? I must assume they did you a grave injustice to call for lethal force to be used against them".

"Yes, they did" Crenshaw said.

"That guy, Manny Laear, he's taken over the town. Got all the stores closed up. His cronies are keeping everyone out. Won't sell anything to nobody. No one voted him into that position. He's the Sherriff and his family owns the store, but he's effectively shut down the whole town like he owns it. He kicked out the town's administrator and now he's confiscating guns from people and he's using force against anyone who doesn't comply. All in support of the Feds. Are you guys on our side or not? Helping me would prove it".

"Briggs, I think you're right. I should help you. For all those reasons and the implied ones too. Under normal circumstances I would help you. But we can't. I have orders that supersede your request. We're on a mission. So where do you want to be dropped off?".

Eight miles farther up the road just off Rout 8, Crenshaw, true to his word, dropped Marco Briggs off at his house along with his two partners Trip and Nevel. They were met with hugs and tears from family and friends who had thought they were dead. All the guns and ammunition from the confiscated lot that did not meet the Patriots standards or were not chambered in .223, 9mm or .308, were unloaded into Marko's garage. That infuriated Donnie who coveted the Inland M1 Scout carbine that was among the weapons given away. The Scout is a modern version of the old M1 carbine the US military used in the second world war, only Inland's newer version is a lot more accurate. Since the Inland M1 is chambered in the .30 caliber round it was not a rifle that Crenshaw allowed in their arsenal. Donnie didn't pout too long though. With a huge smile on his face, he picked out that M1A SOCOM-16 from the cache which he now proudly cradled in his arms. The SOCOM-16 is a really nice compact civilian version of the militaries M14 rifle. This one was made by Springfield Armory and chambered in 7.62 NATO (.308). A little heavy at 8.8 pounds but since they were no longer hiking through the woods that didn't matter so much. Besides they all still had their Keltec SU16 in their back packs for if (or when) they got back to hiking.

Marko had everything he needed to go back and do the General Store job if he so desired. Tears formed in the corners of his eyes when he realized that this was no joke, and he was back with his family.

In the conversation that ensued between Marko and Crenshaw, Crenshaw went into a bit more detail about who the Patriots were and what they had been through. He told them about the militia, and he told them about the attack and their exodus out of Clearwater Farms. Intentionally he left the Academy out of the conversation and of course there was never a mention of the payload they were carrying. Marco must have believed him because he opened up after that. In return he offered details about the ambush they had sprung on the Feds. His whole family and some neighbors were involved in the battle that he described in detail.

Towards the end of the conversation, Crenshaw gave anyone in their group an open invitation to join the Patriots. After careful consideration and some sole searching, best friends Trip Salantro, Nevel Burns and Mack Heedy, decided to join the Patriot militia. Once again, they were three young men who thought that there was some other place they should be, something else they should be doing during this crisis. They believed that God had other plans for them besides a mundane lifestyle in the sleepy little town of Poland N.Y. This was their chance, and they took it. The Patriot team was now twenty-one strong.

After that detour, the convoy was back on the road. They were one Humvee, three men, fifteen rifles and quite a few boxes of ammunition stronger. But it was up in the air as to whether anyone thought the additional vehicle was an asset or a drag on the operation. Because of it, they would now have to find gas if it was to stay with the convoy. Back Door Man contributed one 50 cal belt box from their limited supply to make the second Humvee a viable asset that could bring more fire power to a fight. To make both Humvee's a more valuable asset they would need to find fuel and more ammunition for them both. Because of it, Crenshaw almost decided to leave the Humvee at Marco's house, but Kaiden came up with an alternative idea.

"When I was digging into the Feds paperwork, I discovered that they have a roaming support convoy from which their patrols can hook up and obtain fuel and ammunition. All we have to do is to meet the Feds convoy at one of its scheduled stops and we could, in theory, re-supply. A chart on one of the pages in the Feds paperwork says the fuel truck is scheduled to be in Herkimer this week" Kaiden said.

An impromptu meeting took place in which everyone voiced their opinion. Crenshaw gave his assessment then spoke. "I've weighed out the possibilities verses the risks and I'm going to place a lot of value on taking this opportunity to equip the machine guns with enough ammunition to help punch us through a tough spot. We're going to need 50 caliber ammunition to do that. Otherwise, we might as well ditch the Humvees".

Everyone else voiced their opinion and then they took a vote. It was a go. Hence the reason the convoy was now headed south on Rt 28 instead of continuing west toward Syracuse on 8.

Everyone hoped to God the "Support Convoy" would be at Herkimer as scheduled because the detour would take them out of their way at a point where time and gasoline were not to be wasted. Their success at playing 'Fed' in Poland gave them confidence, everyone believed they could do it again. Ramifications about what they could gain turned the opportunity into something they could not pass up. They were going to waltz in and steal supplies right out from under the nose of the Feds.

It was always a possibility that they would be mistaken for real Feds by some local group and fired upon. Every Patriot dreaded the action they would have to take if that happened. "We will have to defend ourselves no matter who attacks us. As hard as that is to accept, it's the law" Crenshaw told them. "We will have no choice".

The rag tag group of Patriots breezed through the town of Newport without stopping and without any problems. Ciera hardly had enough time to orient the new members of the Militia before they came upon the town of Middleville N.Y. She had given the new "prisoners" the speech and taught them the role of prisoner that they would play when confronted by a hypothetical event.

Middleville was one of the largest towns that they had come across to date. Compared to Poland it was busy. People and cars were numerous. It looked like something was going on. As they cruised down the main street Crenshaw slowed and rolled down the window to ask a female pedestrian a question. She was pushing a baby carriage and didn't stop.

"Hello! May I ask what's going on here this morning Mam?".

She looked at him and the row of federal vehicles behind him and answered but didn't slow her stride. "The towns having a meeting, going to decide whether to put up roadblocks on 28 like Herkimer did".

"Oh, Herkimer's got roadblocks huh? Why would you need a road-block?" Crenshaw asked.

"To keep out the rift raff" she said flippantly. Silently insinuating that Crenshaw and his Feds could be considered part of that group.

So, it wasn't a surprise, they were ready when the convoy reached the road block just outside of Herkimer on Rt. 28. A warning echoed over the Patriots radio… "Road block ahead".

The citizens of Herkimer were ready too, it showed by the number of armed people who manned the road block. It was obvious that it wasn't the Feds who were in charge here. When Crenshaw saw it, he ordered the convoy to halt about two hundred yards away from the barrier.

"Ok here it is people" Crenshaw said over the radio. "We knew it would happen sooner or later. Let's do this by the book".

Kurt Mendel and Robert Metcalf (their appointed sharpshooter team) exited the bus with rifles in hand and discretely hustled over to a spot where they set up an overwatch.

"Back Door Girl, watch our six" Crenshaw shouted over the radio. 'Back door Girl' was the call sign for Betsy Stoiber's vehicle. She was driving the newly acquired Humvee with another Patriot dressed in a Black Jack uniform. "This could be a ruse to get our attention up front and then attack the rear" he added.

The bus and Stoiber's Humvee stayed behind. Everyone on the bus was locked and loaded. Crenshaw's Humvee and the van with six heavily armed Patriots continued up to the block and stopped about twenty-five yards away. Were they anti or pro Fed? That was always the question, and this was as dangerous a moment as any. Would they be fired upon or welcomed? The barrel of the 50 cal was pointed at the barrier ready for whichever way this was going to go.

For a moment neither side moved, which each used to assess the other. From Kurt's overwatch position and through the scope of his rifle he saw numerous rifles protruding out from different parts of the barricade. Some of the men walking around behind it were dressed in black with black bandanas over their faces, they looked just like ANTIFA members. Then one of them stepped out and started walking toward Crenshaw's Humvee. The guy held a rifle in his hands and therefore the cross hairs of Kurt's rifle scope followed him the whole way.

"Take the 50 off him" Crenshaw yelled at Profit. "Raise the barrel to the sky in a show of faith".

Kaiden got out of the Humvee and walked up to the guy and met him half way with his 'new to him' Heckler and Kotch 416 rifle cradled in his arms. "I represent Federal convoy #357. (he got that from their listed designation on the Fed's paperwork). What organization are we addressing here sir?".

"I'm Rawls Laughlin representing the Herkimer government".

"And what are your intentions? Kaiden asked.

"I'm supposed to screen anyone coming through here, check for guns and contraband".

"Doesn't the government of Herkimer know that there is a Federal ban on guns?" Kaiden glanced down at the rifle in Rawls hands.

"Hell, I thought you'd be happy we're helping you out. Aren't you here because of the attack on your men last night".

"The attack?".

"There were casualties and a bunch of damage" Rawls said.

"Ah... yes but... we didn't get any details. We were just told to get our ass over here ASAP. Didn't know what we'd find" Kaiden replied.

"Your friends, they're licking their wounds that's for sure".

"Ok Rawls, let us through so we can get to them" Jerry said.

"Yeah, I can do that. I'll even give you an escort to their location".

Rawls turned around and waved his hand at the barrier. Jerry walked back to Crenshaw who rolled down his window.

"Cap, looks like our Black Jack friends, I'm guessing the ones we are supposed to hook up with, were attacked last night and suffered some damage along with casualties. This guy says he'll escort us to their location".

"Damn. It may or may not be the supply convoy and I'm not interested in meeting anyone else. But we have no choice". Into the radio's handset Crenshaw said "Patriots, collect our sniper team and form up. We're going through".

Obstructions making up the roadblock rolled back out of the way and a path through the center cleared. The four vehicles in the Patriots convoy rolled through with Rawls taking up the lead in a Ford pickup. He waved to them from an open window. "Follow me" he yelled.

"Cap, this guy could be leading us right into an ambush" Jerry said from the back seat of the Humvee.

"Yeah, possible. But why wouldn't they have simply opened up on us here?" Then into the radio Crenshaw said "Keep alert people we don't know what we're going to find going through here".

Rawls took them through a large sprawling suburb before getting to their destination. It was a lot different than driving through the small towns they had become accustomed too. It was strange, driving with no working traffic lights. Every intersection had to be treated like it had a stop sign. Traffic was light. That was the only good thing that could be said about the crisis, it solved the traffic problem. In every block the convoy passed you could see groups of people hanging out on porches or sitting in chairs in the front yard. Even on this cool spring afternoon. Maybe that's another good thing, people are talking to each other a lot more than they used to.

General Gutierrez sat in the passenger's seat without comment the entire trip. Now he spoke with a heavy Spanish accent "If there was an attack on the supply convoy, there will be a call out for aid. You won't be the only patrol responding to the area. The agents at this base and the ones responding are going to want to know why you have not contacted them by radio through proper channels. Who knows what they will think of your arrival".

Crenshaw looked at him a little surprised that he would warn them. When Crenshaw looked at him, Gutierrez shrugged his shoulders and said "Hey you were right, I don't want to die today". Crenshaw handed him the radio handset.

Gutierrez took it and reached for the radio's dials, but his hand cuffs stopped him short. "Channel 42" he said to Crenshaw. Gutierrez held up his chains and said "How are you going to explain these my friend?".

Crenshaw ignored him and just turned the channel to 42 yet he was forced to consider what Gutierrez had said.

Suddenly the air waves came alive with chatter in both English and Spanish. Some of them faint with other bits coming through stronger. Gutierrez spoke English into the handset "Patrol 0357 calling 'special delivery' come in special delivery". The response was instant, and it came back clear. "Patrol 0357 this is 'special delivery' what's your 20?" Then Gutierrez switched to Spanish and started talking fast".

"Cap!" Kaiden got nervous and took out his pistol, pointing it at Gutierrez.

Crenshaw raised his hand and said "Stand down soldier". Then he glanced at Gutierrez who paused and returned the glance with a worried look.

"I think he knows the consequences" Crenshaw said. Then he used a key to remove the handcuffs from Gutierrez hands. Gutierrez continued.

"I don't trust him…" Kaiden said, but he lowered his weapon anyway.

Crenshaw told Kaiden "There are some angry people in this town, I think that hanging out with some Black Jacks might just be the safest thing we can do right now". Kaiden smiled at Crenshaw's use of the nickname for the Feds.

It was 1:00PM when four Patriot vehicles rolled up to the front gate of the Herkimer Post Office. The only incident on the way in was when they got pelted with rocks by a gang of people when they slowed down at one lightless intersection. Their escort stopped out front and pointed his hand at the Post Office. It wasn't a huge building, but the new owners had turned it into a compound with concrete road dividers placed end to end all along the entire perimeter. The street in front of it was closed off with the same barricades. Attached to the top of that waist high wall was a coil of barbed wire, one on each side of the barricade. It made a formidable obstacle against anyone wanting to force their way inside, yet since it was just four feet tall, it wouldn't have stopped anyone from taking shots at the building. Looking more closely you could see that someone had done just that. But it was a lot more than just pot shots. All across the front wall of the building was evidence of a major fire fight. You could see hundreds of pot marks in the concrete wall where bullets had struck. It looked like every window and door on this side had shattered glass with holes in them.

Security was tight. Black Jacks carrying rifles were everywhere. One had a dog that was biting at the bit to sniff Crenshaw's Humvee as it rolled up to the front gate. Crenshaw stopped, rolled his window down and told the guard "Patrol #0357 reporting in. We're looking to re-fuel and re-supply". He handed them some paperwork and engaged the guard with small talk.

"I hear you got attacked last night" Crenshaw said.

The man bent down to the window, looked in and glanced around at the passengers. "Good afternoon. Oh, AIC Gutierrez" he said when he saw him. He gave a short salute. "My name is agent Kendrell. We're glad you're here sir, we could use the extra help after last night's attack".

Crenshaw had to digest the fact that Gutierrez was an AIC, certainly not a 'General' as Gutierrez was calling himself.

"…it was a bit more than we anticipated. They killed two and got into the compound, but we were able to beat them back. Got two of them in return, the bastards deserved it".

Gutierrez spoke to him "Is there any assistance we can give you?".

"That would be up to central. They'll let you know in the briefing".

"Thank you, agent Kendrell. We're here to check up on you and pick up supplies but then we're going to have to get back on the road".

"Sir my orders are to escort your patrol over to a designated area and then to bring the officers up to headquarters for a briefing".

"Ok Sargent, show us the way" Gutierrez said.

Each vehicle was inspected before being allowed to enter. When the bus stopped at the gate two guards walked over to the bus and knocked on the door. Ciera nodded to the driver who pulled the lever that opened it. One of them entered and stepped in enough to peer inside offering greetings to his fellow agents as he went. He looked around and when he saw the prisoners, he committed himself to investigate further. He walked past Ciera and the two Patriot Black Jack guards sitting in the first two seats and strolled down the aisle gazing at the prisoners on each side. The ones he saw had their hands behind their backs with a rope that tethered them. Ciera's heart was pounding knowing that this was it. *"If it goes wrong here the whole gig is up"* she thought.

The guard must have been satisfied because he turned and walked out wishing them a good day. After the last Humvee was inspected and the paperwork was handed back, the Patriots watching knew they were in. All were standing at the ready, ready to instantly switch into attack mode if things went sour. Everyone breathed a sigh of relief. Still, it was a scary ordeal for every Patriot playing a part in this charade. There was a lot of stress in the air due to possible consequences of what some of them thought was an unnecessary diversion from their main mission. Bringing the motherload into the lion's den didn't resonate as a good idea. If one thing went wrong, all hell would break loose.

The guard escorted the lead Humvee and the rest of the vehicles into the compound. They passed a crew of Black Jacks filling sand bags. They were building a wall at the front gate guard station and also one at the front door of the main building. Inside, parked in sections of the lot were a handful of black vans and Humvee's exactly like the ones the Patriots were driving. When he got to a clear section of the parking lot he yelled "Ok, this is you. Stay in this sector. Again, my name is agent Kendrell, I'll be back to bring you up to headquarters".

When he saw it, Crenshaw asked right off "Ahh, agent Kendrell, is that the tanker we fuel up from?".

"Yes sir" Kendrell said.

"And where do I requisition supplies?".

"On the other side of the building, there are three freight trucks parked side by side. Send a man over and fill out the paperwork, the attendant will help you" Kendrell told them.

"Thank you sir, that's just what we need".

"But before you can be issued supplies, the commander wants to see you and your officers. I'll be back to escort you up" Kendrell said.

"Very well agent Kendrell" Crenshaw waited until he left, then mumbled "I wonder what's up with that?".

"How we gunna do this sir?" Jones asked from the back seat. We're going to bring him with us". He tapped Gutierrez's seat with the barrel of his rifle.

"We'll have too" was the reply.

Fifteen minutes later agent Kendrell was back. Crenshaw, Kaiden, Ciera, Jones and Gutierrez formed the group that met him. Kendrell looked everyone over and saluted Gutierrez when he saw him. "Yes sir" he said. "I've come to escort you up. If you would follow me". Without saying anything Gutierrez returned the salute.

Kaiden walked behind Gutierrez the whole way with one hand on his hip just inches away from his holster. Kendrell led the group, oblivious to how serious the situation really was.

It looked like the Feds had completely taken over the Post Office and were using it as their hub. Electricity was on in the building due to a generator humming along on an abundant supply of gasoline. They passed agents building the sandbag wall at the front door and entered the building. They were led up to the second floor and into one of the offices. Sitting at a desk inside was an official looking man dressed in a New Order Federal uniform. It looked like he might have been from any number of foreign countries, take your pick. Maybe not Latin American, more likely the middle east.

Rank for this new regime was designated by insignia of a different order than standard military. Kendrell walked over to stand at the commanders side as if he was his right-hand man. The commander looked up as they entered. "Yes gentlemen" he said with an accent. (He glanced at Ciera but made no correction to the pronoun he used). The four of them stood at attention in front of the base commander as Crenshaw introduced everyone. Then the commander spoke.

"My name is Commander Hanson of the Herkimer outpost; you know my aid Kendrell". He stood and shook hands with Gutierrez and offered him a seat. Hanson continued "We're glad you responded. At the moment, I'm short on men. You know we were attacked last night and we're hoping that the presence of more Federal assets will be a deterrent for any further transgression. But I have another solution for that and that's why you're here. How long are you staying? Oh, at ease gentlemen" he said to the rest. "I'm not used to such strict military protocol around this place. It's refreshing to see though".

"Yes sir" they all relaxed.

Gutierrez went with the program, positively to get his ass in and out of there without an incident that could turn deadly real fast. He told the commander "We are just here to resupply and of course to see if we can be of any assistance".

"Yes, thank you, I'm going to take you up on that. Why do you have a bus among your assets AIC?".

Gutierrez was hesitant and had to search for a reason, he responded "I lost a Humvee, so I commandeered it to use as storage for confiscated weapons".

Crenshaw jumped in to add to the explanation "We also needed a suitable method of transporting prisoners Commander. We turned the bus into a prisoner transport. We've been ordered to bring a bunch of sad sacks back to Central Command. Command wants them ASAP".

"I see. Who are these prisoners?" Hanson asked Gutierrez. Crenshaw answered for him.

"We captured the leaders of a resistance cell in our sector sir".

To Gutierrez the Commander said "Ah, you will be rewarded AIC Gutierrez, you have proven to be resourceful. Last night two of our guards were killed, six wounded. It would have been a lot worse if it hadn't been for an informant. She got word to us a couple of hours before the attack started. Hell, they might have overrun this compound if we weren't prepared. We killed two of theirs and captured two alive. Through interrogation we got one of them to give up the address to their safe house. I want em bad, dead, or alive.

I need you to do me a favor AIC Gutierrez. I want your patrol to pay them a visit and give them every reason not to screw with me again. I want you to dish out some real pay back. Go in guns blazing. Shoot to kill. Can you do this for me?".

"A daytime raid sir? Isn't that risky?" Crenshaw asked.

"You can go whenever you want. But I know that these recidivists are regrouping now and would never expect it. I think they will be quite unprepared for a counter strike after losing those men in last night's debacle. Bring me some prisoners if you can. I want to talk to them. I want these bastards bad and the sooner the better".

"Ahh sir, we're just stopping in for supplies we can't..." Crenshaw started to say.

Now Hansen was getting annoyed that Crenshaw was answering for Gutierrez. "I'm ordering you to do this son, if you don't then you ain't getting jack shit from my supply line" Hanson said. "We support each other, don't we?".

"Yes sir" Crenshaw said.

Kendrell stepped in "Why are we talking to this guy anyway, he's just an agent. He's not an officer". Crenshaw was wearing a low-ranking agents uniform, the only one that fit him. The officers uniforms that became available did not. At the time it didn't seem to matter what their rank designation would be as long as they were all able to dress the part of a Federal agent.

Gutierrez responded angrily and addressed Kendrell to salvage the situation "I was wondering the same about you... agent or whatever you are! I buried my patrol officers. These soldiers have been field promoted. They'll get proper insignia on their uniforms when we get back to Central".

Hanson broke in "Alright, alright. Let's not get into a pissing contest here gentleman. I'm glad you showed up Gutierrez. I also want to hear how it's going up there in your sector".

"We ran into some resistance up in Poland. Lost some of our guys there during a confiscation raid. Nothing we can't handle though. People are cooperating for the most part. We've got the locals helping us with confiscation. It's going as planned, we're making headway into the local governments. We did find that the resistance is well armed though Commander" Gutierrez said glancing at Crenshaw.

"Yes, I am painfully aware of that as evidenced by last night's attack. When I was in the C.I.A. I pushed to start the confiscation program a long time ago, but our do-nothing politicians never could get it prioritized. Now it's coming back to bite us in the ass. It's like there's a gun behind every blade of grass in this country. Command wants us to double our efforts. We need to clear the way for Operation Cover Charge. They're building up now for the big push. Syracuse Command is responsible for securing the territory between Lake Erie and Albany. The better we do our jobs the easier it will be for them" Hanson said.

"Sir, can you give us an update on any news you've heard?" Kaiden asked.

"The latest out of Washington is that they've overcome all resistance in the area and are pushing for us to do the same. President Richardson has capitulated. In return for ceasing all further aggression in the west by Mexico we gave back Texas, Arizona, California and New Mexico. Hell, the cartels knocked down the wall at the start of this and overran all the border states anyway, it would have been a tough fight to get them back. I say good riddance. California was a disaster; they can have it. All the money the old Federal Government spent on helping those sad sacks didn't do a damn thing. The ingrates revolted against the establishment in spite of it. Mobs of homeless and immigrants attacked the homes of the rich and famous throughout the state. Stole everything of value, hacked up the owners and destroyed everything in their path. I heard it was a brutal cleansing. They killed the rich, journalists, professors, the famous, anyone considered to be part of the elite. Hell, they deserved it. No more movies coming out of California for a while. Let's see if Mexico can do any better with it" Hanson said.

"Why is the power still out?" Ciera asked.

"Why? Ha ha" Hanson chuckled. "Don't you know? It's going to give us the leverage we need against the resistance. It's by design. Without the internet and without gasoline the people in the new American Territories will not be able to effectively mount a supported campaign of resistance, soon they will grovel at our feet. Americans will turn against each other and end up doing anything to get the power turned back on. Including hand over all their firearms and swear allegiance. As the reality of this 'new order' sets in the people will start to demand 'us'.

Somebody a lot smarter than me figured out a brilliant way to kick this can; We started off with the virus. Now let them riot, steal and destroy themselves. Shutting essential services down will bring the population to their knees and make them scream for a taste of the old life. Plus, it solved a problem that we couldn't have handled in a better way. The virus and disorder set the stage and killed off the fat, the lazy and most of those baby boomers that still held on to that old patriotic notion and who idolize the free market system. All those white supremacists. Soon it'll be survival of the fittest and they'll be unable to cope with themselves let alone participate in any resistance against us. Once they die off and the population thins out, then we can turn the electricity back on along with the internet and use it as a bargaining chip in negotiations. We'll positively clean up at that point. You watch, people will sue for peace just to get the power turned back on and restore order. Single player political system. We are simply the best solution to this catastrophe and we're the only game in town".

"So, this is a campaign to purge the population?" Ciera asked incredulously.

"Bingo. No more two-party system" Hanson said. "That wasn't working out too well was it. Hell, they couldn't get anything done.

Anyway, I want you guys to get going on this. Our informant says that there are a lot of weapons at this location and the recidivists are there right now licking their wounds. Wouldn't you know we'd find a pocket of patriotism in the frickin fire station. We've got to stamp it out. Ha, get it?".

"The target is a fire station?" Ciera asked with raised eyebrows.

"Yes, and your next mission will be the police station. Anyone got a problem with that?".

"No sir" Crenshaw responded.

"I want you to take out these two main services to add to the chaos and speed up control of this area. After we take them out the citizens will have to come to us for protection and services. Right now, I'm feeling too much resistance from the Police Chief to suit me. Gunna stamp that out too.

To minimize your risk, you have my permission to use the 50 cal for maximum effect. That'll soften up the target".

"It'll destroy it" Kaiden interrupted.

"I'm counting on it" Hanson said. "Then go in and get me some prisoners. They're going to pay for what they did. Don't bring me any medical cases though. I don't want them" Hanson said.

"What do you want us to do with the wounded sir?" Ciera asked.

"Leave em', put a bullet in em'. I don't care. We're going to have to be ruthless to get this job done. I'm surprised you have a woman on your staff Gutierrez, they don't normally make good soldiers because they get too sentimental about these things".

Ciera stood up like the hair on her back. Scorn oozed from her mouth "I can put a bullet in someone just as easily as my male counterpart sir, and I will exceed at the task...".

"Ok Ciera, sit down, sit down" Crenshaw said trying to reel her in.

"Oooo I like that" Henson said with a grin. "No wonder she's on your staff Gutierrez. A wild cat. Put that attitude to use out in the field agent, that's where it belongs.

Here's an address and directions". Henson handed Gutierrez a piece of paper. "Go". Henson stood up. Gutierrez stood up and the five of them came to attention.

"Yes sir, we'll get right on it" Gutierrez said.

"One question sir" Kaiden asked.

"Yes, what is it?".

"You said there was a female informant? I'm wondering why she didn't give you the address of the safe house".

"Ah, good question agent. I see you're listening. She did. We were simply looking for confirmation from the prisoners and anything else we could beat out of them. If you take any prisoners and find her among them, let her go. That one will be useful to us".

"What's her name?".

"She said it was 'Raven'. I don't know if that is her real name or some kind of code name. Female though. Sweet voice, nice ass! Ok agents. Dismissed!".

They all turned to leave. As Crenshaw got to the door he turned and said "Oh, Commander. Can I borrow your prisoners? I might be able to beat some intel out of them. Intel that I can use for the raid".

"If they can walk, you can have them" Henson said. "They're no more use to me". He gave a nod to his aid.

* * *

On the walk back to the outfit all of them were visibly disgusted with what the Commander had said. A lot of 'Why are they doing this?' was becoming clearer. So many times, they all mulled over the thought *"How could this happen in America"*. Now they had an answer. These are the people who are carrying out a planned coup against the government. They walked to the bus wondering how they had become so detached from their fellow Americans.

The many ways that this could be handled swirled in their heads. Only they were silent in front of Gutierrez. First, Crenshaw had

Gutierrez reoccupy his seat in the Humvee as well as the handcuffs. "You did good AIC Gutierrez. Your still alive" Crenshaw told him. Then he posted two guards and left him with a ray of hope. "Keep it up and you just might make it through this". Gutierrez just sat there expressionless.

Right off Crenshaw called his main players for an impromptu huddle. Time was critical. Information obtained from their meeting with Henson was relayed to those who were not there, and the unexpected turn of events was discussed.

Each commented; "Getting supplies now isn't going to be as easy as we thought. We're going to have to do it the hard way" Crenshaw told them.

"It's obvious that someone got fed up with the two-party system and decided to correct it" Jones said.

"It's prime time" Kaiden commented. They're going to make a push now with their main action. We've got to get out of the way".

"If we do this and bring prisoners back here who knows what Hanson will do to them" Ciera said.

"We're not really going to do this right?" Donnie stated more than asked.

They all looked at Crenshaw wondering what he was going to do".

"Here are our options people" Crenshaw said definitively. He laid them out as he saw them and then asked around for opinions. After a discussion with some intense back and forth, an option considered to be extreme by some floated to the top of the list as most likely to succeed. When it came to a vote, the action was approved.

Fifteen minutes later agent Kendrell released a prisoner into patrol #0357's custody. Kaiden asked him "I thought you had two prisoners. Where's the second one?".

"That one didn't make it, and good luck with this one. He ain't talking. We couldn't beat any more out of him." Kendrell said.

The guy was pretty banged up. They got him on the bus and Ciera did the best she could by applying first aid to the prisoners obvious injuries. At least it helped to slow most of the bleeding. Until things could be explained the prisoner could be a threat to the Patriots, so for now Ciera had him tied to one of the seats so he wouldn't be tempted to do them any harm. It was ironic, guards wouldn't be needed, the prisoners on the bus would watch him.

A meeting between the new prisoner and Crenshaw was to take place ASAP but first, Crenshaw was in a hurry to get his team out of there. "Load em up, we're move'in out" he ordered. Then he repeated it over the radio and the convoy was once again on the move.

Mission not accomplished. But it was still possible to salvage depending on how much cooperation they could get from the prisoner. He was in bad shape. The guy could barely sit up, yet Ciera got him to do so. She gave him water and tried to console him. They would have gotten him something to eat but that wasn't advisable. He probably would have thrown it up.

Driving across town, any Patriot looking out the window couldn't help but notice the number of people out on the streets. The city of Herkimer, with its large population, was a lot different than the small towns they had just driven through. One result of the crisis here was that a lot more people were gathering outside either in a neighbor's yard or in some business parking lot close by. At one of the lots they passed, there must have been a crowd of fifty or more people ambling about.

"Wow, there's a lot of people who don't have much to do" Ciera commented to whoever was listening.

Some of the groups of people had gathered around a burning pile of junk which had become the center of attraction. They looked up and stared at the Patriots vehicles as they passed. Some looked frightened, some were angry, some threw rocks at them in defiance. Still others waved and looked like they were friendly and were beckoning the Feds to come over. One of them held up a 'Help" sign. Help with what the Patriots could only guess. Crenshaw kept them on task and had them continue driving.

The convoy turned off onto 'Main Road' just before entering East Herkimer. They had about five blocks to go to the target. Before they got closer, Crenshaw had them slow down and stop in the middle of the road, effectively blocking it off. If there was any local traffic, he didn't want the vehicles to be able to pass and go to warn anybody about their presence. Crenshaw and Kaiden got out of their Humvee and boarded the bus.

"How's the prisoner?" Crenshaw asked Ciera.

"He's one hurtin' recidivist" She said. That might have been funny at some other time. They both looked at the guy. He was barely sitting up in one of the seats in the middle of the bus. When they walked over, the prisoner was the first to speak through his busted lips.

"I want to know what you're going to do with me? None of these guy's will tell me what's going on" (implying the other prisoners).

"Yes, that's what I've come to talk to you about. What happens to you depends on what you are willing to do for us".

"Me? Do for you? Ha, that's a joke. You beat the crap out of me and then what? You want me to do something… for you? I have rights you know!".

"No, your rights were thrown out when you and your friends voted for this shit".

"I didn't vote for this…".

"Oh yes you did. Next to California, New York is the most liberal state in the Union where the politicians you have elected have bowed to an extreme socialist agenda. Wouldn't you know, it's the most highly taxed state in the Union. That fact alone caused an exodus from the state, especially by wealthy people. Their money and their businesses... gone. Don't you know that this is a typical reaction to a Marxist style rule. This state has been so badly governed by Democrat politicians and more recently by progressive Democrat politicians for over seventy years. Where were you and your friends when they started taxing people at 60% of their income and when they implemented the State death tax witch enabled them to take 75% of someone's estate when they die. Where were you when they offered free health care to illegal immigrants and were surprised when dependents started showing up in droves? Tens of thousands of them quickly overwhelmed state run services until they cried for Federal emergency bail out funds. Did you think the $25 minimum wage was a good idea? And that it should be forced on the restaurant industry? Killing it in the process I might add. Were you surprised when half of the restaurants closed? Or when they passed SR-286 which planted so called government 'accountants' into businesses to monitor and identify excessive profit. Upon which the government would swoop in and take for themselves. And we're not even talking about the Green New Deal fiasco, shall I go on? I sure could. How about when you lost your right to own a gun? There's more. Where have the policies you voted for gotten you? Right here where you are you stupid son of a bitch!".

Ciera was surprised to hear that come out of Crenshaw's mouth. Normally he was quite removed from the emotion of it. The situation they were in and what they had to do now put a lot of stress on him. She placed a hand on his shoulder. He looked up at her and understood her message. The guy didn't know what to say. What Crenshaw had just said didn't quite match the persona of a Federal agent.

"Ok, ok. What's your name?" Crenshaw asked.

The guy hesitated but then replied "Marshal, I am Fire Chief Marshal".

"Fire Chief huh. Well Marshal, they call me Captain Crenshaw. I need you to listen to me carefully. The fate of you and all your friends depends on it. There's a few way's we could play this, but I need you to comprehend something quickly… it's this- We are not Federal Agents". He paused to let that sink in.

"Then untie me and let me go" Marshal said.

"Un tie him" Crenshaw said. "I'll let you go. We would like to drop you off at the station on 193 Main Road and just turn around and leave Herkimer. That's probably the smartest thing I could do. But like

I said, there's something else that can be accomplished here, and my guys voted to help you do that before we go home. Plus, we can't do it without you". Marshal stared at him not knowing what to think.

"You say you are not agents. How is that possible? You have prisoners here. You were in the compound. Your wearing…".

"Yes, yes, and yes. I'll explain" Crenshaw glanced up and smiled at Ciera the same way he did when he gave Marko this speech. "Marshal, today's your lucky day…".

"…So, you see, right now we're tasked with hitting your base of operation and wiping you out. But here's the rub. If we don't follow orders, we can't go back and get re-fueled or re-supplied; so we either drop you off and go on our way without, or we capture your pals".

"You what!" Marshal exclaimed.

After an explanation that got him to believe his story, Marshal came over to Crenshaw's side. With this alliance, Crenshaw was able to overcome some heavy skepticism and coerce a partnership. They drove to the fire station and hence were able to meet with Herkimer's Acting Fire Chief Klem Ambrose at Marshal's request. Klem had been appointed in Marshal's place due to Marshal's absence and acted now since Marshal was taken to the hospital. They talked for an hour inside the same station that the Patriots were supposed to attack and destroy. That was an ominous event by itself, but Crenshaw performed another one; on the way back to the Feds compound the Patriots stopped off at the Herkimer Police station to warn them of the Feds plan. At first there was a lot of tension. It ends up that many of the police were involved with the attack on the Feds compound the previous night. Crenshaw had to have members of the fire department go in first and quickly dive into his story to avoid a negative reaction to a visit from the Patriot Black Jacks. That put them half way at ease but there was still plenty of skepticism to go around. APC Halper (Acting Police Chief Halper) had to wade through the possibility that this was some kind of trick after trying to decide who these "Patriots" really were. After all, this could be a trap designed to imprison them all.

Once again thanks to Marshal's support, Halper was eventually convinced, and everyone became intrigued by the opportunity. After much debate, Halper and his men decided that they would bet on the Patriots.

12

OPERATION INSIDE OUT

"This is patrol #0357 calling Herkimer Command Post to report, over".

Static.

"This is patrol #0357 calling Command to report, over".

Static, then "Go ahead 0357 this is Command Post Herkimer, we read you, over".

"Yes, Command this is 0357 reporting on mission payback. We initiated contact with the resistance and have achieved the element of surprise. I can report mission success. Six enemy dead and twelve captured. Zero Federal casualties, zero Federal wounded. We're collecting weapons and cleaning up the Herkimer fire station now, over".

"Roger 0357, good show. We'll be able to get some sleep tonight".

"Roger that Command, when we're done, we'll contact for re-admission into Command Post".

It was around 9:00PM, much later than they planned. Lights illuminated the Post Office building and it's parking lot making it one of the few buildings around that had power. Just as before, Crenshaw's lead Humvee turned into the front gate first. The Black Jack guards responded in the same way and inspected each vehicle as it drove through. The guard who stepped onto the bus to inspect passed five Patriot Black Jacks who had rifles pointing at the seated prisoners. This time the bus was packed full of prisoners who were all tied to their seats. It must have looked legitimate enough because the guard left with only one comment "You got your hands full here guys". The bus along with the rest of the convoy, was allowed through.

What came next wasn't anticipated. After parking, agent Kendrell approached them with a request from the commander. "Crenshaw, the Commander wants their leader along with three prisoners to be brought up to the meeting".

"What meeting?" Crenshaw said.

"The one you have with the Commander… (he looked at his watch) in fifteen minutes. Be there!" Kendrell said.

"What do you want them for?" Crenshaw asked.

"The dungeon of course". Kendrell said with a 'you know what I mean' smile on his face. He turned to go but Crenshaw pressed another issue.

"Sir do I have clearance to re-fuel and re-supply?".

"Yes, you do. And the commander wants any men you can spare to be placed on watch tonight. Just in case. Send your available to the front gate and the AIC there will place them" Kendrell replied and then turned to go. Crenshaw grabbed him by the arm. "That was the Fire Station you know". Kendrell pulled his arm back and got in Crenshaw's face. In an angry voice he said "Yeah, we know. Wherever the bastards are, we will go. Don't get too sentimental, the next job's the Police Station". He turned and left leaving Crenshaw there wondering about the future of America with these type of people in charge.

A meeting with Commander Henson offered them an unexpected method of infiltrating the building. On the spot Crenshaw changed their plans and went over the details with all main players. He asked for three prisoner volunteers from the bus. The ones who responded were prepped and then assembled just outside the bus door. They had their hands tied behind their backs and were standing there when agent Kendrell and his men came to escort them up. Purposely, Ciera had the prisoners searched by a Patriot Black Jack right in front of Kendrell.

Otherwise "The group" consisted of the same Patriots who met with Henson previously, only this time Ciera would stay behind to manage the bus personnel. Betsy Stoiber volunteered to take her place.

When the entire group left for Henson's office, Ciera and the rest of the Patriots wearing Black Jack uniforms kicked it into high gear. She gave the 'Go' to Donnie and his partner. Those two took the second Humvee, over to the fuel tanker to fill up. Then she sent Jerry and patriot Neil Lee in the black van over to the freight trucks to load up supplies.

After they left, Ciera turned and flicked out a sharp knife switch-blade style. She addressed the first prisoner in the first seat leaned over... and cut his hands free. She gave him the knife and in turn he cut the rest of the prisoners free.

"Get set!" Ciera said to them all. Without their restraints the prisoners took their que and came to life. Two of them opened the emergency exit on the blind side of the bus. The rest pulled out rifles hidden underneath their seats and armed themselves. One of them had an M79 grenade launcher they had captured. After checking and loading their weapons, they stood ready. It looked like they were preparing to do a parachute jump out of an airplane and were now waiting for the green light.

Ciera turned to her team and went over the plan. "Kurt, Marsal, Trip and Nevel. Your job is to stay here and protect this bus at all costs. None of these bastards get control of it, you understand!" They shook their heads in agreement.

"Monitor the radio and listen for my signal. Now none of you has fired that 50-cal on the Humvee before, but it's ready to go and it's just a matter of pulling the trigger. Use it if you have too. Pick your targets carefully if you do shoot it. Short 20 round bursts only. Pull the trigger and release. Watch for muzzle rise. Got it?" They shook their heads again. "Remember, be careful, there will be a lot of friendlies out there. That's why we don't want to use the 50 if we can help it" Ciera told them.

Crenshaw had assigned 'Profit' along with Robert Metcalf to do what was considered the most dangerous job of the operation. But when it came time to go, Ciera changed the plan.

"Robert and Profit... change of plans. I'm going with you" Ciera said. Profit was surprised but didn't argue.

Rough estimates were that the Feds had approximately forty or fifty troops presently stationed in and around the site. There could be more. Tonight, there were four agents stationed at the front gate guard house, with four that sat in each of the other four exterior guard stations. One interior station was strategically placed at the front entrance to the building. At each corner emplacement the occupants sat behind mostly completed sandbag walls. Normally Federal bases like this had guard towers but this site was new. It had just been "acquired" and just recently thrown together. To make up for the lack of ideal conditions, the Feds simply parked a manned Humvee with its menacing 50 cal machine gun twenty yards behind the front gate. Because of the attack last night, they manned another Humvee in the back parking lot too. If there was another attack like the night before all the men stationed at the guardhouse had to do was duck. The 50 cal would take care of the rest. Along with their "go to" grenade launcher, the M79, supposedly they were ready for anything.

Donnie and his partner pulled up to the gas tanker attempting to refuel and were met by three Black Jack attendants who were manning it. He made a gallant attempt to engage them with small talk and to get the latest news, but it was tough because two of them spoke very little English. At the same time, Jerry and Neil Lee arrived at the supply trucks. Both pairs of Patriots tried to stall and drag out the process with an abundance of questions and by slowly filling out the requisition forms.

The Patriots had barely enough people dressed in Federal uniforms to attempt this plan. It was absurdly risky to say the least. Ciera thought they were spread way too thin and voiced her opinion at the meeting.

"If they have more men in there than we think, this could go horribly wrong" Ciera warned.

Crenshaw replied "Yes, that's why we can only afford to send two patriots to each location. I need everyone to do their jobs. It's imperative we take out the front gate, the front door position and most importantly that 50 cal machine gun. I hope those guys know how to use that M79 we gave them".

Ciera thought that sending two Patriots to the front gate for such an important mission was not enough and considered it the weak link in the plan. Hence the change of plan, she went with them. As the three of them walked toward the front gate she told Benny and Profit "We're dressed just like them, but I think because I'm a woman I can get us closer to our target than you guys can. Our mission is of paramount importance, we must not fail".

To make her gender more obvious she disposed of the black hat and let her hair down. From anticipation, the walk across the parking lot seemed to take a lifetime just to get to the gate. The Feds Humvee looked menacing as hell with the barrel of its 50-cal pointing towards the entrance. She noticed a man standing in the turret and one sitting in the driver's seat of the vehicle. She gave them an enthusiastic "Hi!" accompanied by her best smile as she walked by.

Arriving at the front gate, Ciera was directed to the AIC on duty. They found him sitting inside the guard shack. "Yes sir" she said with a salute when she found him. "I was told to report for duty".

"What? They send me their women now?" the AIC said in a grumpy voice.

"We were told to send any available and report for guard duty. I was sent to this post sir".

The AIC didn't look happy. "You are all they can spare?".

"Sir, I brought two with me, the others are guarding the prisoners, and the rest were sent to other posts" Ciera said.

"Alright, three is better than nothing. You're assigned to the wall. Go". He pointed to the door.

After looking around her 'post', and when no one was looking, Ciera uttered into her hand-held radio. "This is 'Gate take', I'm in".

"Ah, Crenshaw and... Where's Gutierrez?" Henson asked when the group entered his office. "I wanted him to see this. A lesson on how to tame a rebel". Once again Kendrell was standing by the commanders side.

"Commander Henson" Crenshaw said. "AIC Gutierrez is not feeling well. I was instructed to take his place". The newly acquired prisoners from the fire station entered right behind Crenshaw, followed by two Patriots and then by two of Henson's men who followed them in. Two more of Henson's Black Jacks stood just outside the office door.

"Ah, well it doesn't matter. Good job boys. These are the people I wanted to see anyway" Henson said indicating the prisoners as they walked in. He got up and walked over to inspect them.

Crenshaw presented the prisoners to Henson while scoping out situation details. The commander had a hand gun on his hip and two of his men stood at each side of the door holding rifles with confidence. They weren't wearing Kevlar vests and were somewhat relaxed in the presence of so many fellow agents.

Which one of you is the leader" Henson said to the three prisoners.

"I am" one of them spoke up and stepped forward.

"Ah" Henson said as he maneuvered to stand in front of him. "I'm going to really enjoy this...".

Before any of them could react, Henson pulled out a blade from his waste belt and stabbed the leader in the stomach. It was a disgusting deed accompanied by an astonishing degree of hatred. Not so long ago, such an act directed at a fellow American would have been considered unconscionable. The crisis had fueled evil in a man who fully immersed himself into his role as vanquisher. The intensity of which could be seen by the fuming expression on his face.

It happened so quickly it shocked everyone. Certainly, none of the Patriots were expecting revenge to be dealt out in such a manner right here in his office. Out of the group, only Kendrell maintained a sadistic smile that spread across his face. One that quickly changed when Kaiden reacted by firing a powerful front kick into Henson's rib cage. The kick hit hard sending Henson reeling backwards. The commander turned back with outrage spitting out of his mouth.

"How dare you!" he exclaimed with contortions forming deep wrinkles on his face. He regained his balance, dropped the knife and fumbled at the latch on the holster of his gun. For such insolence, he had no problem shooting the offender.

Kaiden couldn't afford to do anything else, he beat Henson to the draw and had his Berretta in hand before Henson could get his side-arm out. The Beretta fired twice hitting Henson square in the chest knocking the commander back over his desk.

Things went crazy fast. Jones and Crenshaw turned and fired their rifles at the two guards standing at the door. Those two went down before they could bring their guns to bear. Kaiden spun around knowing that this was going to be close. Kendrell had his pistol in hand, and it was coming up fast pointing directly at Kaiden.

A shot rang out and Kendrell was hit in the shoulder. It spun him around just as his gun went off. A second shot hit him in the back. He fell against the wall and slid to the floor in a lifeless lump. Betsy Stoiber was standing there with a smoking rifle in her hands. Luckily the bullet that Kendrell fired hit the desk instead of Kaiden.

All three of the prisoners hands had been rigged to look like they were bound. Getting free was a simple matter of twisting and pulling sharply on the rope that bound them. Instantly, the pistol hidden in the waist band of their pants was in their hands. As planned their responsibility was the guards in the hallway. They ran to the door and threw it open. The two guards on the outside were already in stride and poised to intervene but were cut down with guns that blazed away in their direction. The ex-prisoners searched the dead guards and armed themselves with their rifles and extra magazines.

It happened sooner than anticipated. None of them had time to mourn the prisoner who got stabbed. The Patriots didn't even know his name. Crenshaw got on his hand-held radio and yelled "357 go".

In the shuttle, the Patriots received the message and relayed it to the others. "Go!" they said to the group of ex-prisoners standing by. The whole bunch exited the bus through the emergency exit. Two groups of them formed outside with six in each. They peeled off and went in opposite directions, one going to the front and one going towards the back of the bus. The group at the rear took off at a sprint across the parking lot with their rifles aiming at the front gate. The other group took off to attack the front door of the Post Office.

For a few minutes Ciera, Profit and Robert mingled around at the front gate with the others and tried to blend in playing the part of a Black Jack. One of the Black Jacks told Ciera "If they're going to attack tonight it's going to come from there" the guy pointed across the street. "That's where they came from last night. But if they do, we got this". The Black Jack smiled and patted the M79 grenade launcher he had in his hands.

Ciera took note of that and other details as the three of them strolled around. They introduced themselves and engaged in short conversations. With a pause and at the right moment, Ciera walked over to the Humvee and knocked on the driver side window. The glass rolled down and Ciera gave him a flirty "Hey how's it going?".

Half of the ex-prisoners on the bus were Patriots and half were volunteers who were directly or indirectly associated with the East Herkimer Fire Department. A few of them were ex-military with combat experience. The rest were men who knew their way around guns and wanted to do something about the takeover of their country. All of them had a grudge to settle with these Black Jack intruders due to last night's attack in which two of their friends were killed and their chief was captured and tortured.

Firemen in the first group out of the bus had the job of taking the front gate. They moved in silence across the lot with as much stealth as could be achieved, but that was short lived. As soon as they got within range and had Black Jacks in sight the first shot of the battle was fired. The group pressed forward toward the front gate firing a blistering barrage of gunfire as they went. Two gate guards went down in the first volley. The remaining guards recovered quickly and effectively used the sandbag wall for cover. Popping up from behind it, they returned fire. One of the firemen went down. Added to that, a burst of fire from the 50 cal on the Humvee produced another casualty. That one went down as his group moved across pavement. As luck would have it, it was the guy who carried the weapon they needed the most, the M79 grenade launcher. His loss spooked the rest of them who hit the ground looking for any degree of cover they could find. They found it behind a few vehicles, a large metal mail drop box and a thick cement light pole. Instantly they were all pinned down.

Gunfire was the signal. Donnie and his two men at the fuel tanker suddenly stopped the friendly conversation they were having, pulled out their rifles and pointed them at the bewildered attendants. Two agents raised their hands in the air saying "Que…?" but the one in charge must have thought that this was some kind of joke. He went for a rifle that was leaning up against the table. A shot from Donnie's HK made the guy regret his decision. Then Donnie wagged his finger at the other two and said "No, no, no, no". If not before, they sure knew the seriousness of the situation now. Their eyes popped out of their heads when the Patriots took off their Federal uniforms and replaced their hat with a Cadet beret. Underneath, they had on the Patriot summer green camouflage battledress.

At the supply trucks, when Jerry and Neil heard gunfire, that was the signal. They pulled out their weapons and caught the two attendants completely by surprise. The two Black Jacks in front of them gave up easily but there was a third. That one had gone into one of the freight trucks to get their supplies when the shooting started. "Stay on them"

Jerry told Nick. Jerry went to find the guy. Unknown to Jerry, the attendant had peeked his head out of one of the freight trucks to see what was going on. He witnessed Jerry pull a gun on his fellow agents.

It shouldn't have been difficult to find the guy, there were only three freight trucks parked side by side. *"The Black Jack must be in one of them"* Jerry thought. Walking with caution, he peered around the corner of the first truck and looked inside the freight car with his gun leading the way. Nothing. He walked stealthfully over to the second and did the same. Nothing. Now he knew the guy must be in the third, so he was even more cautious when he moved out in front of the door and pointed his rifle inside. The Black Jack attendant who appeared behind Jerry didn't allow any time for him to react. He shot Jerry in the back.

After hearing gunfire and getting over the shock that there were enemy inside the perimeter, the Feds man on the turret of the Humvee turned the 50 around and aimed it in the direction of the threat. There was a very loud string of noise when the Black Jack pulled the trigger and fired at the group of firemen maneuvering toward him.

Ciera kicked it into high gear. She had to work fast. In an instant she turned from friend to foe and stepped back from her conversation with the more than willing agent sitting in the driver's seat of the Humvee. The look on her face changed and she swung her rifle up and pointed it at the guy's head. More than puzzled, the driver looked at her with no clue as to what was going on. Ciera shot him point blank. She had too, this was literally a do or die situation and she had to act fast to stop that machine gun at all cost or all would be lost.

Without skipping a beat Ciera opened the door. Profit appeared at her side and they both pulled the dead driver out throwing him to the ground. Climbing in she instinctively grabbed her more maneuverable Beretta PX4 from its holster and fired three shots into the guy standing in the turret. The 50 cal went silent as the victim slumped over. Some kind of harness or seatbelt held his body in place. The shots fired had gone unnoticed due to the loud burst coming from the 50. At this point in the battle, it was risky but all three of them tore off their Black Jack uniforms revealing their camouflaged Cadet uniform underneath.

The second group of firefighters were assigned to deal with the guards stationed at the front door of the building. When they maneuvered close enough to see the heads of agents protruding above the sandbag wall, they opened fire. One guard was caught out in the open on the sidewalk smoking a cigarette, he was cut down where he stood. The rest of the guards behind the sandbag wall realized what was happening and were quick to duck and cover and then to return fire. The firefighters in the second group had to take cover and they too were pinned down as they traded fire with the Feds. The Patriots M79 grenade launcher was supposed to help either group deal a knockout blow but now without it they were in serious trouble.

Gunfire was the signal and a popping noise started to emanate from somewhere outside the front gate. It started off sporadic but then erupted into a barrage. A shower of bullets came streaking in from seemingly everywhere hitting wall and sandbags with a 'thud'. Ciera, Profit and Benny ducked inside the Humvee to avoid getting hit and to keep the 50 cal out of the fight.

Each time a bullet hit the wooden guard shack there was an audible 'crack'. Each hit opened a hole in the wall splintering wood and shattering glass. Bullets zipped through the interior of the guardhouse narrowly missing, then hitting the men inside. The AIC was struck in the head, his body went stiff and the gaze on his face froze. The others ducked and took cover, cowering down low. Now the front gate was facing an attack from two different directions which took the pressure off the team of firefighters attacking from inside the perimeter. Unfortunately, explosions erupted both on the inside of the compound and on the outside as the Black Jack with a grenade launcher fired frantically in both directions. The explosions were loud and every Federal agent who heard it hoped that it was doing a job on the invaders, but none of the Feds could understand why the 50-cal was silent.

The Feds did a good job of defending the front gate; bullets hitting the perimeter's cement wall had no effect on the inhabitants, but as noted these were concrete traffic dividers placed end to end to form a 'quick" barrier. It was a short wall probably more like three feet high designed to stop vehicles, the new hastily erected sandbag wall was there to stop bullets.

At first bullets 'thunked' into the bags knocking over a few of the ones on top. It was a quick fix to simply throw them back up. But very quickly the weakness of the design became apparent. A section of the wall fell in exposing the inhabitants to dangerous incoming fire. From there the defenders were picked off by a sniper on the roof top of an adjacent building. One, two, then the guy with the grenade launcher was taken out. One of the guards still alive freeked out. He tore off his black jacket, tore off his shirt, tore off his white T shirt and placed it on the barrel of his rifle. Quickly he held it up and waved it in the air praying to God that it would make the lunacy stop.

As soon as the white flag went up the attackers exploited the weakness and moved in. The corner posts were pinned down with sniper fire as Police cars appeared from down the street and drove up close to the wall. They skidded to a stop where both men and women exited the vehicles and joined the fight from newly established positions. A blue wave of police with helmets and bullet proof vests on, fired their AR-15's as they ran up to the patrol cars and then to the protection of the wall. They placed themselves behind cars, behind the concrete wall and now after overtaking it they fired at the building from behind the Feds sandbag wall. Within minutes they had control of the front gate and took the lone survivor prisoner.

Up in Henson's office on the second floor, Crenshaw and crew had eliminated the immediate threat they faced. Jones tore off his Black Jack uniform and threw it on the floor. "Ahh, it feels good to be back" he said with a smile on his face. Quickly every Patriot did the same and were proud to once again be operating under true colors. To cover their ass and to make sure that none of the Black Jacks were still alive they put another bullet into each one of them. The noise from their attack alerted others in the building.

Before leaving Hanson's office, all fellow firefighters could do was to make an attempt to stem the bleeding coming from their friends stab wound. They did their best to make him as comfortable as possible. Tending to him any further would have to wait until this fight had been decided. Right now, everyone's life was at stake, not only his.

Everyone else was set to go. "Ready? Jones, Stoiber, on me! We go left. Kaiden and the rest of you go right. We got the front door. You got the rear!" Crenshaw yelled as he went.

As soon as they exited the office door and ran into the hallway, the door at the end of it opened and three Black Jacks ran blindly into the hallway. Unfortunately for them they were completely unaware of the danger. Crenshaw opened fire and dropped the first two with well-placed shots. The third tried to go back but Betsy stepped up and shot him before he got very far. That guy was knocked back into the stairwell from the impact and fell down a flight of stairs. The three of them moved down the hall checking the other rooms as they went. A figure emerged from one of them with a gun in his hand. Instantly and at point blank range, Crenshaw put two bullets into him and ended the threat. The last office room before the stairwell door was locked. All three stood outside, turned their rifles on the lock and fired. A scream welled up from inside. Another bullet to the lock made the door fly open. They must have been using the offices as sleeping quarters. The man inside was sitting on a cot half dressed in uniform and he was clutching a wound to his side with one hand and groping for his rifle with the other. Crenshaw fired again, ending the threat. Clearing that section, they fast walked it past the bodies at the stairwell and started down.

Kaiden and two firefighters went in the other direction and cleared the two offices (turned bed rooms) on that side. Inside each room, the desk had been pushed into a corner and there was a cot up against the wall. There was no one in either of them. After they cleared the two offices at the end of the hallway, they used the stairwell to get down to the first floor. At the bottom was a fire door. Kaiden checked for threats through the single pane glass window but saw nothing on the other side.

"On three" Kaiden said. They busted through the door with one of the firefighters pointing left and Kaiden pointing his rifle to the right. The firefighters right side was clear, but Kaiden found himself staring at four agents moving rapidly down the hall coming towards them. He fired before the Black Jacks realized that they should have fired first. Three went down before the third was able to pull the trigger on his weapon. He got off a shot, but the bullet went wide. Kaiden's partner turned and shot the guy before he could fire a second shot.

"Nice going!" Kaiden said. "Hey, I don't even know your names". They lined up three abreast with their rifles pointing down the hall and started walking. "Dean" one of them said. "Chess" said the other.

"Chess, cover our six!" Kaiden yelled. The guy turned and all three continued walking with one rifle pointing to the rear and two to the front.

A short distance down the hall they came to a door that led into the mail room. Busting through, put them all in the middle of a large room that had been converted into the agents sleeping quarters. Most of the mail paraphernalia had been removed yet there was still a conveyor belt system attached to the wall with mail carts lined up in front of it. Some carts were filled to the brim with undelivered letters and paper. In the center of the cleared room some twenty or so cots were lined up in rows. Kaiden's crew surprised the hell out of a hand full of agents that were spread about the place in various stages of readiness. Most were clamoring to put on clothing and equipment, but some were standing at the ready. Kaiden engaged those first, shooting as he dogged to the left. Dean and Chess both fired and dogged to the Right. The two firefighters took cover behind a long table and began firing at the enemy from behind its solid base.

So far, they had been lucky. The element of surprise was their ace in the hole. But now the agents in the center of the room saw the threat and realized that their only chance against it was to become aggressive and move on the intruders. More likely it was because there wasn't any cover for them to hide behind and they had no choice. Two of them moved toward Dean and Chess rapidly firing their HK's as they went effectively pinning the pair down behind the counter. Chess could hardly return fire because of being pummeled with bullets that pinged off the corner of the table. Just when it looked like the Black Jacks would overtake them, Kaiden popped up from between two mail carts and fired twice. Both agents went down, and their guns went silent. By that time four of the men sitting on the cots had stopped everything and had gotten to their weapons. They stood, turned on Kaiden and fired. Kaiden ducked as bullets zinged over his head. More peppered the cart he had just ducked behind, papers inside flew up in violent jerks from bullet strikes.

Dean and Chess stood up from behind the counter and fired at the enemy. A moan describing immense pain came out of each Black Jack when they got hit. Three of them clutched themselves and fell to the floor unable to move. The last able body agent ducked down between two cots.

Searching the room with nervous rifles pointing out in front of them, Dean came upon that last agent lying on the floor. The guy looked up with a scared expression and was repeating something in Spanish. Dean shot him without hesitation. He would have time to think about it later, but due to the intensity of the moment and because it was right after these people were trying to kill him, Dean thought nothing of taking the guy out. Besides, at this stage of the game they had no way of taking prisoners. They all put another bullet into each body to make sure they were dead then took the Feds loaded magazines as their own.

Inside the perimeter at the front door of the building, the team of six firefighters were not making any headway. Without the grenade launcher they were stuck. Their job was to overrun the position if they could but for now, they would have to settle for diverting the Feds firepower and forcing their attention away from the front gate. Only now, the guards they were facing were doing a good job of keeping them at bay. One firefighter shooting from behind a car got hit in the foot and was taken out of the fight. Two down. If more got hit and something didn't break soon, the Feds could very well take the advantage.

From the hallway outside Henson's office, Crenshaw led his team past the bodies, down the stairwell and out into the hall on the first floor. Crenshaw didn't have to tell Betsy to cover their six, her training automatically called for one of the team members to have their rifle cover the rear. Luckily so, because three way too enthusiastic Black Jacks came running around the corner in the hallway behind them. Thinking they were running in to help their compadre's; they ran right into Betsy's line of fire. Hearing her gun go off made Jones turn and fire as well. Their combined efforts took out the unsuspecting enemy.

The hallway they were walking down led directly into the customer service lobby at the front of the building. Two nervous agents were standing there at a counter loading bullets into magazines. Looking up from hearing loud gunfire in the hallway, they were warned and went for their own weapons. Crenshaw and crew came around the corner wearing a strange uniform. The Patriots didn't give them a chance to fire a bullet. Double taps to the upper body took each one of them out of the fight.

Now only two thick glass double doors separated the Patriots from the Black Jacks standing behind the sand bag enclosure built just outside the front door. The sandbags were designed to protect the building from an outside attack without considering the scenario that was about to unfold. Five agents had been assigned to this station and now four of them were busy firing over the wall at some unseen target in the parking lot beyond. After firing, one of them ducked down to reload. He started to, but then he glanced back through the glass door into the lobby and was horrified at what he saw. Crenshaw, Stoiber and Jones were standing there in a line just twenty feet away pointing their rifles right at him. Pure terror flowed through his body when he realized what was about to happen. He dropped his unloaded rifle and reached for his side arm. That's when the Patriot's opened up.

Bullet holes appeared in the thick glass and thousands of crazy cracks splintered the entire piece turning it opaque for just a moment before the entire piece of glass burst apart and crashed to the floor in small pieces. Those same bullets hit some of the agents on the other side making three of them squirm in pain. Two other agents tried to quickly turn their attention to the rear, but it was too late. The teams rapid fire hit each one of them before they could react effectively.

Kaiden and his team hustled over to the rear bay doors. While trying to listen to what was going on outside in the back parking lot adjacent to the mail room. From outside came the sound of a 50-caliber machine gun. That gun had to be stopped. No one could defend against that kind of fire power. Doing some reconnaissance, Kaiden cautiously peered out one of the exit doors. Straight ahead across the parking lot was one of the four rear guard posts installed against the perimeter wall in the corner of the lot. Four or five Black Jacks were huddled down behind a sandbag enclosure with their rifles firing over the top, they had complete command of the area. Various targets outside the wall attracted their attention which was bad news for whoever was receiving their fire. The Humvee was half way between them and the building with a gunner on the 50 cal, that guy was firing at anything that moved outside the wall.

"Guy's, the only way to do this is to take out that Humvee" Kaiden told Dean and Chess. The story about how Brian Hardy's crew had taken out the 50-cal kept running through his head.

"Yeah, how the hell are we going to do that?" Dean asked.

"We're going to have to get up there and shoot the guy" Kaiden said. "Cover me!". To their surprise, Kaiden bolted out the door and ran all out across the open parking lot toward the Humvee. A dangerous move. There were snipers firing at the Feds from outside the perimeter who could have easily mistaken Kaiden for a bad guy. The Humvee's gunner was facing the other way and Kaiden was banking on him remaining that way. He got half way to the vehicle when Dean and Chess prematurely opened fire to "cover" him. They might as well have stood up and waved a flag. When bullets pinged off the rear of the Humvee, their good intentions only served to notify the machine gunner of their presence. The guy in the turret turned and saw Kaiden, then turned the barrel of the 50 cal in his direction.

Caught out in the open, Kaiden froze in place realizing that no matter how he moved the remainder of his time on earth could be measured in seconds. His mind's eye turned into tunnel vision with his total attention zeroed in and focused on what was about to happen. He never saw or heard another Federal Humvee barrel around the corner of the building and stop about fifty yards away. But its presence became obvious when it's 50-cal machine gun opened fire with a deafening roar.

Kaiden hit the ground more because his knees went weak rather than intending some kind of a defensive maneuver. The surprise was that heavy 290 grain, 12.7 x 99mm bullets started plowing into the Humvee in front of him. The gunner in that turret had no chance being hit from the side like that. Kaiden watched as a barrage of lead tore up metal, penetrated through gaps in the armor and smashed through the machine gunners body killing him right before his eyes.

Kaiden looked hard and had to squint. He couldn't believe it. Ciera Lowman was standing in the turret of a Humvee firing it's 50-cal at the threat that would have ended his life. Robert was in the passenger seat and Profit was at the wheel. At that point it was a battle between two Humvee's. Kaiden couldn't have been happier to see three people more in his entire life. He screamed at the top of his lungs "Yeah! God damn right girl!" and shook his fist in the air in a solidarity salute.

Ciera followed her own advice and fired in short bursts to minimize the muzzle rise on the 50 cal. For every ten bullets she fired one tracer round shot out of the barrel. The bullet, accompanied by a brilliant yellow glowing streak of light, sailed through the air and smacked into the side of the vehicle confirming that she was on target. That vehicle was armored but not even armor could stand up to a constant barrage of 50 caliber bullets. Holes appeared in the driver's side door and the glass smashed out. Lead bounced around inside the vehicle taking out the driver as well as the man in the turret. Ciera succeeded in taking the Humvee out of the battle. Without a pause, she turned her attention to the corner guard post on the left side of the lot. The one that was manned by agents that were now taking pot shots at her.

Kaiden turned around to call Dean and Chess to his side, but they were already running up to him. From there, Ciera covered the guard post on the left and Kaiden and his guys attacked the second post on the right side of the parking lot.

Sandbags helped the Feds, but they were not enough to change the outcome. Ciera tore them up with a string of bullets from left to right and the impact knocked down part of the wall. The men inside who weren't hit threw down their guns and surrendered with their hands up. That allowed Kaiden to move up on the right.

Kaiden yelled at his crew "Get down and lay some fire on that post!". The crew found slim cover behind cement parking dividers and laid prone behind two of them. From there they fired at the second corner guard post forcing the inhabitants to duck and keep their heads down. Those men were also taking fire from outside the perimeter wall which intensified their predicament. The combined effort stopped the enemy from firing on Ciera's Humvee. When the Feds saw what happened to the other guard post and the futility of the situation, a white tee shirt on a rifle barrel rose up over the top of the wall and waved back and forth. They were lucky they surrendered before Ciera had a chance to turn her attention on them. Kaiden, Dean and Chess ran up unhindered and took them prisoner.

It was over. Positively for the dead, thankfully for the living. The Combined forces of the Herkimer Police department, participating firemen and the Patriot Militia were in solid control and were now rounding up prisoners in the compound. They roamed the compound freely collecting weapons, prisoners, and evidence about what was going on here. Papers they found in Henson's office confirmed what the Commander had told Crenshaw. The outline of a plan on written orders directed the Commander to infiltrate the local government, obtain compliance and secure control of the area using any method deemed necessary. A quote from one of the orders addressed to Commander Henson stated:

> "We have been successful in eliminating the two-party system in the Federal government. Now we need to expand our control and eliminate all further resistance. The speed in which you accomplish your mission will bode well for your advancement in the New Order".

It was signed by ex-President Richfield, head of the Progressive Democrat Party. This confirmed that America was suffering the aftermath of a successful coup.

* * *

In the aftermath of the battle… Kaiden stood in the middle of the rear Post Office parking lot taking it all in. He had a few moments to reflect during which he closed his eyes and thanked God that he was still alive. Ciera interrupted his prayers when she walked up.

"Lieutenant, I am forever in your debt" Kaiden said as she approached. He got all serious and gave her a formal salute while standing at attention. Tears were forming in the corner of his eyes. She returned the salute and responded with a week smile. "At ease private" she said but broke into a smile when she hugged him. Kaiden twirled her around in his arms. When he finally let her go, he kissed her. Through the kiss he could tell that there was something right and there was something wrong. Ciera had been shaken by the ordeal. Inside more than on the outside. He held her tight, wishing he could make all this go away. But the feeling that this was just the beginning haunted them both.

Neil Lee walked up to Ciera and Kaiden and gave them a report on his situation, informing her of the events that led to Jerry's death.

Kaiden was stunned. He felt emotion weld up inside to the point where he couldn't hold back an outburst "SHIT!" he yelled at the sky.

"Let's report to Crenshaw" Ciera said. Sadly, they all walked to the front of the Post office where Crenshaw was talking to acting Fire Chief Klem Ambrose. His men were lining up the prisoners and stripping them of their gear.

"Ok guys, report" Crenshaw said when he saw them.

Ciera got serious. "We lost Jerry Reeder sir" she said. "I just got Neil's report on the incident. The only Pioneer KIA. Otherwise, five were wounded, two seriously. Three of those were recruits from the fire station".

"Shit!" yelled Crenshaw. He covered his face with his hands and turned in a circle. Then he stopped and looked at them. "From this moment on I'm going to consider each and every breath I take as a gift from God. I suggest you all do the same and celebrate the fact that you are still alive and well. Do not let this death drag you down. I'm sorry it had to be Jerry, he was a great soldier, but I'm also glad it was only one". He shook his head and closed his eyes. "Damn! Why him lord, why him?".

Ciera followed up with the rest of her report and described her experience. The part about her not being able to get the body out of the Humvee's turret explained why that asset did not join the fight against the Feds in the beginning of the fire fight. By the time they got the body out of the turret, Crenshaw's team had silenced the opposition at the front door. That's when Ciera and Profit drove the captured Humvee around to the back of the building where they joined the fight for control of the rear parking lot. Due to the positive outcome, Crenshaw didn't reprimand her for disobeying orders. She outranked him so technically he couldn't condemn the action. Instead, he commended her for being flexible and "adjusting to prevailing circumstances".

A handful of Patriots started to gather around the group. They watched as the Herkimer Police lined up the prisoners and searched them. Every Patriot clutched their rifle as if it was their most valued possession as they watched the prisoners. Everyone was curious …who were these people that they were at war with? Why do they want to kill us?

Herkimer's Fire Chief Marshal Kelly walked slowly up to the group with the help of a cane and a fellow firefighter. He was in obvious pain from the beatings he received during his stint as Hanson's prisoner, but he was bound and determined to be there for the aftermath of this action.

"Even though I didn't participate, this was my battle!" Kelly said with a tear in his eye. Then he explained. "A week ago, Hanson invited all of us here for a meeting. Mainly officials from the City Government, Fire and Police departments. After the Feds divulged their strategy for securing the area, some of us voiced our disapproval. Those in opposition were arrested, taken to the basement, and locked up. I hadn't seen anyone except for my tormentors until you showed up Crenshaw. And I've got to say I didn't think much of you in that uniform at the time to say the least".

Crenshaw added his side "Once I heard there were prisoners, I asked Hanson to release you so I could get more information about the place I was ordered to attack. I figured I would try and get whoever I could out of there. For some reason he gave you up easily. The hardest part was convincing you that we were not actually Federal agents". Patriots standing around them chuckled.

"Marshal, you ended up being instrumental in helping us persuade the firefighters and then Chief Halper to go with my plan. I thank you for that".

"It was an unbelievable opportunity. We didn't know if we'd ever get another chance to pull something like this off. I was skeptical because we had no time to practice the assault, anything could have gone wrong, but you did it Crenshaw! You and yours did really good. It worked. I feel bad that I couldn't participate. Thank you, sir, for your effort". Marshal saluted Crenshaw and Crenshaw returned his salute.

"Your welcome. How'd your fire fighters do?" Crenshaw asked.

"We lost two, with four wounded including Bert the guy stabbed in Henson's office" Marshal said. "He's in bad shape".

"I'm sorry to hear that. I hope Bert pulls through" Crenshaw said.

APC Marvin Halper walked up to the group and saluted Crenshaw. Crenshaw met with him when the convoy stopped in at the Police station for an unscheduled chat on the way back from their 'attack' on the fire station.

Right away Chief Halper shook Crenshaw's hand. He told them "I didn't know what to think of you when you came into my office with your cockamamie story about a Cadet Militia. Then the surprise ending that the group you were describing was 'you'. We had problems with the Feds before. The fact that you weren't really Feds was a relief but hard to swallow at first. And was even harder to accept your plan. Wow, talk about risk. But son of a bitch, it worked. If it wasn't for you, we'd be at the mercy of that asshole Henson for some time to come. You set this town free sir".

"I don't blame you for doubting me" Crenshaw told him. "The experience my guys have gone through must have sounded like a wild made-up story and yes, my plan was definitely extreme. I can apply 'extreme' to everything we've done for the last couple of weeks. I thank you for believing in us and putting Gutierrez behind bars so I could focus all my manpower on the attack. Without all of us working together we could never have pulled this off. How did your guys make out sir?".

"We're tending to six wounded, one critical, but I can report no fatalities as of yet. Thanks to your team Crenshaw, we didn't have to face the full brunt of their force. I want to congratulate the men who took out the 50 at the front gate. That's positively why we didn't suffer more casualties than we did".

"Ah, well here 'she' is Chief, you're standing in front of her. This is Lieutenant Lowman".

Chief Halper stood at attention and aimed his salute at Ciera. "My apologies for the misgender Mam, I should have said 'guys'. My solid thanks to you". Ciera returned his salute.

"And the Feds?" Crenshaw asked.

"The Feds on the other hand took a beating. 33 dead, thirteen wounded. We took fifteen prisoner..." he turned and motioned with his hand to the double line of prisoners forming up in the parking lot behind them.

At that moment, when no one was paying attention. Patriot Neil Lee walked down the line of prisoners looking closely at each one of them. When he came upon one guy in particular, a spark of recognition showed on his face. The prisoner was the third attendant at the supply truck. He was the guy who killed Jerry. Neil yelled "You son of a bitch!", stepped back, and raised his rifle. Then he shot the guy twice in the chest.

When those shots rang out, the entire group of Patriots jumped, ducked down, and turned to look for the source.

"What the hell!" Kaiden exclaimed.

Neil was standing in front of the line of prisoners, with a prisoner lying motionless on the ground near his feet. All the other prisoners had ducked down with their hands over their heads.

Chief Halper yelled "Grab him!". Two of his men that were standing closest leaped over and grabbed Neil by the arms yanking the rifle out of his hands at the same time. He didn't resist. They took his rifle and dragged him over to Halper and Crenshaw. "Neil?" Crenshaw said, staring at him with an angry flare. What the hell are you doing you stupid son of a bitch!".

"That guy killed Jerry" Neil said in his defense. Neil had a far-off look in his eyes.

"God damn it! So, you shoot him!" Crenshaw yelled.

To his guys Halper said "Cuff him and sit him in a patrol car". His men took him away.

"Make that '34' agents killed" Halper said to Crenshaw. Halper stared at Crenshaw and said "We're going to have to resolve this Crenshaw. That's murder and he's going to have to pay the price".

Crenshaw looked at him knowing that this wasn't going to be good.

"I just spoke to the guy" Kaiden said. "Neil told me that after they sprung the trap at the supply trucks and successfully captured two of the attendants, Jerry went to look for a third Black Jack that had gone back into one of the trucks right as the battle started. Just bad timing. Neil heard a gunshot and was distracted. The two Feds he was watching attacked him and tried to get his weapon. A struggle ensued where they were able to wrestle his HK from him, but Neil pulled his knife and stabbed them both before they could turn his weapon against him. He found Jerry's body in the back but never found the Fed that killed him.

"Damn!" Crenshaw yelled. "I can't believe Neil did that, doesn't sound like him. Just shows how all this shit can get into your psyche".

"I don't think that's going to be a good defense" Ciera said.

"Not for committing murder" Halper added. "We'll put him on ice for now but we gotta talk about what we're gunna do about this Crenshaw".

Crenshaw rolled his eyes. "After what we just did, you're calling that murder? Talk about irony. Shit, now I've got to deal with this. And what are you going to do with the prisoners?".

"We can hold 'em right here in the same room the Feds used for prisoners. I've got your Gutierrez in a cell at headquarters, and I'll put Neil in a separate one. I'm dying to talk to Gutierrez. I want to know more about what's going on.

Crenshaw, come with me I have something to show you" Halper said. He led Crenshaw along the sidewalk and back inside the Herkimer Post Office building. Continuing, Halper took him down the stairs into the basement. When they entered one of the basement rooms Halper told Crenshaw "After we got the two guards to surrender, my men found six barley alive prisoners locked in that storage room over there. They had no access to a bathroom or adequate food or water. One among them was dead. One of the men cried with tears streaming down his face when he was freed. Look at this". They walked into another room off of that one and there sitting on a table against the wall were 'tools of the trade' along with evidence that they were used to torture the prisoners.

Crenshaw looked at Halper. "I'm not surprised. When we freed prisoners in Poland, we found them in the same predicament. To the Feds, it's a justifiable means to an end. Don't be fooled, their goal is total domination. If we let them, our society will become one with two classes, the working class, and the elite. The latter reserve for themselves the ability and the 'privilege' of being rich. A typical Socialist MO. Right before our eyes we are witnessing their push to make it happen".

"I believe you now Crenshaw. I didn't see it coming, but now from everything we've experienced and from what you've told us, I believe it. We'll take care of the wounded. I'm hoping your militia can stay on in Herkimer till we sort this out. We're going to need men like you and women like Ciera. There will be more battles to come. I see one forming within our own ranks. Half of my available personnel opted out of this fight due to... well I guess some understandable resistance to going into battle, but also because of opposite political viewpoints on the direction this country should be going. Looks like we're at the beginning of a Civil War. America's second Civil War. Damned if we're not going to see a lot more bloodshed before this is over".

"Chief Halper, this is going to be the biggest challenge this country has ever faced. Under other circumstances I, we... would be honored to join forces with you but we're not going to be able to stick around. I need to fuel up and get the supplies we need and get out of here. My guys and I have got to get back on the road. I'm on a mission and I cannot deviate until it's done. We're going to take the fight to them, that is certain. But first we are going to regroup, pool our resources and then strike back. I want to extend an invitation to any of your people who are serious about fighting this to join up with the Cadet Militia and come with us now. We leave in the morning".

"I understand. I'll pass the word. Where are you headed?".

"East. Massachusetts, Boston. Got a job to do there" Crenshaw lied.

"I hope you make it. I heard it's tough going east from here, but I think they mean it's tough going south east toward the city. If you stay north and then go south into Boston that would be the path of least resistance. I heard Boston is a mess so good luck getting in there, probably the same as any other city as far as that's concerned. The whole country has shut down.

Both walked back out of the building and into the parking lot. "Well Crenshaw, If you find yourselves needing a friendly place to go, please consider Herkimer. You will always be welcome here. Oh, and by the way, I see that the Feds left us three semitrucks of supplies. Take one of the semi's instead of loading up your vehicles".

Crenshaw raised his eyebrows. "Wow, thank you sir. That's a great Idea. I'll take you up on the offer. We've been running into opposition so often; you don't know how nice it is to hear that we have friends we can count on". Crenshaw stepped back and saluted the Captain. The Captain returned his salute.

Crenshaw walked back to the group of Patriots that had gathered in the parking lot and called out to his guys. "One of those semi's is ours. Kaiden, I need you to get it loaded up with everything we deem worthy… get it done tonight. We leave at first light".

Winter jackets, thermal underwear, boots, uniforms, socks, AR-15 rifles, grenade launchers, 40mm explosive shells, .223, 9mm and .308 ammunition, fuel, food and even toiletries were packed into the Patriots semi that night. Afterwards Crenshaw met with his team to discuss their next move.

"People, I have decided to continue our act and stay in character as agents manning a Federal convoy. It's worked for us so far and the paperwork should still be good as far as I can tell. Not sure if they were able to radio out a message from here. I hope not. I see this as our best chance of getting through. Since we have access to Federal uniforms, all of us can dress the part. But don't get dressed now. Black Jacks are on the shit list around here" everyone laughed. "We'll stop shortly after we get out of here and dress the part.

"An order of business I must perform is… a promotion!" He turned to Kaiden. "Kaiden, I am giving you a field promotion to Sargent in the Cadet Militia Organization. You will take Jerry's place on the team.

You've earned it by your unwavering determination and your support for our cause. I apologize for not being able to issue you your stripes at this time, they will be forthcoming".

Kaiden looked around like the promotion struck him in the head. "I don't think I was unwavering sir..." Kaiden started to say.

"I understand. But you can't refuse. It's an order. I need someone who can keep this unit together. You're liked by all, and I'm impressed with your dedication, especially under fire. I want you up front. You deserve it.

Pair up with two Patriots in each vehicle and put three of us on the bus. We're taking as many Humvee's as we can. Once we get going, stay together, stay together, STAY TOGETHER! If we get attacked, our MO for the trip will be for all vehicles to rally around the bus. Protect it at all cost. We're spread thin enough, if we lose anyone it can severely compromise our mission".

"What about Neil?" Jones asked.

"The Herkimer Police got him up on murder charges and we're going to have to leave him here to face the music. End of story. Now go prep for your assignments and then get some sleep" Crenshaw said in an 'end of conversation' manor. Kaiden didn't argue but he gave Ciera a wary glance.

* * *

It was a fine spring morning just before dawn, the Patriots convoy formed up. This time with the addition of a large semi freight truck. Also, Crenshaw repeated his offer for anyone to join up with the Patriot militia. The word got around and two men from the Herkimer police department took Crenshaw up on the invitation. They approached and enthusiastically asked permission to become a member. One of them, Nance Lackland, was on the older side. Must have been around 50 or so. The other recruit called himself "Sky" and said his last name was Winiker. He looked to be about 25, but no one asked their age.

Before Crenshaw gave the word to "Move out", the Patriots, as a group sought out Crenshaw and formed a circle around him. "Captain, what about Neil?" Eric asked Crenshaw. It was a question that was on everyone's mind. "We're just going to leave him?".

Crenshaw looked around and then said "Alright, I see what this is about. Everyone, listen up. I know exactly why Neil did what he did, we all felt like doing the same thing. But we, as Patriots, must control our emotions and act responsibly. We can't throw out the rule of law and become executioners…".

"Why not?" someone in the group said. "Just minutes before we were killing them… what? legally? And then the curtain comes down and we're murders if we kill after? In no way does this make sense. We got to go and get Neil. He didn't do anything that we didn't do".

"Yeah, we got to go get Neil" more of them repeated.

"I hope he's not in there with the other prisoners" someone else said.

"Oh, I see. So let me get this straight" Crenshaw began. "Someone goes up to another person, becomes judge, jury and executioner all in one, and executes a guy for their 'alleged' crimes without a trial and you what? Want to congratulate him?".

Eric replied "No. But we want to reserve the right to put him on trial by a militia jury. This is not a civilian matter. This is a military matter".

Crenshaw was struck by that very profound statement. It put a pause in his thinking because… Eric was right. He realized that he was so willing to give Neil to the Herkimer police just to eliminate the problem that he didn't take the military side of this into account. To simply give him up was expedient. It was 'Problem solved'.

While contemplating a solution, the group was interrupted by a fast-moving car that pulled into the parking lot. It drove in bottoming out on the pavement and bounced past the still smoldering front gate guard house with a speed that made everyone turn and clutch their rifles. All of them were somewhat relieved when they saw it was a police patrol car although they sensed a degree of urgency when it skidded to a halt in front of them. The driver jumped out of the vehicle and trotted in their direction.

"I'm looking for Captain Crenshaw!" he said.

Crenshaw stepped out of the group. "I'm Crenshaw, who's asking?".

"Lyle Ramshaw, Sir". The policeman stopped and unnecessarily saluted the Captain. He was in civilian clothes, but it was a good bet that he was a cop. He said "Sir! I just spotted a Federal patrol on 90. "Six vehicles are headed this way fast".

Crenshaw turned and looked around. His thoughts revolved around an effort to avoid a confrontation and to save as much of their inheritance as he could. Both eyes settled on the fuel trucks. "Can anyone drive that fuel truck?" he shouted loud enough for everyone to hear. No one spoke up. Kaiden would have but he was already slated to drive the supply truck.

After he saw that no one else was going to respond, Lyle spoke up. "I can".

Crenshaw's eyes pounced on him. "Ok, get in that gasoline truck..." Crenshaw pointed to the 5,000-gallon fuel truck parked in the back. His thoughts now focused on taking as many assets out of the Feds hands as he could before they arrived. "Follow us. Let the Humvee bring up the rear" he told him.

With a new found urgency Crenshaw turned to his guys and yelled "GRAB A VEHICLE AND MOUNT UP ON THE DOUBLE!". We're leaving NOW people, NOW!" Back to the Policeman he yelled "Lyle, how much time we got?".

"They must only be about fifteen minutes out" he said.

"Damn! Warn the others!" Crenshaw said as he turned and ran to his Humvee. Donnie followed him and got in on the passenger side. Crenshaw didn't have to bark orders twice. Kaiden ran to the semitruck with Eric. Betsy paired up with Profit in the second Humvee and Reese paired with Vic in the black SUV. Four other Patriots jumped into a third and fourth Humvee.

Ciera and the rest of the Patriots ran to the bus. All remaining personnel who chose to go with the Patriots climbed on board the shuttle or one of the Humvee's. A positive factor was that they were all basically standing by ready to go. All except for the Herkimer Policeman. He stood there for a second looking undecided about the option that just presented itself. He let out a heavy sigh and then ran towards the fuel truck.

Crenshaw's Humvee was the first to line up, the other vehicles fell in line behind him. Then Crenshaw yelled "Move out!" into the radio's handset at the same time signaling with his hand out the window.

On the double the convoy, having grown by the addition of several vehicles, a semi and a fuel tanker truck, sped out of the Post Office parking lot. Immediately Donnie looked up from the map in his hands and started shouting directions. "Go left up here and take that straight down to Myers Park. It looks like that's the best way to avoid running into these guys". Crenshaw turned left.

Myers Park was five blocks down the road. Donnie had Crenshaw stop at the park and position the Humvee so they could look down 'N. Bellinger Street' without being seen. Everyone else pulled their vehicles in behind them in a line and stopped.

"The fuel truck's still with us" Kaiden reported to Crenshaw over the radio.

Crenshaw keyed the mike on his radio and said "I'm not sure what we're going to do with that, I just wanted to keep the Feds from getting it" Crenshaw replied.

From that vantage point, their Humvee overlooked the intersection where main route 5 (called Herkimer Rd. in town) crossed N. Bellinger Street a few blocks south of their position.

"Wait right here" Donnie told them.

"Why?" Crenshaw asked.

"Watch, they should be coming across Herkimer Rd. any moment now. That's the shortest route to the Post Office from the Thruway. Sure enough, a few short minutes later. Six Federal vehicles in a convoy barreled on past the intersection looking like they were in a big hurry to get somewhere.

Crenshaw looked at Donnie. "Nice move. There will be hell to pay when that patrol finds out what happened".

"I sure hope those guys got out of there" Donnie said.

"Ok, now get us out of here" Crenshaw demanded. "The locals are getting nervous".

Looking around Donnie saw groups of people standing on the porch of the houses that surrounded the park. They were looking suspiciously at the convoy.

One vehicle pulled out behind the other and the convoy was on the move again. The news was that the concerned citizens of Herkimer had set up a road block at Herkimer's entrance/exit to highway 90. They chose to block the road and screen cars there instead of setting up a barricade on the highway itself. They voted to let travelers pass through on the highway and just use assets to monitor the traffic coming in or out of their town. Donnie mentioned that they should avoid that checkpoint so that no one there would be able to tell an interested party which direction the Patriots convoy had gone. Crenshaw agreed and told Donnie to guide the convoy through the back streets which eventually brought them out on Route 5 just before they left the town limits. Once on 5, the convoy drove west, in the opposite direction the Feds were going.

Ten minutes into their drive, just outside of Frankfort N.Y., Crenshaw stopped the convoy again to allow everyone to change into their Federal uniforms. "Ok Patriots, dress the part" he said into the radio.

Crenshaw was nervous about stopping, you could tell. He didn't allow extra time to find uniforms for the policeman or anyone else. They would have to go on as civilian drivers or play prisoners on the shuttle. Three minutes later they peeled out and were once again moving fast along Route 5.

Other than the gasoline tanker, they set off with two Patriot Black Jacks in each vehicle. It was Crenshaw's rule to have two guys in each so that one could support the other. During his speech on how they would react tactically, he always made sure that everyone understood they would rally around the bus to protect the motherload if they ran into any trouble.

By continuing west on Rt. 5, instead of turning onto highway 90, they'd be following parallel to the Highway on a less traveled secondary road, first keeping 90 on their Right and the Mohawk river on their left flank most of the way to Utica. Crenshaw had originally intended to travel on the highway but being that it was a toll road, exits and entrances were few and farther in between. There wasn't another entrance until they got to Utica. He believed Rt. 5 would be a safer way to go.

After a rough night before, it looked like the Herkimer Police were going to avoid an even rougher morning. The order went out to vacate the area in the same fashion the Patriots did. Fast. Not long afterwards, Federal Patrol #237 drove up in force and poured into the Herkimer Post Office parking lot unopposed. The Police had avoided a battle that they weren't ready for. The Feds quickly assessed what had happened by beating information out of two captured policemen who didn't make it out of the Post Office building in time. Instantly the Feds assigned blame and sought to apprehend all the culprits responsible for the death of their men and the loss of their equipment and supplies.

13

BACK TO SCHOOL

Peering out the windows, the Patriots constantly searched for any indication that would depict the demeaner of the land they were driving through. They were on alert for friend or foe because now, danger could come from either side. Once again, that familiar feeling that everyone was against them crept up and pulled down a somber mood.

A few minutes out from the town of Frankfort, the Convoy encountered another moving vehicle. It was a large pickup truck passing in the opposite direction. It's truck bed was full of young men with rifles in their hands. That group made no attempt to interact or even flee from the Federal convoy. Surly they must have wondered why the "Feds" didn't stop them and hassle them about the guns. Another car the Patriots saw had a trailer attached to the back of it and was loaded to the hilt with 'stuff'. Positively a family trying to get from point A to B. Ten minutes out the convoy passed a stationary car on the side of the road with no one in it. After the convoy passed it, a group of people ran out from the bushes, started it up and pulled in behind Betsy and Profit's last Humvee.

Betsy radioed it in "Cap we're being followed by that car we just passed".

"See any weapons?" Crenshaw asked.

"No".

"Then they're probably just travelers who consider it a whole lot safer to follow the convoy rather than going it alone" Crenshaw surmised.

A short way down the road from that they passed another abandoned vehicle. It was sticking out in the road a bit, so they had to go around it. There were bullet holes in the glass and dotted puncture marks in the metal. Theories about what happened to the occupants ran wild. Was it an attack or did someone just use the car for target practice after it was abandoned? It became a source of stress not previously encountered during a drive down any road in America.

"We got a situation up ahead Cap" Donnie exclaimed. Donnie was driving. Their Captain had almost fallen asleep in the passenger's seat, so Donnie said it loud enough to shake him out of it.

"Yeah, yeah, what do we got" Crenshaw said before he was even fully awake.

"We're coming up on Rt 5's overpass with Highway 90. Got a bridge with a pickup and a car on each end of the bridge. Looks like there's multiple civvies manning the bridge on its crest". Donnie had good eyes and could make out details even from that distance.

"Stop here!" Crenshaw yelled. The Humvee along with the rest of the convoy came to an abrupt halt. Crenshaw unbuckled his seat belt and yelled "Alright I'm on the 50. But damn it, wait till I get up and settle in there before hitting the gas will ya?".

Crenshaw climbed up and poked his head up through the turret. A pair of binoculars came up to his eyes, he fiddled with the adjustment and focused on the bridge. Men on the near side of the bridge were using the wall for cover and shooting down at something on the east bound side of the highway. "I can hear gunfire" he yelled down to the others. Reports of gunfire accompanied the puff of smoke that came out of the shooters rifle barrels.

"They got weapons!" Donnie yelled.

"I see em" Crenshaw said calmly. He concluded. "Give me the radio" Donnie handed the handset up to him and Crenshaw spoke into it.

"Kaiden and Profit, front and center. Everyone else... defensive posture. Watch the rear Betsy. We're going in".

"Yes sir" came back over the radio.

Crenshaw didn't have to say "bring your rifle". It was their SOP (standard operating procedure) that Crenshaw drilled into them to always have their rifle within reach.

As soon as Kaiden and Profit got seated, the Humvee was off at a decent clip. Crenshaw yelled down to Kaiden "When we stop deploy to each side of the bridge".

"Got it Cap". Everyone put their ear plugs in.

"They see us!" Donnie yelled. They're on the move! Yup... they're gunna run! They're gunna run!".

Half the men on the bridge grabbed their rifles and started running toward their vehicles, one group ran to the far side of the bridge and other half of them ran toward the vehicle on the near side. The ones running toward Crenshaw shouldered their rifles and pointed them at the Humvee. That was a mistake because those vehicles were easily in range. Crenshaw didn't hesitate and opened fire.

Even with ear plugs on it was loud. 50 caliber bullets sailed into the nearest pickup truck with devastating effect. The 4,000-pound vehicle started to shake and jerk from the impact of bullets. Glass and tires blew out. Gasoline that spilled out of a perforated gas tank caught fire with a loud "poof" noise. The truck exploded into flames. The owners instantly stopped and turned to run the other way abandoning the idea of being able to get away with their vehicle intact. They all piled into the pickup truck on the far side of the bridge and took off.

Crenshaw's Humvee came to a halt before the bridge and in front of the burning truck. Kaiden and Profit spilled out to each side. There was no need to take cover because there was no one attacking them, but they ducked low and cautiously advanced anyway. The Humvee drove around the burning vehicle and slowly over the bridge with Kaiden and Profit walking next to it, their rifles pointing beyond, ready for any hostility that might present itself.

Before they reached the other side of the bridge, the bandits were able to put a couple hundred yards between them. Crenshaw fired off a string of automatic fire which stitched a line across one of the fleeing car's trunk and tore up dirt all around it. In the distance they watched as three vehicles suddenly veered off the road, traversed the shoulder and bounced over a downed section of fence. The guys in the back almost fell out of the truck. It looked like they had that escape route planned. Dust formed behind them as they hightailed it out of there. Seconds later the vehicle disappeared into the tree line.

Donnie was ordered to stop yet Crenshaw stayed on the 50 watching the trees on that side of the highway for movement. Kaiden and Profit ran to the side of the bridge and peered down onto highway 90 to see what the bandits were shooting at. On the highway below they saw fifteen or more vehicles strewn around the road in various positions. Many had bullet holes in the windshields. In one vehicle, possibly more, there was a dead body. But the others were empty. Emerging out from one of the cars that sat about a hundred yards away, came two then three individuals. One man and two women. The man waved friendly like, indicating that he believed the (Feds) were friendly because the Patriots had just fought off their attackers.

Kaiden and Profit worked their way down from the bridge to the highway below surveying the situation as they walked out to the civilians. They were in the middle of introducing themselves when the rest of the convoy drove up on the bridge.

"So glad you guys came along" the traveler said while shaking Profit's hand enthusiastically. "Man, I thought we were goners".

"Everyone all right? What happened?" Kaiden asked.

"Yeah, now we're alright thanks to you. We were driving Ok until we came up on these assholes. We slowed down to try and maneuver around these cars when they started firing at us from the bridge. Almost got me" the man said as he wiped blood from where glass fragments had cut his face. "If you hadn't come along, they probably would have killed us. Thank God. We're very grateful".

"Just doing our duty sir, mam" Kaiden told them. He tipped his hat to the two females, but they didn't respond and never approached. They stood well back as if they were afraid to make contact. The answer to the question "How are you doing?" was evident by the distraught look on all their faces. A look that somewhat subsided due to the Patriots presence but it never disappeared. Kaiden was dying to tell them the real story behind the Patriots and the Black Jack uniforms. It just killed him that anyone would get a good impression about Black Jacks. Playing this charade had its drawbacks.

"Which way you headed?" Kaiden asked the one who introduced himself as George.

"Going east but after this I don't know how far I'm gunna chance it. I never thought Americans would treat Americans like this".

"You don't know the half of it" Kaiden said. "How's it looking west from here?".

"Well, we went through a roadblock at the next exit on 90" George said. "But not a problem for you guys. You'll get right through. It took us hours".

"Well, if there's anything we can do for you…".

"No, we're good. We'll just be on our way, that'll be good, you've done enough. Thank you, thank you".

Soon after, the civilians car snaked its way through the litter of cars and got back on a clear stretch of road on the other side of the bridge. The Patriots took advantage of the pause and turned it into a 10-minute break. Everyone got out and took in the view as they looked down on the highway.

Eric urged Crenshaw "We should do something about those bandits".

"No, there's nothing we can do" Crenshaw replied.

Of course, there was something they could have done but it would have taken them out of their way. Crenshaw squashed the idea.

"Captain Crenshaw!" the policeman took the opportunity to corner him for a conversation.

"Yes, ah yes the policeman" Crenshaw said.

"Lyle Ramshaw" he said. They officially shook hands.

"Yes, I'm very glad you came along officer Ramshaw. I wanted to thank you for volunteering to salvage the tanker. Nice move. I guess it's coming with us now. It's a plus to be able to add that to our inventory".

"It worked out. I didn't really know what I was getting myself into though. That's why I wanted to talk to you".

"I hope you're contemplating joining the Militia officer. We sure could use you".

"I heard about your offer last night. Where are you going sir" Arron asked.

"We're on a mission that will take us to an undisclosed location about a day's drive from here. That's all I can say about where we are going. If you stay and help, I can tell you that you would be contributing in a major way to the effort to save the republic. We need to get these supplies to our friends so that we have the ability to fight this. If you agree with our goal, I invite you to come along. If not, feel free to jump out now with no hard feelings. But I must warn you right now. We are at war with these people not because of our own doing, it's positively due to their agenda, not ours. This is going to have to involve you coming to grips with that and accepting the things that happen in a war like the fact that you are going to be called upon to fight".

"I see. Well sir, I joined the force to try to make a difference. I don't see myself accomplishing that in a big way in Herkimer, at least not under these circumstances. I'm impressed with your militia; I'd like to join. But the deal is this- I'm with you as long as things are on the up and up. As long as our principles are aligned, I'll be a loyal member. If you split off… I'm gone".

"That's all I could ask from any of my Patriots. Welcome aboard Lyle". They shook hands again.

"When do I get my uniform sir?" he said jokingly with a smile.

"As soon as we have time to dig into that supply truck, see Kaiden, he'll try and find one for you. Do you have a weapon?".

"Yes sir!" Without losing the smile on his face, Arron pulled out a stainless-steel Kimber 1911 from a holster at his side. "But I could use one of those HK's your guys are carrying sir".

"Arron, from now on consider them your guy's too. Again, see Kaiden, he'll get you a rifle".

Before the convoy left the bridge, Crenshaw let Kaiden pull out one of the M79 grenade launchers to do an experiment. Most had never fired the weapon, and everyone was curious about how it handled, what its range was and most of all, of course, they wanted to see it blow something up. All the convoy's vehicles were moved to the exit side of the bridge and the Patriots took turns firing grenades at abandoned cars down below, even Ciera fired a round. It took three tries before someone hit a car, but everyone learned a lot. It blew one of the car to pieces and set it on fire in the middle of the road.

* * *

OIC Pablo Domingo of patrol #237 and his men released Gutierrez from jail at the Herkimer Police Station after a successful raid on the building. Spurred on by reports that the station was the source of the attack on the Post Office last night and the night before, the Feds wasted no time in striking back. It wasn't that difficult being that there was only a skeleton crew left to man it. Gutierrez was freed from his jail cell in the process and now the two Federal OIC's (Officer In Charge) were able to trade stories and information.

OIC Domingo along with Gutierrez now stood in front of a lineup of men and one women who looked horrified about the position they were in. With the acquired support of Domingo's Patrol behind him, Gutierrez now stood in judgement of some of the very policemen who had jailed him. All of them motionless with their hands tied behind their backs. Among them were the two policemen the Feds caught at the Post Office. Immediately upon learning details about the attacks, Domingo sent a team of agents to Chief Halper's home in downtown Herkimer. They tore the guy away from his family and added him to the lineup.

Gutierrez was mad as hell. He lectured them "You all are guilty of crimes against the Federal government, and you will be punished accordingly. We will find the others who helped you do this, and they will come to the same fate". Gutierrez moved to stand in front of Chief Halper. "I ask you one time only, which way did they go?".

Halper had been badly beaten for the second time now. The guy was hardly able to stand there let alone respond. All resistance was gone. Through swollen, bloody lips he said "East".

Gutierrez raised his pistol and shot Halper in the head. His body crumpled and fell to the ground. Then he turned to the soldier next to him who was wearing a Patriot uniform. They had found him locked in a cell inside the station. Gutierrez spoke harshly to him "But you say they went west". Tell me the truth or you will receive the same fate".

Shaken by what he just saw, Neil Lee was standing there in shock. He was panicking and almost in tears. His voice trembled when he spoke. "Yes sir, I didn't participate in the attacks! I swear to you. I can supply you with information about their movements if you'll let me go".

"Why would you do that, and why were you locked in a cell? In fact, why shouldn't I just shoot you right now?".

"Those bastards arrested me for stealing and left me here (Neil lied to try and save his own ass). I hate them for it. I want to join you, Sir. I can be of great value; I can give you those men".

"If all you got, is that they're heading west then I don't see the need…". Gutierrez started to raise his pistol.

"No! Wait! No, there's more, much more that you should know. They got a bus full of gold and silver that they're taking to their hide-out! Please don't kill me, I can be of assistance to you, I can tell you anything you need to know…". Gutierrez raised his eyebrows and lowered his pistol. "Really? Go on" he said. Gutierrez was all ears.

"Very interesting" Gutierrez said after hearing Neil's story. Gutierrez moved out of the way and turned toward Domingo. "These are the ones we've been looking for. OIC Domingo, you may proceed". Domingo raised his arm and then dropped it yelling something in Spanish which obviously meant "Fire!". A slew of rifles in the hands of an execution squad fired bullets that plunged into Neil and all the bodies of the people lined up against the wall.

At this point, at least in this section of central New York, communication between the Feds assets in the field was made by short wave radio transmissions on the Citizens Band radio. Channel 42 was the official Federal channel. Anyone else broadcasting on the channel was threatened and told to get off. The CB was chosen for communication over other technology because in their spare time, patrols could monitor chatter coming from the local population as well. Ham radio was reserved for city-to-city communication where applicable and it was intensely monitored. Messages were transcribed and coded and then sent from base to patrol, then patrol to patrol or any combination thereof. This meant that a single message could take some time to travel back and forth through the pipeline. Every Patrol helped to pass on news and orders which would eventually reach the intended recipient.

"My fellow OIC, I'm glad you survived" Domingo told Gutierrez. "I will report this to central command through channels, they will want to know details about this group. The Ham radio is gone from the post office. Stolen, and we're too far away for direct communication with truck radio's but we'll send a message through channels" Domingo said.

"No, my friend, don't do that, please hear me out. This news changes everything" Gutierrez told him. "I am not eager to submit a report to command about the loss of my entire patrol and all its equipment. I certainly don't want to tell them it was due to this small band of rebels. Not yet. First, give me a chance to sufficiently correct the situation and bring these rebels to their knees. Allow me to save face. If I can turn this around fast and offset the bad with some good news, my career in this new regime might not be over, if it isn't over already. And since that might be the case, I don't advise reporting the existence of a large stash of gold and silver right now. The two of us can make plans for that. Getting our hands on that can truly set the both of us up for retirement. I suggest we seek to acquire it for ourselves. We'll split the spoils, and the two of us will become rich men".

Domingo thought about it, then smiled.

Greed had set it's hooks into the both of them.

* * *

Someone took a pot shot at the Patriots convoy as they drove by. It put a hole in the side panel of Kaiden's semi. Luckily no one was hurt, and the bullet didn't strike the ammunition. After that whenever they stopped, everyone inspected their trucks for damage. Especially on the gasoline tanker where puncture holes could really be a problem. No further contact with snipers occurred throughout the next leg of their journey. Every Patriot hoped that the single occurrence would prove to be an isolated incident.

During stops, and even in between, Crenshaw continually briefed the crew on their roll and what action he expected from them when and if they encountered various hypothetical scenarios. Especially concerning was the roadblock on highway 90 that they knew was coming up at Oneida. When they got close enough, Crenshaw stopped the convoy at a place where he maneuvered his vehicle to get a clear line of sight. From a distance, through binoculars, he observed the roadblock the Feds had placed across Hwy 90. It looked like every other road block they'd seen up to this point except this one was a whole lot bigger, more organized, and more heavily manned. This one cut down the number of lanes on the highway and funneled travelers into one of the search areas. Inspectors with rifles in their hands guided cars and trucks through the line. Once again there was a semi-truck on the side loaded with confiscated items.

The presence of Black Jacks was not a surprise. When the Patriots had come within radio range, they picked up radio chatter on the Feds channel indicating the presence of a federal force at the Oneida roadblock. Guards manning it were made up of a conglomerate of Federal agents, a handful of local policemen still wearing their police uniforms, and a surprising number of young adults. Even more of a surprise was that some of them were carrying rifles.

"I thought guns were banned?" Crenshaw said out loud. Then he handed the binoculars to Kaiden and told the others to gather around.

"The gun ban is for us, not for them" Kaiden stated.

"Ain't that the truth" Crenshaw replied. Then he addressed his men. "Ok, they've got two Federal Humvee's, one parked on the north and one on the south side of the highway. Those 50's are overlooking the lanes with a man in the turret inspecting 'customers' as they pass. I estimate a patrol size force supplemented by local police and civilians who are doing the physical search of the vehicles. Some of them look like they're fresh out of high school. Roll the dice and it looks like the police in this town came up on the side of the Fed's. Now here's how we're going to do this…".

* * *

No warning or radio contact preceded their appearance so the sight of the Patriots driving up gave the men manning the road block something to talk about. It wasn't a large contingent of Federal agents that manned this station but there were a lot of others in civilian clothes walking around with guns. Crenshaw took note of the Black Jack in the turret of the Humvee. Two more agents were sitting in the front seat and six more were walking among the other men overseeing the physical labor of searching cars and trucks that were passing through. Their Humvee was strategically placed to monitor the action and to facilitate a quick reaction if needed. When the Patriots pulled up, a Black Jack got out of one of the nearest Humvee's and walked over to greet them. He spoke Spanish at first but when Crenshaw said "Hello Sir, how're things going here?" the guy switched to English.

"Greetings comrade. Papers please. Nice to have some backup finally show up, I've been calling for reinforcements for three days now" the Black Jack said. He looked into the cab of the Humvee and eyeballed

Donnie. "Where's your OIC? And why didn't you follow protocol and radio in before your arrival?".

Crenshaw gave him their papers and a viable excuse. "Patrol #357 reporting sir. My OIC was killed in a skirmish at Herkimer, ran into some heavy resistance. We're following emergency protocol and implementing radio silence sir". The guy cocked his head and looked like he was trying to recall that rule. Crenshaw didn't know what the emergency protocol was or if there was an emergency protocol. He figured the OIC wouldn't know either.

"Patrol number 357 huh. That was Gutierrez patrol, right?

Quickly Crenshaw changed the subject "Yes, well I'm sorry to inform you sir that we are not here to reinforce you. My orders are to get these prisoners we have back to headquarters ASAP. We need to re-supply and get another OIC assigned to our patrol so we can get back out on the road and knock some heads". The officer smiled at the last part, but it was quickly replaced by a frown.

"That's strange" the officer said looking at the rest of the trucks in the convoy as they pulled up behind Crenshaw's Humvee. "Then why do you have a fuel truck attached to your patrol? And I thought we had orders not to take prisoners?".

Crenshaw responded on the fly "We kept these supplies out of the hands of the rebels and were able to take some high-level prisoners. Got the leaders of the resistance here. Headquarters wants to see them so they can beat some information out of them. Wants to know what they're up too".

The officer smiled again. "Well, you're not going to be able to get the leaders of the Oneida resistance".

"Oh yeah, why not?" Crenshaw asked.

"They're going to hang him and his traitorous cohorts today at the University's sport stadium. Freedom Brigade got them. The professor and his amigo's. It's the big event... wish I could be there".

"Freedom Brigade?" Crenshaw asked.

"That's these guys here" The officer pointed to the guys operating the road block who looked like high school kids. "They're running the show in Oneida".

"I thought we were running the show" Crenshaw told him.

"We are, but a deal was struck with certain small towns like this one. HQ thought we're better off leaving it to the local labor to cement the lockdown and make the changeover. This way we can bypass the small towns and concentrate our trained agents in the cities where they're really needed. These guys from the college floated to the top as the heavy weights around here so they got the contract to purge the City. Oneida was the first city outside of Syracuse that we took over and implemented the "Renewal Project'. It's working so well that they're going to start it up in every town, possibly some cities too. Weren't you briefed on this?".

"Yeah, but I don't recall the part about giving them guns" Crenshaw motioned to the youth that was standing close by with a rifle in his arms.

"Well, I didn't like that aspect either, but don't worry about that...". Under his breath as if to keep anyone else from hearing, he said "...as soon as they're done with the purge then we'll get those back real fast. It's brilliant, this way we don't need a large army to go in and take over each town. These turds will do it for us".

On the inside, Crenshaw was disgusted, but he replied "Wow, brilliant" with feigned enthusiasm.

Crenshaw was so disgusted that this was happening in America that without consulting anyone else he changed plans right then and there. "Well Sargent, who's in charge? Who do I see about getting those prisoners?".

"That would be the Professor, I mean Chancellor Sonowski. Good luck though. You're going to need it".

* * *

On the outskirts of the town of Herkimer, Gutierrez stood at the entrance to highway 90 taking in what he had just heard. Before him, members of his newly acquired patrol were having a conversation with a policeman who they found manning the road block just south of Herkimer on the entrance ramp to highway 90. The policeman was on his knees with his hands tied behind his back. He yelled "I'm telling you the truth! There was no convoy that came through here this morning". He said it through tears, and then screamed in agony as Black Jack patrolmen from #237 held him down and beat him mercilessly for being a member of the force that had attacked the Post Office. The guy kept screaming "I wasn't there! I didn't attack your men". It didn't matter. They kept beating him until he went silent. With a nod of his head, Gutierrez directed the men to throw his limp body off to the side of the road.

In rapid Spanish, Gutierrez told Domingo "I believe him. Our quarry was traveling south up to this point and were probably trying to get to the highway. That means that these stinking rebels could only have gone west, south, or east from here. The Herkimer police chief told me east. Going south from here would put them on the back roads of central New York which would cost them a lot of time, unless of course their destination is somewhere in the Catskills. But I don't think so. From the things I heard when I was a prisoner, and by gut instinct, I determined that they were headed for the highway. They're in a hurry to get somewhere. The passes they have in their possession will allow them to slip through the road blocks since we're not reporting this to command. They'll be good for another week before they become outdated, so they might not even have a problem passing through Syracuse. I believe they went either east or west on 90. But no, not on 90. Not if they didn't pass through this entrance. They must have taken Rt. 5. We're going to cover both most likely routes; I want to split our patrol and send one team to scout east and the other west. I'll take west, Domingo, you go east".

* * *

It was a cool day with a partly cloudy condition that enabled the partly sunny side of it to make it a pleasant one. Five Patriots in a Humvee drove up to the entrance to the Oneida University Sports Stadium and passed through an initial check point that was manned by the Freedom Brigade. They were waved on through without incident confirming that Black Jack uniforms were as good as a valid membership card. By the look of things, they had arrived at the start of the so called "Big Event" along with hundreds of other people, many of whom mingled outside the stadium on the sidewalks and in the plaza before going inside. To a casual observer it would have looked like there was a game going on. But the underpinnings of this gathering were far more sinister. This would prove to be unlike anything that had ever taken place in America.

Crenshaw got Reese, Kaiden, Profit and Donnie to volunteer for this. Now the four of them drove through the stadium parking lot which was basically empty except for a sprinkling of civilian cars that dotted the lot along with several Federal vehicles parked near the main stadium entrance. A whole mess of scooters and bicycles were parked in different clumps all over the place. A bunch of kids held skateboards in their hands which gave away their age. All the others had probably walked there.

They all noted three or four gangs of people strolling around with rifles cradled in their arms looking like they were policing the event, yet they looked way too young to play the part. The odd thing was that there were a few people throughout the crowd who carried swords. Some had them sheathed at their side and there was one who had a set of swords in scabbards strapped to his back. They looked just like the character in Blade Runner, sunglasses and all. Another was dressed like Mel Gibson in Braveheart complete with the haircut and a long sword. You couldn't tell if they were serious or just imitating for fun.

"You got to be kidding me" Donnie exclaimed. Are these people playing out some kind of Halloween fantasy game?".

"They can't play it on the net, so they got it going right here in real time. Damn, we can deal with the weapons we can see, no problem, but look at that guy dressed like Keanu Reeves in the Matrix. You can't tell what's underneath that trench coat. We've arrived at a fricking costume party!" Kaiden exclaimed.

"Then we'll fit right in" Donnie mumbled.

"I don't know but I don't want to find out if those swords are real" Reese added. "Swords and bayonets give me the creeps".

"I don't see anyone here older than like twenty-five. This is a major college town. They all look like they're college kids. Must have gotten stuck here after the melt down" Donnie theorized.

Crenshaw pulled the Humvee up to the main entrance and parked right next to one of the Humvees overseeing the stadium entrance. A crew of Black Jacks were standing around watching the crowd. The one manning the 50 cal on that Humvee made this whole thing look completely unamerican. The Patriots piled out and acted like they belonged while maintaining an air of confidence just like Crenshaw had instructed them to do.

Crenshaw walked right up to the nearest agent and asked "Who's in charge here soldier, where's your AIC?".

The Black Jack replied "It's Agent Ramone".

"And where can I find him?".

"He's inside the star tunnel with the Chancellor".

"The Chancellor?".

"Yes, Sonowski. I mean 'Chancellor' Sonowski. That's what the Professor calls himself now. Where have you been?" the agent asked.

"We just arrived. Heard you needed some reinforcements. Who's this Chancellor guy?".

"Big shot Sonowski?" the guy looked around as if to make sure no one could hear him. "He was a Professor here at the college before the SHTF. Now he's running things. We only have six guys here, more in the tunnel but not enough if something goes down. I'm glad you showed up. It makes me shiver to see these kids with guns in their hands. They look like they're just dying to pull the trigger. They're going to do just that to a bunch of them constitution thumping right wingers today".

"Yeah, that's what I heard. And that's why I'm here. I'm supposed to pick up some prisoners and bring them back to headquarters for interrogation" Crenshaw told him.

"Oh, I can tell you the Chancellor ain't going to like that. Everyone here is psyched up to see 'em hang. Look..." the Agent motioned towards a guy standing in the middle of a crowd just outside the stadium. "That guy there ain't just cheering for the home team". He pointed outside the main entrance toward the plaza. On the side of the walk way was a young man standing on two five-gallon buckets speaking to a small crowd of people that stood around him. There were four mean looking dudes behind him with folded arms staring at the crowd. The speaker was waving his hands and carrying on like an evangelist minister. His rhetoric was judgmental and laced with condemnation.

"...we never knew the extent..." the guy shouted. "...the extent of just how deep their fangs were into us. The elite are ripping us off and stealing our future! Chancellor Sonowski freed us and gave us a path to a new beginning. He designed this revolution and has rid the government of those sap sucking lawbreakers. You know it, it's the resistance that we all felt. Resistance to helping the real workers of this nation. Us! The ones who deserve more that we are getting. Those people are guilty of holding us down and contributing to the demise of the working class. Sonowski has gotten our student loans forgiven and he's promising free education and jobs for every one of us after things get back to normal. Think about it! Everyone, finally working for equal pay. We can start clean with the Chancelor as our leader. Our government is now working for the common 'Mon'. For the new world!" he shouted. The small crowd cheered his words and enthusiastically gave it back to him.

"Wow. That's not a real happy young man" Crenshaw told the guard.

"Yeah, I can't wait for the second phase, the 'purge', where we get rid of them" the guard said. Crenshaw just stared at him without commenting further. His brain was trying to comprehend what exactly the "purge" might mean.

"You guys can go into the stadium and walk onto the field and over to the home team side. Guards will let you into the team tunnel entrance, it's got a star over the doors. You'll see it. Follow it into the locker rooms. They're in there" the Black Jack said.

As per instructions the Patriots walked into the square past the guy preaching on top of buckets and past the crowd milling around outside the main entrance. There was a totally different feel than what you'd expect at a sports event. And it wasn't a friendly one. There were no kiosks selling food, hats, or tee shirts. Only one place sold water. Here though, the word "sold" had taken on a new meaning. The people on line paid for their bottle of water with red "tickets".

Kaiden grabbed the nearest attendee and asked her "Hey what's up with the tickets?".

She looked at him kind of strange "You mean 'Script'?" she said. "That's what they're paying us with".

"Paying you for what?" Kaiden asked.

"For being here and for the work we do for them" she replied.

"Do all businesses here and in town accept 'script' as payment?" Kaiden asked.

"They have too, it's law" she replied.

Kaiden and Crenshaw glanced at each other, then turned and walked into the first entrance that took them into the stands. Kaiden remembered doing this with his dad when he took him to a ball game at Yankee stadium. Only there, as a kid, he was immediately struck by the bright shade of green from the well-manicured grass on the ball field. Here, the field was brown, trampled down to practically bare dirt by a large crowd of young adults who roamed all over it. Garbage was strewn everywhere. It looked like a dump.

At one end of the field there was a large bonfire burning which, at the moment, was the center of attention for the mob that gathered around it. People were continuously rolling up through the mess with wheel barrels full of stuff. Others took the contents and threw them onto the fire. Upon closer inspection you could see it was books they were burning. Thick school books along with books that had been looted from the library. All of them were being thrown into the flames. Another cart had a stack of paintings on it. With indifference, valuable art encased in expensive frames was piled on. Others walked up and pulled papers out of their packs and threw them in on top of it. The people standing around held up both hands with palms to the fire and cheered as if this was a major accomplishment.

On the opposite end of the field a large stage had been set up. At the center of it and across its entire length ran a thick beam suspended about ten feet high with 'A' frame supports. Eight sets of evenly spaced ropes, each tied in a hang man's noose hung down from the beam. For those who thought what was about to happen was wrong, the scene generated a deep gloomy feeling.

Walking down the steps the Patriots reached the field and were appalled by the nature of the crowd. They got stared down, cursed at, and given the finger by students who resented them being there. Venting anger, a bunch of them were screaming and yelling obscenities while pushing each other around mosh pit style. Some of the ex-students were shirtless. When they caught sight of the Patriot Black Jacks, they stared at them as if they would be their next victim. Many acted and surely looked like they were high on drugs. The Patriots increased their grip on their rifles and moved on through.

Just then a group of four crossed their path carrying a large painting of the schools founder in a magnificent thick flared hand carved wooden frame. When they got to the fire, with a heave ho, they tossed it on. The whole crowd cheered and shouted "down with the system" as it went up in flames.

Crenshaw motioned for them to keep walking until they came to the home team side and found the tunnel entrance with a big star above the double doors. It was easy to find but they had to go through a gate guarded by Black Jacks and a handful of Freedom Brigade members to enter. The guards pointed the barrel of their rifles menacingly at people who walked by but raised them when Crenshaw and his Black Jack crew walked up. There was a Black Jack group and a Brigade group who stood apart from one another and huddled together on opposite sides of the path making it look like there was a rift between them. All of them were armed and everyone turned to look at the Patriot Black Jacks as they walked between the groups. This was positively a "members only" entrance. Luckily none of them hindered their passing.

On the other side of the door there was a long tunnel which led out to the place where sport team buses normally pulled up.

Crenshaw calmly asked one of the Black Jacks "Where can I find Agent Ramone and Sonowski?".

"That's Chancellor Sonowski to you. Who's asking?" one of the Black Jacks asked.

"We're from 357..." Crenshaw said. "Got business to discuss with the Chancellor".

The guard grew a puzzled look.

"We're reinforcements reporting in" Crenshaw added to placate the guy.

"Oh. It's about time" the guard said. "When you get in there, I wouldn't call him 'Sonowski' if I were you. He'll rip your head off. It's 'Chancellor' now".

"Yes, so I heard. Got it" Crenshaw said. The guy let them pass.

Inside and down the hall a ways, the Patriots came to a locker room door. Two Brigade members were standing at the entrance. They too let them pass without a word. Inside, a following of young men holding various weapons looked them up and down but gave them no trouble. You could tell the guns in their hands gave them a sense of power they never had before.

At least there was still some measure of respect. Inside, the group of ex-students parted as the Patriots waded through them to get to a place where they could see and hear. It ended up that they were standing in the home team locker room. Only now it was packed with about fifty young adults sitting on bench seats or standing along the walls listening to two older men standing at the head of the group.

"That's got to be Sonowski" Kaiden whispered to Crenshaw.

Supposedly the guy was a professor, but he looked like an ordinary old man, harmless you might say. He had a scruffy white beard and an overall look that gave his age at 65-70. Right now, he sounded like a coach giving a pep talk to the home team before a game. But a sharp harshness in his voice turned the affair into something disturbing.

Dressed in a Federal uniform and standing next to Sonowski for support was a considerably younger man somewhere in his thirties. The guy nodded in their direction when he saw their uniforms. Crenshaw nodded back.

"A professor? The leader of a revolution?" Crenshaw whispered to Kaiden.

It was obvious that Sonowski commanded a large degree of respect. Everyone sat quietly and listened intently to what he was saying.

"...these people are of the old patriarch; they have been violating our principles for years. They've glorified the constitution and stifled our ability to pursue happiness with their self-righteous indignation. They're working off two hundred year 'old' ideas that once upon a time, were successful in their ability to control us. But not any longer! We will not stand for the disinformation they spew any longer!".

"Yeah!" the group in front of him yelled back at their leader.

"They profit while we do all the work! This we have stopped! Their old-world order is outdated by hundreds of years and no longer applies to modern times. Their constitution needs to be re-written and brought up to modern world standards. The one percent has kept us down, oh they have kept us down. They kept blacks down! Kept women down! Minorities! Brothers and sisters... that will no longer be tolerated.

Someone yelled "No more!" and then the group began to chant. "No more! No more! No more!".

"These people, they sit around in their golden offices with their golden parachute pension plans never realizing that without us, they wouldn't make a dime. THEY DON'T PAY WHAT WE'RE WORTH" Sonowski yelled.

"They sure don't!" someone in the group yelled.

"We're taking over their businesses! And we are going to install a Marxist mindset back into our society. The way it should be. This time people, we will make it work! Their world is crumbling before us!".

To Kaiden and Crenshaw, Chancellor Sonowski sounded the same as the guy preaching on the buckets outside. The irony of the man's claim was that being a professor at a prestigious college like Oneida University meant that he was a wealthy man himself, probably bringing home over three hundred grand a year with a sizable golden parachute pension plan to back it up. He was the epitome of the very thing he railed against.

Sonowski continued. "Now we have an opportunity. We have successfully overthrown the plantation owners and I can now report that we are in complete control of the town of Oneida". The group went nuts and cheered the accomplishment. "We have the power to guide our future on an equal level with those sons of bitches that have been raping us for so long… we've knocked the statues and the elite off their pedestal and brought them down to their knees. They are not better than us. We are all equal!" the crowd cheered again. "But wait! Wait…" he said with a sympathetic glance around. "It's sad. The opposition to our rejuvenation? The bastards that dared attack us? Well, they're not going to be with us much longer. Today we'll see to that! We will not tolerate their malevolence any longer… Any minute now the whole lot of them will arrive here by bus and I want you and your group… Carl (he pointed to what seemed to be the leader of a group standing next to him) to go get them and escort them to their seat at the table". Many laughed at that notion.

"That's a pep talk alright. He's getting them psyched up for the kill" Kaiden whispered to Crenshaw.

Abruptly Crenshaw replied "We got to go. Let's get out of here".

With that he turned and led them back out through the locker room doors, past the dark stares and the eyes of Brigade members and back into the Star tunnel. Once outside and out of ear shot, he instructed his guys. "Reese, Donnie. Go back out the way we came, get the Humvee, and meet us around at the team entrance here (Crenshaw pointed to the light at the other end of the tunnel). Don't get into any trouble that will delay you". "Hurry! Kaiden, Profit, come with me". The two groups went in opposite directions.

Exiting the tunnel through double doors brought Kaiden, Profit and Crenshaw out into the light. They found themselves in a caged area with a wide gate at the other end. It was heavily guarded with a lot of men standing around waiting for their guests to arrive. Some were federal agents but most of them were Sonowski's men.

After waiting a few agonizing minutes, the bus that everyone had been waiting for pulled up and came to a halt with the bus door opposite the opening in the gate. When the doors swung open, three more of Sonowski's men hopped off.

None of it deterred Crenshaw in the least. He told Kaiden and Profit "follow my lead". Playing the part, he marched right up toward the guards at the gate and right up to the men who stepped off the bus. Kaiden was more than apprehensive but did his best not to show it.

Crenshaw addressed the men who had gathered around the door of the bus. "Ok, gentlemen. There's been a slight change of plans" "I've been instructed by Chancellor Sonowski to bring the bus around to the main gate. He wants to march them in that way for greater effect". Sonowski's men looked at each other concerned about the new directive. The other Black Jacks standing around just stared back at him with indifference.

"I know, I know, these things happen but we can take it from here". Crenshaw turned and climbed on board the bus with Kaiden and Profit in tow. One of the agents tried to follow them in. Kaiden turned to the agent and said "We got this".

"Ok we'll send a Humvee with you to back you up" the Black Jack replied. He was about to give that order to his men, but Kaiden stopped him.

"No thanks, we've already got one". Kaiden motioned behind the bus where Reese and Donnie were just pulling up in their Humvee. Satisfied, the federal agents backed off and didn't push the issue any further. But with Sonowski's men, it was a different story, they weren't buying it. Three of them stood firm.

"Sorry sir but we have orders to escort these prisoners in and that's what we've got to do. The Chancellor would have our heads if we don't".

"Yeah, I've heard that before" Kaiden said.

Kaiden's desire to get the hell out of there without a confrontation was overriding. Especially in front of what could become a lot of angry opposition. He didn't know what else to do, so he didn't fight it, he went with it. "Ok, I can understand that. Let's go". With that, three of Sonowski's men climbed back on board the bus.

Inside the bus, stretched across from one side to the other about two seats back, was a hastily built chain link fence divider that was installed as a barrier between the prisoners and the guards. It looked more like a chain link curtain with a split down the middle acting as a door. It was crude but effectively sectioned off the bus. Two padlocks secured the two sides of the chain link curtain together. The front two seats on each side were left open for the guards. A Black Jack was sitting in one of them when Crenshaw and Kaiden walked on board. They immediately noticed the rifle cradled in his arms and the set of keys in his hand. That guy, plus the bus driver, made it 'five' guards that they were going to have to deal with if Crenshaw was going to pull off his spur of the moment ever evolving plan.

Crenshaw scanned over the prisoners and determined that there were about twenty to thirty of them locked up back there. Most were men but there was at least one female that he could see. He locked eyes with a black man who sat up front and stared back at him with contempt. They all had their hands tied behind their backs and the looks on their faces told a sad story about the state they were in. Crenshaw had seen this before; their demeanor was agonizingly familiar.

New 'partners' didn't raise any suspicion in the mind of the Black Jack guard on the bus. The guy seemed to be content. *"Plans changed all the time with this damn crew"* the Black Jack thought. Then he motioned to the seats indicating that they could sit down, two of Sonowski's men did, but one held back and stood by the door. Crenshaw also stood stating "We'll stand, this'll be a short trip". He leaned over to the bus driver and gave him an order to drive them to the main entrance but also gave him directions on how he wanted them to get there. Crenshaw directed him to go around once and circle the stadium.

It only took a few minutes before the bus came up on the turn that would define Crenshaw's real intention. The sign directed that up ahead, a left would take them out of the parking lot and a right would bring them right back around to the Arena's front gate. It was now or never. Crenshaw whispered something to Kaiden who turned and quickly grabbed the lever to the bus door opener and yanked on it as hard as he could. The folding door flew open and the guy standing next to it turned to face Kaiden with a quizzical look on his face. In one motion Kaiden delivered a solid front kick to the guy's sternum sending him reeling backwards. He fell right out the open door. The poor guys hands reached out to each side in a desperate attempt to grab something, but he found no hold that was sufficient enough to stop his predicament. The next thing he knew he was floating in midair for a short time before hitting hard on a moving conveyor belt of solid pavement. His body tumbled in circles before coming to a stop motionless.

Crenshaw and Profit quickly turned their rifles on the guards. Crenshaw waved his weapon wildly back and forth yelling "YOU MOVE AND YOU DIE!" at the top of his lungs until he had their full attention. "Throw your rifles on the floor now!" Stunned and confused, all three obeyed and sat there without moving.

Crenshaw had Profit collect their rifles while he covered them. Kaiden held his rifle pointed at the bus drivers head. That made the driver really nervous, unconsciously he started to slow down.

Kaiden yelled at him "DON'T HIT THE BRAKES OR YOU GET A BULLET! TAKE A LEFT HERE!". Once he saw the driver understood and was complying with his request, he said in a calm voice "Now do as I say or else this is your last bus ride".

Crenshaw yelled sharply at the guards "No sudden moves and you'll all live through this! If you go for a weapon, you're dead. Are those the keys for the pad lock?" he asked the Black Jack. The guy nodded his head. "Throw them to me". The guy did as he was told.

Kaiden kept reminding the driver. "If you speed up or do anything that I don't tell you to do I will put a bullet in you. Got it?" The driver nervously nodded his head.

"How are we doing Crenshaw?" Kaiden asked.

"All's well here" Crenshaw replied. "They're a cooperative bunch".

Crenshaw pointed at one of Sonowski's men. "You... get up and come here... now!". The guy stood up with his hands raised. "Move to the door now. NOW!" Crenshaw yelled. After he did... "Jump!" Crenshaw demanded. Shocked, the guy looked at Crenshaw to see if he was serious when Crenshaw repeated his demand louder "JUMP!".

Turning back to the open door Sonowski's man stepped down and jumped out believing whole heartedly that this would be a better fate than the one he envisioned if he stayed onboard the bus. Every prisoner was watching intently. Half of them cheered when the guy leaped out. Crenshaw repeated the process with the other two guards and the cheers got louder each time one jumped out. After the third Black Jack jumped and hit the pavement tumbling, the crew in the back cheered the loudest. But some of them kept their solum faces not knowing if their predicament would improve with the new warden in charge.

Both Kaiden and Crenshaw focused their attention on the bus driver. He was a young man, probably a student, just like the rest of Sonowski's men. The distress expressed in his face and demeanor was obvious. Even though it was not hot, sweat was dripping down off his brow from imagining various painful outcomes to this.

Crenshaw told Kaiden "I'll cover him. Switch places".

Using the sling, Kaiden flipped his rifle over his back and looked up to make sure they were on a straight stretch of road. He grabbed the guy's shoulder and said "Get up!" The driver let go of the wheel and stood up. Kaiden reached in, grabbed the wheel and slid into his seat.

The bus lurched due to taking his foot off the accelerator. Except for that, Kaiden successfully replaced the driver without a mishap.

No one had to tell him. The driver took one look at Crenshaw with his rifle pointed at him and he walked out the open door all on his own. Another notable cheer rose up from the prisoners as Kaiden manipulated the lever and closed the folding doors behind him.

Kaiden put his foot on the accelerator, and they started to pick up speed. He glanced in the rear-view mirror to look for anyone pursuing them, but only saw Reese and Donnie following in the Humvee. Out loud so that Crenshaw could hear he said "Looks like we're clean away. So far, no one except Donnie in the rear".

"Ok get us on Rt. 5 going west and get us the hell out of here fast" Crenshaw instructed Kaiden. Kaiden hit the gas and the bus sped out the exit road from the stadium's parking lot. Crenshaw unclipped a hand-held radio from his belt and spoke into it: "Number two, this is 'number one' come in, over".

"One, this is 'Two'. We're right behind you. Got your back". There was laughter coming from the radio. "I see you took out the trash..." Donnie said.

"Yes, we're in control of the situation, over" Crenshaw said and then turned to face the prisoners.

Half of the prisoners were chattering up a storm wondering what to expect from this "ST". ST was short for Storm Trooper or Student Trooper which is what both the Feds and Sonowski's men were called in Oneida. The rest of them gave Crenshaw a blank stare. "Wow, this is becoming a habit" Crenshaw said under his breath. Then he spoke loudly through the chain link fence so that even the prisoners in the back could hear him.

"Ok listen up. Now that that's done, I know exactly what's on your mind. Who am I and what the hell's going on here? Right? Well, let me inform you if you haven't figured it out already. These people were going to hang all of you at the stadium in front of hundreds of people. Yes, I said 'hang', they were going to make an example out of you, that was their plan. If we make a clean escape here, and it looks like we might, I can boast that I just saved all your ass's from the gallows. I don't tell you this for my own ego or to elicit gratitude, I'm not even asking for a thank you, I'm telling you this so that you will believe me when I say that I am not your enemy. So please, don't try something foolish like attacking me".

"Cap! We got a problem!" Kaiden shouted in a nervous tone.

Crenshaw turned and looked out the front window to see what was bothering Kaiden. What he saw bothered him too. Three Humvee's trailed by a black SUV were driving into the stadium on the same road coming right at them.

"Ok, stay calm. I don't think they know what's going on here, they couldn't have gotten word that quickly. Let it ride".

Kaiden gave a conciliatory wave of his hand along with a smile in acknowledgement as the line of vehicles drove by them on the opposite side of the road. Crenshaw glanced at the lead vehicle as it passed and was shocked that he was close enough to be able to recognize someone in the front seat of the lead Humvee. It was someone who could have recognized him too. It was General Gutierrez sitting in the passenger's seat.

"Woh!" Crenshaw said as he quickly turned away to minimize the slightest chance of being identified. The convoy past them and continued on to the stadium.

"Holy crap, that was Gutierrez! Crenshaw exclaimed.

"What!" Kaiden shouted. "Did he see us? Did he see us?

"I don't know, I don't think so".

For a long moment Kaiden studied the rear-view mirror and Crenshaw strained to see out the window. None of the vehicles turned around.

"Phew. They're not onto us man" Crenshaw said.

"Gutierrez? What's he doing here?"

"I don't know. They must have sprung him from the Herkimer jail, which means…".

"Yeah, that means that Herkimer's Police Chief and probably the entire Police force, have been compromised and... now we got Gutierrez on our ass" Crenshaw finished his sentence.

"Damn!' Kaiden hit the steering wheel with the palm of his hand.

14

BIRDS EYE VIEW

After driving off stadium grounds and taking a left on the road, the Patriots started to believe that they had pulled off a victory without firing a shot. Donnie, Reese and Kaiden and Profit were jubilant. Crenshaw kept his solum face on. It was a strange mission. No one knew what it was or what the goal was when they got to the stadium. Not even Crenshaw. Everything happened on the spur of the moment, without a plan. A very dangerous way to operate. Crenshaw had no idea what he could do, if anything, to save the condemned men. He just had to go to the stadium and see for himself, not believing that such an execution was going to take place in America. "*Had society fallen that far that quickly*? Crenshaw thought. The answer was "Yes".

"Alright Kaiden good job. Good job". Crenshaw patted him on the shoulder. "Now if we can get back and hook up with the motherload, I will feel a whole lot better". Crenshaw spoke into the radio's microphone he unclipped from his belt. "'Base' this is 'Mission one' over". There was a pause. 'Base' this is 'mission one' come in".

"Mission one, this is Base. Got ya".

Hearing Ciera's voice made Kaiden smile, it told him she was all right. "Base, how're we doing?".

"We're hanging at the stop, no problems to report. How is it on your end Mission one?".

"All good on this end, I'll tell you all about it at the get together. Commence plan 'A' for extraction, we're leaving this town. See you then".

"Roger out mission one".

The sound of one person doing a slow "clap" came from the back which got Crenshaw to turn around. All the other prisoners were silent. The white guy in the first seat sitting next to the black dude was performing a slow clap giving the impression that he was being sarcastic with feigned enthusiasm. It was instantly obvious that the guy had somehow gotten out of his restraints and was sitting there clapping with a serious look on his face. Crenshaw noted that all the prisoners that he could see up front had their hands unbound. He walked up to the chain link curtain to address the guy who was clapping. The man stood up and confronted Crenshaw. They stood there for a moment opposite each other, each one evaluating the other through the chain link curtain swaying back and forth as the bus sped down the road. The guy responded before Crenshaw asked a question.

"We were about to jump those ST's when you showed up. We weren't going to take the chance of letting them lead us into the stadium like cattle to slaughter".

Crenshaw looked him in the eyes while taking keys out of his pocket, looking down for only a moment to insert a key into the two locks that held the chain link shut. After removing them, he parted the curtain and now stood directly in front of the prisoner. Other prisoners moved up in a threatening manner.

"You don't know my situation..." Crenshaw told them. "All you need to know is that I, and my fellow patriots here are not Federal agents. You have my word; you have nothing to fear from us".

After a tense moment of not knowing how the guy was going to react, the prisoner raised his hand. Crenshaw looked at it and then extended his own. They shook hands. A smile broke out on both their face's. A cheer rose up from the other prisoners who were very happy to know that their luck had just changed.

"They call me Crenshaw".

"My names Ramsey. Ramsey Himmel. You don't know my situation either, but there's something I've got to tell you. It's something you've got to understand, and fast".

Two prisoners pulled the chain link fence back and tied it off while another went back and cut tie straps off the wrists of some of the others. Ramsey and Crenshaw sat down across from each other in the two front seats. After seeing Ramsey eye the pile of rifles on the floor, Crenshaw motioned to them and said "Distribute those to whoever is best at using them". Ramsey picked up the Black Jacks HK 416 for himself and handed the rifles the students were carrying to a select few of his fellow prisoners. Those weapons were old era M16A1 rifles, military surplus that the Feds supplied to Sonowski. There was no need for the Feds to hand out up to date equipment like the new model M16A2.

Ramsey spoke quickly and in a serious tone "I am going to be brief because we don't have much time. I am the head of the Oneida Uphold and Defend Movement. Our enemies call us a militia. There's five of us left". He motioned to the men who now held rifles in their hands.

One of them was the black guy who spoke "We're 'The Boys From Oneida'... and we're prepared to do what's needed. When rioters attack your neighborhood 'what's needed' becomes painfully obvious. It got serious for us real fast".

Ramsey continued "That's Merrill Konager, he's a lawyer, or was. A lawyer forced into this shit by these assholes who are trying to take us over. You need to know what you're facing here. I take it you have others with you".

"You've been paying attention" Crenshaw said.

Ramsey flat out stated "You need to believe me when I tell you that all of us, and the rest of your team, wherever they are, are about to get caught".

Crenshaw looked at him with a blank stare. "Go on".

"We found out what was happening months ago and vowed to do something about it. Four years ago, Oneida U won a bid for a sweet contract with the Feds to expand their universities drone program. It was just an elective at the time, now it's a well-funded high-tech program. Professor Sonowski was put in charge. At the time no one realized the significance. But as we know now, it was all part of the plan. As soon as the shit hit the fan, the Feds in Syracuse hooked up with Sonowski and made him king around here. He's overseeing all the reconnaissance for the Feds in this area and has a lot of pull. Commands a 200-mile radius or more. His drones are alive and kicking. They see everything and he's got them up there right now". Ramsey pointed to the ceiling. "As soon as they get word that you... we, are on the loose, they'll be on us like ice cream on a three-year-old".

It took Crenshaw a few moments to calculate what he was hearing. The thought of being captured was devastating. Crenshaw took too long to respond so Ramsey continued.

"We must go right now... right now and attack their base and take out those drones. Take out his eyes and his missile capability. It's the only way. Sonowski's going to hear about our escape somewhere around now. He'll have the drones search and they'll find this bus and your guys real fast. Realistically, we've got about forty-five minutes tops. Could be more like twenty-five".

"Missile capability? Shit!". The wheels were turning in Crenshaw's head. "We can't just attack. We have no intel, no plan. What... we're just going to go in blindly and shoot the place up?".

"Go in, yes. Blindly, no. We've been planning on busting the place for six months before we got caught. Someone snitched, and I know who. With the help of these drones the Feds raided our homes and rounded up what they call 'the opposition'. Caught each one of us alone. Because of it, some of us are no longer with us, but here we are, what's left. Subversion is our crime".

"Any wives or kids?".

"We don't know what's happened to our families, but we know they've confiscated our homes and bank accounts. That's why we're willing to put it all on the line and do this. The only way for us to get back is to knock out their eyes so they can't find us or else we're all dead. We've done some surveillance, got an idea of the layout. This guy 'Will' here..." Ramsey motioned to one of his men who came forward, "...worked at the facility as a technician. He came to us, that's how we knew what they were doing. He's legit, we confirmed it. Now those ST uniforms of yours might help us get in the door, we can pull this off. Actually, with you guys, this is the best chance of success that we've come across".

"I see..." Crenshaw took a moment, then responded. "If what you say is true, I agree. Doesn't seem to be another way".

"Ramsey, I'm going to put you on the radio with someone. I need you to guide her to a staging area near the drones base of operation. Base..." he said into his hand-held radio. "Forget radio code, we don't have time for that. Follow this guy's directions and meet me there".

Ciera and the rest of the team had been holed up at a warehouse parking lot waiting for word. Instructions were to wait for three hours, if Crenshaw and crew didn't show up, she was to proceed to their destination without them. With a sigh of relief, Ciera gave the order to move out and the convoy rolled following directions given to her by Ramsey. They weren't that far away, and their vehicles drove into the staging area four minutes later by pulling out all the stops. The staging area Ramsey chose was a closed-up gas station just off RT 5. A sign on the pumps read "NO GAS".

Crenshaw was in a big hurry and called a huddle as soon as the 'main body' arrived. He told the new x-prisoners on the bus that they were free to leave, or they could participate in the coming action. There was no time for further explanation, but Crenshaw gave it his best shot to try and recruit them.

"If you don't want to, or don't know how to wield a weapon we can still use you as drivers for our vehicles. Remember you were as good as dead in the hands of these people, and you will be again if you are caught. I suggest you fight for your freedom. Your best bet is with us, but no one will blame you if you decide to go".

Four of the new guys ended up leaving sighting reasons like "I got to take care of my family". Over twenty of them stayed along with all five of Ramsey's militia men. They had a bone to pick with Sonowski, and it showed in their demeanor. Everyone who claimed they knew their way around a rifle, was supplied with a weapon and ammo much to the delight of Ramsey and his men. They couldn't believe their luck. And the ones who didn't want a rifle, became drivers for their vehicles. That freed up their trained personnel for the difficult part of the coming action.

Crenshaw laid out information and ideas and got back opinions on how to proceed. From that, they created a plan for their next move.

* * *

"Sky Bird" was the name of the universities drone program. It was funded by a bottomless Federal grant that was designed to develop and enhance the Feds surveillance and drone strike capabilities in America. The north east sectors home base for the entire program was located here in Oneida. All of it under the guise of educational research backed by denials of any political connection or a connection to the military. The grant placed the project in the hands of a private organization giving the Feds non culpability and plausible deniability if their activities were ever exposed.

Therefore, the 'Sky Bird Building' was the name of the brand-new off campus building that had been custom designed and built exclusively for this project. A rather spacious main control room was attached to a large three bay garage. That room contained high-tech computers and all the latest monitoring equipment and antennas of a small airport. It even had a weather room. Other rooms on the second floor accommodated four engineers, eight administrators and eight full time technicians which it supposedly took to run the place. The service department behind the bay doors was plenty wide enough to house the unmanned drones being built. Looking at it from the rear, it looked more like a hanger than a garage.

Multiple drones in various forms of assembly were spread out on tables or sitting on a work jack in the middle of the bay floor. One of their newly completed RF-4 drones with folded wings sat up front facing an open bay door. It's body was long and sleek with a 22ft wing span and propelled by the new light weight Rolls Royce DC engine. It was all electric and 'power extended' with SST technology (solar skin technology). SST is photovoltaic technology that enables the entire exterior to generate DC electricity when exposed to sunlight). It didn't generate enough to make it self-perpetual, but it could extend the RF-4's no load flight time to sixteen hours on a sunny day.

Outside the building a 10,000-watt generator was running continuously to power the building. That generator and the whole rear of the complex were enclosed within a six-foot-tall concrete wall. One entrance gate to the back parking lot was on the east side and a large double gate was situated in the center of the rear wall. That opened up onto a large field adjacent to the building's back parking lot. A field that had a single paved road running down the center of its length. That was set up and used as a runway for launching drones, small aircraft and even on occasion, as a helicopter landing pad.

Depending on timing, if the drone operators were notified and had been ordered to search for a bus fleeing the stadium with a Humvee trailing behind, it might have been in vain. At that moment, the stolen prisoner bus sat alongside the Patriot's bus underneath the gas stations large overhang which effectively hid them from aerial view. The oil tanker was parked next to the station and the semitruck next to that. The idea was that it might look inconspicuous in that setting.

Inside the Sky Bird building, drone operators and their attendants got busy. Ten minutes prior they received a priority one order from Sonowski himself to search for a renegade bus with a Federal military Humvee attached. Their airborne assets had already been committed to another mission dictated by Federal Command, so they had two choices. Reassign their present asset and piss off the Feds or take the time required to launch another RF-4 and piss off Chancellor Sonowski. Since the Chancellor classified the action as CIA (Cleared for Immediate Action) they understood he expected immediate results. No one wanted to piss off the Chancellor, that was not wise, and no one wanted to piss off the Feds. They decided to try and please both parties by allowing their working bird to remain on task and began the preparations to launch a second RF-4B1. But first, the B1 had to be set up and fitted with missiles.

In the control room, men and women were sitting at desks staring at monitors with support personnel fluttering around in the background. Eleven minutes later their airborne asset was pulled back over their immediate territory and from the air they spotted a Federal patrol consisting of three Humvees, a black van and a black SUV driving down Rt. 5. At first, they wondered if this was something they should report. There was no bus in sight, and it looked like a normal Federal troop movement. When more information came in (Gutierrez had the time to relay his story to Sonowski) their target was further described as a federal patrol consisting of Humvee's, possibly two buses, with an oil tanker and a semitruck attached. There was some doubt that this was their target since there were no additional attachments. They hesitated and sought confirmation.

"Set team are you clear?" the drone operator spoke into a microphone on his desk. He was speaking to today's launch crew in the Sky Bird Building which consisted of a technician and four drone mechanics. By directive the five accompanied every launch and landing. It was never a problem getting people to go, the launch was the most exciting part of the procedure and there were always people who wanted to watch. Now, ever since the attempted sabotage had been thwarted, two-armed Federal security agents were ordered to be there for every launch and landing.

"Control, this is 'Set Team 1'. We now have RF-4B1 prepped, loaded, armed, and cleared for takeoff".

"Systems go for launch, set team you are authorized to take her out to the runway, prepare the launch sequence, over."

"Roger control, on the move now. Ready in 3".

Setting the RF-4B1 for launch was just a matter of towing the bird out of the hanger and through the gate to the paved runway with an electric cart. Then all they had to do was to point it in the right direction- down the runway. Once it was on line, the computer took over and everything was automatic.

"Control this is set team. You're a go for launch. It's all yours".

Control set the on-launch mode and the bird came to life. It's long wings slowly unfolded and locked into place. The four sky hawk missiles attached to the main body were impressive. They made the bird look dangerous. It's engine was so quiet that at first you couldn't even tell that it was running. But then, the whirling electric engine noise intensified, and the drone started to move. A burst of engine power propelled it forward and it picked up speed as it moved down the runway. Gracefully, and with so little runway it lifted into the air.

"Sir, I need you to come look at this" a drone operator told his manager. The manager came over to his desk and they both studied the large monitor in front of them. "We've identified the target and we're locked on".

"Ok, yes there's more than one Humvee, but there's no bus".

"...they're on the move sir".

"So what?" the manager said. "Confirm that this is our target and we can get them with our bird anywhere they turn".

"We're waiting for authorization now, but Sir, that road they're driving on...".

"Yes, what about it?".

"It's Rt. 5 sir".

"So what?".

"It's the same road we're on".

"Yeah, what are you saying?".

"Sir, they're only half a block away from us".

They both turned and looked out the front window. Just as they did, the convoy drove up and pulled into their parking lot.

"Sir they're outside our front door right now". The two of them froze and stared at each other.

Another technician sitting at another monitor listening to headphones yelled out "Sir, we just got permission to engage the target. It's a go. "We're hot and ready to fire".

"Wait! Holly shit! Belay that order!" the manager yelled. "DO NOT FIRE!

It took him a moment but then the manager yelled into the intercom "Security! CODE 3, CODE 3!".

It was amazing. On screen the technician and the manager could see details of the Federal patrol pulling into the parking lot of their building. They saw their own personal cars parked out front and immediately recognized the building as the one they were in. When they zoomed in closer, they saw one of the errant Humvee's continue barreling on toward the side gate. It rammed it at full speed and easily smashed it open.

It was enough time to activate security, but hardly enough time for Sky Bird personnel to set up properly for an attack. An attack that they never saw coming until it was way too late. Most of the agents were in the cafeteria drinking coffee. Two of them had escorted the RF-4 out to the runway according to procedure and one was stationed at the front door. Weeks earlier, when the plot to attack the Sky Bird building had been uncovered and thwarted, the Feds increased security personnel from two to eight and added another Humvee. Agents assigned to guard the facility were prepared for an attack in theory only. They set up but never fully practiced any defensive maneuvers believing that their manpower plus a couple of Humvee's with a 50-cal machinegun on them could defend against anything that this sleepy little town could throw at them.

William Dunlop (the Sky Bird technician gone rogue) was sitting in Crenshaws Humvee. He offered good intel about the buildings security measures and the internal layout of the building. Will had worked there since its inception and knew the inner workings.

"Right now, there's a Humvee sitting in the back parking lot of the Sky Bird building" Will told Crenshaw. "But chances are that it sits there unmanned. There's never a man posted inside the vehicle that I ever saw".

Profit was in the turret of the Humvee that smashed through the gate and roared into the rear parking lot un-opposed. Within seconds, they were in the back lot before anyone was aware of their presence. Their main mission was to cover the Feds Humvee and keep it from entering the fight, yet the immediate threat came from two Black Jacks who had escorted the drone mechanics out to the runway to launch the bird. All the involved personnel were riding back to the main building in an electric cart. The two Black Jacks had just gotten the Code 3 warning on the radio, and they came back in 'hot' through the gate with guns up.

Reese, Donnie, Merrill, and Ramsey spilled out of the Patriot's Humvee and used it for cover as they took up firing positions and opened fire.

The two Black Jacks on the electric cart hesitated for a moment when they saw what they thought were Federal agents. They didn't understand what was happening, but the Code 3 plus the sound of gunfire coming from the front of the building told them they were under attack. When the men crouching behind the Humvee that had just busted through the gate started firing, they fired back.

Two of the Patriots Humvees pulled up to the front of the building and came to a screeching halt with the van and the SUV right behind them. Patriots poured out of each vehicle and took up positions. As planned, a portion of them ran around back to support the rear attack.

There was movement at the front door. It opened slightly and someone peeked out to see what was going on. When the barrel of a rifle followed, gunfire erupted.

Patriots launched their initial attack on the building with small arms fire. Windows cracked, holes appeared in the doors and in the building's facade. That elicited a response. More return fire came from the front door, that's when one of the Patriots 50's opened up and blasted the door to pieces. When return fire came from one of the second story windows the Patriots second Humvee blasted that window with similar results. Resistance was short lived, Patriots on foot succeeded in entering the building.

In the back of the building the initial volley put down one Black Jack and wounded two of the drone mechanics. Luckily, none of the Patriots got hit by return fire. The cart came to a stop and the rest of them held up their hands. The remaining Black Jack threw his weapon down and put his hands up.

A side door on the building right next to the Feds Humvees opened and two Black Jacks ran out. They were making a frantic dash to try and make it out to their Humvee. Profit leveled a burst from the 50 at them with devastating effect. Their bodies flew backwards and hit the wall. To head off any other attempt, Profit targeted the door they came out of and fired multiple 20 round bursts at it. His bullets perforated it with ease and two Black Jacks standing behind it were killed.

Within minutes of the Patriots pulling into the parking lot, the entire group of technicians, the managers, and two Black Jacks that were still alive had their hands up and were standing in a line in front of Crenshaw and his men who pointed rifles at their chests. The rest of the Patriots secured the building. The whole attack lasted six minutes.

Will Dunlap had become the Patriots ace in the hole. If he wasn't a militia member before, he sure was now. Previously he was a student at Oneida University and majored in electronics. When he heard about the drone program in his freshman year, he signed up immediately but had to wait till his senior year to get into the class. It was a popular elective. From working as a technician in the program the previous school year, he learned about the inner workings of the new RF4 drone and about its weaponry. The weaponry was a surprise, but it was cool, it didn't bother him. Demonstrations of the drones attack capabilities didn't bother him either, that was the raz. All the innovations were to support public safety, or so he was led to believe.

Will explained to Crenshaw: "I didn't have a problem tweaking and fine tuning the drones surveillance capabilities. It was only when I became aware of the true nature of the missions we were flying, did I become a conscientious objector. The administration keeps details of the missions a secret, but I got a look at surveillance reports, and I was shocked. The missions they were flying surveilled or more accurately 'spied' on Americans on American soil. The reports gave detailed descriptions of individuals movements and detailed information about the individuals preferences with a list of contacts he or she had made. My actions were not motivated by the fact that we were equipping the drone to carry four sky hawk missiles, each one the equivalent of a 500-pound bomb by the way. No. The problem was 'who' was being targeted and 'where' they might be firing them.

Over the next month I sought out and got a good look at more reports and concluded that there was a concerted effort to gather information on Republican and Conservative political party members by the progressive party. They were even bold enough to call some of them 'enemies of the state' in the reports. It was all so one sided, there were no reports on any Democrat or Progressive party members. I knew these people in charge were progressives, but I didn't know to what degree they were willing to take it. At that point, one file I saw really drew my attention. It was a surveillance report on 'The Boy's From Oneida' and their 'Uphold And Defend' militia. It was extensive with pictures, names and addresses of the members. To sum up the recommendation paragraph, it said 'Terminate'. That's when I got in contact with Ramsey and warned him".

Will moved to the front of the lineup and stood between the Patriots and his old fellow drone technicians who were now prisoners. He faced his boss and smiled. "Mace Powers" he said in a nonchalant tone.

"Why you son of a bitch!" Mace yelled and took a step forward like he was going to strike Will. Crenshaw stepped in and struck the manager in the gut with the butt of his rifle. That sent the guy reeling back clutching his stomach.

Will clasped his hands and rubbed them together. "Ok, now that that's done, let's get down to business. I need this man taken out of here..." Will motioned to his old boss and two Patriots took him away. Then he turned to the group of technicians "...and I will need you John, and you Seri, to help me".

"Yes sir" they both said. They were now very eager to help.

"Seri, what's the status of our birds?" Will asked.

"We got two up. This screen shows RF-4A and this one's got B1" she told him.

"Is B1 armed?" Will asked Seri.

"Ah, yes, it is".

"I thought so" Will said. He looked back at Crenshaw. "Those missiles were intended for us". Then he turned back to the monitors. "Seri, sit here and operate this for me. I want to use the B1 to search the immediate area. Pull it up on the screen".

"Sure Will. Anything you say".

The screen already showed in real time a top view of the building they were in, "I see you guys were watching us" Will said. "I thought you would be. Now pan out and give me a search of this area". Will pointed to a road.

With a few clicks on the keyboard Seri had a wide-angle view of the area on screen. "Ok, now follow Rt. 5 out toward town" Will said.

Seri did as she was told. "Ah! Ahh! Right there. Zoom into this". Will looked up at Crenshaw who was looking over their shoulders. "I told you. Look at this!".

On screen was a close up of Rt. 5. On the road you could plainly see a fast-moving convoy of Federal vehicles.

"Just as I told you. They're onto us and moving in fast" Will said.

Crenshaw got nervous and turned to Kaiden "Get the men ready. Go to phase 2 of our plan, hurry". Kaiden gave a curt "Yes sir" and left.

Will smiled at Crenshaw and said "Don't worry, don't worry. Then he turned to another one of his colleagues and said "This is where you come in John. Sit at your console". John obeyed and sat down. "Now I want you to lock B1 in on the convoy and also I want you to plug in these sets of coordinates for the other spears". Will placed a piece of paper in front of him. "Then I want you to transfer control to the remote laptop". John looked at Will and hesitated. All the other technicians and the Patriots were looking at him.

Ramsey had this all planned out in advance. He had intended on doing it with Will's help but when they all got arrested it foiled the plan.

"John, you're the only one who can do this" Will said. "and yes, you will probably lose your job if you do. But John..." Will looked him in the eyes. "That would be far better than losing your life now, wouldn't it?". Will turned and addressed all the technicians standing behind him. "Someone here was responsible for my arrest. Did you know they were going to execute me today? You had no problem ratting me out and literally sending me to the gallows, so I'm not in a very good mood. If I positively knew which one of you did it, I'd shoot you right now". Will pulled a pistol out and held it pointed at John. "So, I won't have any problem at all putting a bullet in you John. Get the picture?".

John no longer hesitated and got busy typing on the keyboards, quickly tapping out a succession of numbers and letters. The screen in front of him jumped and a picture of the same road the Feds were on came up, John zeroed in on the group of vehicles racing towards them. A 'zero' with cross hairs in the center appeared on the screen and the center of the cross locked on and started to follow the lead vehicle in the Feds convoy.

The RF-4B1 flying somewhere above them turned. John let out a sigh and hit the last key in the sequence. One of the Sky Hawke missiles attached to the side of the drone released and dropped off. Three feet away from the bird its engine ignited, and the missile shot away with a hiss.

"John?" Will said giving him a look that conveyed expectation.

"John looked at Will and then back down at the keyboard and tapped More keys. That combination transferred control of the drone to a brief case computer, essentially a laptop, sitting in a black case next to his desk.

"How far are they from us?" Crenshaw asked.

"About five miles" John answered.

"Watch this" Will said to Crenshaw.

"John, put it up on the main screen". All eyes went to a large screen on the wall showing an amazingly sharp close-up view of six Federal Humvees barreling down the road. Each truck had a man in the turret holding onto a machinegun looking like they were ready to destroy. All of the vehicles were filled to capacity with men eager to do battle. None of the Patriots knew it but General Gutierrez was sitting in the lead Humvee edging them on. It showed in his face. He was itching to get back at the people responsible for ruining his career- so he personally led the attack.

Thirty seconds later, just as the lead vehicle entered an intersection, the missile hit between the first and second Humvee. Instantly the first three vehicles disappeared in a massive fireball that suddenly appeared on screen. A huge fireball rose, and the ensuing cloud of smoke, dust and debris engulfed the intersection. Even with its forward momentum the fourth Humvee flipped over backwards and was blown into the air. The two vehicles behind them were smashed with flying debris as they attempted to steer left and right. One of them turned and smashed into a telephone pole. It was an awesome display of firepower. Even the Patriots heard the blast and felt the reverberation of a major explosion from where they stood.

Crenshaw's eyes bugged out as he watched. More than satisfied with the results, he didn't need to see anymore. "Ok people…" he said to the technicians and administration personnel. "Everyone outside on the double. I want this building cleared".

As the Patriots escorted the prisoners outside under guard, others on their team came in and placed four jerry cans filled with gasoline on the floor of the computer room. They didn't open them up and splash them around, they just left them there.

On the radio, Crenshaw got a response from Profit. "We can take the two Humvees they got here and use them for transport. We're moving them now".

Crenshaw spoke into the radio "Finish removing anything of value, deposit our gifts and clear the building". Then he turned to the Patriots standing around him "Make sure everyone's out of the building. Let's go people!".

Outside, and under guard, a group of fifteen drone technicians and administrators formed in the corner of the parking lot. After all the preparations were completed and all vehicles and personnel were accounted for, Crenshaw jogged out to the prisoners who huddled together with intense concern about what fate had in store for them.

"Ok, listen up! These people- your boss, do not deserve your loyalty. They are responsible for forcing you to work for the detriment of you, your family, your neighbors, and your country. They will believe that you helped us and used this technology against them. Believe me, they will not be treating you kindly after this. You all know that this technology is being used against your fellow Americans. I implore you not to participate. If you want to get out from under the heels of these tyrants, then come with us. You are welcome to join us. Please climb aboard that truck or in the Humvee's. Otherwise, you are free to go. Those that do not come with us I want you to turn around right now and start running or walking real fast in that direction". Crenshaw pointed down the street away from the building. "Don't stop or go back into the building, It's going to blow in about ten minutes". Six of the group climbed into the Patriots vehicles. John, with his briefcase, was forced to go with Crenshaw. The rest started moving down the street as fast as each could go.

Profit and his crew had finished their part of the mission. They got the prisoners out, confiscated a few items that they deemed valuable and left four jerry cans filled with gasoline in the bays. It was Profits idea to take the Feds Humvees and add them to the Patriots growing convoy. To see them sitting there with all that 50-cal ammunition and have it destroyed was just unthinkable. When they were done, they joined their fellow Patriots out front, loaded up some people, and the entire attack force took off out of the parking lot heading west on Rt. 5.

A few minutes down the road the convoy slowed down at an intersection and allowed a string of trucks to enter their procession from a side road. It was Ciera. She led the 'main body' of the group and merged with them in turn. Ciera in her Humvee, with the SUV, the gasoline tanker, the semitruck and the shuttle bus tucked themselves into the center of the convoy. They left the prison bus behind believing it to be unnecessary for their needs.

Will was in the back seat of Crenshaw's Humvee with an added guest- John the drone technician. He was sitting sandwiched between Will and Ramsey with the computer on his lap, the display was flipped up. You could tell it was on because it cast a weird light over the men staring at the screen. Everyone in the Humvee except for Kaiden who was driving, turned their attention to John.

"Ok John, I gave you the three coordinates" Will said. John knew what was expected of him. Will made it clear that this is the only reason he remained alive. Amicably, he went to work on the commands. When he was done, he hit the last key in the sequence and looked up. "Ok, it's set" he told Will.

They all waited. Forty-five seconds later a bright flash of light and the roar of an explosion rose up behind them. It would have been spectacular if they all could have seen it. The Sky Bird building was hit with a missile that blew it to smithereens. The blast triggered secondary explosions that were almost as powerful as the missile. It leveled the place and ignited a fireball positively due in part to the gasoline they had left in key areas. All of it in an effort to assure the complete destruction of the building and to keep the technology out of the hands of the Feds. Their whole drone program had been wiped out in an instant and by their own technology no less.

The fire that ensued engulfed what was left of the building. Crenshaw wanted to see it for himself, so John passed the laptop to him. "Woh!" Crenshaw said although he couldn't see much through the smoke. "Ok. I don't believe we will have to go back and finish it. Mission accomplished". Crenshaw looked at Ramsey in the back seat and nodded his head "Good job guys" he said.

As a condition for Will's contribution to the mission, Will asked for and got permission to name one of their targets. The next set of coordinates on the list he gave John was a special request.

The Sky Bird program built MVC (missile vision capability) into its Sky Hawk missiles. That's simply 'video technology' installed in the cone of the missile. John turned the laptop so they all could see.

As it flew, from the missiles point of view; It saw the forest at the outskirts of the town of Oneida and the image followed the contour of the land heading for a set of buildings in the distance. It flew over the rolling hills of the University's campus and immediately after that, the sport stadium came into view. The image coming from the missile focused on it. When it got close, it rose up overhead, refined its search and zeroed in on the gallows at one end of the field. Then it steered right toward it until the wooden structure got bigger and bigger. When the picture went out, the missile struck and blew up the gallows and everything around it with an awe-inspiring display of firepower. No telling how much collateral damage had been inflicted. Switching to an arial view from B1, John showed the whole stadium filling up with smoke like a cereal bowl filling up with chocolate milk.

Next, Sky Bird RF-B1 turned west and focused its attention on Syracuse. It flew for ten minutes until it was within range and then settled on its final flightpath over the city. Pictures of the Federal Hacia building appeared on screen and the bird zoomed in on the grounds that surrounded it. Will and Ramsey were amazed at the clear details the drone was able to pick up.

"I wish I could tell which one of those outlying buildings was for ammo storage" Will mentioned. "I'd prefer to hit that".

Ramsey said "This will do might nice" while pointing his finger at a spot on the screen. "Put it on that, right there".

There was no doubt about what the four round 60,000-gallon tanks were for when Ramsey saw them on the laptop's screen. It was a logical choice. They watched in real time as the missile hit one and were jubilant when John switched to the B1's arial view which captured the explosion. The gasoline tank shook and shuttered and then blew to high heaven with a huge bright expansion of fire that encompassed the tanks sitting next to it. One set off another as three more immensely powerful secondary explosions rocked the area one by one. Even the bird, as high above the explosion as it was, shook from the resultant shock wave. A huge fireball rose into the sky unlike anything anyone had ever seen, even in the movies. It looked like a volcano blew its top. The explosion blew off the entire side of the eight story Hacia building along with others in the area for miles around. The blast and the heat were so intense that it set the rest of the buildings on fire even though they must have been a couple hundred yards away. In the parking lot, overturned trucks and scattered ammunition burned and exploded continuously for over two hours afterward. The ammo storage building eventually caught fire too, it blew up seven minutes later. That was a spectacular secondary explosion in and of itself. People in the surrounding area and the ones who survived thought that the place was under continuous attack long after the initial blast. Later, news reports said that a band of over fifty militia members attacked the building for hours and killed hundreds of Federal employees including women and children. "All of the militia scum were killed in the ensuing battle" or so the report said.

News reports were not verified so the Patriots didn't know how to feel about the death toll. But the physical results were more than the Patriots could have wished for. Two main targets for the price of one not to mention the burning Humvees and all the Federal vehicles and equipment that were now out of commission.

Even with their success, the tough part of this war still loomed ahead of the band of rebels. The burning question: How many people are going to have to pay with their lives for this regimes greedy quest for power.

* * *

From Rt. 5 Kaiden followed Ramsey's directions which led the ever-increasing number of vehicles in the convoy away from Oneida. The guy knew the area well. They drove hard to get themselves far away from the possibility of being discovered by roaming helicopters that probably would be dispatched rather quickly. Betsy Stoiber's Humvee hung back as a rear guard and made sure no one was following. Turning south they drove up to the town of Lenox and took Creek Road south just before entering the town, thus hoping to avoid as many prying eyes as possible. When they hit Peterboro Rd. they jot over to Stockbridge Falls Rd. and continued south on that to avoid going through the town of Peterboro. That slowed them down, but it felt a whole lot safer. They drove for hours making multiple turns on back country roads doing their best to avoid the well-traveled ones. Darkness started to descend yet they drove on.

At times, Crenshaw designated one of the Humvee's as a scout. It drove ahead of the convoy and stopped them more than a few times to play cat and mouse with various groups of people or vehicles that they encountered. All in an effort to avoid being seen. The convoy finally turned south on East River Road and after a stretch, arrived at their destination well into the night around eleven o'clock. Ramsey had brought them to a farm just a way's outside of Morris N.Y. It was a farm that belonged to a good friend of his. Just how good of a friend he was about to find out.

The owners name was Jester Mann. Ramsey and Jester had served together in one of America's many conflicts. Ramsey didn't elaborate, he just said "The war". He chose the Mann's place because Jester was an old-time buddy, but it was mainly due to the characteristics of the guy's property. They needed to hide, and Jesters farm was able to swallow up the convoy underneath a canopy of trees that lined his quarter mile long driveway.

Ramsey was counting on getting his friends cooperation. No one had gotten much sleep recently and everyone needed a safe place to lay low and rest. After the other members of the Patriots crew heard details about what transpired; the destruction of the Feds drone program, as well as the annihilation of the Feds main base at Hacia, they all felt they could now relax a little more without the intense fear of being hunted although the fear of being discovered would never subside. For now, they were far enough away and were confident enough that the Feds no longer held the advantage or could use the degree of technology they once had that could easily locate them.

The farm was in a remote area with a detached barn and a long driveway up to the guys property through a canopy of foliage that hid the vehicles well. Crenshaw had them park under cover and both Ramsey and Crenshaw used the SUV to drive the rest of the way up to the farmhouse. Before he met with the owners Crenshaw took off the Feds uniform and changed back into his camo's, he felt it would look less intimidating. Luckily the owner was home, but they had to wake him up with some rather loud persistent banging on the front door. It was completely understandable when Mr. Mann opened it with a shotgun in his hands. After the shock of seeing an old friend and consequently being rudely disturbed in the middle of the night, Jester Mann and his wife Shelly greeted them warmly. Ramsey called him "Jess" and they gave each other a hug attesting to the fact that they were old friends. After introductions, Ramsey and Crenshaw were invited into the kitchen where the Mrs. offered to make some tea.

"I'm glad to see you, it's been a while" Jess told Ramsey. "Not a big surprise though, I heard there are a lot of people around these parts getting visitors. We've seen strangers roaming around. It's been reported that people are fleeing the cities to get away from the chaos. I just didn't think it'd be you who'd show up on my doorstep".

"These certainly are rough times my friend, let me tell you just how rough..." Ramsey began a story that divulged details about what he had been through for the last eight or nine months. Crenshaw felt sorry for him after hearing how he had lost his family and everything he owned after the Feds raided his home.

Although Jess and his wife were happy to see Ramsey, at first, a frown formed on the man's face as Ramsey's story unfolded. Crenshaw jumped in and helped with some background on what was going on out there as well as giving a further explanation of some of his own experiences. It was all news to the Mann's. They didn't have a clue, all they had was rumors since reliable news was not trickling down anymore after the collapse. Some would say even long before the collapse. After that, Shelly wasn't very pleased to hear about their newly acquired friends, her demeanor showed it.

"So, I've got a small army parked in my driveway" Jess said with raised eyebrows. "One that's on the run too".

"Yeah, I'm sorry to bring this to your doorstep Jess. Sure, I had other places I could have gone but nowhere that would hide us like your place. It's the only place I could think of going. Can you help us out?".

Jess glanced at his wife, then at Crenshaw, then back at Ramsey. "I heard your tale, now I want to hear it from you Mr. Crenshaw or 'Captain' Crenshaw as it turns out. I want to hear why you and your militia are fighting and what you are fighting for".

"Fair enough. You have the right to know. At present we are fighting for our lives. As far as purpose? I believe in the Constitution of the United States of America as written. I will uphold, defend and fight to keep power in the hands of the people and to preserve our authority over the government. These Progressives have just executed a coup against 'We the People'. Right now, we have lost control of our sovereign rights. If we allow it, we'd be giving it up to a minority of authoritarians who want the fruit of this land for themselves. If we let them, the new regime will become our ruler, 'the state' will become the new aristocrat. They couldn't re-set our system by convincing enough voters, so they had to force the issue and back it up with force and the threat of violence. They want us to sit down and shut up. I'm going to stand. 'I' will not go quietly and let this happen".

"Well put. But I've heard that the Progressives are for many of the same rights and privileges that I believe you are touting Captain Crenshaw. They say that 'they' are the ones fighting for the constitution" Jess said flatly.

"Yes. Mr. Mann, some of the old school 'are' fighting for the constitution. At least that's what they claim, I don't believe it's reflected in the way they vote and certainly not in the way they act. If you voted for the Democrats who are in lock step with the Progressive party, then you voted for socialism and gave the green light to a Communist/Marxist style of government. You voted for what's happening here today. Did you know that the Russian Constitution guarantees their people many of the same rights and privileges that our constitution does? Only they have one clause added to theirs that makes all the difference in the world. I am paraphrasing but here's the idea. They list items like: You are free to pursue a living. Free to profit from the sale of goods. You have freedom of speech. Free health care. Free education and free elections. It all sounds great. But the last paragraph says 'You are free to do as you please as long as it does not infringe on the desires of the collective'. Due to that clause and to rid himself of people who didn't do as 'he pleased', Stalin killed 20 to 30 million people he labeled as "the opposition". Their crime was simply- 'Opposition to the Communist party'. So much for free speech. I can give you many more examples of this same phenomenon occurring around the world wherever socialism/communism appears and that's exactly what these people are doing here. They talk the talk but, in the end, you will be under complete State control. My point is that many people will claim they are fighting for the constitution and for the 'worker', what they don't tell you or can't tell you is what version they are advocating for".

"I can back that up" Ramsey said. They tried to silence me and were going to kill me, just for speaking out against the program. I can tell you they do not believe in freedom of speech and obviously they don't believe in the second amendment either. With that evidence, it's plain to see that they don't believe in the constitution as written no matter what they try to tell you".

"Yes, now tell me Jess, how free are the Russian people when you can lose your life for speaking out? And now, how free are we?" Crenshaw continued. "This socialist utopia that these people are forcing on us always ends up with an authoritarian rule that benefits the few, the elite and they tap into the middle class to pay for it. It always, and I mean always, ends up failing due to a very flawed system of ideas. It is quite the opposite of the America that I want my kids to grow up in".

"That's an amazing story". Jess paused to consider it. "Ok, Captain Crenshaw. I see where you're coming from. Since you have proven yourself to Ramsey and have elicited his support, or else he wouldn't have brought you here, I choose to believe you. I can support your vision or should I say your 'version'. I didn't know exactly what was going on out there so thanks for bringing me this information. I can make more informed decisions and it gives me reason to re-consider my stance. This has become a whole lot more serious than I thought. I'm shocked at what I hear, and I don't know what to do about this. Our officials in Oneonta have locked the entire city down due to the crisis. No one can move. They have roadblocks on the main road going into town and they are manned with people carrying guns. It's like Nazi Germany out there. They've taken over to the point where no one can continue doing business. They've committed home invasions to grab guns and I hear they've robbed and killed people".

"Who?" Crenshaw asked.

"The Oneonta Citizens Brigade" Jess said. "We got 'this' in our mailbox about five days ago. Shelly, bring me the notice, it's sitting on my desk". Shelly brought over a document and placed it in front of him. Jess glanced at it with a serious look on his face, shook his head, and then slid it over to Crenshaw so he could read it himself. Crenshaw looked at it and then started to read it out loud.

OFFICIAL NOTICE From:
COUNCIL of THE CITY of ONEONTA

To address the current monetary crisis facing America and to repair the collapse of the Dollar, the Council for the City of Oneonta has mandated that all businesses close (with a few exceptions as noted). The Council will re-open these stores and play a major role in assisting in the process of distributing food and grocery items in stores associated with these essential products.

To distribute food equally and to maintain crowd discipline, our newly formed 'Citizens Brigade' will assist the police in maintaining law and order. You are hereby required to obey their commands and adhere to all local regulations. Protesters and troublemakers will be delt with harshly.

Unless otherwise authorized and directed by the Council- Every citizen is required to stay at home until we can re-set and implement a new system of digital monetary exchange to replace the dollar. The new system will commence when the internet comes back on line. Currency, as it has been known, is no longer valid. The 'dollar' will no longer be accepted as a medium of exchange. You are hereby warned that using gold and silver for purchases is prohibited by the new government. Oneonta will allow private bartering and exchange for gold or silver with a City permit only, except for emergency government transactions. Persons violating this rule will be punished with fines, jail time or both.

City hall is now open. The Council will be accepting applications and assigning jobs to people who apply. Jobs will be given to those most suited for the required work. During this transition, work effort will be rewarded with City stamps or government stamps. These stamps can be used to purchase food at Council run grocery stores. Stamps for work or food products will be issued as compensation. Amounts will be determined by the Council.

TO MAINTAIN ORDER, EVERY CITIZEN IS OBLIGATED TO FOLLOW THESE RULES:

1. Obey all commands given by City officials, the Police, and the Citizens Brigade.
2. Do not congregate in groups of more than five people unless it is with immediate family members.
3. Churches are hereby closed until further notice.
4. Public gatherings will be dispersed by Brigade officers and fines imposed.
5. Essential food producers, farmers, and the like, will contribute a minimum of forty (40) percent of production to the City run grocery stores to maintain an adequate supply of food for all citizens.
6. When asked, citizens will volunteer and contribute various needed items to the community for the good of the community.
7. If deemed appropriate, unused land will be re-allocated and given to people who can produce for the greater good.
8. Every owner must volunteer to hand in all firearms and associated items to our police or a Citizens Brigade member.

9. Earn stamps by reporting transgressions of these rules to your City Council representative, the Police, or a Brigade member.
10. Taxes are still in effect and will be collected by the City Council. Taxes are a government transaction and therefore can be paid with gold or silver in an amount determined by the Council.

Thank you for your cooperation. With your help we will all be able to get through this crisis and back to normal in a safe, timely manner.

Signed
Marvin William Shaw
Chairman of the Council of the City of Oneonta

"There it is". Crenshaw pushed the document away and sat back in his chair. "Socialist medicine laid out as a cure for the crisis".

"I don't know how else to fight this" Jess said. "All I can do is to offer what little I can. You have my support. I'll let you use the barn if that helps. There's a pot belly stove in there, I'm sure you can figure out how to use it. It'll allow you to cook meals if you need to. There's also a stack of horse blankets in there that are perfectly good to use for bedding. They'll keep you off the ground at least. You might need it. Nights are still cool around here. How long do you plan on staying?".

"We're just passing through. A day or two at the most to rest and organize. But before we get off the subject, Mr. Mann, I would like to hear from you too. What's your position on this?".

"I'm a Democrat. I've always voted Democrat, but I never thought the party would go to this extreme. I can't call them Democrats anymore. I would like to continue being a Democrat, but I want to work within the system, not against it. I'm not a socialist so I can't call myself a Democrat anymore. The party has evolved into something that I do not recognize. It's not the party I signed up with. This is something far different".

"Understood" Crenshaw told him.

Then Jess said something unexpected. "I prayed hard for the lord to guide me and tell me what to do. I didn't know what I was going to do if they came here to my farm and tried to take my shotgun and 40 percent of everything I have worked so hard for. My gut reaction is to fight, but what am I going to do by myself? Us farmers out here ain't enough, we're spread out to thin. We would need several of us to get together to form any kind of an effective defense. I've talked to some of my neighbors, and they say they're with me. They 'say' they want to fight this. It sounds sincere but I just don't know how far they are willing to go or if they really have it in them. If it comes to a real fight and there's the smell of gun powder in the air… I have to be honest with you, I don't even know if I have it in me. When the possibility of dying becomes real… it changes everything.

I prayed to God to send someone to help… and then you guys showed up. It's a sign. With you and your army we could fight back and actually make a difference…".

"Wait a minute Jess, I don't know if we were sent here by God, but I do know that we can't get involved in a battle with the City of Oneonta" Crenshaw said.

"Captain, the way I'm seeing it, you're our only hope. You got a cohesive unit, and we don't have the fire power. You've got guns. There are many others who would join us if we just showed some solidarity and some resolve".

"Jess, I've got to get my guys home. To a safe spot. That's my mission. I can't do that while continually fighting a war, even with what we've got. We'll be moving on as soon as we can. Thank you for use of your barn and mam, thank you for the tea". Crenshaw stood up, shook hands with Jess and said "I've got to get going. I'm beat, got to find somewhere to lie down and get some sleep. Thank you for allowing us to stay. It's great to meet a fellow Patriot". They shook hands.

"You're welcome, Captain, but I ask you. Where is there a safe place in all of this?".

Crenshaw looked at Jess and raised his eyebrows. "You got a point" is all he said before leaving.

That night it got down to 52 degrees. Everyone sought refuge in one of the vehicles or the barn with the exception of the Patriots who got stuck on guard duty. The shuttle bus with its bench seats was a coveted spot for sleeping. Throughout the night you could hear the occasional startup of an engine as someone tried to crank up the heat. Some people slept soundly, for others it was difficult and for more reasons than just the cool weather. Recent events banged on the conscience of people who assigned a high level of significance to what they had just been through, those had trouble sleeping, and they were the first ones up early the next morning. For them it was useless to lie there, awake... thinking about what's in store for them now. They tried to take their minds off it by busying themselves with gathering wood for a fire or fetching water. Somehow, someone made hot coffee although there was a shortage of cups from which to drink it.

Kaiden, who was normally an early riser, slept past nine. And no one dared wake Crenshaw who was perfectly content sleeping in the barn with one of those horse blankets under him and one pulled over him. About ten other people lined the floor of the barn all around a pot belly stove which they kept burning all night. Heat radiating from it was the driving factor behind their extended slumber. No one wanted to get up and venture out.

Ciera had taken a seat on the bus and slept somewhat, but not really. Crenshaw had drilled it in her that she was responsible for the bus, so she took it seriously and found it hard to leave it. All the Patriots and even some of the new recruits slept with their rifles by their side. Many also made sure there were extra loaded magazines close at hand too. It was a sign of how bad things had gotten.

15

ONE FOR YOU, TWO FOR ME

As the next morning progressed, slowly there was more and more movement around the Patriots encampment. Everyone awoke to witness the expanded number of members in their group. One by one another who couldn't sleep got up and added themselves to the growing number of people who stood around one of the smoking campfires that sprang up along the side of the Mann's driveway. Hands were either shoved into pockets or their palms were held out to the fire to feel its warmth to offset the cool morning air. Dawn broke and their surroundings became clearer in the light. It was evident that grey skies would rule the day. A misty fog hung around and floated on the farmers' fields making it hard to see clearly in the distance.

Now Crenshaw was up. Right out of the box his thoughts were occupied with how to integrate the new recruits and how to proceed from here. "*It seems we're picking up recruits wherever we go. This merry band of rebels is growing*" Crenshaw thought. "*We're almost at Company strength now*". How to handle them without losing sight of their mission was a concern. He walked out of the barn and strolled down the driveway taking the time to talk to each person or group of people he encountered. Each time encountering another story told with wild hand gestures that described the previous day's escapade. Conversation batted around the possible future of their newly formed coalition and what the plan might be from here on out. Crenshaw had no real answer at this point. 'Where do we go from here?' was the question on everyone's mind.

"From here on out maybe we can ditch the Federal uniforms and wear our own" Crenshaw offered. "I can't stand this ruse. I want to stand as Pioneer Patriots" he told a group standing next to a campfire.

Eventually Crenshaw got around to talking with the two techie's, John and Will. Otherwise known as "The drone guys".

"Ok, now I've got to decide what to do with you two. You did great and were superb in your roll yesterday. Will, I thank you for your effort, your warning. Your actions saved us". Then he turned to John. "John, I thank you for your effort too even though it was coerced. You saved all our lives, I hope not 'inadvertently' as far as you're concerned. I'm not going to ask you for your opinion yet because I don't think you've heard the full story about our group. After you do, we'll talk. Sorry for having to kidnap you, but I'm afraid I can't let you go just yet. I wouldn't advise leaving either, the Feds will think you helped us, and they won't take kindly to that. I believe you're safer with us than going alone out there. I promise, I will let you go, it's just that I'm hoping you'll join us.

You guys aren't going to be able to use your skills in the drone department anymore so I don't know in what capacity you would serve, that would have to be determined. Oh, and by the way, I never asked you John. I thought about this last night. What happened to the drone after it fired the last of its missiles?".

"Well, both drones, there were two of them, would have continued on the last programed flight path and would have flown until they ran out of power and crashed. I would guess somewhere around 75 to 125 miles out with the power they had, that would depend on how much energy the solar panels were able to generate before dark.

Captain, you didn't ask but you're going to get my opinion anyway. I'm not happy about losing my job especially in an attack where people lost their lives. I think you're a son of a bitch for attacking like you did. Don't think it was necessary. All those lives and technology… wasted. It's a shame is all I have to say".

"Ok, I understand how you feel. We ripped your job right out from underneath you. I'd be pissed too. As pissed as I was when the Feds ripped my job right out from underneath me.

Crenshaw explained himself; "After I graduated High School I went into the military, saw some combat. I did my time, got out and tried to get a job as a policeman. Long story short, departments had been defunded and the new Social Service groups like the CAF (Citizens Action Force) were formed to replace them. I call them modern day 'SS troops' because they are essentially left-wing fascist extremist sympathizers posing as social workers. It seems like every towns got one of these groups now. Mr. Mann said they got one in Oneonta called "The Citizens Brigade". Anyway, it was a bad time to try and join the force, every effort was made to make a career on the force as unattractive as possible to new recruits. They purged the existing roster of patriotic conservatives by cutting their pay which got them to quit all on their own. They changed the law and made it so that if an officer made a mistake in the line of duty, they could be sued and convicted in court. It would cost a ton of money in lawyer's fees just to fight it. There went the incentive to be a cop. There's been an all-out war against the police, a concerted effort to transform departments into something that would better serve the Progressive Socialist agenda.

Groups like the CAF were being funded and empowered by left wing politicians. They didn't want ex-military in their ranks either. The job market turned against me, at least in the things that I was good at. When all the shit started to get crazy the Patriots brought me in and I ended up back with the Academy. John, the Feds took jobs away from all of us" Crenshaw waved his hands in the direction of the other Patriots.

With that Crenshaw moved on down the line and got into a conversation with Ramsey and the 'Boys From Oneida'. Some of them were standing around one of the Humvee's and were already in the middle of an intense conversation amongst themselves. Crenshaw felt it important to establish right up front who was who and whether they would be joining the Patriots. That would determine how much he had to explain. Still, he gave them his best sales pitch to bring them on board.

"Gentlemen, this is going to be your best chance at joining a well-regulated and well supplied militia in which you will have the opportunity to participate in the fight against the people who have destroyed your home, your family, and your livelihoods.

Yes, we are a militia. The word and the idea of a 'militia' has inherited a negative connotation perpetrated and perpetuated by the anti-gun, anti-patriot movement. The word militia means 'An armed force comprised of conscripted citizens needed to serve and protect in a time of emergency'. Specifically necessary for when the police or National Guard cannot, it is then the duty of the militia to step up and form our last line of defense of our property and our families.

There has been a steady campaign by the left to demonize the concept of a 'militia'. They strive to obscure the idea that you, citizens, have the right to defend yourself. They endeavor to inhibit us from fighting against a tyranny they say will never come. Isn't that ironic because- here it is.

I consider self-defense a most basic right. The right to protect your family, the right to life. So did the creators of this amazing country. They saw it as such an important tool of personal survival that they stated it 'in no uncertain terms' in our constitution- "The right of the people to keep and bear arms shall not be infringed". What part of that is unclear?

Ah, but I digress into one of my rants. I'm asking you to join our militia with one stipulation and it's a major one. If you decide to join you must accept my authority over your actions. This is a military organization, and you must pledge that you will follow my orders.

This is paramount. I will accept nothing other than strict compliance. It can be no other way. Ramsey, if you would join us, you'd be given the honorary rank of sergeant. It will become legitimate when we can officially induct you into the organization. You all did great yesterday; we'd love to have your support in this fight. We sure do need you.

"Where're we going Captain?" Merrill asked.

"I decided on sticking around here for a few days so we can all get some well-deserved rest. Rest without someone chasing us for a change. It's a nice feeling. We'll move out in a couple of days. I can't tell you where we're going just yet. I ask you to trust me. Can I get your commitment?".

"We were just talking about that sir, and we came to the conclusion that if we can man this here Humvee that we took from the compound then we're all onboard" Merrill said.

Crenshaw smiled "Can you operate that 50?".

"Hell, yes sir!" Ramsey exclaimed.

"Then yes, I think we can arrange that".

"Then I can speak for all the Boys From Oneida. We're with you one hundred percent sir". Ramsey said and gave Crenshaw a crisp military salute. The rest of the boys came to attention and gave a salute of their own exclaiming "Sir!" as they did.

"That's great to hear" Crenshaw gave a quick return salute. "Then I welcome you all as members of the Pioneer Patriot organization. Consider it official, but of course the paperwork will be a little late in coming gentlemen". A chuckle came from the men. "Ramsey, I want you to get together with Ciera. She'll answer any questions and can give you more details about our organization. Merrill, may I speak with you for a moment.".

"Yes sir" Merrill said. Crenshaw took him to the side.

"Listen I'm going to come right out and say it. You might have a little trouble fitting in at first".

"I noticed" Merrill agreed.

"I don't think some of the boys are going to warm up easily to a black man. I mean, a black man who's loyalties are unknown and one that might hold a less than favorable view of his fellow white compatriots. This goes both ways, Merrill. That would be an underlying suspicion and a fair question. Now me, I preach 'Martin Luther King's ideology'. I take ones character as the overriding factor above all else, not the color of his skin. But I have seen and heard about a lot of racism and violence coming from the black community in recent years and so have some of the men. I've heard stories. Hell, I have a story of my own. So, I'm going to need to know where you stand".

"I am here because of what you said on the bus. That you are protectors of the Constitution as written. I want to be a part of that. Any group supporting and seeking to maintain our God given rights is on my side and I'm on theirs. Yeah, there's hate going around these days, but I don't see it as a color issue. Hate is flying every which way. My neighborhood was attacked, and my family was threatened by a crowd made up of both white and black. I'm not proud of it, but we shot both without prejudice. Throughout this whole thing, what I'm mostly mad about is that people have come to believe in stereotypes. Just because of the color of my skin they think I'm a democrat that lives in the ghetto or that I side with Black Lives Matter and that I blindly vote for progressive ideas. Sir there's a lot of us who do not adhere to that philosophy. I'll do my best to establish that for anyone who needs proof".

"Good. Yes, I would advise that you get that message out. It would go a long way in making you a respected part of this group".

"Sir, with all due respect. In a military organization there is no room for prejudice. We all must become one with everyone fighting for the man next to him without discrimination. I suggest that 'you' get 'that' message out".

"Point well taken, Merrill. I'll do that".

After clearing the air, Crenshaw walked on. Passing the shuttle bus, he heard radio squawk coming from the open door. Peeking in, he was surprised to see Ciera sitting in the driver's seat monitoring the CB radio.

"Good morning, sir" she said.

"Good morning".

"They're talking about us".

"Who?" Crenshaw asked.

"The Feds. A non-descript statement came across identifying a problem in Syracuse. Some of their patrols are being recalled".

"They're in defensive mode. That's good to know. For today at least, we can relax" Crenshaw said.

The day went like that. Nothing much to do but lots to talk about. It gave them all a chance to catch their breath. That night they rejoiced around a huge bon fire around which everyone seemed to be celebrating the fact that they were alive. The Mann's butchered a pig and roasted it over the fire to everyone's delight. For the first time in a long time... at least for a precious moment... life had some semblance of a celebratory nature.

* * *

An hour after dawn the next day, the morning progressed as it had the day before for Casey Brown. Over on the 55-acre farm adjacent to the Mann's farm, their neighbor, Casey Brown was done with the morning chores. He was looking forward to coffee and a hot breakfast and it showed in his quick step as he walked from the barn to the farmhouse front porch. Before entering the house, he caught sight of a line of moving cars in the distance. Pausing, he studied them. Six or seven vehicles kicked up dust along his dirt driveway at a speed that angered him. High speeds on a dirt road contribute to the formation of ripples and pot holes that form in the dirt due to spin and wheel chatter. Ripples made his truck shake violently when he drove across them, it was a maintenance problem he addressed occasionally by dragging an old 6' by 8' metal blasting mat behind his truck. That had the effect of scraping the driveway smooth again after he drove the mat up and down it a few times. It did a great job of erasing the ripples and helped to fill in pot holes.

The incoming fleet of vehicles, composed of a surprisingly large number of cars and trucks, continued up the lane towards his farmhouse. Now Casey could see that one of the trucks was a cattle transport rig the likes of which he himself used to take his pigs to a buyer's market or to the slaughter house. He walked up to the front door and yelled for his wife, then went out to stand on the porch steps to greet them. When the line of vehicles pulled up, each one parked haphazardly between the farmhouse and the barn in no particular order. The cattle transport truck continued and parked in front of the barn. The number of people who got out was alarming, the Brown's hardly ever got visitors out here and suddenly there was a crowd in their front yard. When his wife saw them from a second story window, she frowned. Then she gasped when she saw the guns. Instantly nervous, she yelled to their son who was somewhere in the house. "Charlie! Get in here now!". When the boy heard that tone in her voice, he recognized it as something he'd better not ignore.

A group of five young men exited the first vehicle that parked closest to the front of the farmhouse. Cautiously, they scanned the place for any sign of trouble. Each of them pulled out a rifle or a shotgun from the car and held it at the ready. More men got out of the other vehicles and mingled around, some with weapons, some without. The ones without started walking toward the barn. The five with weapons hooked up with an older man dressed in a police uniform and escorted him up to the porch steps. The difference in age between the policeman and his followers was obvious. Casey Brown stood on the porch waiting.

"Are you Mr. Brown?" the policeman asked as he walked up. Without waiting for an answer, he shuffled up the porch steps and held out his hand. "I'm Officer Kent, I'm in charge of this unit of the Oneonta Citizens Brigade".

Casey didn't offer him his hand. He sensed something was wrong, so he just said "Yeah I'm Casey Brown, what do ya want?".

"I was hoping to get a warmer welcome than that, Mr. Brown. We're tasked with coming out here, meeting the farmers in the area and carrying out the peoples work. We can do it the cordial way, or we can get right to it...".

"Mr. Kent... those weapons kind of take the 'cordial way' right out of it don't ya think?

Kent looked down at the ground and chuckled, then looked back up. "Yeah, I guess so. Well okay, then we'll get right to it. On behalf of the City Counsel, we are here to collect. I'm sure you got the notice". He nodded at his men and told them "Boys, go check the house". Then he shouted out to his guy's standing in the driveway "Brian! Go manage the stock!".

The men standing behind Kent walked up the porch steps and strolled past Mr. Brown not waiting for an invitation to enter the house. One of them stopped and stood in front of the farmer with his rifle at the ready. The other three went inside. It looked like they'd done this before and knew exactly what to do.

"Now wait a minute!" Casey exclaimed. "Where the hell do you think you're going?".

Casey started for the door, but the guy moved in front of him and raised his rifle with his finger on the trigger.

"Now, now Mr. Brown" Kent said. "We just have to go in and make sure there are no guns involved here".

"Isn't that ironic" Casey said with a glance down at the guy's gun. "Why don't you just ask?".

"We've tried that before. It didn't turn out so well...".

Casey turned back to Kent. "So now you just bust right in?".

"Yup, we find it much more efficient this way" Kent said with a smile.

"Sally, we got visitors" Casey yelled over his shoulder to his wife.

Shortly after the men entered the house, voice levels rose, and Sally could be heard telling them exactly what she thought of the intrusion. One of them grabbed her as she yelled "Get out of my house! Don't you touch me you @$#%!". Cursing prevailed and then, there was a scream. Her thoughts instantly focused on concern for her son. The guy's partner forcefully brought the woman out on the porch with no let up on the language coming out of her mouth.

Casey moved toward his distraught wife. The guy standing in front of him raised his rifle as if he was going to shoot him. Casey backed off.

"Casey, this is going to be a lot easier on you and your wife if you cooperate. I don't have the time... would you shut her up please!". The guy holding her arm 'back handed' her across the face. She got all wobbly and sunk to the floor. That ended the cursing, but she turned to Charlie who was now standing in the front doorway behind the screen door watching everything. She yelled "Run Charlie!".

A mad look formed on Casey's face. He moved forcefully toward his wife. "You son of a...!" he yelled just before a rifle butt struck him in the stomach doubling him over. He dropped to the floor in pain. "I can't believe this is happening" Casey mumbled through clenched teeth.

"Run Charlie run!" Sally yelled again at the boy who had not moved. Now Charlie obeyed and scooted past the man in the hallway who attempted to grab him but missed. In an all-out sprint Charlie high tailed it out the back door and into the back field. The man ran after him but stopped at the backdoor plainly not interested in running through the field after the kid.

Kent spoke to Casey who was lying on the floor moaning "You see Casey, we're as serious as a cat on mouse about our mission here so come with me and let's get this over with". Kent started to walk toward the barn. His man picked Casey up off the floor and forced him to follow.

As soon as the sun came up it warmed quickly. The Mann's farm was a great place to lay low and was a perfect hide due to the bloom of spring foliage on the trees. Crenshaw praised the more than adequate canopy of camouflage for their vehicles. More than likely the Feds were looking for them and with that in mind, once again he walked around the camp checking on people and informing them of his plan to move out tomorrow.

Cheer and laughter occasionally floated up from around the camp fire or from one of the groups that formed. It was good to hear. Kaiden and Ciera took advantage of the down time to try a little tenderness which had been impossible during the past week with all the fighting. Yet nothing seemed to be the same. The experience had changed them, it changed them all. The killing… this was serious business. It was like a cloud that you can just barely see through, people tried to hide it and not talk about it, yet it hung around in the back of one's mind without dissipating.

Crenshaw came up to another group huddled around a Humvee when a commotion over by the lead Humvee made them all turn their heads. Kaiden shouted "Captain! Captain!". A man and a woman along with a child were being guided over to where Crenshaw was standing. Crenshaw recognized Jess and Shelly at once although he didn't know who the boy was. "I didn't think they had any kids" he mumbled just before they got to him.

"Hello…" Crenshaw started to say.

Jess cut him off "Captain, we have a problem. This here is Charlie, Charlie Brown from one farm over".

"Charlie Br…" Crenshaw started to say.

"Sir we don't have time for jokes. The Browns are my neighbors". Jess pointed to the south.

"Well, how did the boy get here Jess? He didn't come up the driveway, we would have seen him" Crenshaw asked.

"He ran up the boarder lane between our farms. He says there's a gang of people that just arrived at his house. They're roughing up his parents and demanding payment. They're in the process of taking their pigs".

"Payment? Like what we talked about the other night?" Crenshaw asked.

"Yeah, exactly".

Crenshaw knelt in front of the kid. "Charlie, what happened?".

Charlie was out of breath and visibly shaken. He pointed in the direction of his parents farm. "Trucks came with bad men. They hit my mom and she's crying. They're taking our pigs. My mom told me to run so I ran here".

"You did good Charlie, you did good". Crenshaw stood up and looked at Jess.

"Can you help us?" Jess asked. "They'll probably come here next".

That possibility struck a chord with Crenshaw and all who were listening. It was highly possible. *"I can't let that happen"* Crenshaw thought. *"Damn, above all else we have to avoid being discovered"*. Then out loud he said "Ok, we'll help you, Jess. He turned and looked at Kaiden and the Patriots standing around behind him. They all nodded their heads.

"Okay then" Crenshaw said. "Here's what we're going to do…".

* * *

Crenshaw asked for volunteers, Kaiden and Vic were the first to step up. A plan was hatched that involved driving the SUV over to farmer Browns house with the four of them ditching their Federal uniforms in favor of Cadet camouflage. "I don't want to play our hand with the Feds uniforms" Crenshaw said. "No sense in making this more than it is. Let's find out what's going on first" Crenshaw said. Jess had insisted on going with them, he thought he could help identify his neighbor and mediate a peaceful solution to whatever was going on. Afterall Jess was the one who had to live in this neighborhood with the results of their actions. Kaiden agreed that the goal was to gather information, but they still took precautions.

Kaiden drove the SUV up the Brown's driveway. Crenshaw was in the passenger's seat and Jess and Vic were in the back. They parked next to the first car they came upon. Like bees coming out of a hive, five or six men streamed out of the front door of the farmhouse onto the porch and five or six came from the direction of the barn. Four more were strolling around near their parked cars. They all merged to confront the SUV with weapons drawn.

Before getting out Crenshaw commented "These people are not professionals. They're driving civilian cars, and they didn't even post a guard. Well-armed... with a mish mash of different types of rifles I see, but a civilian force by the looks of it".

"One of them on the porch has a police uniform on" Kaiden advised. "Definitely not military". Kaiden had his captured HK 416 government issue rifle with him, but Crenshaw only had his side arm in a holster at his side. Still, before getting out of the car Crenshaw told Kaiden "Leave your rifle, we don't want to spook them. Vic, stay with the car, keep your eyes peeled for trouble". The three of them jumped out and started forward.

"That's far enough!" someone yelled. It came from the older man in police uniform who had walked out of the house with his men in support. He stood there with confidence and smiled with a tooth pick dangling from the corner of his mouth.

Looking like the man in charge, Crenshaw took a step toward him. The response was quick. All the men standing around the policeman raised their rifles and pointed them menacingly at the three of them.

It was serious for a moment until the guy said "Now what do we have here? And what uniform is that? Who are you and what are you doing here?" the policeman asked.

"I was going to ask you the same thing" Crenshaw said.

"My name's Kent, I'm in charge here and I'll be asking the questions. Why are you driving a Federal vehicle? You're certainly not Federal, and you're not police dressed like that" Kent stated. "You're not allowed to be here. You're interfering with City action. How did you get that car?".

"We killed them and took it" Crenshaw said bluntly. Intentionally trying to rattle the guy. It worked. A serious look formed on the guys face. He took the toothpick out of his mouth and threw it on the ground with a grimace replacing the smile.

Kaiden looked towards the barn. Men were loading pigs onto a ramp that led into their transport truck. "Helping yourself to the live-stock?" Kaiden quipped.

"You killed them?" Kent said brushing off Kaiden's comment. He spoke to one of his men "Get his gun".

Crenshaw took a step back and yelled "No one is taking my gun!"

All of Kent's men tensed up and trained their weapons on Crenshaw. "Wow, and with all these weapons pointed at you. You got balls mister; I'll give you that" Kent said.

Jess broke into the conversation yelling "You're the one with balls 'mister'. Coming in here stealing from farmers. Where's Casey?" Jess yelled loudly in the direction of the house. "Casey! Where are you?". Then he turned to Kent and asked in an angry tone "What have you done with Casey and Sally and what gives you the right to bust in here and take whatever you want? This is theft, this is private property!".

"Oh, I'm not stealing anything..." he smiled. "We have Mr. Browns permission". Kent turned to the screen door and said "Bring him out here".

One of Kent's men brought Casey out with a gun at his back. Casey was in terrible shape. His face was bloodied, and he was in pain. He had been badly beaten and could hardly stand up. The guy had to push him to get him to move.

Kent smiled and said "Tell him Mr. Brown. Tell him that you gave us permission to take these pigs in payment for the right to farm here".

Casey looked up and nodded.

"See, of his own free will" Kent said with a laugh. Others from his group laughed too.

"Since when do we go around collecting taxes with an armed gang?" Jess asked.

Kent got mad. He moved closer to confront Jess. "We are mandated by the City Council to carry out the people's business and we're here to collect 'due share" which is needed to keep the people of Oneonta supplied. Now I'm warning you not to interfere with City business".

"If you're not paying for it then you're stealing. What authority could possibly grant you the right to steal" Jess countered.

Now they were yelling at each other. "'Collecting due share' is not stealing! My authority comes directly from the City Council. You farmers have plenty. The Council has mandated that we redistribute the surplus to the people. Anyone found hording or with stored supplies in this emergency is required to distribute it to the people".

Crenshaw stepped in. "Hold it, hold it! Calm down". He addressed Kent "My name is Captain Crenshaw of the Patriot Militia…".

"Oh, you must be part of the militia scum we've been warned to look out for" Kent remarked with a frown.

"I'm here to uphold the rights of the American citizen as granted by the Constitution and the Bill of Rights. It's my job, a job that no one else seems to be doing. I hereby inform you that you are not allowed to deprive citizens of their property without due process of law or without just compensation as stated in Amendment 5 of the constitution. I suggest you read it".

"Ha, that's not law anymore" Kent declared. "The Council is responsible for making law and I'm here to enforce it. By interfering, you are the one in violation".

"I guess that's the question here isn't it: who's law are you following? I contend that our rights cannot be taken away by you or by some City Councilman's stroke of a pen. Laws cannot be created by any arbitrary governing body, only sanctioned Federal and State Legislatures can legally do that. Everything proclaimed by your city council is notwithstanding". Then Crenshaw addressed all the men standing within ear shot. He spoke loudly so they could all hear. "You are all enforcing an illegal order that is destructive to the rights of your fellow Americans, and to the rights that you yourselves are entitled to. I implore you to think and stop what you are doing…".

Kent held up his hand. "Mr. Militia man, haven't you heard? The Feds are in control, and they put us in charge. So, there's your legally created law. Now I demand that you follow it". Kent spoke to the men next to him. "Take his gun, tie them up and put them in the cattle car". His men took a step toward Crenshaw.

"Wait!" Crenshaw yelled while backing up farther. You have no authority to take my gun and I have every right to carry it".

"If you're not going to give up your weapon my men will shoot you and take it off your dead body" Kent said.

"Now you're going to shoot me just because I don't give up my weapon? You're going to be my Judge, jury, and executioner? Is that your 'Federal' law?".

"We've been directed to search and collect any and all firearms we find, it's against the law for you to have that" Kent pointed to the pistol on Crenshaw's hip. "Now give it up or you'll wish you had". He nodded to his guys and one of them stepped forward. The guy attempted to grab Crenshaw's gun, another of his goons went towards Kaiden. Thinking their victims wouldn't try anything while under the gun, Kent's men were puzzled when Crenshaw, Kaiden and Jess dropped to the ground and went prone with their hands covering their heads. They lay there looking like they were giving up. A quizzical look formed on the Brigade members faces, then they smiled at each other thinking this was amusing.

A bullet came whizzing in from the north quadrant of the farmhouse. After the unmistakable sound of a bullet slapping into a man's body a report of gunfire followed a split second later. Kent went down. There was another report, a man on the other side of him got hit. It was a shock to the others. They ducked and froze, then frantically looked around to determine where the threat was coming from. For some it was too late. Another shot, another body hit the ground lifeless before anyone could find adequate cover. Some of them did recover and scrambled for anything they could hide behind. Another gunshot. A scream describing intense pain welled up from one of the now wounded Brigade members. Crenshaw and Kaiden hugged the ground hoping not to get hit in the melee that followed.

Previously… On foot, Charlie Brown led Ramsey, Melvin and seven other Patriot volunteers over to the boy's house. The nine of them ran the dirt road between the two farms as fast as they could under the weight of their equipment while Jess, Crenshaw and Kaiden took to the street and drove over coming in through their neighbors front driveway in one of the Feds SUV's. Ramsey's team only slowed down when they got within 200 yards of the farmhouse. From there, they crouched and crawled the rest of the way to a spot that overlooked the cars parked in the front yard of the house.

Ramsey volunteered to go on this mission. After describing the skill set he learned in the military, there was no doubt that he was the man for the job. Ramsey was given an LR308 rifle with a nice Leopold MK5HD scope and told "Good luck!". The Patriot who lent it to him promised it was zeroed in. Ramsey was exceedingly familiar with the AR platform but could only hope the guy was right about the rifle being on target.

The bad guys on the Brown's farm were so immersed in addressing their newly arrived visitors that the Patriots sniper team was able to move into position without being seen. No guards or lookouts had been posted by the intruders. "Amateurs for sure" Ramsey said out loud. There, at the edge of farmer Brown's field, Ramsey and Merrill lay in a makeshift snipers hide with the remaining Patriots lying in wait behind them. They had hurried to set up in the few minutes they had before Crenshaw's vehicle arrived on scene. Ramsey was watching through the scope on his rifle and had the guy called 'Kent' in his sights. Merrill, Ramsey's spotter, watched through binoculars and mumbled "175 yards, no wind" and gave Ramsey the green light slap on the back. The crosshairs settled on his target and when Ramsey saw the signal, it meant that negotiations had broken down. He fired.

If it was a video game, it would have been fun and would have elicited a chuckle from Ramsey's lips. But this wasn't funny. Every time he pulled the trigger someone went down. After hearing gun shots, members of the Brigade scrambled into various hiding places but since some couldn't tell where the shots were coming from, their hiding place left them partially exposed to Ramsey's sniper rifle. He picked them off one at a time.

After their numbers were thinned out, the Patriots backing Ramsey moved up on the farm. Advancing cautiously, the Patriots fired from a crouched position as they scurried closer to the house. Their bullets plinked into cars and kicked up wood chips when they struck the fence behind one of the places where an intruder was hiding. A few of the Brigade members got off a couple of shots in the direction of the Patriots line, but with the degree of fire power coming at them they quickly realized that they were in way over their heads. When their friends went down after getting shot and a line of what looked like soldiers started closing in on them, they panicked and threw down their rifles. With hands in the air, they hoped to God that the attackers would honor their surrender and thereby end the possibility of getting shot.

Citizens Brigade officers had pulled members from the towns abundant supply of stranded college students and supplemented their numbers with town folk that either adhered to the same progressive liberal mind set or were forced to work for them through unscrupulous means. The prospect of being in charge gave the people who joined the Brigade a sense of belonging and a sense of power that none of them ever had before. Most of them were awfully young and were simply handed a rifle and told they now had the authority to go out and "collect". "Do it for the good of the community" was drilled into their heads.

Four Brigade members were inside the farmhouse. One of them was guarding the Browns, keeping them prisoner in their own living room. When the gunfire started, the guard ran over to the front window of the Browns farmhouse and saw their leader and two friends lying motionless on the ground outside. When their comrades stood up with their hands in the air, he realized the situation was hopeless. He panicked and called upstairs to warn his partners in crime who were searching the second floor for valuables. All four guys ran out the back door in a big hurry.

At first, the advancing Patriots bounced back and forth from cover to cover or hit the ground and lay prone as they fired. They moved in low, standing up fully only when they saw the remaining Brigade members drop their weapons and put their hands in the air. Patriots filtered into the front yard of the farmhouse with their rifles swinging back and forth towards the enemy yelling "Get on the ground! Get on the ground, Now!" at the top of their lungs. There was a shot fired and one of the prisoners went down. It made the rest of the prisoners dive to the ground in a hurry.

At the outset, when the five people loading pigs into the transport truck heard gunfire, they all took off on foot going in the opposite direction. None of them were armed so it was easy for the Patriots to find them and round them up. That group didn't offer any resistance. It was from those men that Kaiden learned some interesting facts about what was going on.

* * *

The Browns were free from their captors. Crenshaw and crew met in the kitchen of the Browns farmhouse for an impromptu briefing on the action. A handful of Patriots stood around on the side with Kaiden and Crenshaw sitting at the kitchen table. One of the Patriots, Kurt Mendel, was standing at attention before his superior officer.

Crenshaw spoke in a tone that told of his frustration. "There's an issue that needs to be addressed before we continue. If I hadn't witnessed it myself, I wouldn't have believed it. You shot one of the prisoners to death when the situation had clearly been contained. What the hell happened Kurt? The guy had his hands up for Christ sake".

"Sir, it was a mistake. I don't know how it happened. My gun just... went off..." Kurt said.

Crenshaw jumped up and got in his face. "That's your excuse! Your gun just went off? You killed a man. Do you understand the ramifications of your actions?".

"Yes, sir I do...".

"Shit! This is just as bad as when Neil killed that prisoner. What the hell is going on here? We are a trained militia. I expect more than that from my men and women. If you want to stay in this organization, you're going to have to prove that you belong here. Now, you're going to have to live with the fact that you have taken a man's life unnecessarily!".

"Just like you will have to for killing innocent people when you bombed the Hacia building…" Kurt said in defiance adding a sharp "Sir!" at the end.

Crenshaw fumed. He turned to all the Patriots in the room and spoke to everyone present. "That decision was made in an effort to save all our lives and to initiate a positive outcome for our cause. What Kurt has done is a blatant act of incompetence. There's a big difference". He turned back to Kurt. "I will have to live with my actions, and in the future if they are deemed contrary to the Patriot code of honor, then I will accept my punishment just as you will have to accept yours for the crime of executing a prisoner. You will hand in your weapons, and you will not be allowed to carry one until further notice. You are suspended, and I will be watching you closely. You're dismissed".

"Yes sir" Kurt said. He turned and left the room.

"Kaiden, report" Crenshaw demanded.

"The bad guys had a total of seventeen men and one woman with them. They suffered six dead including the woman. We took ten prisoners total, two of their fighters were badly wounded. Five of the prisoners are noncombatants, those were the workers who were loading up the pigs. The Browns warned us that three or four fighters ran out the back door after the shooting started. We pursued and surprised them down by the brook, traded fire, killed two and took one prisoner. One got away and that's where Nevel Burns, the guy we picked up in Poland, was wounded. If we can get him to a doctor, I don't think it's life threatening. We didn't pursue the guy who got away, I didn't deem the effort worth it".

"Good, we don't need any more wounded or God forbid killed over this. But have Ramsey set up and scan the area in case that guy decides to return".

"Yes sir, already on it" Kaiden replied.

"How about Nevel?"

"We've done all we can. He needs to get to a hospital".

"Casey Brown!" Crenshaw shouted into the living room. The farmer responded and appeared in front of him a second later. "You are injured I see. Do you know where the hospital is?" Crenshaw asked.

"Yes, of course".

"I need to get you and my wounded man to the hospital. I want you to guide them, so they don't get lost" Crenshaw demanded it more than asked. "I need you to go now". Then he spoke to Nick Malner who was standing next to him. "Get Kurt and have him drive them. Give him the SUV. No guns".

"And what about the two wounded Brigade members?" Kaiden reminded him. "They're both in pretty bad shape. I don't think one of um's gunna make it".

"Ok, take them too".

"But Captain, what's going to happen to Nevel in the hospital if or when they find out what happened here?" Kaiden asked.

Farmer Brown stepped in and objected too "If they talk and they find out that I helped you guys it'll bring the whole lot of them down on my farm".

"What do you want me to do, execute them? There's already one guy on the loose. If he gets back eventually the story will be told. Mr. Brown, you're gunna have to enter the fight against these people if you want to survive. Otherwise, you might as well get out now and leave your farm to them. Eventually they will take everything you've got till there's nothing left. It's the inherent nature of socialism, it's like a black hole that sucks everything in. It's time to round up everyone you know who is willing to fight this and organize resistance".

Mr. Brown stood there in shock. "I can't believe it's come to this. Why me?" he said shaking his head.

Kaiden stepped up to him "All of us have been thrown into this without our consent. None of us asked for this. It's simply our bad luck to be here at this moment in time. It's up to us, we've got no choice but to try to make a difference".

Crenshaw added "Yeah, and I've got no choice but to get the wounded to a hospital no matter what the consequences, I'm not going to just let them die". To Nick he said "Go and get Kurt to drive and drop them off, then get back here as soon as possible. Go".

Casey walked off immersed in his own thoughts. Crenshaw turned to Kaiden... "What about the noncombatants?".

"We got the prisoners locked up in the cattle car right now. A fitting end to their excursion". Kaiden said.

"Ok, Eric, identify the noncombatants and bring one of them here for a conversation" Crenshaw ordered.

Minutes later, Eric escorted one of the prisoners in and sat him down across from Kaiden on the other side of the table. To make the guy feel more comfortable, Kaiden offered him a bottle of water which he took and gulped down in a nervous manor.

Even before Kaiden asked him a question the guy spoke in his defense. "My name is Jeremiah Greein and I'm not part of this man! The 'Brigade' is responsible for that. They're forcing me and many others to do hard labor against our will. We work for them now but it's not a job, they feed us, but they don't pay us. 'It's your duty to serve the State' they tell us. Our reward is that our families will not be harmed. Told me they would come to my house and... not punish 'me' but will pull one of my family members out and whip them right in front of me. So, I 'volunteered' to work. They put me on this work detail".

"Same with the others who were with you?" Kaiden asked.

"Yeah, they call us 'worker shit'. We're sentenced to work as punishment for questioning what they were doing and not going along with the program. We're not allowed to carry on as we did before, and we're not trusted with carrying guns. We do all the heavy lifting like removing the pigs here. I tell you we've been coerced into working for them. It's like being in a prison chain gang with them as the guards".

"Who's 'them'?".

"The Brigade? All the ones with guns here are full-fledged members of what they call "The Citizens Brigade". Their power comes from the school board which rose out of both the College and the local public school system. Both groups became very powerful with union support and Federal stimulus money which they used to build up their organization and enrich themselves. For a while it seemed like they had an endless supply of money. They used it to control politicians and install their own sympathizers. For a long time now, they've undermined parental authority and taught their critical race theory to our kids on the sly. That was their way of getting our youth to hate their parents and to hate America. They taught our kids that their parents didn't have the right to tell them what to do and that today parents are irrelevant. I know, I have kids that were involved in all that. I can see it now; it was a blatant attempt to destroy the family and gain control of our kids by shifting their loyalty to the State. Eighty percent of Brigade members are students, illegals, and local youth. The rest are older Kool-Aid drinking die hard progressives. Yeah, we know how they did it now".

Kaiden looked at Crenshaw and said "That's why we're running into so many youngsters". Then he asked Jeremiah "Why are so many of them South Americans? Many can hardly speak English".

"Progressives have been working that 'come on in' policy for illegal immigrants for more than two decades now. The amnesty program brought in tens of millions of them. We've had to deal with the surge of migrants ever since. They've been given a free bus ticket to all parts of the US. Free welfare checks, free healthcare and yes, free education too. All on the taxpayer's dime. Many of the classes here at the college are, or were, taught in Spanish. Who wouldn't want to come. Oneonta was one of the cities where they bussed in thousands of them. Probably because we had a College here and once upon a time, a good education system. Hundreds were dropped off at the local bus station and simply let loose on the town. Then the virus hit, taxes went sky high. They shut things down, jobs became scarce, and the economy went south. I think they did it on purpose. All the discord, and the demise of a prosperous future was blamed on the old ways and on Capitalism. They've been teaching our youth and the immigrants that our traditions and old white people are the enemy. The anger felt by today's younger generation has been funneled into hatred toward the rich and successful.

By design. By the very same people in control now. Now it's the haves against the have-not's.

"You sound like you know what you're talking about, what did you do before the melt down?' Kaiden asked him.

"I was a teacher. So yes, I know. We went through the "defund the police" movement where our elected officials cut the police force in half. We had our share of riots in Oneonta, they were brutal. Rich homeowners were dragged out of their homes, beat up and even killed by mobs that roamed the city unchecked. It took the police hours to respond if at all. The destruction was so senseless, destroying what other people had because you don't have it. So sad". Jeremiah looked down and shook his head, then he continued.

"As I said, the college school board merged with the local public-school board and out of that came the "Citizens Brigade". A banner under which they all united and coalesced their resources into one effective force. An armed force at that. These guys aren't foolin around. They're not social workers I can tell you that.

For receiving benefits, or should I say in order to keep receiving benefits, students, illegals and the locals, are asked for their loyalty, loyalty to the Progressive party. The Board formed 'Brigade patrols' and they replaced most of the police under the guise that the police weren't doing their job. Funny huh, they de-fund the police, then complain that they're not doing their job. Said the increase in crime was proof. They used that to justify the formation of the Brigade and placed it under their direct control. Brigade patrols went around like Nazi storm troopers enforcing whatever mandate the Board handed out. They are violent and brutal. That's who you went up against today".

Kaiden turned to Crenshaw "Wow, importing illegals was done purposely to fill the ranks with the 'dependent discontented' which became a revolutionary force to draw from when the time was right…".

"And the time is right now" Crenshaw stated. "Jeremiah, how many patrols do they have?".

"Four major ones that I know about. But I'm not one of these people. Me and the four others don't agree with what they're doing, you've got to believe me. This is wrong. We just don't have any way to stop them and we're not soldiers".

"And what will happen if we let you go?" Kaiden asked.

"I can only guess that this will be blamed on me, and my family will suffer. They'll make me pay for sure. It's in their nature, they're modern-day Fascists. They consider themselves to be better than us and they are very eager to rise above and dominate".

"Knowing that, are you still unwilling to pick up a rifle?" Kaiden asked.

Jeremiah stared at Kaiden thinking hard about the question. His eyes stared out, focusing on nothing for just a moment as the debate raged in his mind. He finally said "You want me to join you?".

"Join what?" Crenshaw asked.

"Why… join the fight against these people of course".

"We're not fighting these people. Well, we weren't until today" Kaiden said glancing at Crenshaw.

"You can do it" Jeremiah said. "You have the firepower and the skill to do it. They've been taking guns away from us and blocking the roads so we can't fight or even travel to earn a living. You got guns. You're the only ones who 'can' do it. If it isn't you who stands up against these people… then who?".

Crenshaw fired back sharply "How about you! Why don't 'you' stand up against this? You expect us to go out and fight your battle? This is the problem with Americans today, a pandemic of cowardice has settled in around all of you. You're lazy, no gumption and no spine. That's what put you in this predicament. You're unwilling to do what's necessary to protect what you have. Now it's being threatened and still, still you look to someone else to do what you should be doing yourself".

Jeremiah looked dejected and stared at the floor.

Crenshaw asked him outright "Are you willing to fight for your freedom?"

Jeremiah looked up "I have no choice now. Today is proof that we're well past talking. This is only going to get worse. To help my family it looks like I'm gunna have to join the battle. Somehow, I've got to stop these people from showing up at my house".

Crenshaw turned to Eric. "Eric, bring in the other four workers that were with this guy".

"Yes sir" Eric replied and left the room.

"Jeremiah, who do you report to and where do these people operate out of?".

"They operate out of City hall, that's their headquarters but they're holding us at the YMCA. We're prisoners there. There's over a hundred of us who have been arrested for simply voicing opinions in opposition to their agenda. As punishment they sentenced us to serve in the labor force. It was the school board members and the administrators; they joined up with the city's politicians and the cops that were hip to the program. They run the show now. The bastards. The mayor and such. They rule with an iron fist. They've taken over city hall and got the police under their control too. Kent was one of the cops who joined them. The cops who didn't go along have been sentenced to the 'Y' as well. I know, I know some of them".

"Why do they keep you at the Y, why not just threaten you and the family and force you to show up for work every day?" Kaiden asked.

"Total control" Jerimiah said. "They need total control of the family. They put one family member in prison and threaten the other members with his demise if the entire family doesn't cooperate. This way the family won't skip out of town, and they'll support the program. They got a grip on the whole community this way".

"How many members does the Brigade have?" Kaiden asked.

"Oh, well there were a lot more of them until today. On their own the Citizens Brigade probably has over one hundred thugs and cops in their pockets and ready to roll at their discretion. The Feds had a slew of men and vehicles stationed at police headquarters. That legitimized the council and gave a lot of support with all that firepower behind them. But the Feds left yesterday morning because of some major incident that happened in Syracuse. I didn't get details, but I heard something about a battle that took place between the Feds and insurgents.

It gave me hope that there are people out there who are fighting back. Then you guys showed up and we were ecstatic. You proved, thank God, that there are people out there who are willing to do something about this".

Kaiden looked at Crenshaw and said "Interesting".

"Yeah, we're 'insurgents' now huh" Crenshaw said. "Can you beat that. The ones fighting to assert the Constitution are the ones they call "insurgents". It's time we started calling them 'insurrectionists'. It's obvious now that they're the ones who just pulled off a coup against our government".

Eric led a group of four prisoners with their hands tied behind their back and brought them before his captain. Crenshaw asked each one of them questions that enabled him to confirm Jeremiah's story. They all had a similar disturbing tale that led up to their incarceration. One of them who called himself 'Greek', told of a warehouse where all the spoils gathered by Brigade patrols were brought.

"I've been there and seen it myself. We drop off all the food, water, guns and money that we collect to the Walmart loading dock. It's been closed to the public ever since the riots. They confiscated the building and everything inside to protect it from getting looted and destroyed. Now they won't let no one go in there. Got guards all around 24 hours a day. No one's allowed to go into the parking lot unless you got a pass or you're a city official. I see them selling stuff and making deals with people all the time. They carry stuff out and fill the trunks of cars.

Officials say they're going to distribute the stuff to the people, all except the guns of course. But it's not going to the people, it's going to their supporters. No one I know has heard of any distribution, not for free anyway. They use it to bribe us to go to work for them. Anyone who goes out on a work detail gets paid in food and basic supplies".

Kaiden looked at Crenshaw "They're taking it in the front for free and selling it out the back".

"Nice racket they got going" Crenshaw said. "Probably only selling to their cronies too. I wonder what they're using for money?".

"They can be buying a lot of loyalty with that scam" Kaiden said.

"We drop off a lot of money that we get too. They tell us to look for gold and silver. Dollars are worthless" Jeremiah said.

"You mean 'steal'" Kaiden corrected him.

"Yeah, you're right. 'Stealing' would be a better word for it".

"Alright Eric, take off their restraints" Crenshaw said. Then he addressed the x-prisoners. "Guy's, I'm going to give you a choice, and it's going to be interesting to see which way you'll go. I want you to think about an idea I got, we'll discuss it and then put it to a vote. But first, let's clean this up, bury the bodies and get everyone back to the Mann's farm. Eric, drive the Brigade vehicles over to base, we can use the cattle car to lock up prisoners and I got an idea for the rest of their vehicles".

* * *

Back at the Mann's farm, Crenshaw held a meeting/briefing with everyone in attendance. He informed them about the mornings events, the ramifications of the day's action and why he reprimanded Kurt for his error in judgment.

As Crenshaw spoke, something in his voice told of a change. A change in tone, a change in direction. Today's events had gotten to him, probably like it had gotten to all of the members who had participated in this morning's action along with an accumulation of the effects from everything they have been through since the collapse. Now it's a war game that has become as serious as it can get. With every passing day it's gotten worse and more somber than anyone ever thought possible. Crenshaw reacted... differently than he had before. No longer did he show the same urge to forget everything and push on to the outpost to get the gold back into Patriot hands. That's probably what he should have done. Instead, he told of plans to push back against these people. Push back against the insanity that was pushing on him.

Crenshaw told the group arrayed in front of him "I was planning to stay here and hunker down for a few more days. This was a great spot to lay low, but the problem we have now is just that. It 'was' a great spot to lay low. My decision to intervene in the Brown situation has changed that, and I apologize. I certainly did not plan for it to go down the way that it did.

The Feds have pulled out of Oneonta and have left behind a system of organized modern-day slavery. Slavery! Can you believe it? Once again it rears its ugly head in America, only now it seems it's being inflicted as revenge upon whites, blacks, and all colors of the middle class! There is always a group or class of people who suffer under the thumb of Communism. And that's what we have developing here, an attempt to takeover America. Our new friends… (he waved his arm at Jeremiah and the four standing behind him) have told of the crimes these people are committing against society, the City government has turned the YMCA into a prison and is keeping over a hundred citizens there against their will. They are using them for forced labor. We have freed Jeremiah and his compatriots from this debauchery, and they have expressed a sincere desire to go back and free their fellow citizens of this scourge.

This is it! Now you all have a chance to participate in retribution against evil, but I am not one to force anyone to do something they're not fully invested in. With the Feds gone, we now have the ability to waltz in there under the guise of a returning Brigade patrol. An opportunity that shouldn't be allowed to go to waste, not if you're serious about putting an end to the grip these socialists have on you and your fellow citizens. This is not the American way, no. I ask you to fight it!". Crenshaw directed that last remark at Jerimiah and crew, and then scanned the crowd of people in front of him.

"We need to win one battle at a time against these people if we are to save our republic. Now's the time to fight one of those battles. If or when they get wind of what happened here today our cover will be blown, they will look for us and harden their defenses. Then it will be impossible to get into the City and achieve our goal without a major fight. That, I would like to avoid. We need every advantage we can get to pull this off and having the benefit of surprise in this case makes my plan to take back the city completely doable.

Now. I need volunteers…".

16

DETOUR

The Oneonta Police operated out of a Station located just off Main street on the south end of town. This facility had also been "hardened" by placing barricades in strategic places all around the building. Construction of a similar style wall became a necessity with many Police departments and Federal office buildings in the cities as well as towns after the SHTF event. Police were protecting themselves against what? Their own citizens? To deter what? A suicide bomber? American terrorists?

Here at the Oneonta Police station, barricades in front of the bay doors looked like they kept people in as much as out. Visitors were forced to park elsewhere, walk to the guard gate, stop to be searched and show ID before entering. At 1:45 in the afternoon, a squad car full of police drove up and weaved their way through the barricade. All the occupants got out and escorted two prisoners up to the station entrance and past two policeman standing guard. One of the prisoners was Kurt Mendel. He had his hands tied in front of him and was escorted up to the building with cops on all sides. His escorts looked at the camera on the wall and made a 'request to enter gesture'. The door opened. They handed him off to detectives who were waiting for him inside.

One of the detectives led him into a room and sat him down. The guy removed Kurt's handcuffs and said "Sorry about the cuffs... standard procedure".

Kurt didn't have to wait long, within minutes, Chief Ferenczi himself entered the room to personally assist with this special case. "I understand you have a very interesting story to tell me" he said to Kurt.

Kurt no longer felt any desire or obligation to protect the Patriots. Not after what Crenshaw had done to him. He was pissed. He didn't feel like he was one of them anymore. It was an easy decision. "I'll tell you, but I want immunity" he told Ferenczi.

"You got it" Ferenczi told him.

Kurt sang a song and gave up a story to his interrogators who listened with undivided attention. He got their attention alright, especially the part about the gold and silver.

The head detective took the chief to the side and stated flat out "I believe him. He knows details about the attack on the Hacia building that no one else would know. If the rest of his story pans out, these could very well be the people who did it".

"Yeah, the ones we were told to look out for" chief Ferenczi said. "We got em now. And with a major bonus...".

"Yeah, the gold. Who would believe our luck? It drove itself right into our lap. Details of the carnage these guy's inflicted came in all day yesterday on the radio. 185 dead, 130 wounded. Each time more information trickles in the numbers rise. I heard they're going to have to make a new provisional headquarters in Syracuse because the old one is... gone. These people are trained professionals" the Detective said.

"Yeah, we're dealing with some dangerous people here". The chief looked him in the eye "No matter what, we're going to send a team in to get 'em".

"Why? Can't we wait for the Feds? Let them do it".

"Hell, this is our chance, Rupert. Do you know what this would mean if we captured or kill these guys? And we ain't letting the Feds get the gold, no way. We'd get to write our own ticket with the Feds and to think of what we could do with that kind of money" the chief told him. "Call the boys in, get 'em together and get it done. Go now, round 'em up!" he demanded.

"Chief, you've got half of our squad locked up at the 'Y'... including Sargent Haines".

"No excuses Rupert, Frank Snyder is just as capable of leading the squad as Haines was. Get him on it!" Ferenczi told him.

"Now?".

"Yes, now Rupert, now!".

"What do we do with the prisoner?".

"He knows too much. If this pans out, we'll have to get rid of loose ends. Now go, we go tonight...".

"Tonight?".

"Yes, tonight. We can't let this slip out of our fingers. Don't blow this Rupert... this is too good to be true".

* * *

A hustle replaced the laid-back manner at the Mann's farm. Twenty-two of them, including the five ex-Oneonta Brigade members, prepared the equipment they were given for the mission. Crenshaw emphasized that they had to go... now. "The Brigade probably expects their patrol to report in this evening. This can't wait".

They were forced to improvise because the window for this opportunity would only be open for one night. Every Patriot volunteered to go on the mission, yet Crenshaw ordered four of them to stay behind. That way he was confident there was a contingent of Patriots who he could trust to guard the bus and its contents. Ciera was one of them. She was left in charge. "You're responsible for the team, the bus and the rest of the men and women staying at base camp" Crenshaw told her.

Every Patriot in camp got busy preparing. In between the coming and going, John the drone guy found Crenshaw and demanded an audience.

"Crenshaw, I heard your speech. Really! You're going to set the brigade members free and yet keep me here as a prisoner? You trust them but you don't trust me?".

"I don't trust them to do anything for 'me', but I trust they will do something for themselves. Each one of them had a tragic story about how the Brigade had disrupted their family and destroyed their lives. They're prisoners in their own town for God's sake. Believe me, to do this I had to hear the hate that they had for the Brigade and yes, I heard the tragic details that I know will spur them to action. I would much rather use someone with vengeance on his mind than another who has no connection at all to the goal. Those are the ones who will do what is necessary, those are the ones that have a reason to fight.

One of them told me that the Brigade beat him and then raped his wife right in front of him while holding a gun to his head. The sound of her screams is etched upon his mind as well as the look on her face as she pleaded for help. They threatened to visit her nightly unless he worked for them. At that moment he was helpless, but he's not helpless anymore. Now, he has a chance to even the score.

What's your story John? Do you have one?".

John looked at Crenshaw from a slightly softer angle. "No, mine's not tragic enough for you, I'm sure. But I know where you guys are coming from. I'm not stupid, I too felt the do 'or else' coming from these people but...".

"...But you went along with it anyway didn't you".

"Yes, I did".

"In order to protect your job, you sacrificed your community".

"I sacrificed for the good of the community damn it!".

"Oh yeah John, what good were you going to do by surveilling your fellow citizens, your friends. And oh yeah, those missiles, what did you think when you realized that it was open season on your neighbors?".

John stared at Crenshaw with nothing to say.

"I thought so. But Ok John, you're free to go". Crenshaw turned around and started to leave. John gave Crenshaw a surprised look. Then yelled after him.

"I can go? ...where am I gunna go?".

Crenshaw turned back. "Yeah, you can go. Thank you for your help. Thank you for saving our lives. Of course, I would ask that you don't turn us in and sic the Feds on us. We would all appreciate that. Besides, I'm not sure what they would do to the guy who destroyed the Hacia building... I'm just sayin".

John stood there for a few moments while that sunk in, that along with the fact that he had just been set free.

* * *

"Have you heard anything from Kurt or farmer Brown?" Kaiden asked Crenshaw.

"No. I'm worried but it's not enough to stop the mission. Neither of them is aware of our plans".

"Yeah, but if they've been captured, our target might know about us".

"Even if they talked, I don't think the police can mobilize fast enough to mount a strike against us until tomorrow at the earliest. We are going to give them something much more pressing to deal with way before then" Crenshaw said.

* * *

Jester Mann had given them directions that guided the Patriots convoy through the back roads the same way farmer Brown guided the SUV that took the wounded to the hospital. The roadblock on Route 23 wouldn't have been a major obstacle, but Crenshaw wanted the team to avoid it. They had the power to blast through a civilian manned roadblock and probably a Federal manned roadblock as well, but Crenshaw didn't want to give the Brigade or anyone else any advance warning that a well-armed militia was active in the area. They went around it.

Following directions, the Patriots vehicles silently snaked their way into the west end of Oneonta. Country club road turned into

Roundhouse Rd and as per Browns instructions, they traveled the back roads staying off the main drag as much as possible.

The first stop for the parade of four Brigade vehicles, one cattle transport car and two Humvees, was the YMCA. Only now the vehicles were full of as many Patriot volunteers and recently obtained compatriots that could fit in. All of them armed to the teeth. Crenshaw could have taken them to Walmart first, it was closer, but they planned to put things in motion at the 'Y' before anything else. That was paramount to the success of the mission.

The two Federal Humvees that trailed the Brigade's vehicles gave the group a semblance of validity. It probably helped get them through during a hairy moment after they passed a police patrol car while crossing a main road in the middle of town. Or maybe the police just recognized the Brigade vehicles and thought they were being escorted. Either way, there was no reaction. And here too at the entrance to the 'Y' there was no negative reaction from the men who guarded the gate. Why would there be? They had seen these vehicles every day when they came to pick up labor in the morning and again when they dropped them off with the day's take in the evening. And tonight, the Citizens Brigade is being escorted by two Federal vehicles.

An odd thing about the YMCA's property and the parking lot was that it was now fenced off completely with chain link fence. Some of it was bran new and had been recently installed. You could tell because it was quite a contrast between the old fence in the back behind the building and the new fence around the perimeter of the front parking lot. The rear had been fenced in ever since they built the place. The unusual component was rolled barbed wire that had been added to the top. Some parts of it hadn't been finished yet or they were having trouble getting more wire to complete it, one or the other.

This building was an example of a concept that the YMCA organization tried out in a handful of US Cities. A major portion of the building was a hotel, complete with rentable rooms for a night or for extended stay. The hotel was connected to a section of a building dedicated to member services which included a large gym containing all the facilities you would need to get a good workout. It came complete with basketball courts and an indoor running track that skirted the circumference of the second floor.

Homeless people utilized the YMCA's facilities when they came across enough money to rent a room. When the city came in and took over the building, they kicked everyone out and designated the building for "Government use only". As the Patriots drove along the outside of the parking lot it was a surprise to see fifty or so tents lined up along the outside of the fence. They were all crowded together in a continuous line that covered the short grassy section between the sidewalk and the fence. There, a small community of homeless including illegal immigrants and people who were simply down on their luck, had parked themselves because they had nowhere else to go.

One reason the building was chosen by the Brigade was because it had a massive generator for backup power. A generator they now relied on for all their electricity. Power was turned on to the rooms for two hours in the morning before the laborers were picked up, and for two hours in the evening during the time most of them were dropped off. Normally that was the only time the air conditioning or the heater would be running, but ever since the new management took over, they claimed the air conditioner and the heater were broken.

The procession pulled up to the YMCA's front gate with Crenshaw's vehicle going in first. According to Jerimiah, only the cars transporting laborer's went in to drop them off, so the cattle car and Humvees pulled off to the side of the road out front to mimic normal procedure and not raise suspicion. It reminded Crenshaw of what they encountered at the Post Office in Herkimer. Only the guards here were not Federal agents, it was private security or mercenaries but since they were armed, they were just as much of a danger. The difference was that these guards were tasked mostly with keeping people in, not out. This security team had a mobile office-trailer parked inside the fence just beyond the gated entrance. Guards and patrols rotated and went out from that central location.

Basically, security let the prisoners do as they pleased within the confines of the building. At set times armed patrols roamed the property and hallways of the building to maintain order and enforce the rules as well as a 'Lights out' mandate at 9:30PM. After that, security patrols made sure everyone was on the right side of their door. "You don't want to be caught doing something illegal" Jerimiah told them. "No way man. Consequences for breaking the rules are harsh, you can get a bullet if you're caught out after curfew and punishment is carried out on the spot".

Another reason the 'Y' was chosen to house the forced labor program was because of the "locking system" on the rooms. From the main desk the computer was able to change the system from a manual key card operation to 'master control'. That meant with the press of a key, all the doors to the rooms could be locked or unlocked all at once, instantly turning the place into a prison for the unfortunate people who were forced to serve time there.

One guard inside the security teams mobile trailer was sitting in front of a slew of monitors that showed images of strategic locations around the premises. Being a mobile home, the office had a living room complete with a couch and chairs where patrol personnel gathered and prepared to start their shift.

Tonight, the guard monitoring the front counter saw the vehicles pull up and approach the gate on his main monitor. Recognizing the vehicles, he buzzed them in without giving it a second thought. With a rifle in hand, another guard standing outside the front doors waved at them. He yelled at them "Lights out in twenty minutes!" as they drove up.

On the street outside the property, a front gate guard got curious after seeing the two Federal Humvee's parked behind the cattle car. Walking out the gate and strolling towards them he eyed them up and down.

Patriots manning the vehicles got nervous. "He's coming our way" Eric said.

"Ok, don't get nervous. Just small talk him if he comes up" Proffit advised. The guard came up to the window and knocked on it with his knuckles.

"Hey there, what's going on" the guard said when Eric rolled down the window.

Meanwhile, Crenshaw and his guys got in. "So far so good" Kaiden said to Crenshaw and everyone else in the car. "If we had problems at the gate and had to subdue those guards, this whole operation would have turned into something entirely different".

Crenshaw's vehicle and the one behind him pulled up to the front door of the main building. "Leave the rifles here, pistols only" Crenshaw told them. Everyone got out except the drivers. All ten of them walked up to the front door with two acting as Brigade guard members who normally escorted them up and into the building. A buzzer went off as they approached the door. With a stiff yank it opened. Inside there was what used to be a reception desk for the hotel. Now it was manned by a single armed guard who monitored the traffic going in and out and operated the door. Ramsey and Melvin struck up a conversation with the guard as the rest walked past to the elevator.

Jerimiah had assigned 'a person of importance' for each of his guys to go visit, each contact being someone who was sympathetic to their cause. Instead of going directly to their own rooms they split up and sought out their target. The power was on until 9:30 so they had to hurry and make it before the curfew went into effect. The group of them took the elevator up and dropped off each person at the appropriate floor until only Jerimiah, Crenshaw, Kaiden and Patriot Riley Mason were left. All of them got out on the fifth floor and headed for room #522 with Jerimiah in the lead.

A knock on 522 brought a man to the door who was skeptical about opening it. "Who is it?" he wanted to know.

"Ben, it's Jerimiah, open up". The fact that the guy opened the door confirmed that yes, they certainly knew each other. Ben Haines was one of those 'in shape' burley kind of guys who looked like a bulldog with large shoulders and built-up pecks. He had arms that looked like he'd crush you in a bear hug. Not the kind of guy who looked like he scared easily. But he opened the door meekly. He recognized Jeramiah but the new faces caused a degree of concern.

"What do you want? Don't you know it's lights out in fifteen? What are you doing here?" Ben asked in an irritated tone.

"Yeah, I know, but Ben you're going to want to hear this. I've got life changing news for you, and we don't have much time".

Previously, Jerimiah briefed Crenshaw "I knew Ben Haines long before the meltdown and that this is our inside guy. Ben is the mouthpiece for the resistance. This is the guy you want to get on your side. I went to high school with him, and I know he is as pro American as you can get. Hell, because of it, he was thrown into this dungeon. I know his disposition and I know he would gladly join and lead any effort to thwart the takeover of this City. We've talked about it. Haines is a cop, or was a cop. He's one of a handful of officers who refused to go along with the new management. They didn't like his brand of non-compliance. To get him to go along they must have got some kind of leverage on him. I don't know what it is, it could be the same game they're playing with the rest of us, a threat of harm to loved ones. It's a powerful motivator and they use it to their full advantage".

Ben opened the door, looked around and then let them in.

"This better be good. You've got fourteen minutes to explain before I kick you all out of here. I don't want you locked in my room all night long. You'll have to deal with security after that".

They all entered what looked like a typical small hotel room with two twin beds, two chairs and a dresser. There was a TV, but it wasn't on. That was it. Three other men were there in the room with Ben, one of them was in a sleeping bag on the floor. With the addition of four more people, suddenly the place was crowded. Without bothering with pleasantries, Jerimiah got down to telling a story that grabbed Ben's attention real fast, just like his friends were doing in four other apartments at that very same moment.

Ben Haines stood up and stared straight ahead. After hearing all that, he had to take a moment to process such an unexpected outrageous story. He looked at his watch. Jerimiah was right, it was a life-changing decision and he only had minutes to make it. Either kick these kooks out before lockdown or accept their story and join these so called 'Patriots'. The test would come when the doors were supposed to lock at 9:30.

Crenshaw stood up, walked over to Ben, looked him in the eye and told him "My men and I came all the way over here at great risk. I did it because 'I' had a choice. I chose to help you people who no longer have the ability to help yourselves. Freedom of choice is the very thing that made this country great. Your present situation is typical of what many Americans have lost. We will lose it forever if we don't do something about it. So, here I am. But I'm not going to do this for you. What I offer you is a chance to do it yourself, a choice. What you do with it is up to you. Are your people willing to do what it takes to fight back and turn this thing around?".

"Captain Crenshaw, the people in this city are already hitting a wall with shortages of food, power outages, no internet and this new mindset of a ruling class who wants to control every aspect of our lives. We're not even free to go to work to earn a living. I can speak for them... we're more than ready to rectify this".

At that moment the lights went out and you could hear the door lock go "click". The sound of air coming into the room through vents stopped and everything went quiet. There was a tense moment, and a disappointing moan came from one of Ben's roommates who anticipated that these people had just been locked in their room for the night. Another one said "Oh shit". For if these Patriot people couldn't produce what they had just promised, they now have four strangers for roommates.

One tense moment later, the lights came back on. There was a click at the door indicating that it unlocked. Air started streaming back into the room.

Ben looked at Crenshaw. Ben's seriousness turned into a smile that etched across his lips and puffed out his cheeks. A smile that had been missing from his face for quite some time. But it didn't last long. He turned to his roommates who looked at each other not knowing what to think.

Ben yelled at them "I choose freedom! And if your with me, get your things guys, we're getting the hell at a hea!" Ben pointed to one of his guys. "Nemo, you go over to Mikes and tell those boys what they just told us. Ray, go over to Rinker's room and do the same. Tell anybody who's with us to meet us in the lobby on the double".

"Oh, they'll be with us" Ray said as he dashed out the door. "They'll be with us".

Ben turned back to Crenshaw "We're tearing off the yoke, it looks like we're with you".

"Ok, let's go" Crenshaw said.

"Ben grabbed his jacket and hat and followed the Patriots out and down the hall. Ben's guys were in motion running down the hall knocking on doors. People came to the door, and you could hear one of them in the background saying "I've got some life changing news for you! Listen up!". Someone asked "Hey why are the lights still on?".

The five of them reached the elevator, got in and started down. It stopped on the third floor and when the doors opened there was Greek with four new friends who crammed into the elevator. There was excitement among them from imagining what was about to happen.

"You're one of the Pioneer Patriots?" one of them asked Kaiden.

"Yes, I am" Kaiden answered.

"Is it possible that we can get out of here and put an end to all of 'this'?" another asked.

"If you're willing to fight for it, yes" Kaiden answered.

The guy reached out and shook Kaiden's hand with a big smile on his face. "We're with you all the way man".

That elevator door couldn't have opened quick enough. Crenshaw was cautious and pulled out his Beretta pistol as he exited. Luckily there was no need for it. Melvin and Ramsey were there leaning up against the reception counter. They both had a smile on their face. When Crenshaw looked closer, he saw the guard behind the counter sitting in his chair. The guy was tied up with his hands behind his back and a gag in his mouth. The man looked ghost white with fear. Ramsey had taken the guards rifle and pistol and now handed them to Crenshaw. "He was nice enough to turn the lights back on for us" Ramsey said.

Crenshaw laughed. Turning to Ben he said "Here" and handed him the guards weapons.

Inward, Ben was jubilant. But being a cop, he knew what this meant. Outwardly he became serious because of the ramifications. "You're a man of your word" he said to Crenshaw.

"We have a few rifles for you, but we have to achieve our next goal first in order to arm more of you". Crenshaw told Ben. "Give these to the ones who have the most experience with firearms. Give them to the ones who are most likely to follow you and fight for their freedom".

Behind them, the door to the elevator opened again. It was packed with men and women who poured out into the lobby. Elated wasn't a strong enough word for describing the energy in the air. Especially when they saw the guard tied up and a weapon in Ben's hands. From that point on they knew there was some truth to the story they had just heard. Now there was hope, hope that what people were saying could actually come true.

News spread quickly. Again, the elevator door opened, and a large group of people emerged and mingled with the ones already in the lobby. The doorway to the stairs opened and a slew of people came into the lobby that way. Rather quickly the lobby filled with people. With them came an air of excitement in the form of a murmur that became louder as the crowd grew.

People in the lobby milled around not knowing what to do next. Yet there was an air of wanting to get on with it and do something. Crenshaw picked up on it and addressed the crowd.

"Fellow Americans!" Crenshaw yelled. Silence swept over the lobby. "Fellow Americans! As of this night you have been given... YOUR

FREEDOM!" The crowd cheered enthusiastically. "Do you want to keep it?" he shouted.

"YEAH!!!" they all shouted back.

"Now you can see how fragile it is. How it can be taken away just like that" Crenshaw snapped his fingers. "What you do with it from this point on is up to you. I ask that you, all of you, come with me and fight the plantation owner until you are the ones that are back in charge of your own destiny. Only then will you be able to go back to you families and live free like the Americans you once were. For you to achieve that, you must participate and revolt against this tyranny and fight until they are no longer in power…".

"With what?" someone in the crowd yelled.

"Come with me and I will show you. Come with me and I will feed you. Come with me and I will arm you so you can achieve this for yourselves".

"YEAH!!!" Everyone went nuts.

Proffit and another Patriot exited the Humvee and walked around to confront the guard who had just walked up. The guy wasn't getting answers that made sense from Eric, so he was starting to get suspicious. Especially after seeing that Proffit wasn't wearing a Federal uniform. Proffit offered him some lame explanation, which he seemed to accept. That put him at ease enough for them to small talk him and stall for time.

Eric got a message from Crenshaw on the radio, and the small talk was over. A nod to Proffit set him in motion. Proffit lunged at the unsuspecting guard. He grabbed him and quickly maneuvered around to his back and put the guy into a headlock. Squeezing, it didn't take long before the guy went limp. The two of them dragged him behind the vehicle.

Security camera #3 caught it all. Out at the front gate and right on que at 9:30, Eric, Nick, Proffit and Ramsey led the Patriots in the attack.

The camera angle showed the gate and the area in front of the mobile home that security was using as an office.

Nick was standing in the turret holding onto the 50 cal, his Humvee screamed toward the gate and smashed into it head on. The gate flew apart with the Humvee continuing through. It skidded to a halt in front of the trailer with the barrel of the machine gun pointing at the front door. The front gate guards were quickly overwhelmed by Patriots on foot who flowed in right after the Humvee. The guards who chose to raise their rifles were taken out with triple shots to the chest. The team moved quickly to set up in position all around the trailer with rifles pointing at windows and doors ready to shoot. One of them shut off the generator that was located on the outside of the trailer, all the power went out inside and communication was cut off. Now it was a standoff with the Patriots outside and most of the security team hold up inside.

Previously, just before 9:30, five security team members had gathered in the living room of that office trailer to conversate and set up before going out on patrol. Some of them saw Crenshaw drive by. They were supposed to be out patrolling when the power went out but tonight, they lingered in the comfort of the trailer for a bit longer than they were supposed to. Since this wasn't a real prison, and people were basically forced to work out of here with 'invisible chains', this skeleton crew of security guards is all that was deemed necessary to maintain control. That and the well-known rule that anyone caught outside the building after lights out "would be shot on sight", tended to keep everyone in check.

The Patriots made their presence known to all on the inside of the trailer and demanded their surrender. A shot from an AR-15 that penetrated the front door told the inhabitants that they were serious. They also yelled a reminder that there was a 50-calliber machine gun trained on the building. That was a major motivator. Everyone was silent as they waited for a response. The trailer's front door opened, and the security guards came out one at a time with their hands up. A decision that saved their lives.

In the 'Y', word got around fast. A continuous flow of people came down the stairs and groups of them continuously emerged from the elevators. The lobby filled with anxious people. Crenshaw walked over to the front door and yelled at the crowd. "We need to get moving, everyone meet me at the front gate! Don't worry, you won't get shot, we took out your captors!". Crenshaw opened the Hotel's front door and led them outside into the parking lot. They were jubilant, they were... free.

Crenshaw pulled Ben to the side. "Get your most trusted men, definitely the ones who can handle weapons and meet me at the front gate".

Somewhere between one and two hundred people eventually gathered and stood around the smashed up main gate. They waited for information and were looking for guidance on what to do next. People were all over the place and they were alive with excitement. Even the squatters in the tents outside the fence came out and joined in. No one was happy with the status quo, and everyone felt that finally, here was a chance to do something about it.

It was a good sign. About fifteen men led by Ben showed up and met outside the trailer. Ben and a few of his most experienced men were invited inside for a pow wow. Now a circle of people surrounded Crenshaw and listened intently. He explained the plan and gave out instructions. Kaiden gave Ben and his men the eight rifles, a few pistols and all the ammunition the security team had stored inside the mobile home. He told Ben "This is serious. We heard that you were the guy to turn to so that puts you in charge of your guys. You are their leader. The mob is going to do what they are going to do. You must make sure that your men stick with you and follow your orders. We're at war with these people. They are ruthless, they will kill you, so watch out and show no mercy. Can you do this?".

"These men will follow me. Some are cops that have worked and trained with me for years. Most of us were replaced by the 'Citizens Brigade'. They told us we weren't competent at our jobs and that they were replacing us with social workers. It happened over time and then when the SHTF things moved fast. It was amazing how fast these people took control. Like it had been planned all along. When we protested, we were targeted. Some of my friends are missing, so hell yeah, we can do this! We've all been busting at the seams to do this".

"This is important, and we don't have much time. I need you all to participate. We're going to overwhelm the people who are threatening you and your families. Together we can do this. I don't care how you get there, walk, ride a bicycle, but those who want to join this protest and take back this town, meet me at the Wall Smart parking lot. It's time 'we' do the rioting. We're going to take back what's been taken from us!".

"Yeah!" they shouted and broke like it was a huddle. Everyone went to work.

There had been many riots that occurred all over the U.S. in the prior months. Angry people formed gangs, and multiple gangs formed crowds that roamed the streets chanting slogans against the system with destruction in their wake. Capitalism, they were told, was the catalyst of their problems. This mob, the one that developed here tonight outside the Oneonta YMCA was different. It was made up of a few hundred people who had gone weeks without electricity and without the internet. Food was running out and people were panicking. Many were desperate and wanted to restore the system they had lost and regain the comforts they had. First hand they found out that the alternative created by the progressive socialist party was not all it was cracked up to be. It went from bad to worse. Much worse. Now they had an outlet for their frustrations and enthusiastically joined the movement that promised to push back against the people who took it away. Hatred and revenge motivated the crowd to move down the street toward their goal. A few had rifles, some had hand guns. Baseball bats appeared out of nowhere, others carried sticks and stones they picked up along the way. Ben and his men mingled with the crowd and moved along with them down the street in the direction of Walmart. The ones carrying rifles gave the movement an unmistakable aura of seriousness.

Before the Patriot convoy took off from the 'Y' they transferred their Brigade prisoners out of the cattle car and into the office trailer. There they were placed with the others and held under guard. Nick had to do everything he could to keep people from getting at them, they would have beat them silly if they could. Luckily, most of the protesters ended up leaving with the main body of the crowd. Crenshaw calculated that it would take approximately 30 minutes for most of them to walk the distance to the Walmart parking lot. "That should give us time to achieve our goal" Crenshaw told his Patriots.

A block before the convoy arrived at the Wall Smart building, the two Humvee's peeled off and parked on a side road out of sight to wait for the crowd and a signal. Minutes later the main body of cars arrived at the entrance to Walmart's parking lot. It would have raised suspicion if they tried to bring in the Humvees with the Brigade vehicles, plus, Crenshaw's plan did not involve shooting their way in. That would have been more dangerous and would have put them all at greater risk.

Pulling up to the front gate the Patriots found the layout to be exactly how Jerimiah described it. They were amazed at how 'hardened' the place was. The tall fence around the perimeter looked forbidding with two rolls of barbed wire strung across the top. Some sections had concrete barricades with sharp edge wire strung across it. "This place is more secure than the Herkimer Post Office" Kaiden commented.

Scattered around the perimeter were multiple guard stands that held two or three armed guards at various points along the perimeter fence. To top it off, multiple patrol vehicles roamed the parking lot along the road that encircled the building.

"Someone doesn't want anyone getting in here" Crenshaw commented.

Four Patriot vehicles and the cattle car pulled cautiously up to the front gate. The guards seemed to know them or at least they recognized the vehicles, the guy waved them forward. Kaiden rolled down the driver side window and told him "We got pigs and a bunch of other stuff" while pointing his thumb at the cattle car behind him.

To security they were known as 'Kent's patrol'. Everything looked normal except for the personnel.

"Where's Kent?" the guard asked.

"He's sleeping in the third car" Kaiden replied. "We didn't want to wake him".

The guard thought about it and then waved them on through. After all, this patrol was returning to drop off the day's take like they had done numerous times before. When all the vehicles passed through, the guard closed the gate behind them without being able to see that instead of pigs, there were Patriots huddled inside the cattle car.

"Wow. That saved us from fighting our way in. You were right Cap. Without these vehicles we never could have gotten in here, at least not this easily and not without a major fight" Ramsey said as they drove up to the loading dock located in the rear of the Walmart building.

Crenshaw told everyone in the car "Ok guys, here we go. Let's do it just like we planned". With that, Crenshaw got out and walked up to the loading dock and approached one of the guys standing on the platform.

"These people aren't Brigade members and they aren't Feds. It must be a private security company" Crenshaw noted. A rifle slung over one of the security guards back set him apart from the other workers who were unarmed, plus he was the only one wearing the same uniform that the guards at the front gate were wearing.

"We got pigs today" Crenshaw yelled to him. Where do you want 'em".

"Kent knows where to put them. Where is he? Hey, and what's with the uniform?" the guy asked pointing to Crenshaw's BDU's with a degree of suspicion rising between each question.

"The Brigade's getting official uniforms, you didn't know?".

"No, I hadn't heard".

Crenshaw changed the subject "We confiscated a bunch of rifles today, real nice ones too! Got a lever action Henry. And you should see the gold and silver we got, or should I say that we 'stole' for our cause". Crenshaw laughed attempting to redirect the guys attention knowing that if he was the foreman, he probably skimmed a little off the top of whatever came in.

Taking the bait, the foreman said "Great, let's see what you got".

"Yeah, Kent's around back of the cattle car" Crenshaw told him.

"The foreman jumped down off the loading dock and got in Crenshaw's face. "Don't ever let me hear you say anything about stealing again plow boy or I'll stuff you, you frickin idiot".

Crenshaw saluted and said "Sorry sir, it won't happen again".

The foreman was satisfied with that yet grumbled something while walking toward the back of the cattle car. When he turned the corner, four Patriots grabbed him and pushed him into the vehicle. There was a scuffle and a muffled scream but then… silence.

"Kent's got the day off" Crenshaw said as he looked around to see if anyone saw them. When he looked inside the cattle car, they had the guy's hands pulled behind his back and Kaiden had one hand on the guy's throat squeezing hard on his jugular until he passed out. After going limp, a Patriot of the same size was chosen, and they quickly exchanged jackets and hat with the foreman doing their best to make the Patriot resemble the guy.

With the new foreman at the front of the group, five Patriots fell in line behind him as they walked up the ramp leading to the loading dock. All carrying weapons and doing their best to give the impression that they were Brigade members being escorted up to the main office. Some of the Patriots had on a Federal jacket that they took from the Feds supply truck. It must have been quite confusing to anyone who saw "Feds" walking up the ramp, but it gave the group a greater degree of authority.

The group of them made it all the way up to the office door without a negative reaction from the handful of workers and at least two more guards who were walking around the place. The guards looked quite comfortable working here and were at ease with their rifles slung over their backs, they were unprepared for what happened next.

Four men with the same private security jacket on sat or stood inside the warehouse office busily checking a computer screen or were entangled in a heavy conversation. You could see them through a large clear acrylic window. One of them looked out as the group walked up and recognized the foreman's uniform but frowned and tried to look closer when he saw a different face. It didn't dawn on him that something was wrong until it was too late. The Patriots burst into the office and immediately held the men at gun point. Kaiden pulled the blinds down over the window and they scurried around tying up the prisoners and gaging their mouths.

Now in total control, and at knifepoint, Kaiden asked the guy who sat behind the desk "How many security guards do you have on duty tonight?".

"Six total in this section" the guy said without hesitating. "Please, I'll tell you anything you want to know, just don't kill me".

"I want you to call the others into the office one at a time. If you give any indication that something's wrong, I will be forced to stick this knife in your throat to shut you up. Do you understand?".

"Yes" he nodded.

After punching the intercom button on the phone, over the loudspeaker, a shaky voice said "Jimmy. Come to the office… now".

In the briefing for this mission, some Patriots suggested they just blast their way in. Crenshaw argued it was imperative to take over quietly to keep the place from going on alert for as long as possible. One by one the three other guards came to the office as ordered and were subdued as they entered. So far so good. When all the dock security personnel were taken out of circulation, they figured they only had a few minutes left before someone monitoring security cameras would get suspicious and raise an alarm. They had to take out the camera monitoring room to blind them so there would be maximum confusion when the SHTF.

Crenshaw addressed the same dock manager "Now take me to the monitoring room, the one where they monitor the cameras". "I'm going to warn you one time and one time only. Yes, you could yell to one of your teammates and ruin the surprise. But I must impress upon you that I will put a bullet in you first and you will be dead. Do you understand?".

"Yes, yes" the guy said with sweat starting to build on his forehead.

Crenshaw surprised Kaiden and told him he was going to do this by himself. "This is the best way to get past any suspicious personnel" he said. Crenshaw traded weapons with one of the patriots and stuffed it under his jacket. Crenshaw left his men in control of the dock and walked with the prisoner in front of him trying to make it look like he was being escorted by the dock manager. The room where they monitored all the cameras was located inside the building just down the hall, so the walk wasn't that big of a deal. But there were offices along the way with people in them as well as people in the hallway which they had to pass through, that was the tricky part.

One person they passed in the hallway going in the opposite direction said "Hey Mark" to Crenshaws escort. Mark was so nervous that when he didn't answer, the acquaintance turned and frowned wondering what was going on. The fact that Crenshaw had a weapon hidden underneath his jacket didn't help. It bulged out noticeably. Further on down the hall they came to a door which said "Security" on the outside.

"This is it" Mark said.

Just then someone opened the door, and an armed security agent came out. Crenshaw grabbed Mark by the arm and pulled him down the hallway to try to avoid a confrontation. But the agent walked toward them and passed them in the hall. The guy stared at Mark as he went by and Mark, in his freeked out state, couldn't help but give the guy a nervous look. Either on purpose or by mistake Mark gave the agent cause to suspect something was wrong. The agent turned and looked at the two of them.

"Hey..." the guy yelled at them.

Crenshaw wasn't taking any chances. To stifle the possibility of discovery, he pulled out a knife he had at the ready and attempted to solve the problem quietly. He lunged at the guy and stabbed him multiple times. The guy sank to the floor clutching his stomach and neck, then curled up into a ball as he withered in agony. Agony so intense that he couldn't even cry out. The slice to the throat ended him. Mark fell back against the wall and slid down to the floor with a look of pure fright on his face. Evidence that he pissed his pants showed when a puddle formed underneath him.

Crenshaw threw the knife down, opened his coat and pulled out a loaded M79 grenade launcher, one of the ones they inherited from the Feds. He aimed and fired a 40mm HE round at the security room door and hit it square on. The explosion created a fireball that was all encompassing and blew the door off its hinge's. It disappeared in the smoke. Not having enough experience with the weapon, Crenshaw was way too close to the door when it blew. The explosion knocked him back on his ass and he slid across the floor and slammed into the wall. Everything went blank.

A mob of protesters reached the outside of the main gate to the Walmart parking lot. Slogans they shouted and the noise they generated along the way created a scene that attracted more and more people to their cause as they went. Even at that late hour, people came out of their houses and added to the mass of people flowing down the street in clear defiance of the 9:30 curfew. Their numbers grew and so did the volume of the slogans they chanted.

A mass of people reached the front gate of the Walmart parking lot, the fact that it was a protest, and the size of the mob surprised the guards. They only had a brief warning due to the noise that preceded the mob before the protesters appeared in front of them. The crowd descended on the gate and started beating it with sticks and baseball bats. The guards called it in and reported the disturbance with a nervous tone in their voice and shouted over the radio "We got a mob at our gate! All available personnel converge on the front gate now!".

Within minutes multiple security vehicles pulled up to the inside of the front gate to confront the developing situation. Three security guards jumped out of the first car. They unstrapped their rifles and held them in their arms in a ready position. "What's going on?" the leader yelled over to the guys on gate duty.

The explosion from Crenshaw's M79 rocked the building. Instantly all the secrecy and the hiding were over, the explosion was the signal. All the Patriots waiting in the vehicles at the loading dock jumped into action. Ten piled out and ran up the ramp and onto the loading dock to join the others. Kaiden and his team kicked it in gear and the five of them burst out of the loading dock's office with rifles ready. They bee lined it over to the door leading to the interior of the building and kicked it open.

The sound of an explosion came from the main building. "Holy crap what was that?" one front gate security guard said to another.

"Woh, somethings going down!" the guard screamed. "We got a situation on our hands!" he yelled into his hand-held radio.

"Call the office. Get some help down here!" the second guard yelled.

One of them leaned out of a little guard shack by the side of the gate and yelled "I just called the office, no one answered!". "Shit!" the driver of the security vehicle said. He ran back to his vehicle and was about to get into his car when a machine gun came to life just outside the front gate. Two Humvee's pulled up parting the crowd as they went. When the 50-cal opened up, people in the crowd screamed and ran out of the way.

Bullets sung through the air over the heads of running protesters. Lead passing through the gate generated sparks whenever they hit metal. On a straight trajectory they slammed into the three security vehicles on the other side. The guy inside the first car had no chance, he was cut down as he sat with a string of bullets that pelted his vehicle. The same thing happened to anyone still sitting in the second vehicle. The guy standing outside his car was struck and killed as he turned to run. The line of bullets swung over to each of the cars and then to the guard shack instantly killing whoever was inside the wooden structure. One of the vehicles burst into flames. After placing the guns attention on the lock that hung on the gate, the thick metal chain bounced around and broke into pieces. The two metal sections of the gate swung open giving the Humvee's an invitation to continue on through. Smashing their way through the armored vehicles, they veered around the burning car. One Humvee drove left and the other went right. Materializing from out of the crowd came Ben with his men right behind him. They fell in line and followed the Humvees on foot. When the Humvee's turned in two different directions, right along with them Ben's group split in two with each group following one of the Humvees in front of them.

The Patriots Humvee's sought out targets as they drove rapidly around the perimeter of the parking lot. When they came upon a guard house, they shot it up. When they came upon a security vehicle, they shot it up. Ben's men trailed behind them in support and finished off any wounded with a shot to the head. No prisoners were taken, and no mercy was given.

One of the security vehicles patrolling the area saw what was happening and stopped in their tracks. Four men exited and took up firing positions at each side of the vehicle. It was a gallant attempt, but they didn't know what they were up against. They fired shots that pinged off the Humvee striking the metal shield and cracking the bullet proof windshield. That was seconds before the fifty-cal turned in their direction. It wasn't a pretty sight. The gun chewed up the ground, the vehicle, and the people in firing positions around it. After the security vehicle was incapacitated, rifle fire was still coming from the position, but the Humvee moved on. They were on a search and destroy mission mimicking the extremely effective German blitzkrieg technique. They drove through the parking lot shooting anything that gave or could give them resistance, moving fast before anyone could mount an effective response. Mopping up was left to Ben and his men who came up behind the Humvee's and laid down an overwhelming barrage of suppressive fire that either killed or made the remaining defenders drop their weapons and give up. Those too were shot, and once again, the blaring question of morality rose to the forefront. But all of Ben's men knew that this was a skirmish in which their lives and the livelihood of their families were at stake, and at this stage of the battle there wasn't enough men to spare to look after prisoners so none could be taken.

Once each team did enough damage to the roaming patrols and the guard houses, they turned their attention to the main entrance of the Walmart store. There they found an unknown number of enemy defenders who had gathered at the entrance to repulse the attack. They fired at the moving Humvee from the large three section front doorway. No one knew it at the time but the fifty cal on Nicks Hummve had gone silent for a reason. Nick yelled down from the turret "It's jammed! Give me the blooper!". Someone handed him a loaded M79. As the Humvee drove by the entrance at a fast clip, Nick fired the first grenade at the door.

"Ka-boom!" the grenade hit one side of one of the glass doors smashing it to bits. Someone in the Humvee handed up another 40mm grenade, Nick cocked the M79 just like a break action shotgun, ejected the spent shell and inserted a new one. He snapped it shut as the Humvee turned to make another pass. This time Nick fired at the center of the front entrance in drive by fashion. The round exploded with a shock wave that shattered glass in every direction. Two defenders were cut down by shrapnel giving Ben and his men a chance to move up. As they did, they were met with rifle fire coming from just inside the doors. One of Ben's men was hit, and he went down, the others went to ground and took up firing positions. A blistering barrage of bullets went back and forth between the two sides.

The Humvee came back around, but this time it swerved to a screeching halt right in front of the front entrance. Nick's head popped out of the turret followed by the barrel of the M79. He fired, paused to reload and then fired again as fast as he could. The explosions made the entrance disappear in a cloud of smoke and the return fire stopped. Ben gave the signal, and his men charged the door. They pushed through the cloud of smoke with glass crunching under their feet. A dead man lay in a pool of blood by the front door and another on the inside. Behind a cement column was a man who sat there motionless, dazed and confused. He was just staring into space. One of Ben's men shot him. There was more firing on the right. Ben shot and killed a man who stood up in front of him and fired his weapon. Luckily the guy missed him, but the defender wasn't so lucky. Bullets from two different directions hit the bad guy in the upper body and he dropped like a rag. The mixed group consisting of Nick and Ben's men entered the building together, firing at anything that moved.

* * *

"I think I'm dead" Crenshaw said to himself. There was no sound and everything was black. Then he realized his eyes were closed. He tried to open them, and a blurry picture appeared. It was an out of focus view of a man's face floating around right in front of him. The guy was pulling on him. He was pulling him up into a sitting position. He felt hands on him. His whole body felt weird. The guy was saying something.

"Captain! Captain!" he thought he heard.

His vision started to clear; the blurry face looked just like… Kaiden.

"Captain, wake up! Are you all right?" Kaiden asked.

Crenshaw was bleeding and didn't even realize that he was trying to answer. What came out was just a mumble.

"Sir, wake up" Kaiden told him. "He's in shock" someone said.

"Take him out to the vehicles and see what you can do for him" Kaiden demanded from a Patriot standing next to him. He told Crenshaw "Don't worry sir, I'll take it from here".

Rifle shots came from inside the security office down the hall. Two Patriots had entered the smoldering mess of a room and shot two security guards who were barely alive but moving around enough to be a threat. Then they shot up any equipment that might possibly still be working. Two Patriots came out saying "Clear". More sounds of gun fire came from down the hall. Patriots were going room by room shooting anyone who raised a gun in their defense.

At first the Patriots had the element of surprise on their side. Guards they encountered came around the corner looking to join in to control the rioters at the front gate, some didn't even have their guns at the ready. Others brought them up to bear when they saw the Patriots but were cut down before they could fire. None of the defenders expected to see armed intruders inside the facility. The mob at the gate did their job, it had drawn attention and resources away from the interior of the building.

Still, members of building security who heard gunfire eventually realized what was happening, and now the situation had become more difficult for the Patriots as well as the defenders. For them, putting together a coordinated response to the attack was impossible after the buildings communication system had been taken out.

Kaiden's group came to the double doors that divided the administration offices from the large main retail section of the store. They dove through them and spread out to each side. When the defenders inside the massive store identified them as intruders, they sent a hail of bullets in their direction. A Patriot went down while others returned gunfire and moved from location to location, pumping bullets at enemy positions as they moved. As more and more Patriots entered and joined the fight the battle intensified. A defender stood up to shoot and got shot in the chest. He fell backwards and lay on the floor motionless. Another guard got hit in the shoulder and spun around losing his rifle just before he got shot again. That guy shook and then collapsed.

The Patriots had the momentum. They encountered a lot less coordinated resistance than they otherwise would have if they didn't have the element of surprise on their side. Moving through the store one isle at a time they gained ground. It must have been quite nerve racking for the defending security team to suddenly see a large group of well-armed soldiers coming at them with guns blazing.

Nick had disembarked from the turret of his Humvee and was now walking into the building alongside Ben's men. He was credited as a major reason why Ben didn't lose more men on the way in. Consistent effective aim with the M79 produced an explosion in the area where security forces were arrayed against them. A strike anywhere near the enemy's position tore up the area and eliminated the threat. Debris flew and bodies fell. The defenders couldn't believe it. A situation they never thought would happen was suddenly playing out right in front of them. It showed in the expression on their faces- *"I might die tonight"* was a thought that went through their minds. Then, right next to that guy, a fellow security officer gets hit, he goes down. It was unreal.

Ben and his team were able to move further into the building after each explosion, shooting their way in they pushed everyone back as they went. More of Ben's men came in from behind and added to the assault. Some of them were cops who knew what they were doing, the others just copied what the man in front of him was doing. A crescendo of noise made it sound like an army was assailing the building from the amount of gunfire and explosions. Some of these hired security guards had no major investment in what they were doing. It was the only job available, so they took it. Gunshots made the job way more dangerous than they ever believed was possible; a sickening feeling came over them. A few started to panic. Then a few more. Panic triggered a flight response that promised to remove them from the possibility of bodily harm or even death. It became so powerful that many had no choice but to obey the desire to give up. Those men threw their rifles down, put their hands up and ran in the opposite direction of gunfire. Unfortunately for the others, they stayed, and fought, and died.

Patriot Nick Malner proved to be a highly motivated soldier. He turned up the pressure with his M79. One hit took out four security guards firing from behind a cash register. That stifled some of the main resistance and allowed Ben's men to move deeper into the isles of the store. It was difficult to discern between workers and the security guards. Innocent people were present, and they were unarmed with no stake in defending the place. Some were hit with stray bullets; others lay flat on the floor with their hands over their heads as Ben's men rolled over them. They were shaking, some were crying. In total there must have been twenty-five or so defenders assigned to the interior of the building, a high number which was an indication of how important this operation was to them.

One of the security guards zeroed in on Nick and got off a shot before he himself fell from a bullet to the head. Nick and his M79 went down and out of the fight. Still, defenders saw the futility of the struggle and more and more gave up with hands in the air, this was too much to ask for what they were getting paid. A few holdouts fled towards the back of the building, but they eventually resigned themselves to a hopeless situation. The amount of gunfire arrayed against them made it clear to all remaining that anyone who resisted would be taken out. The eight remaining defenders gave up with their hands in the air. The battle was over.

Mopping up consisted of treating the wounded, confiscating weapons, and placing prisoners into the employee's cafeteria under lock and key. A fire in one of the store isles had to be put out. Riley reported in to Kaiden and informed him that Nick had been killed and three others were wounded including Crenshaw. Ben's team suffered one man killed with four wounded.

Kaiden and Ben met to assess the situation. "I'm not sure what we can do now" Kaiden told Ben. "Our captain's down. Our second in command… dead. Ray and Zack were hit, I don't know how bad. They took out our two top officers".

"There's no time to mourn their loss" Ben told Kaiden. "We must decide what we are going to do next. Figure out who will step up and take command of your guys. No time to lose. We must take over the Police station next, so they won't be able to continue to support the politicians in this town. I know how to do it. But I will need your help. Here's what we do; send the mob over to city hall and the administration complex, it's just down the street about the same distance as it was to this place. We'll get Jeramiah to take the building and hold it. If we get that and the station, we got em by the balls".

"Damn, this shit never ends does it" Kaiden said. He thought for a moment. "...but that sounds logical. Our wounded will be vulnerable at the Hospital if we don't take it over. I'm going to go and take control of the hospital and secure it, then we'll help you take the station. Yes, I agree we're not done. We're going to have to control the turf or else all of this was for nothing". Kaiden thought about Kurt, Nevel, Crenshaw Ray and Zack and what could happen if they didn't have control of the hospital.

It took some time to coordinate before Ben got back to Kaiden. "Ok, I've talked to my men and we're ready to go. Controlling this city will depend on taking back the station. We know the set up and I got a plan for getting in there". Ben explained the plan and finished with "Thanks for your support, we won't be able to do this without you. Besides, you started this, now let's go finish it".

"Yeah, I wish I could finish this. But yes, let's go" Kaiden agreed. "Send a man to get Jerimiah and his guys. We'll be needing to bring them in too".

Kaiden looked around the warehouse as Ben briefed one of his men. Ben sent the guy to inform Jeramiah of the plan and to get him and his men to start the crowd moving in that direction. Kaiden sent Riley Mason to gather the wounded and get them to the hospital. After their runners left, Kaiden looked around and commented "Look at all this. This is where they stored everything they stole from the public". Both Ben and Kaiden looked down the isles at row after row of some common Walmart store items stacked alongside piles of stolen goods.

Ben confessed "I felt guilty as hell participating in this. But now I'm going to make it right. This is where we brought everything we took from the public. First, they confiscated all the merchandise in the store and then added everything we stole. Look they even got it categorized. Nonperishables over there, some fresh food stuff up front and all sorts of tools and equipment piled up over there. This is where the 'elite' come to shop" Ben said.

"Ben, come with me and look at this".

Kaiden led him a few isles over, they took a left and walked to the far corner of the "store. "Holly shit!" Ben exclaimed when he saw it.

"We passed this on the way in here, couldn't believe it. This is where they stored all the confiscated guns and ammo" Kaiden said.

Laid out in front of them were shelves upon shelves holding weapons of every type imaginable. There were hundreds with a large pile of guns in the middle of the floor where they dumped the latest ones they had confiscated, either that or they were the discarded weapons that didn't meet their requirements, one or the other. There was also an isle dedicated to ammunition. The shelves were stacked full and there were six fifty-five-gallon drums sitting on the floor filled to various levels with loose bullets representing six major calibers.

"Some of this stuff they must have gotten from the Feds" Ben said.

Kaiden looked at Ben "Let's get this into the hands of people who can help our cause".

"Gladly, but that brings up an issue. My men are holding back what's turning into a crowd at the front of the building. The 'people who can help our cause' are about ready to tear down the walls to get in here. We can't let them do that. Certainly not with all these weapons in here".

Kaiden looked at him- thinking.

"I told my men to keep them out at all costs. We can't just let everyone have a shopping spree in here, it would be a mad house and they'd destroy the place. I gave them orders to lock this place down, we'll figure out how to deal with this later" Ben concluded.

A string of gunshots came from the front of the building. The sound of screaming could be heard all the way from where Kaiden and Ben stood. Instantly they bolted and ran towards the front entrance. That's where they found six of Ben's men holding off a crowd of protesters at the front door by firing their rifles into the air. The very crowd that helped them take down the front gate, now had faced off with Ben's men. Oddly, Jerimiah and his guy's stood opposite Ben's men, both groups were in the middle of a heated argument.

"Avery, what the hell's going on?" Ben yelled at his messenger.

"They were going to storm the entrance, Ben! They started throwing rocks. We had no choice, we fired into the air".

There was a lot of tension. Jerimiah yelled at them "If you want us to take City Hall, we're going to need weapons. What do you think this is? You think you have the right to keep everything? We deserve to have everything in that warehouse distributed among us, especially the ones here who helped take this place down".

Ben and Kaiden stepped up between the two. "Jerimiah!" Ben exclaimed. "All of us took this place down and there's more to this than you know". Ben grabbed him to attempt to calm him down. "We will distribute these things, I promise you. But we can't just let a mob in there and allow them to have a run at anything they want. That would be disastrous…".

Jerimiah cut him off. "These people deserve to have a run at the people who took it from them. Allow them their due!".

Kaiden stepped in "Jerimiah, we found a cache of weapons inside, hundreds of them. We can't just let them loot the store and take what they want".

"Why not? You gave us weapons. Why can't we arm them?" Jerimiah said it while waving his arm at the crowd behind him.

"We won't know who we are giving them too or their experience with them" Ben replied. "We don't know, we could be giving weapons to Federal sympathizers".

Jeramiah didn't have to think about it. "No. No man! I know these people. They are inspired by what we've done here. They think they finally have a chance. Give it to them! Give them a chance against these people! We need weapons. We are going to need them to hang on to what we've gained here and positively if you want us to take City Hall. I need weapons!" Jerimiah yelled.

"I agree" Kaiden said.

Ben looked at Kaiden with a "I can't believe you're agreeing with him" kind of look.

"Look, Ben… we need to give them the tools they need to take back what's theirs" Kaiden said. "We need them on our side".

"What? Give them the weapons they could use to take this warehouse? I don't think that's a good idea.

Kaiden looked him in the eye. "Have faith Ben. Have faith in the people who have faith in you. They deserve this… this moment. A chance to get their freedom back, besides, we need them".

"And what, just assume that they'll do the right thing?".

"Yes" Kaiden said looking hard into Ben's eyes.

"Ahhh…" Ben exclaimed waving his hand as he walked away in disgust.

Kaiden turned to Jeramiah "How many do you have who can handle a rifle?".

"Give me all you can and plenty of ammo… But now that I think about it, I will agree. If you start handing out food, we'll never get these people to march on City Hall so you're right, we can't do that. We'll have to tell them they'll get the spoils if they help us take City hall. That'll be a motivator for sure".

"Yes, good. Promise them. Jerimiah, I'm placing you in charge of handing out the weapons". Jeramiah smiled. "Then ASAP- get the crowd moving. Tell them we will distribute the food at City Hall to those who help us gain control of it. We'll do this right and get the food to people who need it and deserve it" Kaiden said.

"Ok you got it, but you've got to assure me that this is not the 'new boss same as the old boss' or we are going to butt heads for sure".

"That I promise you. Now let's get this building secured, hand out the weapons and move on to City Hall" Kaiden told him.

After putting out that fire, Kaiden got back with Ben and continued their conversation. "Ok, let's kick this plan in gear" Kaiden told him. "My guys are on the way to the hospital with the wounded. I'm going there myself to guarantee that the hospital is hospitable. One of my guys brought our wounded there today. I've got to go and check on them".

"Ok, hospital first, then the station" Ben concurred.

"You think we can do it?" Kaiden asked him.

"Take the police station?

"Well yeah but I meant 'take the city'" Kaiden corrected.

"Yes, I do. But our opponents have probably been warned. My guys tell me there's a patrol car sitting on a side street just beyond the crowd here. Looks like they got a heads up and are watching" Ben said.

"Then it looks like they've been told to stand down too" Kaiden added.

"Yeah, that's strange isn't it. I can't figure out why they haven't responded in force. They normally would have unless they thought that no one could take this place and they were just monitoring the situation. I'll find out. I got a plan" Ben said.

"I'm sure you do; I see the wheels turning" Kaiden remarked with a grin.

* * *

An officer that Ben knew well was sitting in an Oneonta police patrol car on a side street just off the main road leading to Walmart. In the distance the cop watched as a commotion of people swarmed across the street and around the front gate to the Walmart building. He was constantly on the radio talking back and forth with dispatch giving them updates.

"TJ, we got a whole lot of hostiles here at the gate. They've broken through and have entered the lot at will. There're continuous reports of gunfire, multiple shots fired, I even hear explosions. Over" the policeman said into the radio's handset.

"Isn't security holding them back? Over" TJ responded.

"No, no one is stopping them. I can see some security vehicles just inside the gate, but they aren't moving. One of em's on fire. Over".

"Are the rioters armed? Over".

"Yes, I've seen weapons. I also heard explosions and it clearly sounds like an automatic weapon if you can believe that. Does Walmart security have machine guns? Over".

"No Jake not that I know of. Not unless they've inherited one recently, over".

Suddenly there was a startling knock on the window. Jake jumped. He hadn't seen the guy approach and was disturbed that someone could get that close before he saw them. It was a man. He must have come up right through the blind spot on his vehicle. Jake's hand automatically went to his sidearm. Relief showed on his face when he recognized the guy. He relaxed a bit and rolled down the window.

"Sargent Haines?" The officer stated more than asked.

"Jake" Ben said in return.

Sergeant Ben Haines had been Jakes superior officer before the melt down. As a 'new be' Jake trained under Ben until he got his wings and was authorized to work on his own. Jake was a 25-year-old recruit who was more attracted to the idea of a new world order than his counterparts on the force. He never got along with Ben's flavor of conservatism, and it showed in a few instances of heated disagreements. When push came to shove Jake sided with the station chief who just happened to be his father- Chief Danial Ferenczi. In front of Ben was Jake Ferenczi, the Chief's son.

Oneonta Station Chief Danial Ferenczi was a fervent progressive. He labeled everyone on the force and knew exactly who conformed to his agenda and who didn't. When push came to shove, and when everyone was forced to pick a side, both Ferenczi's endeavored to support the Progressive movement. Hence the reason why Jake was still on the force and Ben had eventually been coerced into slave labor.

"I heard you are doing time at the "Y" Ben. What are you doing out past curfew?" Jake knew the answer but asked anyway. Before Ben could answer Jake continued "Something to do with this I suppose?" He nodded toward what he had told dispatch were "rioters".

Ben squatted down to the same level as Jake and assumed a non-threatening posture. "You mean these 'peaceful protesters'?".

"Yeah right" Jake muttered.

"I'm here to seek justice Jake".

"I don't have to remind you that it's well after curfew for you and these rioters. You know I have the right to 'shoot on sight' for anyone who violates curfew and gets in my way, right Ben?".

"No, you don't, you need to think about what's right and wrong here Jake and you know that's not right".

Tension between the two was obvious. Jake addressed it. "Alright, step away from the vehicle". This was going to feel good. Jake had wanted to put this guy in his place for quite a while. Now he had his chance. Jake opened the driver side door and forced Ben to step back. He placed his hand on his side arm to prepare for any form of resistance. None came. Ben just stepped comfortably back and allowed Jake to exit the vehicle.

"Ok, hands over your head and interlace your fingers. You know the drill" Jake ordered.

"Jake, you think you have the right to order me around and even to shoot me?".

"I know I do, so I'm warning you, do not resist".

"Who gave you that right? God certainly didn't, and neither did the good people of New York".

"Ben, I'm not going to debate you. The curfew was put into effect to stop crime and it has worked very well…".

"Yeah, all except the crime our politicians and you are perpetrating right now. You know what I mean. The movement to de-fund the police and the blatant resistance to prosecuting criminals. After being arrested the bad guys are back on the street within hours, ready and willing to do it again because they know they won't be going to jail. You and I experienced it. The police aren't allowed to protect citizens and the citizens are not allowed to defend themselves because their guns have been taken away. And from 'law abiding' citizens I might add. The only ones who have guns now are the criminals. Then when public outrage reached a fever pitch those same politicians prescribed a cure that was gratefully swallowed by a beleaguered community. At that point they would have accepted anything, anything that promised to stop the level of crime they were experiencing. But Jake, the cure they prescribed, the solution offered, turned into total control of our lives. This is the implementation of Marxism at its worst Jake. It's so un–American I can't believe you and the others fell for it".

Jake took out his gun and pointed it at Ben. "Alright, I'm done, shut up and put your hands on your head" Jake demanded.

"Yeah, just shut up and obey at the end of a gun. Don't you see what you're doing?".

"I know exactly what I'm doing and if you don't comply, I'm going to shoot you and take you in with a bullet in you. You're either going down or downtown. Which one will it be?".

Ben put out a loud whistle by blowing through his teeth. Then yelled "Jake!". It made Jake pause. "Jake, I was hoping not to have to resort to this. I want you to drop the gun, turn around and put your hands on the car. I'm informing you that this is a citizen's arrest".

Jake chuckled. "You're kidding me right" he said with a laugh.

"No, I'm not. Now I'm warning 'you' if you don't comply I 'will' have you shot".

At that moment two men appeared about twenty feet away on each side of the two of them. One of the guys yelled "Jake, drop the gun or I will shoot". The other one yelled "Jake, we got you surrounded, drop the gun".

The two men had crept up on the vehicle from both sides while Ben distracted Jake with conversation. Now they were standing there at close range with rifles pointing directly at Jake's head. Jake turned to one side then the other and looked at them. He was disgusted that these people had gotten the jump on him.

"You got a choice, drop the gun, or take your chances in a shootout. I think you will lose if you go with plan B" Ben said.

Jake chose plan A and dropped his gun on the ground. Ben quickly stepped in, kicked the gun away and forcibly turned Jake around. Then he shoved him up against the patrol car.

"Put your hands on the car and do not move" Ben said while he frisked him. Ben found a backup pistol in an ankle holster and confiscated it. Then he took Jakes handcuffs and cuffed his hand together. Ben turned him around and got in his face.

"Understand this. You just told me you would have no problem shooting me. Well back at ya. If you deviate from anything I tell you to do, either one of my partners or I will shoot you dead and leave your body where you fall. I got no sympathy for you, and I don't need you alive, got it?".

"Yeah, I got it" Jake said in a defeated sarcastic tone.

"Ok Jake, get in, let's go, you're coming with us".

* * *

After the melt down the architects of America's demise succeeded in their quest to float to the top and emerge in control of the government. Designers of the crash decided that supermarkets were second on the list of places they needed to secure and tightly control if they were to survive (Walmart for example). The community hospital was third on the list. The police and the police station had been number one. Due to Chief Ferenczi's full cooperation, they had that in the bag even before the SHTF event. Since they controlled the Police station and the Brigade teams, everything else fell into place like a good bungie jump.

Earlier that year, a security team made up of policemen who were 'on board' with the new world order, had been assigned to and were hence stationed at the hospital. They were tasked with monitoring traffic and keeping a list of employees names as well as the patients themselves. Hospital staff hated the intrusion. The cops stuck their noses into everything and enforced new regulations that came down from the Mayor's office. Medical care was now distributed by politicians, not by doctors. New regulations restricted how medicine was distributed, the quantity given out and who was allowed to get it. It got to the point that all medical services were controlled. New rules made it so that hospital staff had to file a permit for permission to render surgical procedures except in the emergency room. Restrictions got to the point where Doctors had to seek permission for just about everything they did. Politicians dealt out services and made decisions on who would live and who would die.

Sargent Williams was stationed at the hospital as head of 'security' for a reason. He had no problem with Chief Ferenczi's agenda and was good at his job. He enjoyed his new position of power and relished the idea of being able to control the process at the hospital. It was an important position. One which attracted bribes designed to obtain favors. He was a flaming liberal who was a passionate gun control advocate but always wore a gun on his hip to remind the staff of the power behind his authority. "Guns for me but not for thee" he would say with a smile. It was the reason he took notice and placed special attention on any gunshot victims that came in to the emergency room. He wanted to know where the gun was that caused the incident, then he sent his guys out to confiscate it.

Patriot Riley Mason had been assigned to drop the wounded off at the hospital. Kaiden directed him to go to the emergency room without a weapon and to try his best not to make a scene. It was believed they would get faster and better attention for the wounded that way.

Thirty minutes after they took the Walmart building, Kaiden showed up at the Hospital emergency room entrance with two Patriots driving one of the Brigade's vehicles. Kaiden was delayed by having to finalize the plan for taking the police station and had to assign someone to take Nicks place on the Humvee's 50 Cal. There would be time for mourning later. Ramsey claimed he might be able to clear the jam on the Humvee's M60, so he was their man. Ramsey also inherited the responsibility for Nicks M79 grenade launcher.

Quite a few injured rioters had been dropped off at the hospital making a flurry of activity in the emergency room. Treatment had begun on the wounded Patriots and on Ben's men, automatically security had been alerted due to the nature of the injuries. Gunshot wounds and in Crenshaws case, a wound caused by shrapnel. All of it was a red flag to the Oneonta police.. The cops on duty were very interested in the why, what, when, and where.

Security was quick. Two armed cops in uniform were already in the emergency room aggressively questioning Riley at the nurses desk. They had Riley backed up against the counter and it looked like they were about to man handle him.

Kaiden entered the emergency room and started to walk toward Riley but passed a bed where he saw Crenshaw lying there in obvious pain. Crenshaw's 'room' was created by simply closing off curtains on three sides of the bed. There was a nurse at his side prepping him and removing the rest of his cloths, she had addressed some of the worst bleeding from the head wound and was in the process of cutting off the rest of his clothes with scissors to get to the other lacerations. It was obvious there was more work to be done.

"You can't be in here!" the nurse said when she saw Kaiden standing there. "We're prepping him for surgery. We're trying to get a surgeon in here now".

"Yes mam, I don't want to get in the way, but I need to talk to him".

"Are you family?" she asked.

"Yes mam, this man is definitely part of my family".

"Then you've got two minutes" the nurse said.

"Thank you".

Crenshaw was staring into space when Kaiden moved to his side. Occasionally, a cringe formed on his face. Blood-soaked bandages had been pressed onto a major wound on the side of his head. It was ugly.

"Captain". Kaiden waited and had to say it again before Crenshaw responded. "Captain".

Crenshaw turned his eyes in Kaiden's direction and tried to mouth some words, but they did not come.

"Don't speak. We got everything under control. We took the Walmart building thanks to you. Success. The plan worked".

He understood. The news empowered him to speak. "Is everyone Ok?" he asked in a stronger voice.

"We lost Nick. Two others wounded" Kaiden told him flat out.

Crenshaw stared at him. As the reality of that sunk in, tears formed and dripped out of the corner of his eyes.

"I never…" he coughed and cringed from the pain.

"I know Captain, don't speak".

But there was something Crenshaw had to say. "I'm out. It's up to you now Kaiden" he said in a whisper. Kaiden had to lean in closer to hear better. "You take over, you got the team".

"But Captain, I…".

"People will follow you. You're a natural leader. Just give them something to follow and a chance to come around".

Kaiden stared at him.

"Get the bus back to the outpost" was Crenshaw's last words before a loud beeper went off on the monitor he was hooked up to.

The nurse spoke frantically into a microphone she unhooked from the wall. "Code three code three, bed 2!" Then she turned to Kaiden. "Get out now!" she yelled.

Stunned Kaiden stepped backwards until he was standing in the middle of the isle. Two orderly's ran down the hall with a cart and positioned it at Crenshaw's side. They hovered over him setting up for emergency treatment. Another person in white ran down the hall and into the room. That one looked like a doctor or a surgeon. All of them helped wheel out Crenshaw's bed. They moved fast down the hall with one nurse holding a liter of fluid high over the bed.

In a daze Kaiden walked down the hall towards the two guards who were pressing Riley for answers. The look on his face turned from sympathy to anger.

"You're not being straight with me..." the policeman was saying. "I'm going to ask you again, what's going on and how did they get these wounds? Ok, never mind. You're coming with us".

Kaiden was in a different mindset now. His focus turned the hall he was walking down into a tunnel with the guards, Riley and the nurses desk at the focused end of it. Everything started to move in slow motion. After seeing Crenshaw's condition and hearing that emergency signal constantly beeping, emotions welled up inside him. Hatred moved to the forefront, and it fueled his actions.

The policeman, Williams, reached out and grabbed Riley by the arm. Kaiden walked up and surprised the cop by grabbing the cops hand and twisting it to an odd angle, pain shot up his arm and into his shoulder. He cried out and grabbed his arm with the other hand to stop it from being twisted any further. With his attention focused on his arm he never saw the kick coming. A crisp snap to the guys groin was all it took to completely incapacitate him. He bent all the way forward clutching his groin with both hands letting out a groan that would have made any man watching wince. The kick was one of Kaiden's favorite techniques and he used it very effectively.

As the man started to slide slowly to the floor Kaiden grabbed the gun out of the cop's holster, turned it around and pointed it at the second security guard who was shocked at how quickly it happened. It was a Glock pistol which only needed the operator to pull the trigger to disengage the safety. Kaiden was familiar with the gun from previous experience and was perfectly willing to pull that trigger.

"Stop!" Kaiden yelled at the second security guard who at that moment was going for the pistol in his holster. Riley reached out and grabbed the cops hand, stopping him for just a second but it was enough for Kaiden to get the drop on him. Kaiden pointed the pistol at him, and the cop knew it was over. He stopped struggling with Riley and raised his hands in the air. Riley took his gun and pointed it back at him.

"Riley, search em" Kaiden told him.

Kaiden bent down to Williams level and observed Riley as he was searching the officer. 'Williams' was written on the guy's name-tag. Their weapons, radio, belt, and uniform were confiscated. Within minutes they were sitting on the floor in their underwear. Taking the uniform off the enemy had become standard procedure, the enemy's uniform seemed to come in handy.

Kaiden covered them while Riley secured the officers hands with their own zip ties and had them both sitting on the floor with their backs up against the nurses desk. Hospital staff were grateful, some of the nurses clapped. A staff member came up to Kaiden and told him "I'm so glad someone finally put these guys in their place, they've been terrorizing the staff ever since they were stationed here. They bully us and tell us what we can and can't do, who we can treat and what we can use to treat them. They act like they're doctors. We're sick of it. That one there (she pointed to Williams) has sexually assaulted nurses on my staff".

Kaiden changed the subject "Nurse, my guys brought in some patients this afternoon, I need to check on them".

"Oh, the ones with gunshot wounds? Those are your guys too? Yes, we've been treating them. Two are critical and one is satisfactory".

Kaiden knew which one was which and was relieved that Nevel's wounds were not serious.

How many does security have on duty?" Kaiden asked her.

"Normally there's four or more of them at any given time but tonight there's only these two".

Kaiden turned and asked Riley "Did you find it?".

"Yup" Riley said. He handed Kaiden a set of car keys.

Kaiden got up and turned to go. The cop that Kaiden had kicked in the balls shouted after him "Who the hell do you think you are? You're not going to get away with this".

Kaiden thought about it, and he remembered the words. They came back clearly in his mind just as Crenshaw had said it. He turned back to the cop and shouted at him "I am the Captain of the Patriot Militia! And I am fighting to uphold and defend our freedom and to reinstate the American Constitution and the Bill of Rights for the people of this great nation. The question is, Why the hell aren't you doing the same?". Kaiden turned away. Clapping and whisps of agreement rose up from the hospital staff standing around nearby.

Kaiden addressed a Doctor who was standing there clapping. "You all are now free to operate this hospital as you wish. Use any drug or treatment as you see fit. Please treat my wounded men the best way you can. Here's a down payment for services". Kaiden handed him a plastic baggie with a stack of coins in it. We'll make sure these guys will not bother you anymore". Kaiden motioned to the cops on the floor and then turned to go.

That infuriated Williams who shouted "It's not going to work! I'll get out of this and I'm going to come find you wherever you are and put you six feet under IF IT'S THE LAST THING I EVER DO YOU SON OF A BITCH!". Williams yelled the last part at the top of his lungs like a mad man.

Kaiden stopped in his tracks and turned back around. In his inflamed state of mind this cop became the embodiment of the people arrayed against him, the essence of all the people who were killing his friends and ruining the country. Proven by what he just said, this was someone who would come after him and kill him if he could.

Kaiden walked back, pulled his silenced Beretta 92 and pointed it at Williams head. Kaiden looked like he was mad enough to pull the trigger. After a tense moment, the pause allowed Kaiden to see through the insanity and think about what he was about to do. Neil Lee came to mind, Kurt Mendel and the shock surrounding the killing of prisoners. Suddenly he knew exactly how they felt and why they did it. Here, right in front of him was a prisoner that he was going to kill… "*A prisoner that would kill me if he had the chance*" Kaiden told himself. That thought boiled up inside, and he burst out "I GOT NO PROBLEM KILLING YOU RIGHT HERE AND NOW!" he screamed. The gun shook in his hand. Williams cringed at what was coming next.

"I came to grips with killing" Kaiden said out loud. "I justified it. It was either 'me or them' and I swore that I was going to make it 'them'". He clenched his teeth and shook the barrel of his gun at his adversary. His finger tightened around the trigger. "He deserves to die" Kaiden said softly.

But in a moment of clarity, a moment where things suddenly switched in his mind, he knew he couldn't kill the guy. Not like this. The gun stopped shaking and he lowered it to point at the ground.

"You come after me and I'll kill you" Kaiden said calmly.

Williams stared at the ground in a sweat knowing how close he had just come to death.

"Lock him up somewhere, then meet me outside". Kaiden said to Riley, then he turned and walked out.

Thank God for guiding Kaiden to an acceptable conclusion. Killing the cop would have turned the entire hospital staff against the Patriots no matter how legitimate their cause.

17

DOWN BY THE STATION

Using the protesters as leverage ended up being a smart tactical move. Now though, it could easily backfire. A show of force was needed at all entrances to the Walmart building accompanied by a threat to shoot to make it clear that the building was off limits to looting. Protesters became increasingly frustrated; they started throwing bottles and rocks at the building to vent some of their anger. Many wanted to storm the building and take what they needed.

Jerimiah stepped up on the bed of a pickup truck and spoke to the crowd with fiery rhetoric designed to redirect their passion. He yelled "The real way to put an end to this is to strike a major blow at the heart of these people and their operation. That 'heart' is located just down the road- City Hall! (He pointed in that direction). We now have food which we will hand out to those who help us. We also have weapons! I will hand them out to my friends who know how to use them. Step up and get yours!". That got their attention, and their approval. They joined with Jerimiah's purpose and screamed for blood. The clincher for the 'rabble' in the crowd was when he yelled "We will destroy City Hall!". In the background, from the bed of that pickup truck, his men were handing out AR-15's to people they knew and people who knew how to use one.

Redirecting the momentum toward another goal worked to defuse the desire to take out frustrations on the Walmart building. "Next stop… City Hall!" Jerimiah yelled while enticing his people to repeat it and get his men to lead the mob down the street towards the down town district.

Instigators fanned the crowds fervor by yelling slogans and starting chants like "City Hall you're gunna fall" and "Tear us down, you won't be around" followed by "Do us right, we'll win the fight". The intensity built-up steam like a Railking Locomotive on the move. Citizens, armed or not, were infused with the possibility of throwing off the yoke of this dark cloud that had settled over them. They became willing participants in the effort to start the process of taking back their lives. It was well after eleven o'clock now but instead of petering out, the crowd grew in numbers. People came out of their houses and joined the march. After all, what else did they have to do? They had been sitting at home under lockdown and restricted by a curfew ever since the collapse. This was their chance; it was like letting a lion out of its cage. For others, like a shark smelling blood, the crowd shifted and rolled along in waves toward City Hall.

City Hall, the heart of the new regime's operation. Progressive politicians used the building as a base for their party, and to concoct their schemes. An agenda that inflicted emergency 'stay at home' orders on the city brought commerce to a halt, restricted the right to travel, and took away freedom from the citizens of Oneonta. Politicians used the emergency to tighten their grip on the population, thinking that it would make constituents more dependent on the government. A dependency that they could exploit.

The city administration complex was two miles away in the down town district. Approximately the same distance as the march the protesters made to the Walmart building, so it was well within their reach. Protesters in the crowd cheered and chanted as they walked toward their target. "Onward! Vacate, vacate, we are gunna liberate! City Hall you're gunna fall!". "We can do this!" people shouted. The appearance of members of the crowd who were carrying weapons empowered the rest and instilled a sense that their quest for freedom could actually come true.

Then they all shouted in unison "USA! USA! USA".

* * *

Ben was now a passenger in his recently acquired police cruiser. He gave officer Jake explicit instructions on which streets to take and how to act while driving to police headquarters. Jake's hands were cuffed to the steering wheel which was amusing. Ben chuckled at Jakes attempt to steer with them on. The whole way there Ben had a gun pointed in Jakes' direction. The police chief's son was a prisoner in his own patrol car.

Five Patriots including Kaiden were also driving 'their' newly acquired police patrol car that they lifted from the hospital parking lot. Acquiring it fit nicely into the plan which seemed to come together nicely as they went.

It was dark and it was late. No one was out and about in the neighborhood located directly behind the police station. The two patrol cars met up about two blocks away from their goal. Kaiden pulled up and got in line behind Ben. Both cars drove passed fellow Patriots and Ben's men who were sitting in cars parked on the side of the road- waiting. There were ten of them with two Humvee's mixed in. The group of them would have drawn attention if anyone cared. A few citizens noticed, but no one made a point of it.

After the two patrol cars passed the vehicles that lined the street, the signal was given. Men jumped out of the vehicles and took up positions on both sides of the street. First, they walked, then they started to jog behind the patrol cars as they moved on the police station. The Humvee's followed a safe distance behind so as not to be seen and slowly crept along with the men.

For the last two weeks it has become apparent that only government buildings have electric power. That is except for some well-prepared citizens who had the foresight to install a gasoline storage tank in their back yard. Other than those, most people were running out of the small stores of fuel they had on hand to power generators. Street lights were no longer on, and homeowners ran their generators sparingly contributing to the unfamiliar darkness that engulfed the City. The Oneonta police station stood out. They had their generator going full bore with lights on, even the parking lot was lit up.

Ben's patrol car cautiously pulled up to the front gate of the station. Beyond the gate you could see the building with lights shining through some of the windows indicating that yes, someone was home. Normally there was a policeman standing guard at the gate, but not tonight for some reason. No further action was needed to get through, it was all automatic. A camera installed on a post was watching the unmanned gate. Jake didn't even have to roll down his window. A device on the windshield, like a toll pass, triggered the gate. This was the same system they had in place when Ben was working there. Their car rolled in with no problem and wound its way through the new strategically placed cement barricades that forced them to swerve back and forth, left, then right. They drove past the obstacles then through the parking lot and rolled up to the front door of the building.

"There's no one around Jake. What's up?" Ben asked. Even at this time of night there was normally some traffic, some movement.

Jake didn't answer.

Ben took off Jakes' handcuffs and pulled the keys out of the ignition. "Do not disappoint me" Ben warned. "You know what I want you to do. I'll have a gun on you the whole time. If you try anything, you WILL be shot. Jake, it's not worth it to try and be a hero here. You might thwart my plans, but you'll be amongst the non-living, unable to experience life beyond this moment. Got it?". Jake didn't say anything.

They both got out. Ben placed his hands behind his back with the gun hidden as best he could in his rear waist band and kept that side away from the camera on the wall. He made it look like he was Jakes prisoner and was being led into the station. The ruse must have been convincing enough. When the two of them paused and stood at the front door, a buzzer went off. Jake reached for the door, opened it for Ben as if they were on a date, then Jake escorted Ben up to the front desk.

An officer well into old age looked up from the book he was reading and took off his glasses. He was sitting at a desk behind a bullet proof glass enclosure that separated him from visitors.

"Jake! What the hell? I've been calling you for half an hour now with no answer. What's going on?". A small speaker above the window amplified his voice so you could hear him through the thick glass.

Ben gave Jake a look.

"Ah, yeah, I was busy. I picked up this guy on a curfew violation. I'm gunna book him".

"Well, well, well. If it isn't Ben Haines" the officer said when he recognized who Jake had dragged in.

"Ben Haines" the dispatcher said again. I'm surprised Jake didn't shoot you".

"Hello TJ" is all Ben said.

"I heard what happened to you Ben. Sorry it went down that way Ben".

"I'm sorry about a lot of things TJ, at any other time I would shoot the shit with you over a cup of coffee, but things have changed and this ain't one of those times". Ben kept his response short.

"Yes, they sure have..." there was an uncomfortable pause in the conversation. "Well, ok, take him in Jake".

A buzzer went off on the metal door to the left of the desk and Jake opened it. Ben followed Jake into a lit hallway with multiple doors on the left and right side. Immediately to their right was the open doorway leading into the dispatchers booth where there were multiple monitors that TJ was sitting in front of. Just as the two passed the door, Ben surprised Jake by grabbing him and forcefully pushed him inside. Jake stumbled and fell against TJ who was almost knocked out of his chair.

When the two of them looked up, TJ was shocked to see that Ben had a gun pointed at his head.

"Both of you, do not move or reach for anything. TJ, keep your hand away from your gun and that buzzer under the counter or I'll plug you to stop you from pressing it. I'd hate to have to shoot you". Ben knew about the emergency button underneath the counter, and he knew exactly what TJ was thinking.

"TJ, pull your piece out slowly and lay it on the floor, comply and everything will work out nicely".

"Ben, what are you doing? You'll go down for this; you know that don't you?" TJ said as he complied and laid his pistol on the floor.

"TJ, I can only go up from where I was and from what I was doing. Now Jake… pull him away from the counter and cuff his hands behind his back". Jake did as he was told and then Ben sat Jake down in another chair and cuffed Jake and TJ together, then he cuffed them both to the counter on the opposite side of the room. On one of the monitors Ben could see the second police patrol car coming through the front gate.

Two Humvee's raced in right after it and they all pulled up to the front door followed by more vehicles that carried the Patriot team and Ben's men. They tore out of the vehicles forming what looked like an army of men that swarmed around the building and then through the front door.

Ben pressed the button that released the lock on the interior door. It opened and Kaiden burst through with his beretta in hand. Two Patriots were right behind him. Ben's right hand man came in next eager to get word on their situation. Ben put his hand up and motioned for him to wait. In turn his man put his hand up and made the men behind him pause before going any further into the building. "Now TJ how many are on duty tonight?".

TJ answered in a defeated voice "There's only four of us tonight. One in booking, one in the jail house and Jones is roaming around here somewhere".

Walking up to his right-hand man, Ben informed him about what they were up against. The guy nodded and turned to relay the information to the others. He gave a signal with his hand and Ben's men continued down the hall training their rifles on every door and open space.

Getting back to TJ, Ben asked him "Why are there only four people on duty tonight? There's normally double that. What's going on? Answer me quickly. I don't have time for bullshit, and you'll regret telling me something that ain't true. Why are you here alone without backup? Why isn't Ferenczi responding with all hands-on deck to the riot at Walmart?".

"It's just bad timing" TJ said. "We don't have the manpower tonight. The Captain called in the entire team; they got wind of a terrorist cell hiding somewhere out past West Laurens. He needed every man that he could spare to respond for this one. There's just a skeleton crew here now. The others are on their way to take out the cell".

"Holy shit he means us!" Kaiden yelled. They're on their way to attack the convoy!"

Ben ignored it and kept drilling TJ "Everyone? Even Mark's sniper team?".

"Well Mark Evens is not with us anymore but yeah, especially the sniper team. They're all with Ferenczi. Even the Chief went on this one".

"Wow, I didn't think anything could get Ferenczi out of that chair" Ben said.

Full of worry Kaiden interrupted shouting "Ben! They're going after the other half of my team! I've got to get out there".

"Wait..." Ben said to Kaiden. "You could be walking into some shit" then back to TJ "TJ, tell me straight up. What did you report to Ferenczi? What does he know?".

"When the Captain reported in about fifteen minutes ago...".

"What's his status? What was their position?".

"He said they were in striking position and were about to move on the target. I told him that there was a riot going down with shots fired at the Walmart building..." TJ paused.

"And...?".

"I told him security was handling it".

"He doesn't know that the building has been taken over?" Ben asked.

"Oh my God. They took it...?" TJ said.

"We took it!" Kaiden said. TJ looked astonished. "I gotta go..." Kaiden repeated.

Ben's right hand man walked back into the dispatchers room. "All clear Ben, we got everyone and took the building without firing a shot" he said.

"You find Jones?".

"Yup, got all three of them. Locked them in the jail" he told Ben. Then he addressed Kaiden "One of the prisoners they had locked up claims to be one of yours Kaiden. Got the same uniform as you". He motioned to his men standing outside the door.

"Bring him in" Kaiden told them.

If only for a moment, a smile formed on Kaiden's face when Kurt walked through the door. "Kurt! Man, it's good to see you. We didn't know what happened to you. Looks like you got yourself into some trouble".

"Don't count me out yet Kaiden. Listen, that son of a bitch farmer Brown ratted me out".

"What? What happened?".

"That guy called the cops on me at the hospital. He's working with them" Kurt said. Kaiden looked shocked. "Yeah, Brown and the cops were waiting for me when I left the hospital. He told them about us and where they can find us". Kurt spat out his rendition of the story:

"Right after I handed off the wounded to the hospital's emergency personnel, I told myself 'I'd love to stick around', but when I saw the cops, I slid behind a corner in a corridor of the hospital...".

"Kurt, I don't have time for this, give me the short version".

"Ok. Three policemen came around hard looking for me cause I was the man who brought in the wounded. Stealthfully, I snuck out through a back door and made it into the parking lot. All three of the cops hauled ass after me.

I made it to the parking lot where Farmer Brown was waiting for me. He was there with the SUV in the first row outside the main entrance. I saw him standing outside the vehicle, so I started running to him. The hospital security team busted out the door right behind me.

Just before I got to the SUV, farmer Brown yelled out "there he is". I couldn't believe it. Two more security guards with guns in their hands popped out from between the cars and ran at me. I stopped dead in my tracks, instantly realizing that I had been ratted out and now I had nowhere to go. All I could do was raise my hands and surrender".

"Damn, I can't believe it!" Kaiden said. "That rotten son of a bitch!". Kaiden turned to TJ "Did a man called Brown come in here?".

TJ looked at Ben. Ben and TJ had worked together in the past and considered each other friends before all this went down. TJ didn't have a problem with Ben. In fact, he felt really bad that the system came down on him hard like that. But that wasn't enough to pull him to his side. He felt no need to tell the truth.

"Yeah, Brown was in here today. He was really worried about his farm, that's all I know".

"Ok that does it" Kaiden said and then referring to Kurt… "Someone put a rifle in this man's hand and let's get the hell out of here".

"Wait!" Ben said.

"Ben I've got to get out there now!" Kaiden exclaimed.

"Ok, ok, hold on Kaiden" Ben put his hand on Kaiden's shoulder to stop him from marching out right then and there. "I got a plan. We can win this if we're smart about it. Otherwise, the team we are up against will eat us alive. They got night vision. Hear me out, I know how we can win this".

"I'm all ears" Kaiden told him.

18

CITY HALL

It was almost twelve o'clock in downtown Oneonta before the first wave of protesters reached Main Street and turned south towards the Cities Administration Complex. On the way Jerimiah coalesced his group of people with weapons and counseled them on the plan. His accomplices walking briskly along with him listened intently. This was serious, and everyone knew it. It could turn ugly at any moment. There was a heightened air of excitement among them.

Who knew that Jerimiah would step up and become a leader. His advice was reassuring. "Check your weapons, load your magazines, stay with me and all of you, converge on me and do what I do".

Jerimiah could count on the people around him that he knew, it was the others in the crowd that he was worried about. "It's essential that you back me up. That we back each other up. We will be much more effective if we stick together and move as a group". After looking around and witnessing a protester throw a brick through the window of a parked car, he had his doubts and wondered how this whole thing was going to end up.

"At this time of night there should only be a janitor in the building" Jerimiah assured them.

"Yeah, but what do we do if the cops show up?" his buddy asked.

"If the cops show up, we're gunna do battle. We're gunna give them a taste of their own medicine" Jerimiah said.

"Yeah!" they all yelled enthusiastically.

It was easy, at first. Yes, there was only one janitor in the administration building and the police didn't even make an appearance. In the past that's how it was with the riots that were attached to the progressive agenda like BLM or the NWO group (New World Order). For them, the cops were told to stand down. Their so-called peaceful demonstrations were given the freedom to destroy property and set buildings on fire. But if it was a peaceful conservative demonstration held by a group such as "Uphold and Defend" the cops were directed to use whatever force necessary to quell the "unrest".

This protest was different. It was made up of pissed off citizens from many groups but yes, mainly from the conservative side who now realized that their silence in the past has produced the chaos of the present. Protesters who wanted to right the wrong, gathered here and swarmed in front of City Hall to make a point. They wanted to take back their city, by force if necessary. Their numbers strengthened and that strengthened their resolve. Things they normally would never have done, they did tonight. The more energetic antagonists of the group proceeded to vandalize the outside of the City Hall building. None had any problem smashing windows and doors. They picked up and used anything they could get their hands on to attack the place. None of the levelheaded could stop it, nor did they want too. Four rioters carried a park bench up the sidewalk and used it as a battering ram against the front door. Eventually it gave way and the crowd spilled into the building.

It wasn't part of the plan to control it. The protest turned into a riot and the angry participants tore the place up. All the frustration that had built up since the SHTF event was being taken out here, on the place they blamed their troubles on. Their mayor, this government, the police. They smashed phones and computers, threw chairs and turned over desks shouting "Out with the bastards, liberate the people!".

If they could have left it there, it would have been easy. The Patriots had freed and secured the Hospital, a conservative band of police had taken over the Police station, and now citizens had taken over the entire City administration complex as well as occupying about five blocks of the down town area. All of it accomplished within the span of one evening. There was no one to stop them, the police still hadn't showed up. Protesters had their run of the place.

But then their luck changed. A substantial group of people on the opposite side of the political spectrum were able to coalesce in mass on the other side of town. That group came marching up Chestnut street on foot heading towards Main street. Members marching with the group held baseball bats and were threatening anyone in their path as they walked. If protesters got to close, they were threatened or beaten which created the desired effect- people got out of their way. What made them 'substantial' was that many of them were carrying AR-15's or some kind of firearm. These were members of the Citizens Brigade who were the force behind the socialist movement in this town. Word got out about the riot and these people were told to band together and confront the insurgents. They were fired up and hell bent on kicking the rabble out of their city at any cost. Controlled and paid for by the towns wealthy elites, the word came down for them to "Do whatever it takes".

Turning onto Main street the rather large group of Brigade members quickly found themselves confronting a thick crowd of equally angry antigovernmental protesters, protesters who no longer moved out of their way. At first, the two groups butt heads and antagonized each other with taunts and threats, vulgar language and fights that demonstrated a major degree of hate dispensed from one side against the other. When rocks started flying, the bat wielding Brigade members moved to the rear and the ones with rifles stepped up.

Without warning and totally unexpected, the Brigade fired a volley into the crowd. Instantly there was panic. Anti-gov protesters made a mad dash down the street to get away from the deadly gunfire. Some fell to the ground, wounded or dead. The Brigade advanced looking like a Police riot squad except without the uniforms and riot gear. They pushed forward in line forcing people to run before them. Both Brigade and the protesters were soon stepping over bodies in the street. The Brigade continued shooting and moving forward with smiles on their faces depicting their pleasure at the power they wielded. But as it turned out, in the dark they could not distinguish between a dead person or a live one lying on the ground. When the crowd dispersed before them, the Brigade came across a number of bodies lying prone on the ground.

When the shooting first started, Jerimiah took his group (the ones who would listen) and moved up the street towards the shooting. From the sound of gunfire, and from fleeing protesters, he got the gist of what was happening. Jerimiah directed his people to lie in a prone position on the ground in the middle of the street as the antigovernmental protesters ran past them. Yes, some of Jerimiah's men had to endure being stepped on, and had to hold as bullets passed over their heads. As soon as the protesters passed them and it was clear, they raised their rifles and aimed. The Brigade came up on them in the dark thinking the bodies on the ground were dead without realizing the danger. Before they knew what was about to happen, the line of men lying on the ground fired.

Many Brigade members in the front line lost the smile on their face as a bullet tore into their body. They fell to the ground one by one as a crescendo of concentrated gunfire struck their line of advance. It shocked the participants and stopped them in their tracks. They had been told the protesters were unarmed.

"Holy shit they got guns!" a pro-government Brigade member yelled. That guy turned around and started to run in the opposite direction. None of them expected the protesters to shoot back. This was supposed to be a "piece of cake walk".

It turned into a nasty skirmish with the progovernment crowd on the losing end of the ordeal. That instilled courage into a handful of armed antigovernment protesters who walked up on each side of the street and joined Jeramiah's men in their attack on the Brigade. Those were the 'more cautious' of the group and used the building (and anything else they could find) for cover. They joined in and began shooting at the Brigade when they had them in their sights. The battle intensified further, forcing Brigade members to break from their positions and run for cover. Some kept running not wanting to be in an all-out battle where the odds weren't stacked totally in their favor. When their friends fell to the ground it made them re-think their involvement in this and created a panic that made them turn and flee. Soon, the whole pro-government crowd was in full retreat, routed from the streets due to a blistering round of return fire. Jeramiah's guy's stood up and used the momentum to move forward and apply pressure to keep the Brigade members moving back. They backed them up until all the attackers ran down Chestnut street and disappeared. None of them wanted any more of what they had just experienced.

"Victory!" Jerimiah yelled and pumped his AR in the air. His men joined him, celebrating with elated shouts echoing a common sentiment and praise for the fact that they had just survived a serious gun battle. Yet some didn't. One of Jerimiah's guys knelt by the side of a friend lying dead in the street. Filled with emotion, he pulled the dead guy up into a sitting position and cradled him in his arms. Then he softly laid his friend down. Anger rose up inside him. He stood up with a wild look in his eyes and walked over to a wounded Brigade member who was wallowing in pain just twenty yards away. He picked up a baseball bat lying next to the guy and with an overhead swing, struck him with a powerful blow to the head. Blood splattered, and the wounded whimpering man went silent. There was no one to stop him and no one blamed him. Everyone standing around watching thought of it as "deserved retribution". The victorious mob treated many of the others the same way.

19

MY FRIEND, THE END

Jester Mann's farm and what had become the Patriots campsite, was relatively quiet. All of the Patriots had volunteered for the mission into Oneonta, so Crenshaw had to order four of them to stay behind to guard the bus. Someone had to. Most of the others at the campsite had just settled down for the night. Cozy camp fires made the evening a bit more comfortable for those who stayed up. A few gathered around one of the fires and chatted late into the night, hanging on to the sought after 'campfire effect' consisting of the great smell of burning wood, the occasional pop coming from a burning log, flames that hypnotize, and glowing sparks that rose into the night to join the stars above.

The four remaining Patriots didn't have the luxury of hanging out around a campfire, Ciera assigned them the task of guarding the bus and were either out on first watch or had gone to get some sleep before it was their turn. Ciera staked a claim on the first padded seat behind the driver's side of the shuttle bus. Before laying her head down she sat there staring out the front windshield. This way she could watch the door and keep a better eye on things. She looked at the weapons she had leaning up against the dashboard. One was a fully loaded AR-15 with spare mags sitting in a go bag right next to it. The other was one of the M79 grenade launchers they had captured from the Feds. In addition to the three shells strapped to the stock there were more in the bag. Even though she had only shot the blooper gun once, it gave her a sense of security to have that kind of firepower within arm's reach. She smiled thinking about the name "Blooper". When she test fired it on the bridge the other day it made a distinct "Bloop" noise when she pulled the trigger.

Ciera coordinated guard duty and shift changes with the three other Patriots. Assignments for the night had been set. Betsy Stoiber was on the first shift on the outside post along with Glenn Greenwise. Patriot Andy Finn and Ciera herself would be on the next shift. Those on guard duty automatically got seats on the bus so Ciera could easily check on them and make sure shift changes went smoothly. Also on the bus were about eight other people who had requested and got permission to use the bus for shelter. Padded seats made it a popular place to crash and a roof over their heads guaranteed that they would stay dry.

Ciera made sure that two Patriots would always be awake which meant that none of the four would get much sleep tonight. Two hours on, two hours off. In theory she had gotten four people from other groups to rotate on guard duty, but she didn't have much sway over them and couldn't count on them to follow through with their promise. So, she sat there in the front seat of the bus worrying and trying to envision what Kaiden and the team were going through.

Standing at her post as ordered, Betsy Stoiber pulled her jacket up around her neck, not so much to keep warm as to keep the bugs from biting. There was a cool breeze tonight that she appreciated because it helped to keep her from falling asleep. Tonight, the moon was out but when the clouds rolled in, all the features of the land disappeared into darkness *"I can't see a damn thing"* she thought. It was her responsibility to keep an eye on the vehicles and that was going to be hard to do. At first, she walked around to stay awake but then settled down on the tailgate of a pickup truck near the beginning of the line of vehicles parked along the driveway. It was a great seat thanks to a Brigade member who didn't need the vehicle anymore. *"My how we've grown"* Betsy thought when she looked at the number of vehicles they now had.

Glen Greenwise and a new member of the group, one of Ramsey's crew, were on guard duty on the other side of the driveway up a ways from Betsy and closer to the main road. Glen's friend was one of the newcomers from Oneida who promised Ciera he would stand on guard with them tonight. They were tasked with watching the main road and the driveway coming off the road. The two of them were positioned near the first vehicle in line to get a good view of the driveway looking out in that direction. Or at least as good of a view as could be had. Both welcomed each other's company and passed the time with the distraction of flippant conversation.

Every so often Betsy stood up and looked through the night vision scope she was given. It was one of a few different types of available technology that they had the good luck of finding on the Feds supply truck. The one she held was a 'Sightmark Wraith'. This one uses digital night vision technology and has proven to be very effective for hunting, most notably used for hog hunting. When it was brought to Crenshaw's attention, he stared at it and commented "I'm surprised to see this as part of a military units inventory. This was never intended or designed for military use. More than likely, it was confiscated rather than issued. It'll come in handy though. This one's easier to use than the other type we found on the truck and it's easier to sight in".

The only problem was that no one had taken the time to mount it on a rifle. It had simply been handed to Betsy with an order to "figure it out". So, she ended up holding it in her hands and used it like a telescope. She switched it on and off to save battery power and now placed it against her eye to see. Scanning the area, she was amazed by the clear image. Trees, brush, and the outline of the rolling landscape, all could be seen with enough detail to easily determine if there was anything alive or moving out there. It's effective range was about two hundred yards give or take. Digital image technology doesn't detect heat or give a thermal picture, it digitally enhances the view by highlighting the small amount of light that is available and contrasts it against the dark aspects giving the viewer a perceptible view. With digital technology the smallest amount of available light can be magnified into a discernible picture, but yes, if there was no light available at all, the picture you get would not be satisfactory.

Tonight, the moon intermittently went in and out behind thick grey clouds, so to the Sightmark went back and forth between producing a good picture sight and nothing but nothingness. Betsy quickly got bored with it and looked around for something else to occupy her mind. That's guard duty in a nut shell, there's nothing to do.

Betsy thought she heard something, but then didn't hear it. The sound of a car or truck. It came back again, faintly in the distance at first, then got somewhat louder. Crenshaw? Probably. She placed the scope against her eye and scanned the open field that led up to the road. Nothing. She dismissed it until she heard what sounded like a car door. It went on like that for a few minutes, ghost noises that she couldn't really identify.

Looking like the professional SWAT team they were, a large group of police in dark uniforms exited their vehicle's. Immediately, two armed men ran up the road to scout ahead of the main body. Two groups of them formed up quickly and when ready, one group walked into the trees that lined the road, the other broke off and walked over to the entrance to the Mann's driveway. Tactfully, the first group emerged on the other side of the trees and started across an open field. Slowly, the second group walked up the Mann's driveway, stopping occasionally to "stop, look, listen and smell". Each one wore a bullet proof vest, a steel helmet, thermal imagery goggles, gloves, and knee pads. All of them had black rifles in their hands. Some were 223, a few were chambered in 300 blackout and a scattering of AR10's completed their armament.

At first Betsy couldn't make out what it was, but when she did, she couldn't believe it. A large group of dark figures separated only by a few yards between each emerged slowly from the trees that lined the main road. They entered the field across from her and headed in her direction. "Who in the world?" she said to herself and thought *"Would Crenshaw do that?"*. "No" was the immediate answer. Her question was definitively answered when she heard gunfire coming from just up ahead near Glen's position near the first vehicle in the convoy. A second after, when a bullet came streaking her way and struck the side of the truck right next to her, she jumped and sprang into action.

Neither Glen nor his friend had night vision capability, both never saw or even heard the intruders before gunshots rang out. Two fully armed men popped out of the shadows just thirty yards up the driveway from where Glen stood. They had gotten that close without being seen and were on top of Glen and his friend before they knew it. These guys were the scouts, their job was to detect and locate the enemy and then wait for the main body to come up to initiate the attack, the main body of men in their team were following close behind. Although it wasn't part of the plan, the scouts felt they had to, or they simply wanted to be hero's and couldn't wait. Either way they fired the first shots hitting the vehicle as well as Glen who was standing right next to it. The first volley missed his friend who froze in place not knowing what to do. It registered that he was being shot at, but his brain couldn't conjure up a thing that he could do about it. Hidden by shadows, the attackers were not easily seen, yet with sophisticated night vision thermal technology they had their targets in their sights. They fired again. Multiple strikes hit Glen's friend who instantly fell to the ground dead. Glen suffered the same fate just seconds later.

Ciera woke with a start. She realized she had fallen asleep sitting up in the front seat of the bus. Her head slumped and fell to one side. It jolted her awake. Or was it something else? It took a few moments to realize that the popping noise she was hearing was gunfire. Then she heard it loud and clear. Someone suddenly appeared at the door of the shuttle and rapidly banged on the glass.

"Ciera! Open up, we got trouble. Ciera! Open the door!".

It was Betsy, in a panic. Ciera operated the lever that opened the shuttle door and Betsy tumbled in. "We got incoming! I thought it was the Captain, until they started shooting. They're dead!" Betsy shouted. She was out of breath, struggling to gain control of herself.

"Who's dead and who the hell is shooting? Calm down Betsy, breathe". The girl was visibly shaken. She took a long breath and blurted out "Cars, they came up the road and parked out by the driveway entrance, must have done it with their lights off. I knew it was strange, but I thought it was Crenshaw..." Betsy took another breath. "...Next thing I knew there was an army of them coming at us... shooting! Ciera, they shot up the first two vehicles in the convoy. There were people in there! They got Glenn. He didn't have a chance".

"Ok, calm down...". The sound of more gunfire came from the driveway. It was louder and closer. Ciera grabbed the night vision scope from Betsy's hand and put it up to her eye. It was still "on". She looked out the side window into the large side-rear-view mirror and was able to see two men about a hundred and fifty yards away. They were walking between parked vehicles along the driveway with rifles in their hands. With each pause, they shot into one of the cars. Ciera freeked. Looking beyond she realized there were more dark silhouette bodies moving in behind them. Many more.

"Shit, shit, shit!" Ciera said out loud as she grabbed her rifle. With a serious look on her face, she took a moment to think. Then she told Betsy "If it's the Feds who found us then they most definitely have night vision technology, they would have to if they're attacking at night. And if that's true then we're all screwed. The best thing we can do now is to try to save the bus. That's my mission. Save the bus at all costs. It's what Crenshaw ordered me to do".

Ciera laid the rifle back up against the front dash within easy reach and climbed into the driver's seat. In a major hurry she fumbled with the keys and got the engine started. "Get in!" she yelled at Betsy. Betsy wasn't in all the way when Ciera put it in gear and hit the gas. Much to the surprise of everyone else sleeping on the bus, the tires began to spit dirt and the bus jerked to life. With some quick maneuvering it sped out from its parked position between two other vehicles and slid into the tracks of the driveway. The bus tore off in the direction of the farmhouse.

There was no time to warn the others. Ciera honked the horn in a frantic attempt to relay some kind of emergency message and continued barreling up the driveway flicking her lights on and off and honking the horn. As the shuttle passed between the barn and the farmhouse, they witnessed a few people standing around the barn door. Ciera skidded to a halt in front of them and she yelled out the window "We're under attack! Prepare to defend yourselves!". Shocked, they stood there as if they didn't believe her, but then they turned and ran into the barn.

It wasn't a fair fight if there ever has been such a thing. The attackers had night vision goggles mounted on their helmets and the snipers had it mounted on their rifles. They used the technology to make sure they would hold a significant advantage over their opponents and to assure their tactical superiority. First, the snipers easily took out unsuspecting members of the group who were sitting around two separate camp fires. Those people never knew what hit them. Dark silhouettes moving up the driveway shot into cars and picked off people as they opened their doors to get out. Some of the people who reacted to Ciera's warning were able to somewhat respond. They blindly shot back but were altogether ineffective, it wasn't enough to stop the force arrayed against them.

Ciera drove on past the barn like she was in a dirt track derby. On the other side of it the dirt driveway turned into a lane that led out into the back field. Instantly it turned rough and violently bounced everyone around as soon as they turned onto it. The shuttle flew down the lane going way too fast encountering large pits in the road that jolted the inhabitants every time the shuttle sank it's tires into one of them. It didn't help that Ciera kept the lights off to avoid being seen. Guided by moon light alone, the bus bounced back and forth on the sides of the road like a ball bouncing off bumpers in a pinball machine.

Everyone inside got thrown around like rag dolls. John Pearlman the drone operator, who at first took solace in the fact that they were getting the hell out of a bad situation, was now feeling only remorse about his decision to take shelter on the bus. The bone jarring roller coaster ride slammed him against the seat in front of him causing a shooting pain to travel up his arm. The bag he used to hold all his things fell off the seat, its contents spilled out onto the floor. Bending down to look, another bump forced him off the seat and he fell to the floor where he frantically searched for his laptop. Each time they hit a rut his head smacked into the underside of the seat.

The lane they were on was the same one their team had used to hike over to the Brown's farm earlier that morning. Ciera hit the gas instead of the brake and soon found herself careening down it at what felt like over 50-mph, a lane that only supported the Mann's tractor at 5, certainly not a bus traveling that fast. Panic prevailed. They got about three hundred yards out when the bus hit a major pot hole that ended their ride. First the bus dove into it, they bottomed out, then it launched out the other side and they sailed off the road like jumping off a skate board ramp. The bus flew in the air and came down hard on the front wheels which dug into loose soil. The bus came to an abrupt halt which made everyone inside smash into the object in front of them. Ciera hit the steering wheel hard which knocked the wind out of her. Her face smashed flat against the windshield. She sat there in the aftermath bent over the wheel with blood dripping down from a cut on her forehead. Her diaphragm had spasmed and locked up tight from the blow, so much so that she was unable to take a breath. She sat there desperately trying to breath but could not.

Hands gripped Ciera's arms and she was pulled upright. It was Betsy who got to her first. Ciera's face was turning red from the lack of oxygen. Betsy grabbed both her arms and pulled them up in the air over her head. That straightened out her chest and stretched her diaphragm which released its grip on her lungs. The technique enabled her to open up and breathe. She took a long desperate gulp of air.

Betsy was injured too but she didn't have time to address it. She bent down to Ciera's level and looked at her to determine the extent of her injuries. Ciera was rolling her eyes in a daze. Betsy stared into her face and tried to bring her back around. "Ciera, Ciera" she said while trying to shake her back to conciseness.

Oneonta's police Chief Ferenczi was with his unit looking through an expensive set of night vision binoculars. He alternated his attention between them and a live laptop he held in his other hand. The Laptop connected him to the technician in the police surveillance van parked on the main road along with their parked cars. The technician inside monitored a drone they had in the air above for mission support, it relayed information and thermal pictures of what they were facing. The drone was a top-of-the-line C142 Thunderbird built by Skyline Enterprise. It was a drone designed for the military and therefore one would instantly question what the Oneonta police department was doing with one in their possession. It had the capability of carrying a mini hellfire missile and did so on this mission just in case they ran into any stubborn resistance. Chief Ferenczi wasn't taking any chances on this one, he was determined to bring everything he had to this fight to assure victory.

Gunfire ahead signaled that his scouts had made contact. Ferenczi frowned, "You aren't supposed to start firing until the main body comes up you idiots" he said out loud. Ferenczi spurred his men on with a wave of his hand. Still confident that they had achieved the element of surprise, he felt elated by what was about to transpire. With this win he could rise through the bureaucracy of the new order. He could feel it. Wide eyed he walked down the driveway with sweeping success well within his grasp.

Ferenczi spoke into his hand-held radio giving the signal to his snipers "Commence firing". Two snipers were in position with thermal night vision scopes trained on the Patriots convoy. Each sent a bullet down range into unsuspecting targets. One rebel standing around a campfire was alive one minute and dead the next. A woman walking around a car was just about to claim her spot to lie down for the night. She stood up and looked around for the source of the gunfire when a bullet hit her square in the chest. She fell backwards over the hood of the car. Under 'cover fire' from their snipers, a swarm of SWAT members moved confidently forward.

Now that their presence was known, the line of police automatically picked up the pace and moved forward toward their target. The sound of gunfire intensified when the bulk of them came up on vehicles parked on the side of the Mann's driveway. Rambo style they stood in a line and shot blindly into them. People sleeping inside were killed when they were hit with bullets that pierced through glass and metal alike. No one was safe except maybe the lucky ones inside the Humvee. Thick steel plating and bullet proof glass on those vehicles offered better protection. Even then, a sniper shot someone who peaked his head out of the Humvee's turret to see what was going on. That guy never knew what hit him.

Other members of the convoy woke up from the commotion and emerged from their cars completely unprepared to confront the onslaught arrayed against them. At least unprepared with any kind of organized defense. Most were new additions to the group and didn't even have a gun to fight back with. The few who came up with rifles had no real targets to shoot at. Muzzle flashes were the only thing they could see. One defender who did have a rifle fought back while seeking cover behind a car, a police sniper cut him down with a single shot.

Each warm body signature registered as hot orange in the snipers thermal night vision scope. The victims were easily discernible as well as any other heat source like a warm car engine. Sometimes even warm foot prints can be seen in the dirt. Gravely mistaken was the rebels belief that the darkness of night would conceal them. Not being certain where the stroke of death was coming from, people started running for their lives in the direction of the farmhouse. One of them was shot in the back and the guy tumbled to the ground never to move again.

Terrified individuals who were successful in getting away from the attack ran up the driveway to the barn in a desperate panic. Some had rifles, most didn't, some were dressed, and some had escaped in only their underwear. All of them looked over their shoulders with fear in their eyes. A few of them ran past the barn door and screamed at the people who were standing there "They're coming up the driveway! They're right behind us! Run! They're shooting everything in sight". They didn't pause to elaborate, they just kept running towards the perceived safety of the farmhouse.

Police swarmed over each vehicle in line along each side of the driveway shooting anything that moved as they went. Turning on any one of the vehicles lights wouldn't have helped the defenders; all of the vehicles had pulled in facing away from the attackers.

A side door to one of the vans in the Patriots convoy opened and two policemen walking by turned to face the movement. Whoever was inside the van got off a flurry of shots with a hand gun that dropped both policemen in their tracks. One small victory in a futile effort to fight back, although amid the slaughter it was no consolation. The men behind the downed officers opened up on the van ventilating the people inside Bonnie and Clyde style.

Police snipers eventually became ineffective from their position as their brethren moved up and they lost the line of sight on viable targets. Ferenczi looked to his laptop for an aerial view from the drone which hovered overhead. It showed heat signatures of the enemy running up the driveway towards the farmhouse. He yelled into his radio and at the men standing around him at the same time. "Move up and take positions for a move on the farmhouse. We've got em on the run boy's, watch the ones in the barn. Some of the bastards are headed for the farmhouse. Take the battle to them. Take em out!" Ferenczi shouted to his men.

A surprised individual exited a vehicle towards the end of the convoy just before the cops swept through his position. Being unarmed, he saw the futility in running and gave up instantly with his hands in the air. They had him. He stood there expecting to be taken prisoner. One of the cops standing in front of him shot him where he stood.

Ferenczi's orders were to take no prisoners "This is going to be sweet payback for the Headquarter bombing" he told them in the briefing for this mission.

By that time the handful of people who took refuge in the barn for the night had enough time to understand what was happening. Gunfire told them all they needed to know. Everyone who crashed there was now wide awake and scrambling. They grabbed the few rifles they had and placed themselves in defensive positions at the barn door and in the immediate area. Someone started a car out front and drove it the few feet needed to turn it around and point it in the direction of the attackers. It's headlights came on illuminating the driveway and it's approach to the farmhouse. Two beams of bright light caught the advancing line of police out in the open, who by this time weren't experiencing much in the way of resistance at all. This stopped them in their tracks. Bright headlights shining directly into their night vision monocles was no problem for their thermal technology. The headlight just showed up as a bright orange hot spot. If they had digital scopes, they would have been blinded. Yet unfortunately for the police, the defenders had uncovered viable targets to shoot at if not only for a few precious moments. A crescendo of gunfire erupted when the cops fired on the vehicle and the defenders fired on the cops.

To anyone within range it would have sounded like a major battle. Both sides traded gunfire in rapid succession. 308, 300 Blackout and 223 rounds went off like a string of loud fire crackers without end. A cop went down. A headlight blew out from a bullet strike. Bullets raked the side of the barn going through the old wood like butter. One of the defenders firing from behind the barn door got hit. He moaned, dropped his rifle like it was red hot and started walking slowly out in the open toward the farmhouse. Another bullet found him, and he dropped to the ground.

Quickly the defenders that remained in the barn realized the ineffectiveness of their resistance. One of them succumbed to a level of fright that forced him to run from the barn without making a conscious decision to do it. The others followed the few that made it up the driveway and soon six of them were in an all-out sprint toward the farmhouse. Another bullet found the remaining headlight and the place went dark again except for what must have been candlelight coming from a window in the farmhouse. One of the retreating defenders got shot in the back and he went down, his body sprawled out across the front walkway. One of the defenders shot back from the hip at the danger as he walked backwards to cover the others and possibly give them a chance to get away.

Mack Heedy, and Toadie, two of the new members that joined the Patriots at Poland NY and Lake Pleasant, were lucky to have made it thus far. Upon trying the farmhouse front door, Mack found it locked. Without knocking he, along with Toadie, kicked it in. The front door burst open, and they led the group inside the Mann's house. The ones with a weapon moved to snuff out the candle and set up to cover the window that faced their attackers. Another ran up the stairs to the second floor to get to a window. Others roamed the house not knowing what to do.

Seated in the corner of the kitchen at a table, Jester Mann and his wife were holding hands while staring at a lit kerosene lamp in front of them. Their bodies jerked from fright when the front door was kicked in. To console his wife, Jester rubbed her hands and tried to focus her attention on him rather than the people who just broke into their house. "Darling don't worry, we'll get through this" he told her. But she wasn't having any of it. She cried hysterically and looked terrified at what was happening.

Sounds of heavy gunfire came from the front yard. An unseen defender in the front yard traded fire with the attackers. Whoever it was got the worst of the exchange and was eventually silenced. Everyone who resisted fell to superior technology and a wave of trained men who overwhelmed their position.

Glass in the front windows of the farmhouse smashed out and a rifle barrel protruded. Return gunfire started up again replacing that of their dead compatriots in an angry attempt to inflict casualties on the people who dared to do this. What they got in return was a multitude of bullets that popped through the exterior farmhouse walls striking objects and people in the room they were holed up in. One defender went down with a groan. Bullets continued through and struck items in the kitchen as well. The Mann's cringed as things popped all around them. Bullets struck and splintered the wooden cabinet door. Glasses and plates exploded into bits and pieces. A hole appeared in the refrigerator door, Jester grabbed his wife, pulled her to the floor and covered her as they got down low and hid under the table.

Under these circumstances the farmhouse became untenable real fast. Mack yelled out "They're everywhere! If we stay here, we die. Everyone! Run out the back!". There was no problem convincing anyone. A handful of them who were still alive and within earshot, agreed. A lone defender shooting from a second story window fired at the attackers to stall them and to cover their retreat, then he turned and ran down the stairs to join the withdrawal. They all tore out the back door.

* * *

From the shuttlebus, crippled and now stranded in the middle of the Mann's back field, Betsy Stoiber stared out the side window of the bus with the Sightmark scope she still clutched in her hands. Looking through it she could easily make out the outline of the rear of the Mann's farmhouse and she studied it intently. One insignificant light was on inside, but it helped her see the structure in the little light that was available. From the other side of the house came the sound of a raging battle.

"We're getting the shit kicked out of us" Betsy said to anyone listening. There were about eight other people in various condition in the bus who were recovering from the crash. Some were complaining and moaning. John was bruised with a sharp pain in his arm but relatively okay. Somehow, he had found his laptop and even with all the chaos around him, he was lying on the floor staring into the cracked screen worried that it might not be working. As if nothing else mattered, he vigorously tapped on keys, and made it come to life. "Oh, thank God" he said while poking a few more keys.

Ciera had semi recovered, sort of. At least enough to meander over to Betsy. With both hands holding her head she said "What the hell…?". Hearing the intensity of gunfire coming from in and around the far side of the farmhouse they could only guess what their friends were going through. Flashes from the barrels of rifles could be seen lighting up the night around the house like there was a bunch of tourists taking flash photography.

From a window on that side of the bus, Betsy watched through her Sightmark scope. Within her view she saw the rear door of the farmhouse fly open. Those that survived the carnage inside ran for their lives out the back door. Mack Heedy ran from the farmhouse and beckoned everyone to follow him. "Fall back! Let's get the hell out of here!" he screamed. Running through the kitchen on the way out, they had run right past the Mann's who were still crouching down under the kitchen table shivering uncontrollably.

Almost immediately after the last defender exited out the back, twenty SWAT members busted through the front door and began a room-to-room search. In the living room a wounded rebel was lying on the floor breathing hard and bleeding out. One of the SWAT members walked up to him, pulled up the night vision technology attached to his helmet and looked him in the eyes… then he shot him with two rounds to the chest to make sure the guy would complete his journey to the other side. "Living room- clear!" he yelled. Another yelled "Dining room- clear!". "Hallway- clear!" yelled another. Men split off from the team and climbed the stairs with guns pointing up. Others entered the kitchen and came really close to shooting the Mann's as they lay cowering on the floor.

"Don't shoot, don't shoot!" The Mann's yelled. Their hands poked out from under the table in an 'I surrender' gesture.

SWAT members doused the kerosene lamp on the table and all available light went out in the house. They took up positions at all the rear windows and the back door. Glass broke out and instantly muzzle flashes appeared at those locations as they shot at the retreating figures running away through the back field.

* * *

Chief Ferenczi entered the front door of the farmhouse and immediately started shouting orders as if his men weren't following them already. "Search the house! Cover the back! I want them all!" he yelled. His sniper team came in behind them all and instantly Ferenczi yelled at them "Sniper team! Bring it in and set up here, there's targets in the field. ON THE DOUBLE!". Way over confident, he then turned to one of his men and countering what would have normally been 'standard procedure', he ordered the officer to turn the lights back on.

"Snyder, light some candles will ya. I can't see a thing" Ferenczi was yelling as he walked through the house to the back door. Seeing his men standing around the kitchen made him mad. "Get out on the porch and get into firing positions" he yelled. "Fire! Don't let them get away you fools". He looked at the drone's thermal image on his laptop and yelled "They're in the field, fire!".

Betsy turned to everyone in the bus and yelled as loud as she could "Get ready to defend this bus!". She walked over to someone sitting on a seat holding their head. "Find a weapon, Now!" she said harshly. The ones who could, scrambled. There were plenty of rifles to be had but they were strewn about the bus in disarray. Some of the survivors lost their footing stepping on personal belongings and loose bullets that littered the floor. After they armed themselves with what was available, they moved into a position at one of the windows facing the farmhouse. Windows opened, rifle barrels stuck out and they waited to fire in the direction of an unseen enemy.

Betsy was able to watch the events play out better than anyone else. She never took her eyes off her scope that was aimed towards the rear of the farmhouse. Flashes of light started coming from the farmhouse windows, and now there was a light coming from the kitchen window.

Then she saw dark figures spill out onto the back porch taking up prone positions on the wooden deck. Soon little sparks of light came from those positions too. One member of the convoy in an all-out sprint away from the farmhouse threw up his hands and fell to the ground, shot through the back by the evil that pursued him.

"They're ours! They're running toward us in the field, don't shoot them!" Betsy warned. "Watch your aim! The assholes have taken up positions in the farmhouse. Concentrate your fire on the windows, doors, and the porch! Ready... Aim... fire!".

Ferenczi walked out onto the back porch of the farmhouse after he deployed his men there confident that he had the rebels on the run and that this threat had all but been eliminated. "We're in mop up mode now boys" he said to no one in particular. "Snipers! Set up here and fire when ready". Ferenczi was secure in his position by the way he stood out in the open without bothering to conceal himself. "Fire! Fire! Fire!" he yelled at his men. "Cut them down. I want every one of them on a slab by morning!".

No sooner had he said it than a volley of bullets came streaking his way. They cut through the air with a distinctive 'zip' and landed with a crisp 'smack' into the side of the farmhouse in various places. One buzzed by Ferenczi so close that it made him duck and cover. He went down to his knees with his laptop and his hands over his head like it was raining, thinking his laptop would shield him. Then he crawled back through the porch door and scooted inside on all fours. Once inside, he stood up. His number one in charge of the squad was standing there in front of him waiting for orders with the rest of his men behind him at the ready. His number one thought it comical to see his Chief crawling back into the kitchen and couldn't help a slight pucker that formed on his lips, one that held back a slew of laughter. Ferenczi thought he saw a hint of mockery and got mad. When he heard snickering from the men behind him, he was furious. Ferenczi fumed and became irate. He yelled at them "Snyder get your men out there in the field or I'll have your ass! Pursue the enemy! Don't come back until you get every last one of them. Now! Now! Move it! Move it!". Snyder and his men jumped. They filed out the door onto the porch and scampered down a set of stairs leading into the back field.

Betsy, along with everyone on the bus, kept firing in the direction of the farmhouse and at the scattered position of muzzle flashes coming from that direction. Only when the moon came out did they have better illumination and could focus in better on targets. Yet the moonlight was fleeting, it didn't last but seconds at a time.

In their hurry to do something and help their fleeing compatriots Betsy inadvertently gave away their position. Good intentions came back to haunt them. As soon as she ordered her men to fire, their position was compromised. Identified by their own muzzle flash signatures, the attackers now had another target to shoot at and quickly zeroed in on it. A bullet struck the shuttles window cracking the glass, another popped a hole in the side wall right next to where Betsy was kneeling on a seat.

Holding her head but recovering more every minute, Ciera saw what was happening and realized that they were all in big trouble. If more of the attackers shifted their attention onto the shuttle, it would just be a matter of time before they were on the receiving end of a bullet. Looking down on the floor her eyes came upon the M79 which had been rolling around throughout the ride from hell. Knowing she had to act to stop the inevitable. Ciera climbed out of the driver's seat and yelled at her team mates "We're not going to make it!" she said. Bending down she grabbed the M79 and then opened the bus door.

Blood was trickling down her face and she was walking funny as she moved slowly toward the farmhouse. "*I would love to get closer, but I don't have time. Can't wait any longer. Got to do something*" she thought. As anyone who knew her would tell you, Ciera hardly ever cursed. Here during this ordeal in which she thought she might not make it out alive, she spoke out loud "Ok you mother fuckers..." as if the fact that no one could hear her made it ok. While walking into oncoming fire she de-cocked the M-79, took off one of the three shells still attached to the buttstock and loaded it into the weapon. Cocking it shut with a snap, she placed the buttstock of the M-79 into her gut and pointed it at the farmhouse. Because she had only fired the weapon once before on the bridge and didn't know it well, she raised it up higher so she wouldn't hit anyone running towards her in the field, then she pointed it in the direction of the farmhouse and fired.

"Bloop!" a shell shot out of the gun and streaked across the field in an arc. It came down just short of the farmhouse and exploded in the field with an impressive burst of firepower.

No sooner had Snyder led his men into the field than an explosion erupted just twenty-five yards in front of his men. "Shit! They got mortars!" he yelled. He didn't need to tell his men to halt or duck, everyone automatically dropped and hugged the ground. No one got hurt but the blast effectively stopped their advance.

Not to be deterred Snyder quickly stood up and yelled at his men "Get up. Let's go. Keep moving!". His men were hesitant. So far, they had the upper hand in every aspect of this attack which fueled their confidence. There were casualties yes but none of them felt they were at a disadvantage at any time, until now.

Another shell exploded just out in front of them. It was closer this time and the foremost of Snyder's men were showered with dirt and debris. The mortar attack was a deciding factor. Snyder's men questioned their own mortality. Suddenly no one felt like moving. Going forward towards that didn't seem like a very smart thing to do.

Now Ciera was walking briskly toward the farmhouse. Fuming with rage she pulled the last shell from the pouch and loaded it into the launcher. Still ignoring the pain in her body, she stopped and placed the buttstock into her gut to steady the gun and to better handle the kickback. She leveled the barrel a little more thinking it would help her get more distance and enable it to hit the farmhouse... then she pulled the trigger.

Police snipers settled onto the porch in prone positions and focused their rifle scopes on the bus. "Two fifty yards" one of them said to the other. A thermal image of the bus came into view.

Chief Ferenczi stared at the aerial night vision view on his laptop and quickly determined the origin of enemy gunfire. The drone was right above them now and it produced a great birds eye view. There was a large bus in the field with defenders using it as cover to fire on his men. He radioed his drone technician and moved the crosshairs on his screen over the bus. "Fire the missile at these coordinates. Now!" he yelled into his radio.

A drone that looked exactly like the Feds RF-4 out of Oneida, turned and maneuvered into position. The release on the missile it held under its wing snapped open and the sleek silver cylinder with tailfins dropped away from the craft. It lit and shot away at a speed twice that of the drone itself.

Ben tried to stop Kaiden from leaving the Police station. He pleaded with him. "Listen to me. Ferenczi's got too much technology on his side for us to go head-to-head against him, we will lose that battle. To do this and win we're going to have to be smart and hit them when they aren't ready for it. We'll take control of the City roadblock outside of town on Route 28. We must negate his night vision advantage and attack them when they can't effectively use it against us. We'll set up an ambush at the roadblock and wait for Ferenczi's team to return from their mission. They'll definitely come back in through that check point. Taking the road block from the Brigade members manning it will be easy. They don't know what they're doing, they have no experience for this shit. They'll fall apart when we attack. We'll claim it and hold that position. When Ferenczi returns we'll have a major surprise waiting for him. It's our best chance of defeating him, his men will be vulnerable when they stop. They'll be unprepared to deal with an all-out attack and we'll have the element of surprise on our side...".

"Ben, stop. They might have prisoners with them, that would put them in harm's way. No can do. My people are being attacked right now. I got no choice, I gotta get to them".

"That's a mistake Kaiden. Your men have probably already been taken out, Ferenczi will be on his way back here soon, we've got to…".

"Doesn't matter. I've got to try; I couldn't live with myself if I didn't try" Kaiden said. Kaiden turned to his fellow Patriots who were standing around listening. He told them "Alright, you heard the man. Everyone at the Mann's farm might already be captured or dead, I don't know. From his death bed, Crenshaw made me Captain of this squad. I am now responsible for your safety and our people at the farm. I'm going to try to help them if I can. No one is obligated to follow me if they don't want to, I will understand. But I'm going. If you want to help take these bastards out, then come with me, I sure could use your support". With that Kaiden marched out to the Humvee. Every Patriot there, including Ramsey and Merrill, turned and went with him.

Three cars and two Humvee's drove fast out of town via route 28. Kaiden's Humvee with the working 50 cal machine gun was in the lead. When they came up to the roadblock, they didn't stop but barreled on towards it. When they were within range, they opened up with the 50.

Block Operators as they were called or just "Blockers", were mostly made up of students from the school. They were just kids who got off on their new found position of power. Here, where they were allowed to carry guns, it was a rush to be able to force people to do what they wanted. They celebrated nightly with drugs and alcohol and used the location as a place to gather and party while conducting "business". In between the beer and the drugs, they would play cop (and robbers) and harass any vehicle that tried to pass. Orders from the City Council were to screen all traffic and document who was coming and going, as well as where they were going and with what. They were also tasked with collecting the road tax, which ended up being anything they wanted to charge or confiscate.

The party they had going on tonight took a turn for the worse when the Patriots Humvee suddenly appeared in the distance and barreled down the road towards them with Ramsey firing away from the turret. That was a sight that not many citizens have ever seen before. Huge fifty caliber bullets streaked towards them and busted up the party in a way that no one would have imagined a party could be busted up. Any form of resistance to their passing evaporated as people jumped out of the way and scrambled for cover against the onslaught. Superior firepower tore up boys, men and women who were unlucky enough to have been assigned Blocker duty tonight. Their vehicles, parked on either side of the road, were riddled with bullets. One of the cars burst into flames, starting a fire fed by a leaking gas tank.

Kaiden had a look of determination on his face as he drove the Hummer hard and busted through the fire and the flimsy barricade that had been set up. He roared past without major resistance, and without paying the toll. After recovering, some of the blockers returned fire, but by the time anyone who was still alive could effectively react, the Patriots vehicles were already out of range.

That look of determination stayed on Kaiden's face the whole way. He didn't know what he was going to do when he made contact, but he knew he was going to fight anyone in his way, he would fight until he knew what happened to Ciera. Yes, this wasn't very smart. No there wasn't a plan. Just go until you hit 'enemy', was the driving factor. He clutched his H&C 416 in one hand and the wheel in the other.

Pausing to watch the strike point of the 40mm shell, Ciera wiped the blood out of her eyes so she could see better. She whispered "Right down your throat you fuckers".

Moonlight brought out the silhouette of the farmhouse and distinguished it against the rolling hill it sat on. Hoping to God, she could hit it from where she was and somehow fight back against this horde, Ciera waited for the shell to land. To her utter amazement... the farmhouse suddenly exploded in a huge fireball that mushroomed into three times the size of the house itself. Sharp, bright light lit up the sky making her shield her eyes from the intensity. A deep deafening noise followed. The entire wooden structure was consumed along with anyone in it in an explosion that decimated even the foundation it stood on. The place tore up and blew apart with pieces flying for a hundred yards in every direction. Half the detached barn collapsed on top of itself from the shock wave. The thunderous noise almost split Ciera's eardrums, the ground shook like it was an earth quake. It was tremendous. The resultant shockwave knocked her back on her ass, a wave of surging heat came rolling in right after. It was amazing that the heat was that strong with her being a couple hundred yards away.

Debris fell from the sky, some of it landed quite close. She sat there on the ground stunned, then looked down with wonder at the M79 she held in her hands. Getting up slowly and wavering on her feet, she stared at the destruction in front of her. Out of ammunition, the M79 was useless. She threw it to the ground and walked toward the fire that engulfed the ruins that was once the farm house. Just a few steps is all she took before collapsing to the ground unconscious.

"Woh, look at that!" Kaiden exclaimed to everyone in the Humvee. In the distance just ahead of them a bright flash of light lit up the sky followed by the resultant thunder of a major explosion.

"Damn!" Merrill said from the passenger's seat. "What the hell was that?".

"I don't know but that was powerful" Kaiden commented. I think it came from the Mann's farm. It's just up ahead". Kaiden hit the gas and roared straight towards danger fully committed to accept whatever the consequences would be.

Just minutes later, Kaiden's Humvee came upon a large group of vehicles parked on the side of the main road just outside the Mann's farm. Some of them were civilian vehicles but others were clearly marked 'POLICE'. The entrance to the Mann's driveway was a mere one hundred yards on the other side of their position. In the middle of the mass of cars was a rather large black boxcar type van that had "POLICE" written on the side of it. Definitely a support vehicle designed to back up an initiative and used to transport equipment, personnel, technology, and weapons to a remote site. Kaiden doused the lights and came to a halt about fifty yards away. His crew jumped out with rifles at the ready. Three other vehicles copied and pulled up behind Kaiden.

Kaiden gave Ramsey the signal to be ready on the 50. He motioned to the driver and gave the order to "Follow us". With everyone set and in position, the group moved on the vehicles in front of them.

"I want to run up to the farm, but we've got to get through whatever this is" Kaiden told Merrill who stuck close to Kaiden's side. As they came upon the first vehicle Kaiden signaled "Check it" to his men. Finding no one inside, they walked past and then checked each vehicle in line thoroughly to make sure there were no combatants inside. When they got to the large SWAT type van, they stood around the rear entrance in a semi-circle. Muted voices could be heard coming from inside the van. Someone was almost yelling and because of it they were able to make out what he was saying.

"TJ! I'm telling you; something went wrong. The whole place just blew up!". No response. The voice continued. "No I don't know how many or who is dead or alive but I'm telling you this thing was far bigger than anything we could have done…".

When everyone was in place, Kaiden signaled to open the doors. Two Patriots pulled on the latch and threw the doors open. The people inside turned to look, shocked to see men standing there with rifles pointed at them. By the look on their faces, they knew they were in serious trouble.

"STOP WHAT YOU ARE DOING! DO NOT MOVE!" Kaiden yelled.

Three men inside the van were either standing or sitting around a bench where four computer screens were set up in front of them. A keyboard sat in front of the man sitting in a chair. All three of them were staring at the images trying to glean information when they were interrupted. The man sitting at the console had headphones on and was talking into a strap on microphone secured around his head. Two rifles leaning up against the counter was proof that the men were not expecting any visitors. Especially these type of visitors. Two of them glanced at their rifles.

"Go for those guns and it will be your dying wish. Hands up!" Kaiden yelled. The two decided against doing anything rash and simply put their hands over their heads. Their side arms were taken away and they were escorted off the van as prisoners. Kaiden walked up to the guy in the main chair and took the headphones off his head. Putting one ear piece to his ear he spoke into the microphone.

"TJ, put Ben on" Kaiden said.

"Yeah, I'm here, is that you Kaiden?" Ben asked.

"It's me. We took the equipment van without a fight. Don't know what's going on yet. I'll let you know, out". With that Kaiden turned to the guy sitting in the chair who was now wondering what the hell was going on and how there could be someone else on the radio besides TJ.

Kaiden was in no mood for delay. He pointed his Beretta at the guy's head and said "Tell me what's going on here and don't lie to me or I'll blow you away".

"Ok, ok!" the guy said with a cringe on his face. "We don't exactly know what happened but look for yourself" he nodded toward one of the monitors. "We got the word to fire a drone missile at... (he hesitated) the enemy, and the shit hit the fan. Something big time blew up and we don't know what it was. We almost lost our drone in the shockwave". He brought up the video clip of the explosion from the drone's point of view and played back the video. The video recording in infrared mode was as clear as technology could make it considering that it was recorded in the dark. Only after the explosion engulfed the screen did it shake, and the picture was lost.

"That couldn't have been our drone's 'Minni 5 missile'" the technician said "It's just not that powerful. From the sound of that explosion and the intensity of the shockwave ... it must have been... I don't know... something else. We think the rebels had stashed their bombs in there and the place blew to high heaven. A propane tank could have added significantly to the explosion, I don't know".

The drone operator switched back to "live view". Kaiden watched as the drones night vision camera panned across the wreckage. The pictures showed where the farmhouse once stood. "Holy shit!" Kaiden said out loud. Everything was on fire, giving off light that illuminated the area.

"Where is everyone? Can you get a thermal image? Kaiden asked the operator.

"Yes of course" the guy said. Tapping a few keys, the picture changed, and the inverse view of a thermal image came up. The layout of the Manns farm was evident except for a large fire in the spot where the farmhouse once stood.

"Pan around the area" Kaiden demanded. He studied the screen and then turned and ran out of the van yelling at one of his guys as he went. "Put this guy on ice after he lands his drone. The rest of you come with me".

Supported by his fellow Patriots, Kaiden walked cautiously up the Mann's driveway with his rifle pointed forward. A large fire in the distance took the 'pitch black' out of the darkness but still it created shadows. "We don't know who's who, so be careful" Kaiden told his guys. "We don't want to shoot our own" he repeated more than once.

"Hold it!" Kaiden said in a low tone. He held up his fist signaling for them to stop. Ahead of them, two people were coming in their direction carrying a wounded man up the driveway. The two had their rifles slung over their shoulders and they were concentrating on carrying their comrade fireman style back to get medical attention. As the three got closer it became clear that it was two policemen dressed in SWAT gear carrying a third. The policemen never even considered that they would run into anyone else but their own men, they kept coming without noticing who they were. When the three got right up on the Patriots and realized that the men in front of them weren't dressed in familiar uniforms, they dropped their comrade like a sack of potatoes and went for their rifles. That was a big mistake. The Patriots opened fire and killed all three of them.

"Wow! Night vision goggles!" one of the Patriots said after searching the bodies of the three dead officers. He pulled the technology off one of their heads.

"Ok" Kaiden told him. "bring it, but don't go off halfcocked and start shooting every image you see. That thing will tell us if someone is there, but it won't tell us 'who' it is. It might be one of ours. Lay eyes on them and identify friend or foe before pulling the trigger".

"Yes sir" he replied.

Continuing up the Mann's driveway the Patriots came across the first of the vehicles in their convoy. Thermal images in the newly acquired night vision goggles showed the still warm bodies of their friends lying around the car.

One of the Patriots turned a body over. Looking up he told Kaiden "It's Glenn Greenwise".

"Shit!" Kaiden said. A frown formed on his face. It was one of their own. He worried they would find Ciera among the dead. They all continued on angry that they were not here to help defend the position yet determined to find out if there are any survivors.

"The shuttle is missing" someone said. "It's not where it was parked when we left". That gave Kaiden some hope. The group of them continued up the driveway checking the cars as they went. The bodies they encountered horrified them.

Up ahead, the farmhouse was burning and there was debris all over the place. It gave off plenty of light that allowed them to see the full extent of damage that the Mann's farm had suffered. The farmhouse was no longer a farmhouse and the front section of the barn had collapsed. The Patriots moved slowly and cautiously, snaking their way between the cars and trucks using them for cover as they ventured closer. More bodies. Two of the ones they found were members of the SWAT team, the others were members of their group. None of them were still breathing.

* * *

Ciera sat up and strained to see. It was a different unfamiliar world. She was in a big field and dawn was just now shedding light on her surroundings. Everything was quiet, or so she thought because there was no sound, but actually it was due to the shock to her ears. She couldn't hear a thing.

"I must have been sleeping. How long was I out?" she wondered. There was a thick acrid smell of something burning. The sun was coming up and she could see wisps of a white smoky fog that floated all around on the still morning air placing an eerie effect on the scene. In the distance smoke spiraled up from the place where the farmhouse once stood. Fires still burned in the rubble.

"Ohhh!" she cried out when she tried to stand up. The pain in her leg stopped her. But she tried again. Making it up on two feet she limped slowly forward toward the remnants of the farmhouse. Everything hurt like hell. An invisible magnetic 'pull' drew her towards the unknown. She staggered forward for over a hundred yards before coming across the body of one of Ferenczi's men. *"Is he knocked out or dead?"* she wondered. Ciera should have picked up the rifle laying on the ground next to him, but she didn't. She wasn't thinking like that, she was trying to remember the sequence of events from the night before. She kept walking.

Up ahead on her left, a body was lying on the ground. It was dressed in SWAT gear and lay there motionless. A few yards further up there was another in the same condition. Continuing on she came across someone dressed in the same black uniform only somehow, this one was still alive. The guys clothes were bloody and shredded in some places. The rifle he had previously held in his hand was missing. Upon further inspection, she saw an object protruding from his side. Through all the pain, the guy was doing his best to brace himself and try to remain sitting up. One arm was badly mangled. He was disoriented and confused about what had happened. It showed in his face, a face where blood flowed down into his eyes from a serious head wound. That and the dirt made him look absolutely hideous. He was unable to focus on anything for more than a few seconds at a time. His ear drums were blown out turning his world into a silent horror film.

Ciera walked toward him with sympathy in her heart but could not think of anything that she could do for him under the circumstance. He saw her, and through all the pain recognized her as... the enemy. He became animated and frantically searched around with his eyes looking for his rifle. Not finding that, in a panic his good hand grappled with the holster at his side. Somehow, he managed to get a pistol in his hand. Trembling, and with the barrel shaking wildly, he pointed it at her.

Staring at him the whole time, Ciera walked up within a couple of feet and knelt in front of him. Tears came to her eyes when she saw the condition he was in. The futility of everything that had come before and everything that led up to this moment became clear. In front of her, a human life in such agony. *"For what? How had it come to this?"* she asked herself.

The wounded policeman pushed the pistol forward toward Ciera and wrapped his finger around the trigger. The expression on his face fluctuated back and forth from external to internal with intent momentarily erased by pain until he re-focused on the task at hand. Ciera knelt there without moving and stared at him with tears flowing down her cheeks.

"I'm so sorry" Ciera either said or thought. Neither of them would have known which.

Ciera was so physically and psychologically beat up that at that moment she didn't care if he pulled the trigger or not. After a long tense moment without knowing if the gun would go off, Ciera slowly reached out with one hand and touched it, not to block it or push it to the side but to simply connect with the thing that would end her life. By doing so she accepted her fate.

Yet destiny wasn't done with Ciera. Looking beyond the gun into the man's eyes, she felt his pain as her own. Whatever the man saw looking back at her, it turned into a 'fading out'. There was a discernible loss of light, a drain of the very life force that fueled his being. Or maybe he simply gave up. The gun he held lowered to the ground without going off. He closed his eyes and started to fall backwards. Ciera leaped forward and grabbed the man, lowering him slowly to the ground, cradling his head with her hand so it wouldn't hit the ground hard. His eyes stared up at her and then, at the sky. Then they went lifeless. Ciera stared into his eyes and watched as the man died.

* * *

Something tugged on her arm. There was a muffled sound. Ciera's hearing was starting to return. How long she was sitting there next to the dead man she did not know.

"Ciera. Ciera" Kaiden was saying as he shook her.

Coming out of a trance. She turned and looked at him. Recognition came slowly, but when it did, she broke down. "Oh Kaiden!". She turned and weakly threw her arms around him. "I thought I was dead" she said loudly due to her loss of hearing.

"I'm here Ciera" Kaiden said as he hugged her passionately. "I thought I lost you". He broke down with her and they both cried together. Tears flowed freely, from the pain, and from the atrocity that had just transpired. It all came out in emotion that stuck in their throats making both unable to speak.

Two Patriots stood behind Kaiden, watching. A rifle shot rang out coming from somewhere close by. Kaiden didn't react but kept staring at Ciera indicating that he wasn't worried. It was his Patriots doing the shooting now.

It was a good sign; Ciera heard the gunshot. "What was that?" She cried out.

"Don't worry" Kaiden said. "They're putting them out of their misery".

Ciera looked off into the distance in disbelief.

20

JUMP TIME

For the people still alive it was painful and took some time to sift through the remains of the Manns farm and their camp. Solemnly painful to equate the stupidity of human nature against the loss of human lives. More than two thirds of the civilian personnel camped out at the Mann's farm with the Patriots were dead. Bodies were everywhere. They found six civilians that were wounded yet still alive, some were the ones who joined up with Ramsey. Three were from Poland NY, Trip, Mack and Toadie. They were alive but Mack had been severely wounded. Three of the Patriots and three civilians on the bus were wounded including Ciera. Some were taken off the bus on makeshift stretchers. As they exited, their comments praised Ciera for her fast thinking and the decision to move the bus. "Ciera saved our lives" they said. They called her a hero.

From piecing last night's events together, it was determined that the police drone's Minni 5 missile had been fired at the bus and would have blown it to pieces if not for the mystery blast that blew the drone and the missile off course. The Minni 5 exploded forming a crater they found just beyond the spot where the bus was stuck in the field, yet it hit close enough to do some damage as well as wound the three onboard from shrapnel and flying debris. Everyone on the bus was lucky to be alive.

Two badly wounded SWAT members were taken alive. The two were part of the group that Ferenczi ordered into the field and were found walking around in a state of shock amongst their dead and dying comrades. With the amount of shrapnel and chunks of farmhouse that littered the ground around them, it was amazing that they survived at all. A few of their fellow SWAT members were found mortally wounded. They were so horrendously maimed that it was considered an act of kindness to shoot them and put them out of their misery, those would never have made it to the hospital anyway. After the Patriots saw the carnage left by the ruthless attack, none of them had any problem with shooting them.

Ferenczi's SWAT team suffered a total of 36 dead. The number had come from information gleaned from the prisoners because many of the bodies had disintegrated in the explosion and were never found. Both Ferenczi's body and the Mann's were among the ones missing. That was the case with anyone who was in the farmhouse at the time of the explosion.

Kaiden oversaw the Patriots who were taking the wounded off the bus. Among them was Betsy Stoiber with a bad shrapnel wound.

"Good job Betsy" Kaiden told her with a kind hand on her shoulder as they took her away.

"I wish I could have done more Kaiden" she said with tears in the corners of her eyes both from the pain and from the sadness she felt.

John the drone operator from Oneida walked down the steps and off the bus right after the wounded were taken off. His arm was in a sling, and he wasn't moving very fast. He too was in pain, and it showed. Still, he clutched the laptop in his hands.

Kaiden commented "We'll get you to a hospital to have that looked at John, don't worry, maybe you'll get enough downtime to play some video games on that thing".

"I don't need a hospital but yeah, that will be a nice break from playing real life video games" he replied. John looked out at where the farmhouse once stood and followed the trail of smoke into the sky with his gaze. "It wasn't a game for those people now was it" he said.

Kaiden stared at him "What do you mean?".

John calmly said "Let's just say that they ran out of 'lives' and this time they're not going to be able to reset, get another chance, and go on to play again".

Kaiden was curious. He stared at John waiting for more of an explanation.

John tried to shuffle on past Kaiden without clarifying. But then he stopped and turned back.

"I'll lay it out for you Kaiden" John's expression changed to serious. "I was lying when I told Crenshaw the Skybird RF-4 drone probably crashed after it fired that last missile at the Hacia building". John paused for effect and stared at Kaiden. Kaiden raised his eyebrows and waited for John to continue.

"The RF-4 has CARP, 'Continuous Advance Return Programing'. It's built in. It's designed to kick in automatically. The bird will return to the main base or one of three pre-set service fields that have been equipped with supplies and the ability to receive and service this type of technology. In layman's terms, it will auto-return to the closest base to be serviced in a power down emergency. That night I gave it a command to fly on past Syracuse knowing that it's emergency programming would kick in and it would automatically land at our north west facility before it ran out of power. It was dark by then so it couldn't get power from the sun. Luckily, we had that option available, if it returned to our main base in Oneida, it couldn't have been resupplied and it couldn't have been re-launched".

Kaiden looked at him with suspicion "You mean you knew the bird was still operational and you didn't tell us?".

Without acknowledging Kaiden's comment, John continued. "When this bird landed at the airfield, the crew on duty there was pre-disposed to charge it up, re-arm it and get it ready for re-launch".

"You son of a bitch" Kaiden exclaimed excitedly. "You're the one who blew up the farmhouse didn't you!" A big smile formed on Kaiden's face. He moved forward and grabbed John by the shoulders. Kaiden was suddenly happier than he had been in weeks. John winced from the pain in his arm and tried to hold Kaiden off from hugging him with the other.

"Wait, wait, wait" John told him. "I didn't do it for you or your people. Actually, I was planning on using it to take you and you crew out at my earliest convenience..." John paused and let the smile fade from Kaiden's face. Kaiden released John from his grip.

"Kaiden, I didn't think very highly of what you guys did. Being kidnapped, the killing and being held prisoner wasn't on my list of favorite things to do".

Kaiden looked dejected from a rollercoaster ride of up and down emotion.

"I placed the bird on 'standby' in the computer. That means that the odds were, if the protocol was still in effect, the RF-4 would be reset, and it would be ready to launch. All it needed was my command. I was lucky, hell we were all lucky, that the Feds didn't have enough time, or they didn't know enough to shut down the support bases. Maybe they don't even know they exist now, I don't know.

Yesterday I launched the bird. It was a success. Didn't know if it was possible to get it in the air again. But I did it. I surveilled the area to see if we were being followed but at the time I didn't see these guys coming (John nodded toward the farmhouse). Honestly, I didn't see any threat. Last night when I realized we were being attacked I knew I had to do something to stop the assault that was about to kill me. Kaiden, I blew up the farmhouse to save my own ass".

"Why are you telling me this John? You could have spun a story that would have made you a hero around here".

"I need you to know the truth, I'm just that kind of guy, come hell or high water I'm gunna be straight with you. Can't go round any longer with people thinking I'm something I'm not. Got enough of that going on as it is. But Kaiden, you have to listen to the end of the story before you come to a conclusion. Crenshaw set me free. Even though you guys destroyed my life as it was, I realized that he set me free. I no longer had to play their game. When Crenshaw sent the injured to the hospital, including the two wounded Brigade members, I changed my mind about you guys. In the last few days, I have come to know some of you, and I know that you are not the bad guys the Feds have made you out to be. A lot of what you stand for, I stand for too. I just got sucked up in the machine and I couldn't get out. But you guys set me free, and I thank you for that. There are many people out there just like me. Hell, I could have taken you out on your way to Oneonta, but I decided not to".

"Well, I don't know whether to kill you or kiss you John". Kaiden broke out in a smile. John did too. They both laughed and Kaiden patted John on the shoulder which made him wince again.

"Oops, sorry" Kaiden said. "John, I owe you one, we all owe you one".

The two of them had come to an understanding. One they could both live with. "What will you do now John?".

"I don't know, I might just follow you guys around if you don't mind Kaiden".

"I don't mind at all" Kaiden said and then paused to think. "John, we took over a vehicle, a van the police used to operate their drone. It's got a lot of technology in it. I'm wondering if we can bring it with us and if you could use any of it to help run their drone or even your drone? Could you go and check it out?".

"Sure, wow, if nothing else they will probably have something I can charge my laptop with, something else besides solar power would be nice".

"Yes, the sun can be a hard thing to find at times in these parts" Kaiden said.

"By the way Kaiden, I'd advise that we get out of 'these parts' fast. That explosion could have been monitored. They might be on their way as we speak".

"Understood. I'm on it" Kaiden replied.

John turned and started to go. Kaiden stopped him. "Oh John. One more thing. Is that bird still up there?".

John chuckled. "Yup" he said before walking on. Then, over his shoulder he added "But I don't know for how long".

Kaiden chose the closest Patriot standing next to him "Victor!" and put him to work.

"Yes sir" Vic replied.

"Get Eric, he knows mechanics. Try and start up the bus and see if you can get it to run. If it does, get the Mann's tractor, it's on the other side of the barn, I think it's still intact. See if you can use it to pull the bus out of there. Fix the tires and get it rolling as fast as you can. Get whoever you need to help you. Go now!".

"You got it Kaiden".

The two SWAT prisoners were taken to join the others and were held under guard. The wounded were taken to a temporary aid station set up under the trees on the side of the Mann's driveway. Those were given as much first aid as was available. That's where Ciera and anyone else who needed medical attention were taken.

Kaiden walked to the temporary aid station and sat down next to Ciera who was sitting on a blanket. She had a bandage on the side of her head held on by tying a strip of cloth around her head. Kaiden briefed her on the casualties.

"We found four people alive from Ramsey's group in addition to Mack Heedy from Poland, Toadie and Trip Salantro from Lake Pleasant. They were all hiding in the field or wandering around out on the far side of the Mann's property. We gathered them up and brought em back to join the other survivors. You had Vic Coaler on the bus, he's OK. He's the only one with you who wasn't wounded. Betsey and Andy both were wounded, and I told you about Glen Greenwise and the others".

"I'm going to miss Glen and Nick" Ciera said pausing in a moment of sad reflection.

"Bill and Fife from Lake pleasant were killed Ciera. Shot dead in the van they were sleeping in. I don't know how I am going to tell Brian Hardy. The good news is that Jen and Toadie are alive. Nance Lackland is dead. So is Sky Winiker. Lyle's right over there, wounded pretty bad". Kaiden stared at Ciera as they both sat there digesting what happened.

There was more wounded laying or sitting on both sides of Ciera. "I don't even know the names of some of the others, there hadn't been enough time to get to know them" Kaiden told her. He turned to one of the wounded sitting next to them and as if to try and make up for it, he said "Hey, hello. What's your name?".

"Saco".

"How did you join us Saco?".

"I was on the bus in Oneida. Came in with Ramsey and his guys".

"I'd shake your hand, but I see you're injured" Kaiden said. "What happened last night?".

"I thought I was lucky to get a spot in one of the Humvee's. Then the shooting started. No one in there knew how to operate the 50 cal. Hell, Gene peeked his head up out of the turret to see what was going on and he got his head blown off. That's when I got out and ran. I ran to the farmhouse. They pushed everyone to the farmhouse, then they pushed us out the back. We just ran. Man, bullets were flying everywhere. I thought that any second, I'd get hit. They were shootin at us from the house. Then it... it just blew up and all the shooting stopped. That was the luckiest thing that ever happened to me in my life".

"Hey, I'm glad you're still with us. It's good to know your name Saco" Kaiden told him.

Kaiden turned back to Ciera. "Ciera, we've got to get you and all the wounded to the hospital, and we've got to get the bus out of here. Can you travel?".

"Hell yes, I can travel. Get me out of here".

"Looks like you'll be needing stitches on that cut of yours. I'm putting you on one of the cars going to the hospital. Don't worry, I'll get everything together here and I'll follow". Ciera smiled. "I've got to find out if we have to move the motherload to another vehicle" Kaiden added.

Kaiden didn't have to get anyone together. Donnie Canter, Andy Finn, Reese Johnson, Robert Metcalf, Riley Mason, were all standing close by. Vic, Kurt, Merrill, Ramsey and the rest of the Patriots and the new recruits were there in the background as well. All of them waiting for word on what they were going to do next. Now that Kaiden was in charge there were always people hanging around him looking for answers.

After speaking with Ciera, Kaiden got up and started giving orders. "Donnie, get some of the survivors, whoever can drive, and get them to take the wounded to the hospital. Drive em' in those marked police cars, that might help keep you from being hassled along the way, see if you can find the keys, if you can't, use the vehicles we confiscated from the Brigade. Ramsey, collect all the weapons you can find. I spoke to Ben on the radio. He says they've got control of the City but that doesn't mean there aren't elements out there that wish to do us harm. Be on the lookout.

Kaiden turned his attention to Andy. "Andy, you're wounded".

"Yes, but I can still drive".

"Good. Go with Donnie. You're one of our designated drivers. Take as many vehicles as you need and take the wounded to the hospital. Have someone look at that wound while you're there. Go, now. Get the wounded out of here on the double. We'll follow and meet up. Look for me on the radio. You know the codes".

* * *

One of the Mann's neighbors drove by and stopped on the street to see what was going on. That prompted Kaiden to spur the guys on to work faster to clear the bus from the ditch it was in. Ok, people. Let's go, let's go! We got to act fast and get out of here as quickly as possible. Move your ass and move that bus!".

After a lot of effort, the Patriots finally pulled the bus out of the field with the Mann's tractor. Luckily, they were able to retrieve the tractor from the portion of the barn that hadn't collapsed. If they didn't have that tractor, it would have been nearly impossible to salvage the bus. It took everyone together and a lot more time to free the bus than Kaiden wanted to spend. The engine was ok, Eric got it running. The axil was ok, they got it moving. There was damage to the body and to two of the tires. Multiple bullet strikes and shrapnel holes pot marked the metal side panels and there were holes with major cracks in some of the windows. Both the gas tank and the radiator were punctured and leaking. Addressing that would be of utmost importance. They found that if they didn't fill the gas tank up all the way it didn't leak that bad. The radiator was another story. They were going to have to nurse it through until they could find someone to repair it. Replacing the flat tire with the spare gave it a thumbs up ready to go status. The only other option was to transfer the motherload to the newly acquired Police van and abandon the bus.

"We're not going to abandon the bus" Kaiden decided. "That thing is the best troop carrier/prisoner transport we have. And it doubles as a mobile hotel. We're going to take it into Oneonta for repairs. Kurt, you and I are on the bus. Hey Kurt, what the hell are you doing with that rifle?".

"You gave it to me at the police station!".

"Oh yeah, I forgot, you're not supposed to have one. Crenshaw put you on probation and you'll remain there until I tell you otherwise".

"Awe hell you'd figure under the circumstances you would let it slide Kaiden".

"No. Hand it over".

Visibly upset, Kurt handed it to Kaiden. It was a Heckler Kotch 416, a prize of a weapon.

Kurt, you and I will drive the bus with Robert and Eric to guard the prisoners. Vic, you Reese and Ramsey are on the three Humvee's. take Profit, Trip and Kurt with you. Can I get a volunteer on the semi? Who can drive the semi?".

"I can" Merrill spoke up.

"What? Merrill the lawyer can drive a semi?".

"Hey, I had quite a few other jobs before I became a lawyer".

"Ok, great. Terry, I want you on the tanker. Don't worry, it's not that hard to drive. John, the Police van is your baby from now on. Everyone else choose a vehicle and let's get out of here". They all split up and went in different directions. John took the opportunity to pull Kaiden aside.

"Kaiden, I need to advise you of another option. I told you that my drone was re-supplied at one of three designated emergency airfields. The police van and it's equipment is perfect; I can operate very nicely out of it since their technician was so eager to cooperate and give me the passwords to their software.

Anyway, I trust you see how much of an advantage we had by having this technology to use against them last night. I would say the drone is more important than even that gas tanker or the supply truck that you're dragging along with you. To exploit a glaring opportunity, we should, excuse me, you should, drop by the southern emergency center on your way and secure the essential items that I need to keep the drone airborne. It would be a very effective weapon to have in your arsenal. Besides, I need a place to land it. I could set it to land there, and we could go secure it".".

"Does the site have missiles?".

"I don't know, but it's supposed to be capable of re-supply to some degree".

"Well just fly the bird there and get it re-supplied like you did before".

"That's not a good idea Kaiden. My computer tells me that the site has been disabled. If we fly our bird in there, it might be captured, and we won't be able to get it to launch again".

"Where is this site located?".

"It's in Greene N.Y., just north of Binghamton. I know where it is, I helped build it".

"I see. John, I'm going to have to get back to you on this. I don't know if I want to take the chance of another detour, even for that kind of firepower. Why are you telling me this, I thought you were on the fence about all this stuff. Aren't you itching to get out of here".

"Ahh, don't tempt me" John said with a smile.

Even though they had plenty of gasoline in the tanker truck it was considered a sin to leave cars with gas in them. Still, Kaiden felt pressured to leave the area quickly and therefore decided not to waste time syphoning gas out of the vehicles they were going to leave behind. The grim task of burying their friends was performed but Kaiden ordered them not to waste time on burying the bodies of their enemy. Instead, they concentrated on gathering up indispensable supplies and weapons which were loaded up on the vehicles designated as an essential component of their convoy.

After packing all they could comfortably carry, Kaiden and crew formed up the convoy and road out towards Oneonta in search of repairs, leaving the carnage and all else behind.

END PART III

Part 4- Will the Patriots ever make it to the Outpost, or will vengeful government troops and angry mobs stop them from their quest? Kaiden drives to the Oneonta police station to assess the aftermath- will he be arrested for stealing the Police van or be received as a hero? Will Kaiden and Ciera ever be able to find love in this new screwed up world? Find out in Part 4 of the continuing "Uphold And Defend" series.

A Taste of Part IV

Riding into town past the shot-up unmanned roadblock was somewhat less stressful, only no one knew if a Federal patrol or members of the City Brigade would show up and make everyone's life miserable. The question on Kaiden's mind *"What elements of Oneonta's progressive governing regime are still viable?"* They certainly didn't just disappear.

On the way the convoy stopped three times to deal with the bus and its leaking radiator. That became the first thing on their list of things to do; fix it. Just inside Oneonta's city limits on Keith Street, they came across an auto repair shop with large bay doors. It was closed, deserted looking and all locked up, but it had what they were looking for; an electric generator attached to the building outside, and welding equipment that could be seen through the window. The Patriots broke the lock on the front door, got in and opened the door to the largest bay. The bus didn't fit all the way in but after moving a few things around they were able to set it up so they could work on it.

Repairs would be impossible without electricity, so everything hinged on that. After checking the generator, no one could figure out how to start it up. Kaiden sent Reese in search of the owner or one of the employees whose names they found in an office filing cabinet. Reese concentrated on finding employees with an address that was close by. He got lucky and found the manager, Ray Morris, who lived just a few blocks away. Reese was tasked with driving over to convince Ray that it was in his best interest to come over and open the shop. Ray agreed but was visibly upset when he got there and saw that they had broken in.

"Hey, what do you think you guys are doing breaking in here? It's against the law you know. You can go to jail for breaking an entry".

"Ray, that would be correct if these were normal times. Do you know we're at war Ray?" Kaiden asked him.

"War? What war? At war with who?".

"Ah, the golden question. At war with who? Kaiden said.

"Hell, we just need the government to…".

"To do what Ray? Haven't they already done enough? Your conception of what the government was or is supposed to be doing, is no more. The economy has collapsed, and you are expecting the people who are responsible for that to fix it? Don't you think that's a bit naive? Wake up man! They did this by design. All of us here, we're fighting back. Yes, it's a war alright. They made it one".

Ray looked puzzled. "I heard about some trouble down town last night but I didn't think we were at war".

It was normally Crenshaw who gave "the speech", now it was up to Kaiden to take a crack at it.

"Ray, this is what we know: The government has been taken over by the progressive socialist party. The first two things they did was to turn the military and ban citizens from owning guns. Gun confiscation effectively weakened the possibility of an armed response by the populace. Under the guise of confiscating guns, they set up their hit squads that I'm sure you've heard about. They went around arresting the opposition and commandeering their property. Getting the military on their side was accomplished by initiating 'woke' policies within the ranks which effectively kicked out loyal patriots and installed Marxist sympathizers in key positions. Just like they did in America's universities. In tangent, the push to de-fund the police effectively kicked out all the conservative leaning personnel from the force; the ones they knew would never go along with the program. Then they staged their coup and forcefully kicked out the opposition in government. They knew the general population would resist turning on fellow Americans, so to consolidate their power over the rest of the country they hired hundreds of job hungry illegal immigrants and gave them vacant jobs on the police force and put their comrades in key positions. From their base and from kids fresh out of public indoctrination schools, they formed armed occupation patrols that are at this very moment, going around forcing local governments to conform.

They drew form a pool of downtrodden illegals who were more than willing to work for just about anything and would have no problem enforcing martial law on the populace. Smuggled in "mercenaries" are what they really are. Some cities even put them on their police force. Ray, it's not 'We The People' anymore. It's 'They the ruling elite'.

Now, it's either them or us. By 'us' I mean people who want to restore the United States back to the way it was, the way it was originally founded. We want to restore and enforce the Constitution and the Bill of Rights and re-declare it the supreme law of the land. We have drifted far away from the original intent, what we are experiencing now, is the result.

Every one of us has sworn to fight to give this country back to the people. The only question now is, are you going to help us?".

Ray didn't know what to say. All this was shocking news. News had been slow to circulate around these parts and nothing this intense had reached his ears. "Wow, that's a lot to digest. All I knew was that things were going to be shut down for a while until the government can fix it" Ray said.

"We broke into your shop, Ok, sorry about that. But this is war. We either take what we need, or you can make it easy for us and start the generator so we can fix our vehicles. I'll pay you in silver coins for your service. We're desperate to fix the radiator and gas tank. What do you say?".

"Your cause is something I agree with, I just don't know if we have any real chance of changing the outcome of this. I mean, you're going up against the government. That will be a monumental task. But I'm with you, I'll do my small part. I'll get Victor, he'll start the generator and do the welding for you".

"Thanks, Ray".

* * *

“I’m leaving” Kaiden told Profit along with a few members of the group who were standing around while work was being done on the bus.

“Why, where are you going?” Proffit asked.

“I’ve got to see if Crenshaw is going to make it and I’m going to get Ciera. Gotta make sure our wounded are being taken care of. Profit, you’re in charge while I’m gone. Pull the trucks around back and keep everyone out of sight. Minimize your footprint. If I don’t come back…”.

“What? You are coming back right Kaiden?”.

“Nothin these days is guaranteed. With all that’s happened… things change quickly. We’ve got to have a plan B. Get the bus fixed ASAP, then if I’m not back here when you’re ready to leave, drive a half hour south on East River Road, find a secure place to hang out for a while. If I don’t show up in two days, drive another hour south. Monitor the radio, I’ll follow and contact you guys somewhere down the line”.

“Keep a small footprint?” Kurt blurted out. “Kaiden, as our new unelected leader of the Pioneer Patriots, you’re making a mistake. And by the way, did anyone else here witness Crenshaw placing him in charge?”. No one spoke up. “I didn’t think so”.

“OK, Kurt, I understand, you’re mad at Crenshaw. He put you on probation, but that is entirely your fault. No one else to blame but yourself. But I’ll let you speak. What’s my mistake?”.

“You’re not asking anyone else for their opinion or input”. Kurt told him right out. “There’re a lot of smart people here, look around you. I, for one, have a suggestion”.

“Ok, Kurt I’m listening”.

“You said ‘Minimize your footprint’ but all we’ve been doing since we started this vacation is picking up baggage along the way. Look, now we even got a police van, did you know there are thick white identification numbers painted on top of that van? Our ‘footprint’ has grown to the point where it’s no longer ‘small’ and that’s a problem. I understand the desire to keep all this shit, I do. It’s easy in ‘war’ as you call this, yeah, you just take it. Now it’s dragging us down and making us conspicuous. We need to shed this stuff and drive straight back to the post".

"Really? Do you realize that if we didn't have this 'baggage' as you call it, that we'd all be dead or captured by now? But ok, so, what do you propose?" Kaiden asked.

"We split up, that'll make us harder to find. The trucks go one way, the bus and the patriots go the other. Like it was when we started. The paperwork we got with the pass is probably no good anymore anyway. We keep it light, keep it simple and we'll have a better chance of getting through. Back to basics man".

Kaiden thought hard about what Kurt just said. *"He could be right. One thing he was right about was that I don't ask for input. I was hell bent on continuing what Crenshaw started and got hooked on the idea of bringing all the spoils back to the Pioneer Outpost, not just the motherload. What Kurt said makes sense"*.

"What do you think guys?" Kaiden asked everyone. Everyone sort of mumbled in agreement.

"What do you think Profit?".

"Sounds tactically sound and risky at the same time. But everything we do is risky, no matter which way we go. I agree. I think we should shed some weight and split up. We'll be much faster that way, and harder to detect".

"No!" Merril said.

"No, what?" Kaiden asked him.

"You got me driving the supply truck. If we split up that means me and my truck are more vulnerable to attack. I'm not going to drive that truck without the full support of everyone in this convoy, that would be suicide man. We are going to need everyone here to survive the next battle, and believe me, there will be another battle. Splitting up is stupid man".

"Ok, both you and Kurt have a point. I'll decide when I get back. In the meantime, the plan is as stated. And John... spray paint over the lettering on that police van will ya". John gave Kaiden a salute off the brow.

“What if I don’t hear from you?” Profit asked Kaiden.

“Then it’ll be up to you. Keep going. Get the motherload to the Outpost at all cost” he replied.

END OF- Taste of PART IV

www.ingramcontent.com/pod-product-compliance
Lightning Source LLC
Chambersburg PA
CBHW070642310726
48982CB00001B/378
* 9 7 9 8 9 8 8 4 6 6 3 7 6 *